WHIRLPOOL

NEW YORK TIMES BESTSELLING AUTHOR

CHERRY ADAIR

Have fun with Peri & Finn
Cheers,
Cherry Adair

WHIRLPOOL
 This edition published by arrangement with Adair Digital Press.

Library of Congress Control Number: 2017950590
ISBN-13: 978-1937774479
ISBN-10: 1937774473
www.cherryadair.com
shop.cherryadair.com

REVIEW SNIPS

ABSOLUTE DOUBT. Action, extreme adventure and romance. So much good stuff in this book. A counter-terrorist organization against a sociopath. A hero and heroine who both are honorable, stubborn and loyal and instantly attracted to each other. Totally loved reading this book. It is part of a series, but absolutely can be read alone. ~Fantasy Books

GIDEON. Gritty and action-packed from beginning to end, this is a classic Adair tale, so readers can be sure that the sex is sizzling and the danger relentless! ~Jill M. Smith Romantic Times 4 1/2 * top pick

HUSH Packed with plenty of unexpected plot twists and lots of sexy passion, Cherry's latest testosterone-rich, adrenaline-driven suspense novel is addictively readable. ~Chicago Tribune

HUSH delivers non-stop action, hair raising adventure, and titillating dialogue that will have readers poised on the edge of their seats waiting for what happens next. Ms. Adair has created a memorable couple whose antics are a pleasure to read about. Emotions run high in HUSH, making for an amazing read full of surprising twist and turns. ~ Fresh Fiction

Adair's BLUSH . . . sizzling chemistry adds to the heat of Bayou Cheniere, La., in Adair's knockout contemporary romantic thriller. ~Publishers Weekly starred review

UNDERTOW is full of action and suspense! Cherry Adair did such a great job making the reader feel as if they were part of the experience. I felt like I was right there diving into the water looking for the buried treasure with Zane and Teal. ~Hanging With Bells 4 Bells

WHITE HEAT "…latest in Ms. Adair's T-FLAC series, roars out of the starting gate at a fast gallop and never breaks stride in a thrilling, no-holes-barred roller coaster ride of heart-pulsing suspense and hot romance featuring a delicious, to-die-for hunk…"

"Ms. Adair skillfully weaves an exciting tale of explosive action sprinkled with twisty surprises around a sensual love story laced with gobs of fiery desire. A must for readers who like their romantic suspense hot... and the heroes even hotter!" ~Romance Reader At Heart

HOT ICE is a sure thing! Ms. Adair's characters are well supported by the secondary T-FLAC operatives that assist in the mission. The villain is equally well developed as you come to learn how a man like Jose' Morales became so twisted, that you almost feel sorry for him...almost! Ms. Adair weaves in clever tools and ingenious methods to solve this assignment. There has also been great detail given to the locations/settings, which span many continents. And the ability to bring it all together in a pulse-pounding climax will leave the reader breathless and well satisfied by the time you close this book. ~All About Romance

ICE COLD. Adair continues her wonderfully addictive series featuring the sexy men of T-FLAC with this fast paced and intricately plotted tale of danger, deception, and desire that is perfect for readers who like their romantic suspense adrenaline-rich and sizzlingly sexy. ~ Booklist

WHITE HEAT. "Your mission, should you decide to read it, is to have a few hours adrenaline pumped excitement and sizzling romance with the new T-FLAC suspense by Cherry Adair."

"You'll not want to put this book down as the plot twists come together and explode into a fantastic ending. With the spine-tingling danger, stomach churning suspense, bullets flying from every corner and red-hot romance you get White Heat. Cherry Adair has once again created a heart pounding read with extraordinary characters in extraordinary circumstances that will leave the reader hungering for more. White Heat is an excellent novel and one that I recommend as a keeper." ~ Night Owl Romance

Cutter Cay Series Titles by
CHERRY ADAIR

Undertow
Riptide
Vortex
Stormchaser
Hurricane
Whirlpool

ONE

Bernardino Rivadavia Natural Sciences Museum
Buenos Aires
Argentina

The exhibit closed yesterday." The raised voice, precise, female and annoyed, came from the shadows at the far end of the long, narrow exhibit hall. Out of sight, packing straw rustled. "It's no longer open to the public."

Phineas Gallagher paused just inside the door to the *Mystical Treasures From the Sea* exhibit, surprised to find someone else there when he'd been told he'd have the place to himself for an hour. Finn wanted to see the artifacts before they were crated and disappeared to God only knew where like the other two similar exhibits.

He wasn't in the mood to chat with a stranger, nor share the moment. He was on a fact-finding mission, on his way from point A to point C. His pilot had the jet's engines figuratively idling on the tarmac, and a car and his driver waited for him outside the building to whisk him back to the airfield.

"I'm not the public," he said shortly, striding across the flotsam and jetsam of loose straw and packing materials littering the marble floor. Stacks of wooden packing crates, some open, some already sealed, were piled haphazardly nearby. Black fabric covered the walls, and freestanding, evenly spaced display cases, most of them dark, ran in two parallel lines from one end of the room to the door where he stood.

Finn paused to allow his eyes to adjust to the gloom. Interior lights from half a dozen cases fell across the white floor like zebra stripes. The rest of the place was atmospherically in shadow.

"Unless you work for the museum, which you don't," the woman said crossly, "You're not allowed in here while they're packing up the exhibit." Her high heels struck the hard surface of the floor as she shifted in the shadows, and now Finn was able to see the pale oval of her face illuminated by her white shirt. He doubted a museum collections manager would be wearing high heels during de-installation of an exhibit, and she'd said 'they'

"Unless *you* work here," he said, intrigued enough to advance, "which *you* don't, neither should you." She didn't deny it. So what was she doing back there messing with the crates of packed artifacts if she wasn't employed by the museum?

"Head's up. Not only is security a yell away, *I'm* armed, and not afraid to shoot you if you come any closer or attempt to steal any of the artifacts."

Her husky voice was American. Tourist? Expat? "I'm not here to steal the artifacts, Annie Oakley." Amused by her threat, Finn narrowed the gap farther with a few more steps. The thought crossed his mind that this could be a setup. Anyone who knew him knew how much he liked a challenge. And the woman's husky voice, and the way she kept herself hidden in the shadows was a tempting lure.

Still, all he had to do was raise his voice, and his bodyguards, waiting outside, would be inside the room in seconds. Not that he couldn't take down a woman by himself if the need arose. But it wasn't out of the realm of possibility that she was merely the bait, and had other people hidden back there with her. "Just want a quick look. I'll be out of your hair in less than half an hour."

"Why?"

"Why will I get out of your hair?"

She made a derisive noise. "Why did you break in to see *this* exhibit? Qin Shi Huang's Terracotta Army exhibit is open in the next hall. You should go. It's fascinating."

He'd seen them *in situ.* "Not interested. I'm curious about these particular artifacts. There are other concurring *Treasures From the Sea* touring shows that also closed this week. One at the Muséum National d'Histoire Naturelle in Paris, the other, at the Ditsong National Museum in Jo'burg. I want to see how this one compares. Have you seen either of the others?" Who was she, and what, if anything, was *her* dogged interest in the *Mystical Treasures From the Sea*?

"In Paris and Johannesburg? Of course not."

"Read about them?"

"I'm not going for a Ph.D. in Maritime Archeology. I just freaking walked in off the street an hour ago."

"And you're rummaging through packing crates? You don't think someone would find that odd?"

"It's none of *someone's* business."

Intriguing. "Aren't you curious as to who amassed all these artifacts? Don't you find the lack of specific detail in the descriptions odd?" He sure as hell did.

"There's *plenty* of description for each one of them."

"Only a couple of things missing," Finn said dryly. "The name of the ship on which each was found, and the actual location of the wreck."

"There's enough pertinent info here for me," she told him. "I wanted to see them for the last time before they were packed up forever."

"There's a sizable fortune tied up in these touring exhibits. Maybe the artifacts are finally being sold."

"Maybe."

"Maybe they were stolen."

"Maybe."

"Without provenance, it'll be tough for this mysterious benefactor to get top dollar."

Finn enjoyed a challenging puzzle, and the identity of the shadowy patron who'd sponsored the lavish exhibits of centuries-old artifacts from various shipwrecks was a puzzle he was determined to unravel. At the moment, however, he was sparring with an enigmatic woman whose throaty voice conjured up candlelight, rumpled sheets and vigorous, sweaty sex.

Finn attributed his tolerance of the game to his feelings of restlessness for the past few months. He frequently felt as though he was hurtling at a breakneck speed toward an unknown destination without knowing where or what the fuck that destination *was*. This interaction was a momentary respite.

"There's a mysterious benefactor?"

Finn frowned, half annoyed, half amused by the exchange. Straw flew from the shadows like a snow flurry. What the hell *was* she doing back there? "Of all three exhibits."

"If you say so. Clearly, *money* wasn't the motivation for sharing these artifacts with the public."

There were still a few relics in the lit cases. Finn paused to glance at a jeweled gold chalice, a heavily embossed, six-inch gilded silver flask, and a silver-hilted ceremonial dagger. Five minutes ago, the pieces would've elicited interest, but now it was her siren's voice that drew him.

She muttered, "Ow. Shit."

He smiled. "Are you packing or unpacking?"

"Neither."

He paused at a case to look at a suite of gold and emerald jewelry as she muttered another curse and wood struck wood as though she'd slammed the lid on a box. For all he knew she was back there pilfering the artifacts herself. He didn't give a shit what she was doing. Just wished she was doing it somewhere else. "I don't suppose you can come back in fifteen minutes?"

"I was here first."

"Can't argue that. Need help back there?"

"No thanks. Get your looking done, then check out the soldiers next door. They were buried with new, and fully functional military equipment. Go take a look at the crossbows, swords, lances, halberds- "

"Subtle." It had been a long time since anyone had tried to get rid of him.

"It's an excellent exhibit."

"Hmm."

The next display case was dark, but the one across from it was lit, and Finn strolled over to see what it held. A two-thousand-year-old pickle jar and a bunch of Carthaginian bronze coins. Not that interesting. He considered offering her money to get out and leave him alone. But since what he'd seen so far proved his point that the artifacts here were similar to what he'd seen in the other two and didn't answer his questions of who the sponsor was, he didn't bother. This side trip was proving to be a waste of time.

Most of his hands-on business ventures seemed to have reached a simmering point simultaneously. He was heavily invested in the upcoming salvage with the Cutters. Four brothers who'd made names for themselves by salvaging, and selling, invaluable artifacts they'd fished from the seas. Much like the artifacts displayed here at the museum. He was confident his money was in good hands.

The anticipation of the upcoming salvage, the new corporate acquisition he was finalizing, coupled with the top-secret rocket launch in a few months, should be plenty enough to keep him entertained. Yet something was missing.

Driven, he'd spent the better part of his life trying to fill a void he couldn't name. Maybe his subconscious needed a vacation from all the intellectual, brainiac work. He'd been climbing two-thousand feet to the summit of *Siula Grande*, in Peru for the last couple of weeks. Long enough for his ship, *Blackstar*, to sail from South Africa to South America to rendezvous with the Cutter's dive ships off the coast of Patagonia.

Finn lived onboard and ran his multinational company from the three-hundred and fifty-foot gigayacht. The Blackstar Group was the umbrella held over four hundred companies, in more than thirty countries. The Group showcased Finn's diverse interests. From new forms of energy, to a game reserve, to his passion: space travel.

"What are you *doing*?"

"Looking at this embossed sword." *Trying to figure out who you are, and what the hell you're doing back there.*

"Why are you so interested in these particular artifacts?"

He was halfway down the length of the hall, but she had yet to emerge. "Curiosity." Now he was curious about *her*. "The artifacts are rare, of significant historical value and priceless," he said easily, as he attempted to get more than a shadowy glimpse of her face. "Someone possesses enough relics to support three traveling exhibits circling the globe at the same time. Aren't you curious about the mystery backer? Clearly, the artifacts interest you, too." A thought occurred, "You're not the benefactor, are you?" he asked, as more straw flew.

"If I were, I'd be lying on a beach somewhere with hot and cold running waiters bringing me umbrella drinks as I work on my tan," she said, sounding amused. "We're both too late. As you see, pretty much all the pieces have already been dismantled and packed."

"Are you going to hide back there until I leave then?" He'd already walked halfway to where she hid in the shadows, and she'd made no move to show herself.

"You're Irish."

Not only did she have a good ear, she was damn good at not answering questions. "East Coast?" *Boston?*

"Not specifically," she responded, unhelpfully. "And I'm not *hiding.* I'm back here *looking.*"

Move into the light so I can see you.

Whatever she said after that was muffled by the blood thrumming through his veins as she emerged from the darkness.

Finn's heart stopped. Time slowed.

Bloody hell. A shock of awareness surged from his head to his toes. Then settled in between. His heart resumed beating. Harder. Faster. She stole the breath from his lungs. She was stunning. Striking. Almost otherworldly. Tall and slender, she wore jeans too tight to conceal a weapon, and an open-necked white shirt. Pulling off white cotton gloves, she strolled from shadow into light sliding a smartphone into the back pocket of her jeans. Had she been back there taking pictures, or calling the cops? One thing he knew for damn sure- she'd been handling the packed artifacts.

But whatever the hell she'd been doing two minutes ago was immaterial, as Finn's breath snagged in his lungs. The glossy spill of her hair, falling well past her shoulders, was orange flame, mixed with the red fire found deep inside an active volcano. He wanted to feel the silky glide of her long hair over his throat, over his thighs.

The mind was a cybernetic system, it needed a targeted goal. He'd just found that goal. As his heartbeat accelerated, his vision tunneled, until all he saw was her. Only her.

Lust at first sight. He didn't realize he'd closed the distance between them until he was engulfed in the heady fragrance of her skin and hair. Casablanca lilies. As cool a color as her hair looked hot. He wanted to drown in the scent of her.

Her profile was delicate, straight nose, slender neck- and all that *hair.* Hair made to be tangled in a man's fists.

Hyperawareness. Instant attraction magnified to the nth degree. Finn's muscles tensed as his blood pressure rose. His balls tightened. All his senses heightened. He had the mad urge to scoop her up and carry her to his lair like a horny fucking caveman. He wanted to peel her out of her clothes. Wanted to fill his hands with her breasts, wanted her to wrap his naked body in all that gorgeous, flaming hair.

Intoxicated by the scent, it took all his self-control to keep his hands off her. With her incredible hair waving down her back, she looked as sensual, as exotic as a mermaid.

"History is fascina--Hey!" Startled, she turned to look at him as, unable to check the compulsion, Finn ran his hand down the length of her hair from crown to the small of her back. The strands felt thick, heavy, silky and cool to the touch.

She stiffened. But the sudden flush, and bloom of goosebumps on her throat and the V of exposed chest, showed she wasn't unaffected. "What the *hell* do you think you're do ..." her voice trailed off.

Allowing his fucking impulses to run amok was what he was doing. This was not the behavior of a perfect stranger, nor the behavior of a man in his right mind. He'd been attracted to women many times, but not like this. *Nothing* like this. *Seeing* her had turned him on, but *touching* her ratcheted up a primal need. He felt crazed, reckless, and horny as hell.

Their eyes locked. Braced for recognition, he held a disappointed breath. If she knew who he was, it was game over.

She wet her lips as if to moisten a mouth suddenly gone dry. "You're awfully freaking handsy for a total stranger." Her voice had turned huskier, lower, more aware.

A tilt of her head and their mouths could touch.

Ah, Jesus, she smelled so good he almost groaned out loud. Pheromones. It was as if the very essence of her had bonded to his DNA. Unprecedented. "You feel it, too." How could she not be experiencing the same mind-blowing attraction that he felt?

"Right now, I'm feeling. . ." She shrugged. "A little overwhelmed, to put it mildly. It's as if I just gulped a cup of Death Wish coffee, and I'm dangerously over-caffeinated."

Yeah. I know the feeling. "Is that a good thing or a bad thing?"

In her mesmerizing sea-glass colored eyes, he saw the confidence of a woman who recognized, and was comfortable with, admiration from a man. A woman who enjoyed a light flirtation.

There was fuck-all *light* about this flirtation. He wanted her. She couldn't possibly mistake his intent. His visceral response to her was so powerful, he imagined he lit up in the fucking dark.

"It's an... *intriguing* thing." Her direct appraisal said seduction wasn't a *fait accompli*. Still, it was impossible to miss the pulse throbbing at the base of her throat, or the small shiver that moved through her as her gaze rested on his face. Lowered to his mouth, then captured his eyes again. After a moment a slow, delicious tilt appeared at the corner of her mouth.

Good. She wasn't backing away. Better - she didn't rip her hair from his hands. Best - he thought he detected a challenge in her gaze. As in - exactly how far are you going with this?

All the way. All the fucking way.

Working his thumb over a silky strand, he searched her expression. "It feels cool, I almost expected it to singe my fingers. I've never seen hair this color. MC1R, a gene mutation, causes red hair and affects only about one percent of the world's population. This is a shining example." Probably dyed, but still, mesmerizing.

Unable to stop touching he let the strands sift through his fingers. Static electricity made the filaments cling to his hand as if they couldn't bear to let go either.

"It's just hair." Her sassy smile carried the force of a sucker punch. Her hair was an O classification star color. The hottest, brightest, fastest burning star out there. The stuff of Finn's new fantasies. "*Awesome* hair, but just hair."

Finn smiled back. "Not *just* hair, it's spectacular. Otherworldly." His pulse raced. He noticed the small, dark freckle on her clavicle, bared by the open collar of her crisp white shirt, and the way her long, dark lashes cast shadows on her cheeks. "Never has the phrase 'crowning glory' been more apt."

Water-clear eyes danced with amusement. "God's reward for my fortitude in resisting so many of His deadly sins over the years."

"How many?" he asked, voice thick.

"Ten minutes ago, I was at fifty-fifty."

Inhaling the heady fragrance of lily, he held it greedily deep in his lungs, exhaled, then drew in the scent again. Desire, detailed, and immediate flooded his body. He needed to strip her naked, and fuck her right there, against the glass case holding a golden challis encircled with emeralds that paled in comparison to her eyes. He wanted to watch them haze as she came apart in his arms. "Have dinner with me."

Pushing up the cuff of her shirt she glanced at her bare wrist, then smiled up at him. "Don't you mean lunch?"

His breath snagged. She was so damned beautiful she made him forget civilized behavior. There was no need to *ask* if she felt the same gravitational pull. Her pulse pounded at the base of her throat, and her pupils were dilated. Even more telling, her nipples peaked the thin cotton of her shirt.

"Dinner." He splayed his hand on her hip, felt her muscles tense, then relax, felt the warmth of her skin through the fabric of her jeans. "Tonight."

Holding his gaze, she acknowledged his blatantly dominant declaration, by not stepping away from his light hold. Instead, she gave him a challenging look. A look that said- I can walk the fuck away anytime I want, and leave you holding your painfully erect dick in your hand. She was in the driver's seat, and the fire under all that jade coolness in her eyes said she damn-well knew it.

"Are you married?"

"No. You?"

"No." She tilted her head, giving him an assessing look. "Are you loyal, brave, and trustworthy?"

Finn held up two fingers. "As a Boy Scout."

"Oh, I sincerely doubt you were ever a Boy Scout." She scanned his face, mouth soft and inviting. "I think you were the rebel. You hated the uniform and thought the rules were made to be broken. Are you always prepared?"

Very intuitive. "Always."

"To keep yourself physically strong, mentally awake and morally straight?" she teased. "I have a brother, I know my Boy Scout lingo." She sobered for a moment. "You're not a serial killer, are you?"

He shook his head. "Sailor. You aren't a siren luring me to the rocks, are you?"

She shook her head. "Can't carry a tune in a bucket, you're safe with me."

"About that dinner--?"

"It's two in the afternoon. What will we do until then?"

"I have about sixty-nine ideas."

Her smile was slow and sensual. "Do you now?"

It was impossible to stop touching her. He wanted to bury his face in her hair, brush kisses over the tender skin of her nape, fill his hands with her breasts. "Here's one. . ." Wrapping his hand in her hair, Finn tugged her close, then bent his head to her lush mouth. Without a nanosecond of hesitation, her velvety smooth lips were instantly responsive and as eager as his as he stroked his tongue slow and deep. Her mouth tasted sweet, she'd been eating chocolate, and the scent of her skin made every muscle in his body tense with ravenous need.

The pleasure of kissing her shot to Finn's head like fine whisky, then raced through his veins in a heated rush to pool at his groin. It wasn't the kiss of strangers, it was carnal, mind-blowing and dick-raisingly intimate.

Rising on her toes to slide her arms around his waist, she slid her fingers under the waistband of his jeans at the small of his back. The feel of her smooth, cool hands on his bare skin was electrifying. He felt the hard peak of her nipples against his chest, and his fingers flexed in her hair.

The cavity of her mouth was hot, the slick glide of her tongue as it came out to duel with his, eager. Addictive.

Combing his fingers through her hair at her temples he let the cool fall drape over his arms as they kissed hungrily. They were both breathing hard when Finn broke away.

Sliding her hands free as he stepped back, their eyes locked. He felt as though he'd run a marathon, and her eyes looked glazed as her chest rose and fell.

Reaching into his pocket for his phone, he held up a finger. "Give me a minute."

He turned, then strode back across the hall. Not just for privacy, but because he couldn't trust himself not to strip her and take her on the floor. Or against an exhibit case.

When his assistant answered after one ring, he instructed, "Get me a room in the closest hotel. No. Right *now*. No, not a suite. Leo Major, regular room. You go ahead, I'll see you on board. Send the plane back for me. I'll contact Kathleen directly when I'm ready to leave. Oh, and – call off security. I don't want to see them. Give me the name- Great, thanks." Leo Major was one of many aliases he used to avoid the press following him everywhere he went. Today, it would serve a better purpose.

With a jolt of excitement, he hadn't felt on a personal level in a long time, Finn realized he had a unique opportunity to be with a woman who had no idea who he was, or any idea of his net worth.

He stalked across the marble floor like a lion approaching a gazelle. Except she wasn't prey, nor was she a victim. She'd had ninety seconds when she could've run. Instead, she waited, exactly where he'd left her.

"Shouldn't we exchange names?" she asked, as she slipped her hand into his, they walked towards the door.

Charmed by the innocent gesture, Finn couldn't remember when he'd last held hands with a woman. Unfortunately, his body wasn't getting the 'innocent' message and reacted as if she'd reached out and wrapped her fingers around his dick instead of just threading hers through his.

"You can be whoever you want to be."

They exited the historical building housing the museum into the early afternoon heat and headed down the cement steps to the street. Her hair was even more vibrant in the sun, and her smile shot through his body like an electrical current.

"I *like* being me."

God, he had it bad. He was transfixed with the way her lips moved as she spoke. By the way the sunlight showed her lightly tanned skin, overlaid with freckles as if she'd been dusted with cinnamon. Discovering the location of each one would be as irresistible a challenge as discovering new stars in the cosmos.

Passersby, male and female turned to give her a second and third look. A mild southerly breeze played with the long strands, transforming it into dancing, living flame. His libido responded with the certainty that once wasn't going to be enough.

"Be you. But let's maintain the fantasy. Make up an alter ego." He wanted the same freedom to be whoever he wanted to be with her. No expectations, no preconceived ideas. "Let's freefall for the weekend."

Laughing, she skipped a step to keep up with him. "Wow, you *are* optimistic. A whole weekend? You have that much stamina?"

Ignoring his waiting car and driver, Finn flagged a passing cab. "I told you sixty-nine reasons. Sixty-eight to go." Taking out his phone he glanced at the text before returning it to his pocket. "Four Seasons," he told the driver, as they got in. "We're in a hurry." He immediately wrapped his arm around her, tugging her close against his side as they pulled away from the curb.

Yes," he told her. "I have *that* much stamina. A few days might not even make a dent."

Splaying her hand on his chest, she stroked him through the linen of his shirt. "Do you always get your way?"

Finn captured her exploring hand to hold it still. Already on the razor's edge of insanity, her light touch was enough to drive him over the fucking edge. "I hope it'll be your way as well in a few minutes. Second thoughts?"

"I'm a full speed ahead kind of woman. No second thoughts." Resting her head against his upper arm, she slid her arm around his waist, hugging him against the soft pillows of her breasts. The hard point of her nipple against his arm had him stifling a groan.

The traffic was light as it always was at this time of day as they headed to the La Recoleta district. Modern buildings interspersed with hundreds-of-years-old stone structures housed businesses, homes, and hotels on either side of the wide boulevard. Pedestrians clogged the sidewalks, walking in packs, or enjoying the sunshine at outdoor cafes. Buenos Aires was famous for soccer, the tango and its raunchy nightlife. Been there, done that. Even during daylight hours, the city pulsed with a musical beat that put a spring in people's steps even as they performed their mundane daily activities.

The city was an interesting mix of old and new. Finn didn't give a damn. He was fixated on the way the sunlight pouring through the smudged side window illuminated her skin and set fire to her hair.

She looked up at him for several seconds without speaking, then said softly, "You can call me Persephone."

"Ah, Goddess Queen of the underworld. Excellent choice." He would've thought she'd have chosen Aphrodite considering where they'd met. Either was a mouthful and since he planned to have his mouth full of some part of her for the foreseeable future it didn't matter what she wanted to be called.

"What should I call you?"

"Leo." Low Earth orbit. It would do. He tightened his arm around her as the driver, taking Finn at his word, screeched around a corner at a breakneck speed. Two elderly women shook their fists as the cab careened past them with inches to spare.

"That's not very –fantasy-like."

"It trips more easily off the tongue than Persephone," he teased, brushing a long, fiery strand of hair behind her ear, then lingering to trace the shell with the tip of his finger.

Cheeks flushed, she shivered in response to his touch. "How about shortening it to Peri?"

"I like it." His driver, with his two personal bodyguards, pulled his rental car up discreetly behind their cab. After a glance at the meter, Finn pulled out a wad of pesos and handed it to the driver.

"Keep the change." He suspected he'd just tipped the guy the equivalent of his annual salary. Worth the speedy trip.

Handing her out of the cab, he wrapped an arm around her waist and led her into the hotel. He checked in as Leo Major and was handed a small folder with the room number and the key tucked inside. He glanced at the envelope as he returned to Persephone's side. "Second floor."

She tugged his hand to steer him toward the sweeping staircase off the marble, gilt and palm-filled lobby. "If we don't walk off some of this energy we might kill each other when we get to the room."

"Trust me, darling, walking's not going to make a dent in this energy." Finn tucked her more firmly against his side and redirected her to the bank of gilded elevators. "I have to kiss you again. And if I do that on the stairs I might lose my mind completely and forget we're in public." The doors opened silently, and he pulled her inside. For a man known for his control, he was out of his damn mind. The doors hadn't even closed before he started kissing her ravenously.

Their floor chimed. Reluctantly they broke apart. He'd kissed off her lipstick, and her mouth was pink and slightly swollen. Her eyes, more aqua than green now, looked dazed as the doors opened.

About to step out, Finn was surprised when she grabbed him by his shirt front and tugged his head down for another mind-blowing kiss. The door bounced on his back as they blocked it from closing.

Drunk on the smell of her skin, the taste of her, the feel of her slender body in his arms, he was a starving beggar at a feast. "We might not *make* it to the room," he murmured, mouth too occupied to make the words coherent.

Wrapping her arms around his neck, she whispered, "Don't care."

TWO

8 days after Buenos Aires
Onboard *Blackstar*

Holy shit. Holy shit, holy freaking shit! Persephone Case's excitement had nothing to do with being onboard the luxurious gigayacht hosting the party, or the illustrious, deep-pocketed, influential guests attending the event—bigwigs, museum people, buyers, the usual groupies who gathered around a major salvage like this. No, her excitement had everything to do with the reason for this swanky celebration.

The anticipation for the spoils of the "Cutter Salvage" had been hyped in the press as the biggest antiquities haul in history. Expected to far surpass the wealth and prestige of the Atocha wreck off the coast of Florida––a salvage that had been going strong for more than thirty years, to the tune of over four hundred million dollars.

Now all people could talk about were the *Nuestra Señora del Marco, Santa Ana* and *El Crucifijo.*

But, *four* ships lay at the bottom of the freaking ocean. They didn't mention *Napolitano.*

Had any of these people contacted *her* during the last five years while she was salvaging *Napolitano*? To offer investment money? To interview her? To get *her* take on what *she'd* already salvaged? Not a one. No one knew *her* name, but everyone and their uncle knew the damned Cutters.

Peri didn't want fame and fortune- or no more than the average salvager- what she wanted was recognition. She wanted to finally be *seen*. This was the closest she'd ever come to achieving that goal.

Dizzy with exhilaration, she hadn't felt this much of a rush since she'd stolen that first artifact - a pretty little gilded silver flask - from right under Zane Cutter's nose seven years ago.

That had been the beginning of her life of piracy against the brothers. She'd started off subtly. Targeting a Cutter's dive location, waiting for him to return to his ship for the night, then diving in, and helping herself to a few choice pieces before they could be brought to the surface.

They couldn't miss her sleek black boat, *Sea Witch*, as she lay at anchor well within the legal limit of one mile. Each damned brother had ignored her antics as if she were a pesky fly they couldn't be bothered to swat. Their blatant indifference had resulted in Peri's thefts becoming dangerously bolder. She'd think, *do you see me now? a*s she stood on the deck of her ship, giving them a good long look at her.

She'd dreamed of this confrontation for seven long years. The anticipation, and constant disappointment, had been exhausting. She'd miss the adrenaline rush, but she wouldn't miss the constant battle with herself as to the right and wrong of what she'd been doing.

Given this opportunity to meet them all at the same time, in her own backyard as it were, she was fine knowing her pirating days were over for good. Bearding the lions in their own den was even more of a thrill than stealing from them. It would be *impossible* for them to ignore her now.

This was the last step of her rehabilitation.

"*Dios*, have you ever seen such a ship?" Dr. Thiago Núñez whispered as they entered the crowded salon of *Blackstar* for the dive's inaugural party.

The elegantly appointed room was crowded with well-dressed guests who'd apparently had no issue making the two-hour trip from the mainland to attend a party. Wide windows and open French doors framed lights that glittered on the calm water surrounding a yacht the size of a small island, casting a pale purple wash over rippling navy-blue water. Spring in the Southern hemisphere brought dusk late, and at nine at night the violet and apricot sky wrapped around the ship like a diaphanous silken scarf in a showy display of color.

"Incredible." *Understatement.* "I need a big glass of wine and about a dozen of those shrimp canapes. I'm starving." Discreetly, Peri removed Theo's hand from her ass. On the rare occasions they appeared in public together, he "forgot" that they'd broken up more than a year ago and became possessive and handsy. They were the same height when she was barefoot, and if he wore lifts in his shoes. Since he was self-conscious about his five-foot-six height, she'd worn flats when they dated. Tonight, she wore five-inch sandals and towered over him.

Distinguished, with classic Latin features, and dark hair, prematurely graying at the temples, Theo looked like the professor of Antiquities that he was. But it had been his intensity and love of relics that had attracted her, and that shared interest had kept her distracted when the gloss of their relationship had worn off.

No matter how attractive he was, she didn't want seconds. He made a better associate than a lover. The only reason he *was* the Minister of Antiquities was because when Peri had discovered the four ships off the coast of Patagonia five years earlier and had to register the find with the Ministry of Cultural Affairs, Theo had been a mid-level employee with an archeological background. Because of the anticipated dollar, and cultural, value of what Peri had discovered, they'd given Theo a title and his own department to oversee the salvaging of the four ships.

He'd given her an advisory position because she'd asked for it as part of the deal of cutting him in on a small percentage over and above what the Government would get. Peri had considered it an excellent bargain.

"If I didn't tell you before, *mi amore*, you look delicious tonight." He was eye level with her cleavage.

"Theo-" Peri said warningly as she scanned the room for familiar faces. *Cutter* faces.

He gave her a soulful look. "When we're together in a social setting like this it is impossible to remember that we are no longer lovers."

"I'll keep reminding you," Peri told him dryly, deftly removing that wandering hand again. "I work with you, Theo. And soon everyone here will know it. It would look very bad for the Ministry if we behaved unprofessionally."

His smile was wistful. "It is not that we are no longer lovers, though, is it?" he said softly, black eyes searching her features. "You were never comfortable with displays of affection unless we were in the bedroom, *mi amore*. And even then ... a man needs to know the woman he's with feels the same heat."

She'd had no such qualms with Leo. Theo wouldn't have recognized *that* woman, not in his wildest dreams. *She* didn't recognize that woman. Peri had never had sex with a man she'd just met, never had a one-night stand. In fact, she'd had more sex that weekend with Leo, than she'd had in her entire *life*. The weekend in Buenos Aires seemed like a dream now. It was the first time in her life she'd felt totally. . . *free*. No shackles to the past, no second thoughts, nothing but two anonymous people having glorious sex, then walking away.

"We make better friends." She took the glass of wine he handed her, plucked from the tray of a passing waiter, her gaze falling on the small, black, swirl tattoo on the web of his right thumb. A whirlpool, he'd told her at the beginning of their relationship. She'd never bothered to ask the significance of it and didn't care now.

"Even so, you have always been guarded with your emotions. A man looking at you sees fire when there is really ice."

That stung. "You didn't complain when we were together."

"I thought I could melt you."

You couldn't, but somehow a stranger I'd just met, could. "I'm sorry, Theo." He was a nice man. He'd treated her well. But he'd never turned her on. Not the way Leo had. "I told you right from the beginning that I was lousy at relationships."

He flashed her his flirty, seductive, very Latin smile. Theo could be extremely charming when he wanted to be. "But to tempt a red-blooded man with such a dress. . ."

Peri had chosen her dress with care. Not to be sexy, but to boost her confidence. The strapless, floaty dress, in shades of red and orange, looking like a column of flame, bared her shoulders, and brushed her toes. This evening she flew her vibrant hair, loose down her back, like a red flag to a bull.

I'm here! Ignore me now, you bastards.

How long would it take for them to recognize her? She'd bet less than a minute. She'd mentally rehearsed this momentous meeting- Hell, no amount of rehearsal could possibly prepare her for what was about to happen. Braced and ready, or as ready as she could be in such an unpredictable setting, Peri casually did another scan of the salon.

Him? No.

Maybe that guy over there? Damn, she wasn't sure.

The brothers might not recognize her face, but her hair was a dead giveaway. They'd know who she was right away. There were a couple of other women here with various shades of red hair, but none so bright, or as long as hers. It was pretty freaking distinctive. Even so, would they identify her without *Sea Witch* anchored nearby, to make the connection?

In the years since she'd been stealing from them, she'd never been this close. Peri had gone through several phases of pissed-off-ness in the six months since she'd learned from Theo that the Cutters, too, had staked claims up and down the coast of Patagonia. *Her* damned claim. All of that pissed-off-ness had led her to this night.

Reckless, she knew. But she was sick of the cat and mouse game she'd been playing for so many years. During that time, she'd thought she was the cat. It wasn't until she saw their names on claims *she'd* discovered that she realized who had been playing whom.

Damn it. She'd staked her claim for salvage, bought property nearby, and worked her ass off for five freaking *years* on her wreck, *Napolitano*. Then, out of the damn blue, *they* showed up to scoop up the other three wrecks! What the hell were the odds of *that* happening? But then again, these were the Cutters. Low-down, thieving bastards who had manipulated her family out of fortunes time and again for years.

Still, it was damn hard to justify her annoyance when she'd been pilfering from them as well. And it wasn't as if they could possibly know that the Koúkos Corporation, the one that had claimed *Napolitano*, was also Persephone Case.

The minute they saw her, they'd realize their lives were about to get a lot more interesting. And if Peri had her way, this dive was going to serve their cockiness and bravado back to them, on a silver platter, carved and ready to eat.

She could describe each man's ship to the last rivet, but she wasn't sure she could pick any of the brothers out of a lineup. She'd watched them through her binocs, she'd seen their pictures in various international news outlets. But had never been close enough to touch.

Being a fly on the wall to see their response first hand was going to be freaking epic. Like walking a tightrope over rocky, shark-infested waters, but fun nevertheless.

Peri had always known that, like a house of cards, the whole mess would come tumbling down at some point. Even though the house she'd built with cards of deception was an architectural masterpiece, if she did say so herself. Better to control the fallout than be taken unaware.

The weekend she had spent with Leo had been incredible. Magical. But that Sunday morning eight days ago, as she'd anticipated joining him in the shower, she knew she didn't want to maintain one more lie. She was already juggling several layers of deception. The Cutters didn't know the identity of the owner of Sea Witch. *Yet.* They sure as hell didn't know that the pirate on board *Sea Witch* was related to their nemesis, Rydell Case. Her brother.

Tightrope. Sharks. Rocks.

THREE

Ankles crossed, Finn leaned against the rail on the aft deck of his ship, *Blackstar*, which was anchored forty miles off the coast of Patagonia. Nearby, *Blackstar Two,* his dive ship, lay in position over the wreck of the galleon, *Nuestra Señora del Marco.* He and his partners, the Cutter brothers, had started the salvage two days earlier.

He had zero patience for waiting. Each hour of his day was planned for and filled to capacity. Just the way he liked things.

Now he waited for word from his private investigator.

Eight days had passed since the anomaly in Buenos Aires, and he couldn't stop thinking about the incredible redhead and those thirty-seven intense, heart-pounding hours they'd spent together. He'd returned after a solo shower on the third day to find the room empty. She'd left nothing behind but the faint, evocative scent of lilies on the still warm sheets to remind him of something he'd never forget.

No note, no goodbye.

Fake first name, no last name.

Fuck. Fuck. Fuck.

"You look cheerful." Nick Cutter came outside carrying two beers. He handed a bottle to Finn. "You remember this is a celebration, right?"

Finn drank, giving his friend the evil eye. "You bet me they'd all be gone by eight."

With a grin, Nick shrugged. "I owe you ten bucks."

"Should've made it a thousand," Finn laughed. "I knew you'd lose your ass on that bet, you lying sack of shit."

"Whatever the bet," Zane said as he, Jonah and Logan joined them at the rail. "I'm in."

Nick took a canape off the platter Zane held, and said around a mouthful of bruschetta crostini, "Yeah, well since *you* actually *like* people, you weren't included in the bet."

Finn had first invested, on a calculated whim, in one of Zane's dives a decade earlier. He'd doubled his money. Then met, and became friends with, middle brother Nick and oldest brother Logan. Jonah had come on the scene later. The brothers had a close bond and had included Finn into their tight-knitcircle. The Cutters had become good friends and damn good business partners.

Now, surrounded by his friends, and the lively sounds of a party going on inside, Finn wondered what *she* was doing at nine P.M on this Monday evening. Was she looking at the same lavender and apricot sky he saw shimmering off the still water, and reflecting the dying sun over the Atlantic Ocean?

Where the hell are you? How the fuck do I find you?

Around them, the lights of various ships, boats, tenders, and assorted seaworthy craft, huddled together, having deposited smartly dressed guests to drink his booze and eat his food. Good publicity. What they salvaged from the three wrecks would be sold to the highest bidders.

"See that heavyset guy?" Logan indicated, with a jerk of his shoulder, a guest standing inside, visible through the window. "He's the buyer for that Saudi Prince with serious bank who put the ten million in escrow for the chance at right of first refusal. The blond woman to his left is head of the Major Acquisitions committee at DC's Smithsonian Museum of Natural history. The other blond is a reporter for Quaternary Science Review."

"These people aren't just here to drink your booze and shoot the breeze. They're here to claw their way into position to be the first; to buy, to scoop, to report."

"Making nice is how our bread is buttered and thickly layered with honey," Zane added.

"I like the honey just fine," Finn said with a smile. He knew how to play the game even if having all these people tromping all over his ship was annoying. "Any sighting of Dr. Núñez and his sidekick? I presume the Argentinian government doesn't expect us to house this oversight person for the *duration*, right?" Finn took a slug of his beer. He glanced at his friends, none of whom looked happy about the prospect. "They're aware this salvage could take *twenty* years, right?"

"Fifty, if we're lucky," Jonah said with a wide grin. "Come on, we'll *smoke* Mel Fisher's Atocha salvage. Thirty-two years, and *still* going strong? Almost five-hundred million so far?"

"We'll beat that." Zane clicked beer bottles with his brother as if they'd already won the race. "Fuck, we have *five* dive boats and *three* wrecks. Slam dunk."

With the Cutter's track record, and the artifacts and coins they'd retrieved just in the last two days, probably. "*Estimated* five hundred-mil." Finn was assured his investment would have a healthy return. Didn't mean he wanted to stick around and watch each real brought to the surface. "The thought of staying put that long gives me heartburn."

Like a shark, he liked to keep moving.

"As long as *Blackstar Two* stays right there," Nick indicated Finn's two-hundred-foot dive boat anchored nearby with his glass of soda. "we're good."

Finn smiled. "Now I feel like a twenty-dollar whore."

"Try a twenty-million-dollar whore. Take the money and run, Rocketman." Jonah placed his bottle on a nearby table. "But you'll at least hang for a few weeks, right? Or are you off to scale another mountain? Or build a high-rise on the moon?"

"For the Moon, we'd need to invoke in situ resource utilization. Supplies - oxygen and water - would have to be manufactured on site before anyone could live there. Easier on Mars. The polar ice caps can be melted for water, and oxygen can be extracted from water electrically. The moon has nothing and would be harder. You can't fit enough oxygen and water for a colony in a supply rocket." He looked around at the smiling faces of his friends. "TMI?"

"Always interesting, but that question was rhetorical," Jonah smiled. "Is there a minute of any day that you're *not* thinking about space?"

"I'm thinking this better be the last party I have to host," Finn said without heat as the sound of voices and glasses clinking spilled outside.

"We have to make a decision before the oversight guy shows up," Logan reminded them. "He's not going to commute from the mainland every dayfor a four-hour round trip. One of us is going to have to play innkeeper."

"He could come once a week," Jonah said. "Then we wouldn't need to waste a bunk." He brightened. "Even once a month..."

It wasn't unusual for a local government to keep an eagle eye on their percentage of salvaged treasure. It was part and parcel of treasure hunting. But none of them particularly wanted a stranger on board, monitoring their every move for the unforeseeable future.

Jonah tried again. "Maybe we could switch every couple of weeks? That seems fair--"

"I should be exempt." Zane shot his oldest brother, Logan a hopeful glance. "Trust me, other than my lovely bride, no one in their right mind would want to stay on board *Decrepit* for weeks on end. Worse if it turns out he's a woman."

"First, we don't know if Andersen is a man or a woman, and we've been through this," Logan said. "None of us wants anyone looking over our shoulder 24/7. Five of us. Five straws. Winner is the short straw, losers pay him five grand a piece. Who wants to go first? "

Like himself, the Cutters thrived on competition. Even straw pulling. Finn eyed the toothpicks fanned out like porcupine quills in Logan's fist. "Seriously?"

"You've known us for a decade." Zane's distinctive blue eyes twinkled. "When have we *not* taken a bet seriously?"

"Art form." Finn agreed, plucking his broken toothpick and palming it.

"What if this Andersen's some six-hundred-pound guy who smells like garlic?" Zane pulled out his toothpick.

"You'll have to suck it up, buttercup." Nick's Cutter-blue eyes held a devilish glint, as if he knew something the rest of them didn't. "If you pull the short straw you'll have to learn to live with whatever the guy smells like."

They each held up their wooden sticks of various lengths.

With a grin, Logan gripped Finn's shoulder. "Rocketman it is."

Eyeing the toothpicks and realizing he had the shortest, Finn shrugged. "Not a big deal. I'll house him on *Blackstar Two* and pretty much never see him."

"You really want some government watchdog with *that* much unsupervised access?" Zane asked.

"Plenty of security. I'm not worried."

Privacy was a paramount concern in his life. Even though *Blackstar* was a three hundred and fifty-foot behemoth, with six decks, more than sixty permanent crew and a full complement of office staff, he didn't want an unknown quantity onboard. *Blackstar Two* was close enough.

Finn operated in all his business dealings with fairness and integrity, as did the Cutters. He'd have nothing to hide when they continued pulling ancient relics and valuable treasure from the sea whether a government oversight person was on board or not. No matter what they scored, the Argentinians would get their cut, honestly and fairly.

Finn had his own team of twelve divers aboard *Blackstar Two* and had allocated three hours a day to dive with them. He'd be busy morning, noon and night. Perhaps he could juggle his schedule to squeeze in a quick trip back to Buenos Aires and another visit to the museum. . .

"True." Nick's teeth flashed white as he smiled. "Since you happen to have a ship the size of a fiefdom. More room for her to disappear in. You won't even notice one woman on ..."

"The six-hundred-pound garlic eater is a *woman*?" Zane scrunched up his face comically, his distinctive blue eyes alight with mischief. "Jesus, I bet she has a thick black mustache, hairy warts, and ..."

"Don't make up shit." Logan elbowed his brother. "We don't know if Andersen is a man or a woman yet. Dr. Núñez, head of the agency will introduce us tonight." He glanced inside, through the open doors behind Finn. "They may even be here by now. We should go back in anyway."

The darkening sky displayed a strip of brilliant orange.

Delicate and fiery, like. . .

They'd shared two sunsets, three dawns and only gotten out of bed to shower and eat. The rest of the time they'd made love. For Finn, the experience was like watching the brilliance of a comet streaking through the sky on a clear, ink-black night, knowing it wouldn't appear again in his lifetime. Weird, because he'd never felt that for a person before. Celestial bodies, yeah. But never a woman.

You got exactly what you wanted, dickhead. Hot anonymous sex. Foolish to linger over an anomaly. Yeah, the sex had been phenomenal, but it was just pheromones and sexual attraction to the nth degree.

Just? Jesus. Not *just.* The entire experience had consumed him. *She* had consumed him. Wiped his mind clean, exhilarated every cell in his body. Since Buenos Aires, he'd spent an inordinate amount of time remembering details while his people searched Argentina from one end to the other. To find her. She'd been like a potent drug, and his body, usually so disciplined, was in the grip of a powerful withdrawal.

Annoying and unlike him.

Shit, for all he knew she could've been specifically sent to lure him to a hotel for some nefarious purpose his security people had, as yet, been unable to confirm or deny. Fucking impossible to find a redheaded ghost in a country with a population of over forty-four million people.

She could be anywhere. Anyone.

He didn't do one-night stands- too much of a liability. He enjoyed the personal connection in a relationship. He hadn't had one of those in over a year. He lived onboard his ship. Hard to make connections when he had a strict rule not to have romantic relationships with his staff or his crew.

"Yo." Nick snapped his fingers under Finn's nose. "Never lose focus with this lot. You'll find yourself accepting a bet to French a Great White by default."

Drumming up amusement, Finn blinked the brothers back into focus. Damn, he never lost focus. Why did this one-and-done experience in Buenos Aires still have such a powerful hold on him? He heard them with one part of his brain, while he thought about *her* with the other. Persephone. Queen of the underworld. With her interest in salvaged artifacts, perhaps she would have lingered if he'd told her about this salvage five hundred miles down the coast.

Several occasions over the course of their short time together, he'd been tempted to invite her onboard. Spend more time with her. . . But he'd been the one to stipulate, no real names, no personal details.

It had been a magical weekend precisely because "Persephone" remained a mystery, and because she'd *appeared* to have no knowledge of who he was. There was something ultimately freeing in that. She'd given him everything without ever knowing, or asking, about his bank account. It was a rare gift to have that kind of anonymity.

Unfortunately, Finn wasn't naïve. Maybe the weekend had been as pure as he'd wanted it to be. Maybe it wasn't. Wishing it, didn't make it so. His PI should be able to ascertain who she was, and if necessary, uncover her play.

Find her for fucksake. I'll ask her myself.

The salvage had officially started, but there was still a crapton of prelim work to do. Once things got more interesting, and he got more involved, Finn hoped she'd fade from his mind. With his regular day-to-night work and the salvage, he had enough on his plate to distract himself.

Still, he speculated how much she'd enjoy this sunset, turning her face up to the cool breeze coming off the water, the open French doors spilling soft lights and music out to the deck where he and the others gathered at the aft rail. The scent of the ocean and spicy food rode the breeze. The cool, salty air stroked his face and ruffled his hair, reminding him of the feel of her fingers against his scalp.

Peri. Sassy, sexy. Did her real name suit her as well?

Overlapping animated conversation, laughter, and glasses clinking, lent an air of excited anticipation. Divers from their five ships, and peripheral hangers-on, including some press, milled about Blackstar's expansive main salon on the third deck, drinks in hand. Too damn many people crushed together in one space.

More than thirty divers had done their first dive that day across the three wrecks - Finn's and the Cutter's - covering more than fifty nautical miles of ocean up and down the coast of Patagonia. A small selection of their spoils was now displayed under the watchful eyes of four security guards. Some of the impressive bounty -a handful of the hundreds of ancient gold and silver bars, gold jewelry fit for a queen, and emeralds bound for Europe, had been hastily cleaned of their dark crust for this evening's event. For the first day of a salvage, the magnitude of the haul was unprecedented.

The potential for historically significant treasure, artifacts that no one had seen in hundreds of years, had drawn Finn to this investment. He'd built a career–thrived in fact–on new, unexplored territory, be it in the sky, or in the depths of the ocean. If what he and the Cutters suspected was true, he'd get a return on his sizable investment. Several times over. A nice bonus, and a definite win-win.

"Your cleaning crew did an excellent job processing the stuff on display," Jonah told Finn. "The s--"

Jonah's words dissolved like mist over the water. With what felt like a small explosive charge, Finn's heart shuddered like a multistage rocket hitting outer space as it did a second-stage drop. Deaf, mouth suddenly dry, Finn's focus zeroed in on a waterfall of fiery hair, creamy, freckled skin, and fuck-me jade eyes that were unmistakable. His gaze slid down her body, and the dress of flame that defied all the laws of gravity.

Persephone.

"Ariel?" Theo gave her a worried frown. "Are you alright?"

Peri's heart gave several excited knocks of anticipation as she blinked him back into focus. Ariel was the only name Theo knew her by. She always used it if she wanted to put some distance between her doings and her brother. Just in case things went sideways. It had never been more necessary than now. Her first confrontation with the Cutters.

"Just taking it all in," she told him easily, as she visually tracked the guests. "The ship's spectacular." An understatement. *Blackstar* was beyond a megayacht, it was a gigayacht. The superyacht of superyachts. Over three hundred feet of sleek black hull, six decks, and miles of gleaming brightwork. It must take a veritable army to run it. Peri was impressed, and if she wasn't so tense, she'd love to poke around and see more.

She knew she wasn't going to have that opportunity. Not once the Cutters recognized her. Not that they could do much about her presence, other than try to make her life difficult. She represented the Argentinian government. It wasn't as though they could fire her.

The invitation to the party had come from the Cutters, but this wasn't one of their ships. They'd brought in a new big gun for this salvage.

Peri accepted another glass of white wine from a passing steward, then rubbed the back of her neck when she felt someone watching her. Surreptitiously glancing around, she froze as a tall, dark- haired man headed for her like a laser guided missile.

Dizzy, dry-mouthed and sick to her stomach, she suddenly felt light-headed, confused. Exactly the way she'd felt that time she'd surfaced too fast and got the bends.

Holding her gaze, his grey eyes glittered like polished steel as the party guests parted for him like a kelp forest before a shark. He moved with a familiar self-assurance. Self-assurance that came from knowing who and what he was. He was the king of the world, and he and everyone around him knew it.

Her stomach fluttered,her heart raced, and her lungs burned because she forgot how to breathe. Holy crap! *Leo*?

Her first thought was; how the hell did you find me? Quickly followed by a fervent: Please God, do not be a Cutter!

Then he was there. Close enough to touch, engulfing her in the faint, clean scent of citrus, sea and man. His molten, quicksilver colored eyes ran over her face and body like a lover's eager hands. The naked hunger she saw there stole her breath and sent her heartbeat into overdrive.

Her body instantly reacted to the visceral memory of his hands and mouth all over her. Hot, sweaty sex. The feel of his sweat-dampened skin sliding over hers. Peri's nipples tightened, and her breath caught.

He looked a lot more dangerous now than he had a week ago. More in control than the insatiable man who'd taken her against a wall, in the shower, on the balcony, on the floor of their hotel room. A mental flash of their gyrating, sweaty bodies, his mouth between her legs, the weight of him in her hand, his fingers in her hair, made her tense like a bowstring.

A prickle of unease mixed with the instant flair of sexual hunger. Her knees went weak, responding to the pull of his blatant sexual power. Nothing had changed in her response to him since she'd last seen him. His maleness beckoned to every female atom in her body to respond. And boy, did she.

His dark hair brushed the collar of a white dress shirt, casually open at his strong, tanned throat. His hair was the only soft thing about him. His features were chiseled, and his Roman nose only added to his sex appeal. His jaw was shadowed, and his eyes remained fixed on her face. Towering over her, Leo extended his hand to her as if a week ago that hand hadn't explored every millimeter of her body. Inside and out.

Peri's eyes dropped to his unsmiling mouth.

"Finn Ga--"

"Phineas Gallagher, I know," Theo said with his American-educated Spanish accent, as he intercepted the other man's outstretched hand to give it a vigorous shake. "Doctor Thiago Núñez, Minister of Antiquities. It's an honor to meet you, sir. I've read your articles in scientific journals over the years. I'd be very interested to learn more about your space exploration. I might be interested in purchasing a ticket-"

"Theo, you hate heights." Peri was hardly aware she'd spoken. God, this was surreal. Anticipation, tempered with fear, heightened her senses and made her head swim.

His face a taut mask, Leo's poker face was exceptional. If one didn't see how his eyes devoured her features one by one. A muscle pulsed in his jaw.

Her heart thudded violently. His elegant features appeared more austere than a week ago in Buenos Aires, maybe the white-hot heat in his eyes was a trick of the light? Wishful thinking? There was something coiled and dark behind the silver-gray. Something she hadn't seen, or hadn't noticed when they'd first met. "You're never going to set foot on a spaceship, no matter how exciting it sounds."

Unless he had an identical twin, her passionate lover "Leo" was multibazzilionaire inventor slash philanthropist slash god-only-knew-what-else, Phineas Gallagher. Large and commanding. He looked as though he owned everything around him, and he probably freaking-well did.

God, no wonder he'd looked vaguely familiar at the museum. She just hadn't put it together because it was so random and out of context. She'd heard of the Blackstar Group. What the hell had he been doing at the museum in Buenos Aires picking up a strange woman? Why would a guy with serious bank, a guy who looked like *this*, moved like him, smelled like him-need to have an anonymous weekend fling?

On the other hand, that weekend had been an aberration for her. As daring and adventure-driven as she was, she'd never done anything like *that* in her life before that weekend. She was a normal, healthy, single woman, and she hadn't had a lover in well over a year. The sparks he ignited had been off the charts. It would've been impossible to ignore, and she hadn't tried. A hot- flaming hot, interlude had been offered. She'd grabbed it- him- with both hands.

Now she wondered, fatalistically, if he'd connect the dots. Between her presence at that museum, at *that* exhibit, to her presence on board his ship, and her involvement with the Argentinian government? And any minute, the confrontation with the Cutters?

When Peri extended her hand, Leo -*Phineas*- wrapped his fingers around hers. The contact of skin to skin felt like holding onto a live electrical wire. She wet her dry lips with a sweep of her tongue and was gratified by the flare of heat in his eyes as he followed the movement.

"Ariel Andersen, your liaison with the Department of Antiquities." Proud of how steady her voice sounded, Peri smiled.

He did not smile back. Instead, he raised a brow. "You know this could take twenty years or more?" The hint of Ireland in his voice gave her goosebumps. It was several seconds before she realized his deep voice carried a message her befuddled brain couldn't quite decipher.

Even a football-field-length gigayacht would become a very small space indeed if she was sequestered on board with him for any length of time. Peri felt every hard knock of her heartbeat and covered the base of her throat with her hand, sure everyone could see her rapid pulse.

Her cheeks grew hot at the thought of the Cutters outing her in front of him. The wine glass felt slick in her suddenly sweating palm as she gave him a level look, her heartbeat skittering in her chest.

Longing. Panic. Embarrassment.

Damn it, *excitement* seeing him again.

"I'm fully aware, Mr. Gallagher." Boy, she was going to win the Best Actress Award any minute. "Don't worry, I have no intention of interfering with your day to day operations. You won't even know I'm onboard." *Because any second now you're going to find out who I really am.*

Okay. That sounded good. Cool. Competent. Not panicky at all. "Have you worked with the Cutters before?" But it was too freaking late for cool. Did she have a fever? Her skin felt hot and tight. The blood in her veins was on fire, surging through her in pulsing waves. If just looking at him made her wet, she was in trouble.

She was in big, big trouble.

"Yes, many times. Their ventures usually prove profitable."

Because the bastards were pirates of the worst kind. "They seem pretty sure about the value of this one. There's a lot of equipment coming in, a lot of salvage ships gathered. Do you know how they heard about this particular location?" Might as well get all the questions in before the shit hit the fan.

"You'll have to ask them. There's Zane now, want me to call him over?"

"No." *Chicken.* "This is a social gathering. I'll have plenty of time to ask my questions over the next few weeks."

God, this was awkward. How could her much-anticipated confrontation with the Cutters possibly work with *him* in the mix?

"And it's Finn."

She blinked.

"My name's *Finn,*" he repeated.

"Right. I'm merely here to observe, Finn." She didn't want to talk about the Cutters and scrambled mentally for some sort of civilized, impersonal, cocktail party exchange. "I must admit, I'm also intrigued to hear about your race to Mars." She probably would be if her brain wasn't behaving like a squirrel on a wheel as she fixated on the way his mouth moved. Peri wanted to feel it on hers, needed him to touch more than her hand. Wanted Theo to vanish and take all the party guests with him. Her nipples, painfully aroused, pressed against the lace cups of her strapless bra.

"The first flight is half a year away."

"Ariel loves heights." Theo tried to wrap a possessive arm around her waist, but she adroitly sidestepped so his hand dropped to his side. "I can't even walk across her living room," he smiled. "This girl has nerves of steel. Lives on a bluff and half her house is a glass box suspended over a cliff. A ten-story drop to the rocks below." He shuddered dramatically. "Can't do it."

"I'm not a girl, as I keep reminding you." She pinched his forearm in warning to keep his hands off her. "You're missing out, Theo. Two-inch thick tempered glass, cantilevered over a bluff. I have the most spectacular views in Patagonia." Finn didn't care, and she was talking too much and too damn fast because she was a nervous wreck waiting for several other shoes to drop. "Three sixty views- nothing but ocean and sky. You should've built there yourself. Your loss, my gain."

The memory of Finn's hard naked body, hips pounding into her, was as visceral as if they were in the act there and then. All her body parts responded with alacrity. She remembered the scent of his skin, the heat of him pulsing against her. Remembered that his lightest touch could make her come. And had. Multiple times that weekend.

In serious lust, she couldn't drag her gaze away, couldn't stop her body's reaction to him. She decided to just enjoy the experience solo. "Theo and I met when we both bid on the same piece of land several years ago." *Shut up, Peri! This is TMI. Cocktail party. Polite 'nice to meet you' convo, not my freaking life story. He doesn't care.*

"I got my peninsula," she continued a little breathlessly, and as though she hadn't just given herself that little pep talk, "a spectacular bluff view, and this -" Did his lips just twitch? "This job with the Department of Antiqui---" She let out a little yelp when Finn grasped her upper arm, cutting off her inane chatter.

"Excuse us," he said with utmost insincerity to Theo. Plucking the wine glass from her nerveless fingers, he shoved it at Theo before propelling her through the crowd. Heads turned at their passage.

Startled by the abruptness of his gesture, Peri tried to yank her arm free. "Wait. What-"

He shot a terse, "Shut up" over his shoulder.

She dug in her heels. "*Excuse* me?!"

His fingers merely tightened as he plowed between his guests like a guided missile. Head's turned, people jumped out of their way as he pulled her out into the wide corridor beyond the salon where a dozen or more people clustered around a bar in the curve under the stairs. Everyone there turned as one to watch their progress.

Peri's cheeks flamed. "Maybe-" And maybe *not*. He wasn't stopping for anyone or anything as people parted like the Red Sea.

Finn almost crashed into a steward dressed in a black uniform with the ship's white logo on his pocket. The large tray, with filled wine glasses, swayed and dipped. Disaster was averted without them slowing as the waiter pressed back against the paneled wall, holding the tray over his head so they could pass without incident.

Slapping his palm on the third door to the right Finn manhandled her inside without a word. Darkness enveloped them when the door slammed shut. Without pause, he walked her across the small room, then pinned her between his hard body and something cold and metallic at her back.

The heat of him enveloped her. The world shrank in the cocoon of darkness, and the rasp of their heavy breathing.

Gathering her hair at her nape in one fist, he used it to arch her head back. "Do you know how *fucking* long I've been trying to find you?"

FOUR

God," Finn murmured, breath hot against Peri's throat. "You taste so-" He took her mouth in a ravenous kiss, as if he'd been unable to wait a second longer. The kiss was so hard, so aggressive that Peri almost came right there in the darkness.

Wrapping her arms around his waist, she kissed him back with all the fervent longing she'd felt since they'd parted. She didn't want to stop. She'd dreamed of this for eight days and nights, but reality far surpassed the memory.

Their lips crushed, the kiss mutely rough. Not merely hungry. *Starving. Yes, please, and thank you.* The taste of him was a match to her tinder. She welcomed the slick heat as his tongue dueled with hers and his fingers gripped her butt through the flimsy fabric of her dress, pulling her tightly against his erection.

She made a soft, urgent sound when he released one hand from her butt cheek, to pull her dress and strapless bra down around her waist. Bending his head separated the juncture of her thighs from the promise of that erection, but the sensation of wet heat as his mouth touched her naked breast compensated.

Plumping her breast in the cup of his hand, Finn curled his tongue around the erect bud, then sucked. The sharp, sweet sensation shot to her core, making her head thrash against the heated metal at her back. Tightening her fingers in his hair, she urged his mouth harder against her skin.

The familiar intoxicating scent of grapefruit and ocean shot through her veins like hot brandy as the heat of his damp mouth trailed from one breast to the other. Peri was so consumed and distracted, she at first didn't notice he was bunching the flimsy fabric of her dress in his other hand. Not until she became aware of the cool, silky glide of fabric as he skimmed her long dress up her thigh.

Lifting his head, he buried his damp mouth in the crook of her neck, and unerringly tore the delicate silk of her thong free from her body.

As he tugged the wisp of fabric from between her legs she felt how wet she was and freed one arm, her hand going to his zipper. The hiss of the metal teeth of the zipper being tugged down mingled with their heavy breathing. It was no easy task to get the small tab over his impressive erection. She used the time to explore, lingering to see if everything was as she remembered it.

He hissed in a sharp breath and caught her wrist. "I won't last ten seconds if- Jesus, woman." As he locked their lips in another punishing kiss, she slid the zipper down. One. Tooth. At. A. Time. Finn shuddered, pushing against her fingers. Eventually, the hard length of his velvety penis jerked free and Peri was able to take him in her hand. He was huge, rock hard, and pulsing. Better than she remembered.

Without breaking the kiss, he nudged her legs apart and gripping her butt in both hands, half lifted her to plunge to the hilt, deep inside her.

Peri came apart in his arms.

"Breath," Peri begged on a meager sip of air as the first climax shook her. Instead of stopping, his hips continued to pound against her, building a rapid succession of escalating peaks, threaded like pearls on a string, culminating in a climax that felt as though it lasted to infinity.

Limp and out of breath, she attempted to suck air into her starving lungs. "Mercy! I'm melting like an ice cream sundae. Wait until I get back to solid form before you--"

"You drive me crazy." Reaching between them he touched her clit. Her back arched as a shudder of pleasure raced like fire along her nerve endings. "Can't get enough of you."

Her entire body felt as live as an electrical current. "I can't come again."

She was wrong. Swells of pleasure cascaded through her in a fresh wave as he stroked her. The man had the stamina of a lion.

This time the climax was short and sharp, plunging her into a dark void where she couldn't hear, think, or respond as her body took on a life of its own.

When she could move, and as small aftershocks tightened and released deep inside her, she dropped her forehead to his chest. She breathed in the intoxicating smell of hot skin and sex. His damp shirt smelled pleasantly of musk and starch and clung to his skin. His chest rose and fell in counterpoint to her own. His body was hard and heavy as he pressed against her with his delicious, full weight.

Drunk on the feel and smell of him, she loved that he was as sweaty and out of breath as she was. "Can a person die from pleasure?"

Finn crooked a finger to lift her chin, then kissed her softly on her swollen mouth. "I'm willing to work at it."

She managed a choked laugh as she adjusted her ankles in the small of his back for a better hold. Not that she needed anything more than her legs, since he had her pinned like a butterfly against what she presumed was a refrigerator. "You locked the door, right?"

"You mean between the time we slammed it behind us and now? No." He kissed her neck just under her ear, sending a ripple through her body. Deep inside, his penis responded to her reaction and her body clenched around him.

"So, anyone could just walk in?" She angled her head so he could better reach the juncture of her neck and shoulder, which gave her the opportunity to taste his skin. Salty. "Where are we anyway?"

"Pantry." Finn cupped her breast, his thumb leisurely tracing her turgid nipple.

Now that she knew where they were, Peri could smell the savory hint of the spicy tapas they were serving at the party, and a trace of booze. "We have everything we need. We could live in here for a month."

She felt his smile against her jaw as he kissed her neck. "I think people would miss us."

They'd miss him. No one knew who she was. No one would notice if she went missing. Her brother never knew where she was for months on end. He was used to her disappearing. The thought was a bit depressing.

"We didn't use a condom." In Buenos Aires when they'd depleted the dozen in the mini bar, he'd called down for more.

"Too much of a hurry, and I wasn't prepared. I guess I'm not that good of a Boy Scout after all. I have a clean bill of health—"

"So, do I, but still—"

"It's extremely hard - hard being the operative word here - trying to think when you do. . .that." His thumb glided over her painfully hard nipple making her tremble. She used her teeth on his shoulder and slid her fingers into the hair at his nape.

"All the booze is in here, too, right?" Came out almost breathlessly. How was he still standing? If he wasn't pinning her against the fridge, she'd be a puddle at his feet… An interesting possibility she'd explore later.

"Makes it more exciting."

"To have wait staff to-ing and fro-ing while my dress is up around my waist and you have your pants down around your knees? Sure." She was only being half sarcastic. "Way more exciting."

"Damn it, Persephone, I couldn't find you. You left without giving me your real name or any contact information."

"I like when you call me Persephone when you're inside me." Peri had given him her real name, Ariel was the lie. "Do you want me to call you Leo when we make love?"

"You can call me any damn thing you like, as long as I have you like this. You didn't say goodbye. I went to the airport, car rental places- tore the city apart looking for you. I wasn't ready for our weekend to end."

She'd driven the five hundred miles back to her house in Patagonia with heart palpitations and sweaty palms. Hoping, but also dreading, that the man who'd introduced himself as 'Leo' would follow her and ruin what had been a magical time by allowing reality to intrude. "You said no names, no reality. I figured you'd also want no goodbyes."

"Changed my mind."

At least he admitted, albeit tacitly, that had been his original intention. "Nothing that hot could sustain," she told him.

"Well if we'd left it there, we'd never have had the opportunity to find out, would we?" He nipped at her lower lip, then stroked the sting with a sweep of his tongue. "Now we do."

"I'm on the oversight committee." Peri combed her fingers through his thick, dark hair. She wished she could see him, read his expressions, but there wasn't a scintilla of light in the room. She had to settle for the feel, taste and sound of him. It was almost enough. Certainly, enough to keep this lovely fantasy alive a little bit longer. "That's a conflict of interest."

"I don't give a flying fuck." Pausing to push her hair over her shoulder, he lingered to rub a strand between his fingers. "If you quit, would they send someone else?"

"Of course." She started unbuttoning his shirt. Theo would come out every few weeks or months to see what was going on. But Peri knew him. He wasn't the most conscientious Minister of Antiquities she'd ever encountered. He was happy to sit in his office in Buenos Aires, or at his sheep farm in Patagonia, playing fantasy soccer on his computer, raking in the government's percentage of the findings, taking some on the side, and going to nightclubs until three every morning.

Pushing the edges of his shirt clear, she buried her face against his hard chest, inhaling the smell of his skin.

"Quit. I'll pay you to take a holiday." Slanting his mouth over hers, he kissed her with raw, ravenous hunger. A perfect reason for her not to respond to the offer.

Still erect, and deep inside her, Finn lifted her, his hands under her butt. Peri wrapped her legs more tightly around his waist to maintain her balance. He moved through the darkness, apparently knowing what might be in his way to trip him up. After a few moments, she was set on a cold flat surface.

"Do people eat on this table?"

Gently lowering her so her back met another metal surface, he kissed his way across her chest. Caught between the cold stainless steel and the furnace heat of his body, fresh waves of arousal stole her breath. He sucked her nipple and her entire body arched into him.

Cool air caressed her where his mouth had been, an indication he was looking up at her in the pitch darkness. "No," he murmured against her breast, his breath as ragged as her own, "but it'll get cleaned after the party anyway."

That sounded highly unsanitary to Peri, and she tried to close her legs and squirm off the table. "With industrial strength--"

Finn repositioned himself between her spread knees as he readjusted her hips. He moved slowly, deliberately, until she didn't give a damn about the table or anyone entering the pantry without warning.

"Everyone must be wondering what we're doing in here."

He chuckled. "No one has any doubt whatsoever about what we're doing in here."

"Then let's exceed their wildest imagination."

"Let's." He laughed as he pulled her against the blazing furnace of his naked chest. His grip was unyielding, as if he feared she'd disappear the second he released her. "You don't know any of them, why do you care?" His voice was rich with amusement as he stroked his hand down her hip, urging her even closer.

"Good point." But she *did* know Theo, and very soon she'd confront the Cutters. Having Finn in the mix was guaranteed to complicate *everything.*

It had been three days since Peri had fled *Blackstar*. Her cheeks still flamed hot remembering how, when she'd opened the door, two security guys had stepped aside to let her pass. No wonder no one had come into the pantry while they were having wild, unprotected, monkey sex. It was a little too freaking late to hope that the room was soundproof.

She'd had to return to the party but made no eye contact with anyone. Grabbing Theo, she'd insisted they return to the mainland because she had a headache.

A six-foot-four-inch, silver-eyed headache.

Finn Gallagher was a complication she couldn't have anticipated. Three days away from him hadn't been sufficient time to figure out just how she was going to weave yet another complicated thread into an already overly complicated tapestry.

And maybe she shouldn't. But then she'd have to stay on one of the Cutter ships, and that would prove a whole hell of a lot more awkward. Or she could scrap this whole crazy plan, say to hell with it, and toss seven years of trying to get their attention into a file labeled, *Massive Waste of Time and Energy*. Negative energy.

She could ship their artifacts back to them anonymously and be done with the whole ill-advised freaking mess.

She'd had a nightmare that night when she'd gotten home. She hadn't had one in years, but that night, after being with Finn, the old nightmare had followed her into a restless sleep.

The hard grip of her mother's fingers grabbing her arm as she dragged her from her hiding place in the hall closet, had hurt physically. The slaps, the screams, the sobs, hurt emotionally. Her parents yelling, always the same indistinct jumble of angry words.

Her high-pitched, "Daddy, take me with you!" The slam of the front door as he left without a backward glance, always jolted her awake.

As she always did after a nightmare, she woke, chest heavy, heart racing, clammy with sweat. Being told, repeatedly that she was unwanted, had carved a deep psychological scar that never went away. She carried a hollowness inside her, sleeping or awake. No wonder she was lousy at maintaining relationships. Other than her brother, there were few men she trusted. No wonder she'd been a willing participant in anonymous, unemotional sex where she'd had zero expectations other than exquisite pleasure.

She'd been five when their father left. Adam was twelve and Rydell fifteen. Ry became mother, father and brother to her and Adam. He was her anchor in a rocky sea as their mother had become increasingly unavailable. A year later their father committed suicide.

She wasn't the only one with scars. When he died, their father left his salvage ship to Ry. Rydell had been barely sixteen when he'd taken the dive boat out on his first salvage. She'd tried to understand, but at that age, all she knew was that her beloved brother was leaving her behind, too. Ry had worked his ass off to keep the company afloat. He succeeded, and then some, making his first million at the age of twenty. He'd also secured a name for himself in the salvage circles.

But every two steps her brother took forward in the salvage business, the Cutters beat him back one.

Paying the Cutters back for every shitty, underhanded thing they'd done to her family was Peri's way of silently compensating her brother for their rough childhood.

Zane, Nick, Logan and Jonah Cutter would get back every damn artifact she'd taken from them. Cleaned, polished and curated. But not before she threw who she was, and what they'd done to her family, in their smug faces.

Ironic that Finn had caught her at the museum as she was saying a final goodbye to the pilfered Cutter artifacts. Of course, she hadn't known who he was, nor his connection at the time. But if she had, would things have turned out any differently?

Probably not.

The heat between them was off the charts. There'd been no stopping the inevitable.

She couldn't put off returning to *Blackstar* much longer. In her official capacity, they'd expect her there, doing her job. So would Theo.

But for today, she could enjoy seeing her brother and have the pleasure of showing him their wreck for the first time.

She was about to blow his socks off.

Last night, unable to sleep for the second night in a row, she'd looked at the black moonlit water through her powerful telescope from her vantage point on top of the bluff.

The lights from *Blackstar* cast a halo effect around the enormous ship. What was Finn doing now? Had he also been too restless to sleep? Was he thinking of her, and as horny as she was? The ache she felt between her legs and the tenderness in her breasts didn't diminish because he wasn't touching her. Just thinking about him, turned her on unbearably.

This was crazy.

She was on hormone overload exactly when she needed her wits about her.

South of Finn's ship, the lights of Logan's *Sea Wolf*, Zane's crazy, *Decrepit,* Nick's ship, *Scorpion* and Jonah's *Stormchaser* lay at anchor, lights twinkling on the black water. The Cutters and Finn shared the salvaging of the other three wrecked carracks. *Nuestra Señora del Marco, Santa Ana and El Crucifijo.*

The three Spanish ships, accompanied, oddly, by her Italian *Napolitano*, had been loaded with gold, silver, precious stones and artifacts bound for the return trip to Spain. Shortly after sailing from the port of Buenos Aires on the 8th of November, 1489, they'd disappeared without a trace.

Peri, through diligent research, and following the tiniest leads, had discovered the wrecks, hundreds of miles south of where anyone had ever looked for them, forty miles off the coast of Patagonia. Hundreds of miles south of where anyone had ever looked for them. They'd been untouched, undiscovered for over five hundred years.

She resented like hell that the Cutters had made the same discovery several years later. It pissed her off that, probably due to Finn's incredibly deep pockets, they'd been financially able to secure the rights to three of the four wrecks.

She'd love to see the look on the Cutter's faces when they learned that their nemesis was about to join their ranks.

Hours later, she'd watched her brother's ship *Tesoro Mio*, slip into position and drop anchor near *Napolitano.* She'd barely been able to wait until dawn to leave the house to see him.

Action would get rid of this hollow feeling.

She'd figure it out. But for now, she'd enjoy time with the two people she loved most in the world.

"Ahoy maties!" Peri called out as her runabout bumped the edge of the dive platform on Rydell's ship. After the hour and fifteen-minute water commute from her house, her clothes and hair clung damply to her skin from the sea spray and early morning mist rising off the silvery surface of the water.

The sky was a pale milky wash, and the air still retained the night's chill. She shivered, more from anticipation than the cold.

Holding hands, Rydell and his wife Addison waited for her on the dive platform. Peri imagined cupids and little cartoon hearts popping up around them. The two were dissimilar, yet so perfect for each other. They'd had a hellish couple of years, and Peri's heart swelled with love seeing them again - together.

Love had won after all.

Ry had cut his hair since she'd seen him almost three years ago. He was tall, dark and no longer brooding. Addison was as beautiful as ever. Wearing a yellow maxi-dress and wrapped in a large beach towel to ward off the chill, her strawberry blond hair swung to her shoulders in a glossy bob. She gave Peri a big smile of welcome, motioning her to hurry so she could give her sister-in-law a hug.

Family.

It was impressive that Ry and Addy had salvaged their love, despite all that had happened between them. Peri couldn't comprehend a love so powerful it could withstand the storms that had struck them.

Rydell stepped to the edge to meet her. "Hey, Magma." Emotion deepened the slight British accent he'd never lost. But then he'd lived in England longer than she had.

Seeing his unshadowed smile as he called her by her childhood nickname, made Peri's own grin widen. No matter where they were, Ry would always represent unconditional love and a sense of homecoming to her. Ten years older, he'd borne the brunt of their dysfunctional family on his shoulders. He was one of the good guys. Her example of all that was good and right in the world.

As she grabbed her bag and prepared to board, she was suddenly overwhelmed by all she'd done in the last seven years. It was like flipping a black page to a white page. What she'd done was cheap and tawdry, and flew in the face of all the principles he'd tried to drum into her as a kid. A hollow nasty swirl took hold of the pit of her stomach. God, she hadn't felt this guilty since she was nine and Ry had caught her stealing a comic book out of Adam's room.

It wasn't as if she didn't know her day of reckoning would come. And *now* that cataclysmic event was tangled up with reconnecting with Finn. Once the cat was out of the bag, he'd know she wasn't at the museum in Buenos Aires as a visitor. He'd know exactly who the benefactor was. How would *he* see her when he discovered the truth? Not in a favorable light, that was for sure.

She'd been living in denial for years. One glance into her brother's clear blue eyes told her she'd painted herself into a corner from which she would not escape unscathed.

"It's so good to see you guys," Peri put a lilt in her voice. "I've been pining. Here, catch." She tossed him the bag holding her gear. Once he dropped it to the deck, she threw him the rope to secure *Witch Craft*, to the platform.

After efficiently tying it off, he extended his hand, hauled her up beside him, then pulled her into his arms for a tight hug. "Missed you, too, monster child," he murmured against her hair. "Something we'll discuss in depth later."

Ignoring the threat, no matter how lovingly couched, she hugged him back, just as hard. Damn it to hell, she had tears in her eyes and hurried to blink them back before he saw and started asking questions.

She punched his arm. "I'm about to make you a multi-gazillionaire, so don't mess with me, big brother. I almost raced out here when you arrived last night, but I figured you needed all the beauty sleep you could get."

Ry was the person she loved the most in the world: She'd do anything for him. Up to and including keeping a secret that would destroy him if he ever found out. A secret she'd take to her grave. But there were other semi-secrets she'd better fess up to, sooner than later.

Her brother was too smart to be fooled for long. Unless she changed course, she was about to sail directly up shit creek. Without a canoe or a paddle.

Reaching up to cup his smoothly shaven cheek, Peri gave him a misty smile. "Ugly as ever I see." Turning to her sister-in-law, she opened her arms. Addy walked into them, enfolding her in a gardenia-scented embrace. Unlike herself, Addy's redheaded complexion was almost freckle free. "You, on the other hand, get more beautiful every time I see you."

God, she'd missed them. They'd married, had baby Sophia, mourned the baby's death, divorced and finally remarried, and now had a newborn son. Peri hadn't been present for any of it. "Where's my favorite nephew-"

Baby Adam was her only nephew. Her sis-in-law stepped aside and with a dramatic sweep of her hand indicated the portable crib in the shade. Peri walked over to look down at the sleeping six-month-old.

She'd never particularly been a baby person, but this little guy was the prettiest little human she'd ever seen. Her heart melted, and her throat tightened. That they'd named the baby for the brother they'd loved so dearly, and lost, made the child even more precious.

"Oh, my God, Addy, he's. . .He's perfect!" Allowable tears stung her eyes as she leaned over to marvel at his impossibly small hands and his full cap of silky dark hair. Wearing a fluffy blue outfit with BORN TO DIVE on the front, he was sprawled on his back, arms and legs extended, like a little blue starfish.

"Go ahead." Addison draped her arm over Peri's shoulder. "Pick him up. He needs to wake up. He's a typical Case. Not adhering to anyone's time schedule but his own."

Peri shook her head. "He's too freaking. . . breakable."

"You won't drop him. How can you resist kissing on him for hours?"

Considering they were a mere ten feet away from water that was eighty feet deep, Peri would pass. She felt light-headed just thinking about the responsibility. "Resist I must." She stared, drinking in the wonder of this incredibly small human. If she had one of these she'd never sleep. "I'll wait until later, when I'm sitting on something large and soft. Then you can hand him to me."

The thought of having children had never crossed her mind. But suddenly her biological clock was chiming like Big Ben. She ignored it. She remembered that she and Finn had had unprotected sex three days ago. She ignored that, too.

Of course, the option might already be out of her hands since they hadn't used a condom the other night, and no birth control was one hundred percent foolproof. What was Finn thinking about the situation? As little as she knew him, it didn't take a rocket scientist to know he was a very cautious man. With his wealth, he'd have to be. She believed him when he'd said he'd never had unprotected sex before her.

She was in the midst of the most exciting salvage of her life. Not only was there no time for children or a relationship like her brother's, she hadn't even had a real date in eighteen months. Having wild monkey sex with Finn didn't count.

"Deal." Eyes glowing, Addison looked incandescent with happiness. "He'll be awake, and therefore full of beans by the time you two get back. You can hug and kiss him to your heart's delight then."

"Ready to suit up? A couple of my divers just went down." Ry shot Peri a smile as he stroked his wife's hair.

Peri yanked the damp sweater over her head and unzipped her jeans, revealing a white bikini and a lot of goosebumps underneath. "Already?"

Later it would be a gorgeous sunny morning with just a light chop on the water. Perfect for diving. Now it was cold and not bright enough to see much of anything beneath the glossy surface.

"Momo and Kev couldn't wait. Thanks for rigging the spotlights already, good job all around." He narrowed his eyes. "You haven't been diving alone at night, have you?"

"No, but that doesn't mean I haven't been tempted!

He booped her on the nose. "I'm shocked and impressed that you showed so much restraint waiting for me."

She and Ry began to suit up to join the others on the ocean floor. Addison walked over with the sleeping baby in her arms. Rydell paused, drysuit half on, and leaned forward to kiss his son on the forehead.

Taking in the tenderness of the lingering kiss, the way her brother gently touched the infant's hair, Peri fought to keep her jaw from dropping. Ry looked more interested in domestic bliss than diving. He looked more rested and relaxed- hell- happier than she'd seen him in years. He was going to be a whole hell of a lot happier when he saw what lay below, just waiting for him.

Recovering from the shock, she managed to glance into Addy's eyes and share a smile over the two dark heads. Clearly, loving and losing made his family even more precious to him.

Was Finn thinking about her? She dismissed it as foolish fancy. They'd had sex. *Exceptional* sex. No reason for him to suppose it wouldn't happen again, and as often as he liked, when she returned to his ship. She'd take a bet that if- *when*- that happened, he'd have a lifetime of condoms on hand. She'd bet he wasn't a man who made the same mistake twice.

"Are you okay?" her brother asked, "We're not diving if you don't feel well."

"I feel peachy, thanks. *Napolitano* awaits." She made a sweeping gesture to the water, and pushed aside the scorching heat surging through her blood at the mere thought of sliding a condom onto Finn's impressive erection. "Be prepared to have your socks blown off." Telling him, and showing him, were two different spheres –like being on the surface breathing air, and being under the waves breathing through a regulator.

Heartbeat elevated, and hyper-aware of the four Cutter ships, now hidden by the black bulk of the *Blackstar*, Peri should've been feeling the adrenaline rush that came with a dive. Instead, she just felt that nasty sense of dread that came with having to deal with something unpleasant.

It pained her to know *she* was the thing that was unpleasant.

Had Finn told the Cutters about the redhead he'd met at the museum? Had he mentioned that the government oversight person was a redhead? Had they put two and two and redhead together to come up with *thief*?

Damn it to hell. Pushing aside the niggles of self-doubt and foreboding, Peri reverted to her old standby feeling of up-from-the-bootstraps bravado.

With Ry's unnecessary help, Addy settled onto a nearby lounge chair with Adam in her arms. "I can't wait to see Callie, it's been *years*." With a warning glance at her husband, Addison said, "You'll play nice, Rydell Case."

Eyes serious, he looked at Peri as he stroked Addy's cheek with his knuckles. "I'll always love Callie."

Callie had been married to Rydell and Peri's brother Adam, who'd died of leukemia several years ago. She was now engaged to Jonah Cutter. They'd planned on marrying in Switzerland last year, but the wedding had been postponed. Peri wondered what Ry had had to do with that. She hadn't seen Callie at the party, but if Jonah Cutter was here, Callie would be, too. She'd show up sooner or later.

"Regardless, Ry, we're a family. We have to make an effort." Her love for Callie ran deep. Probably because she'd had to work really, really hard to overcome the resentment caused by the fact that her mom had loved Callista like a daughter. Supremely unfair when she'd treated her own daughter like an unwelcome guest in her own home.

Still, over the years, she and Callie had formed a tight bond and were as close as real sisters. Peri wanted her to be happy. But when Callie married into the Cutter family, she'd be firmly ensconced in the enemy camp, and the last connection they had to her brother Adam would be gone forever.

Ry arched an eyebrow in reply as he picked up his tank from the rack.

"No, seriously." Addy lay the baby back into his bassinet, then positioned her laptop on her thighs. "For Callie's sake, we really must *try*. It would be cruel to force her to choose between us and the man she loves."

"I have no problem loving Callie exactly the way I've always loved her." Ry checked the valves on his tank. "That love doesn't extend to a Cutter."

"You're a bullheaded ass. But I love you anyway," his wife told him, pulling a light blanket over the baby, then tightening her towel cape around her own shoulders.

"There's no reason for me to be in the presence of any of those lying, cheating bastards." Ry shot a glance in the general direction of the Cutter ships. "Callie's always welcome to come and visit *Tesoro Mio* if she wants to see us. I'll welcome her with open arms. Just not her future husband."

With a serene expression, Addy glanced from Peri to Ry. "I'm going to welcome the man Callie loves to the family, so live with it. Peri, tell your brother to stop helicoptering so I can enjoy my vacation." Comfortably ensconced, Addy took a sip from a mug of what must be cold coffee by now, before opening her laptop. Even a beach towel slung around her shoulders looked like a million bucks on Addy, who always looked as elegant as a model in an upscale magazine.

"She's already forgotten we're here," Peri smiled as her sis-in-law started typing. "Come on, Ry," she teased, yanking up the zipper of her drysuit, "we're only going down for a couple of hours. They'll both be here when you surface. Let's go."

It was her brother's first official day here, but Peri had a five-year leg up. She'd found the scattered remains of the *Napolitano*, first. Then other carracks on subsequent dives.

To grant the necessary permits and permissions, the Argentinian government had insisted on being paid an estimated future value of the treasure. Even low-balling what she thought her salvage would net, she didn't have the resources to stake a claim on all four wrecks.

Even with her brother's help, it would've been impossible. Peri had to choose which ship she wanted. The Italian ship was the most intriguing to her. She'd left the three Spanish ships, figuring she'd make enough money on the first ship to cover the other three. Then the damn Cutters had swooped in and laid claim to them.

Tesoro Mio and *Sea Witch's* claim straddled the miles-long spill of the *Napolitano*. Peri had hired a group of divers to build the grid and, under her direction, do the prep work for the dive. They'd painstakingly created a topographical map of the sea bed and marked the search areas in a grid that spanned their claim. Over the last few years, as the prep work had been accomplished, Peri and her small team of divers had salvaged hundreds of thousands of dollars' worth of treasure. Relatively easy pickings.

Based on what they'd retrieved, she'd bet it was merely a drop in the bucket of what the rest of the wreck would give them.

Salvage sites were required to register with the Ministry of Antiquities of the Argentinian government, all a matter of public record. So, Peri had known almost as soon as the Cutters had staked their claims a year ago. How they'd discovered the location of the wrecks was a mystery.

If she were in their position she'd want to know as much as possible about who was salvaging so close to their dive site. To that end-they were shit out of luck, because Peri and Ry had shell companies inside shell companies.

"Any prods?" Ry asked.

He was referring to the Cutter people trying to ascertain who else had filings for salvage. "As to who Koúkos Corporation is?" she smiled. "They tried. Several times. My business people in Greece disavowed any knowledge. They'll never release the information."

"Good. Let them wonder."

Peri rubbed her arms through her drysuit. "Get the lead out, I'm getting goosebumps on my goosebumps here."

Ry paused, giving his sister a narrow-eyed look. "Now, that's a smile to put the fear of God into a man."

Peri's smile widened. "I was just thinking about their reaction when they see *Sea Witch* and *Tesoro Mio* so close together. You know they're already gnashing their teeth and sticking pins in voodoo dolls seeing you show up. I'll just be the cherry on top of their misery sundae."

"And when do you plan to do that?"

"A couple of days, I think." Coiling her hair on top of her head she stuck several long pins into the mass to keep it in place under her helmet. "I'll lull them into a false sense of security, and then, *bam*!"

"Evil."

"True." Drawing a deep breath, she hesitated before going forward. "And in spirit of full disclosure-"

Closing his eyes, her brother rubbed the bridge of his nose. "Oh, God--"

"No big deal. I'm working temporarily as Theo's oversight person, so he doesn't have to take up residence for the duration. A big plus is I'll be able to monitor what they're doing as they do it. Plus, we have the home team advantage."

"Jesus, Persephone. Why would you do something so damn stupid? Unnecessary even. Worse, dangerous."

"It's short-term," Peri placated. "Don't worry. Nothing will go sideways, I promise. Just until I figure out what they're finding. It's all very low key."

"They're aware that you're my sister?"

"Theo only knows me as Ariel Andersen."

"A fake identity?" Ry asked, sounding less than happy. "Peri, what the hell are you doing?"

"Are you still dating that guy?" Addy called out.

"Not since forever. No. But this suits him just fine. He wants to know the value of the artifacts they find."

Looking across the water, Ry commented, "They seem to have a big gun, that's Phineas Gallagher's *Blackstar*. The space exploration guy, right?"

"He's the one. Big-time Cutter investor, apparently. When he's not adding to their piles of exploration capital, he's working on colonizing Mars."

"Then what's he doing on a deep-water salvage? Especially one that could take decades?"

"Good question, I'll ask him later this afternoon when I see him." If he allows me back on board or sweeps me off my feet to have wild monkey sex with me in a closet somewhere.

Ry gave her a stern big brother look. It had never worked on her, but she loved him for trying. "I don't like the subterfuge, Peri. It's unnecessary and could prove dangerous." He held up a hand. "Shouldn't have said that because obviously, that's why you do this shit. I want you to stop whatever the hell you've put into motion. Especially with Callie on her way down here. I mean it, Persephone."

"I'm just going to check on what they've found for a couple of hours a day. It's not forever."

"No, it'll just be until they figure out your dual role and someone drowns you."

Something she'd taken into consideration. "Good thing I'm an excellent swimmer, then, isn't it?" She pulled the hood over her hair and stuffed loose strands inside as best she could. Her hair tended to have a mind of its own. "If you like, we can go to the house soon so I can show you what I've already found." Better to change the subject sooner than later. "Not just coins, and some impressive emerald jewelry, but all the other artifacts I told you about as well. Your minds will be blown."

"Looking forward to it. But it would've been nice if you'd kept me informed of where you were and what you were up to during the last three years." As they donned their tanks in unison on the edge of the platform, Ry gave her a stern glance.

"If I'd known you were going to play cat and mouse with the Cutters I would've done everything in my power to dissuade you. They're not good people, Magma. I don't want you pulling their tails just for sport. Stay the hell out of their way. For my sake. Please. I've lost too much in one life. If I lost you, too . . ."

"A week - max," she agreed, surprisingly not as reluctant as she would've thought. This new Ry, the one willing to acknowledge emotions in words, confirmed what her gut had been trying to tell her for months. It was time for her to get over the Cutters. Time to move on. Time to be free of the Cutter albatross around her neck.

She was the only one left in the world who knew who she truly was, and why she was hellbent on dogging the Cutters. But now that her brother was here to hold up a mirror .. did any of that really matter? Would any of the things she'd done over the last seven years serve to turn back time and rewrite her life?

"Theo really needs the information. I'm a subcontractor to the Argentinian government, so I'm there legally."

Peri felt bad for worrying Ry when he already had so much on his plate. And she had no illusions about how her honorable brother would feel if he ever learned she'd been a pirate for the last seven years.

There was only one person in her life she could depend on, and that was her brother. He hadn't heard the accusations their father had hurled at her that day. She'd never tell her brother how worthless she'd felt, how scared, how absolute and utterly isolated and alone. And she never would. She'd always put on a happy face around him.

The last thing she wanted was for him to think less of her. He'd reconciled with Addison. They had a new baby. He was happy. Ry hadn't had any problem not seeing her for three years. He'd drifted away. Into a new life, with a new family. As it should be.

She'd learned early and hard how little she could depend on anyone but herself. She'd better pull up her big girl panties and deal with this as quickly as possible and get it the hell over with. No point dragging it out. She'd tell them this afternoon. Be done with them once and for all.

"But when they find out, they won't come after this Theo guy. They'll come after *you.* Stay the hell out of their way. The fact that they're here now shows us just how cutthroat they are. I just fucking spent the better part of a year in South Africa fighting their lawsuit about wrongful ownership of a salvage. Be extra careful, Magma. The Cutters are bad news."

"Got it. Are we diving or chatting? I'm freezing my ass off here."

FIVE

With the dawn sky lightened enough to get a better visual, Finn ignored the steaming mug of strong, black coffee and the contract he'd been reading on his tablet in the dining room on board *Blackstar*. Instead, he picked up the Swarovski EL Range-finding binoculars.

In a few hours the restaurant-style dining room would be filled with his office staff enjoying breakfast before they started their day. He'd been up at his customary four-thirty a.m. Spent exactly one hour in the gym on the pool deck, showered, dressed, and taken two video conference calls from Europe in his office.

For now, he was alone, sitting in semi-darkness at his favorite table, beside wide windows with an endless view of pale, colorless sky reflected in the still water.

He'd drink a second cup of coffee, reread the contract, catch up on a few emails and enjoy the solitude before going back to his office for the hour and forty-seven minutes until his breakfast meeting with the Cutters. Between sending the contract back to his lawyers and the meeting, he'd do as much work as someone putting in half a day.

He was in the midst of a multi-company buyout, and much of his time was spent on phone calls and video conferencing. Thanks to his investment in satellites, and pioneering data link technology he had interoperability with his associates and business partners globally, and unfettered access to secure, jam-resistant data links. So he stayed connected with unparalleled levels of situational awareness at all times. He scheduled his calendar in fifteen-minute increments. Not a moment wasted. Even his leisure time was scheduled.

He was accused of being an alien life form and having a twenty-five-hour day. He wished. But until that happened, he crammed in as much as he could every waking hour. Finn rolled his shoulders. Ariel Andersen had been a delicious detour, but taking that three day bite out of his work week had set him back.

Worth it.

The rush of primal lust he'd felt that weekend in Buenos Aires hadn't lessened one iota. Which was both intriguing and a little bit fucking terrifying for a man who considered himself a scientist, and not prone to wild impromptu love affairs.

That loss of control *must* be tempered next time he saw her. They had to coexist, or at least have contact, for a long time, longer than most of his relationships might last. And God only knew, nothing could possibly burn that brightly without incinerating them both.

He couldn't keep his hands off her. Hell, he didn't want to. She'd disappeared after the incident in the pantry, and he hadn't seen her for three fucking days. Would she make him wait on tenterhooks for *eight* days as she had last time? She was supposed to be here. On board *Blackstar*, working. Spending her days overseeing the artifacts, and her nights in his bed.

The other night they'd had sex - several times - without a condom. The last time Finn had gone bareback was the first time he'd had sex at age thirteen with Bridget Moran in old man Frazer's horse barn. It had been amazing then, but bareback *now* took sex to another level. He never wanted to wear a condom again. The sensation of Peri - *Ariel's* slick vaginal walls pulsing around his cock brought new meaning to lovemaking. He'd always enjoyed the act, condom-less took the sensation supernova.

It would be difficult to ignore her when she stayed onboard, but he needed to rein in his lust. *Blackstar* was the size of a hotel. Plenty of space for them to keep their distance. Perhaps she'd be agreeable to a once-a-week liaison, and he could... Jesus. He really had lost his fucking mind, given that he'd hauled her into the pantry in front of a hundred guests at the party the other night. He hadn't given a damn if they heard her scream every time she came.

Clearly, once a week wouldn't be sufficient. He needed to check his schedule, see what could be moved around. . . Satisfied that he'd find a viable solution, Finn settled back in his chair. Now that it was light enough to get a better look, he adjusted the focus on the lightweight magnesium-alloy frame binocs to better see the tri-deck megayacht, *Tesoro Mio*, which seemed to have materialized out of the darkness overnight. He'd noticed it anchored several miles to the south when he'd gotten out of the shower earlier.

Three people stood on the dive platform. Two already in drysuits. Early to dive, and still cool at this hour. He presumed the tall, dark-haired guy in the black drysuit was Rydell Case, owner of *Tesoro Mio*. With him were an attractive strawberry blond and a slender redhead in an orange and pink drysuit reaching for her tank.

As he focused on her laughing face, he felt as though he'd been kicked in the chest. So much for his resolution. Could he clear more time to spend with her now that she was back within his orbit? He had to. At least long enough to get her out of his system.

"Well, hell," Finn murmured, watching Ariel fasten her tank, then give a jaunty wave in his general direction before jumping off the platform. "Cheeky."

He knew damn well that from that distance she couldn't see inside *Blackstar* to observe him sitting at the window. But she'd waved anyway, as though she felt him watching her. He understood that Case would come under the same government regulations as himself and the Cutters. Which meant she had to check on Case, too. But Finn didn't like how friendly she appeared to be with the guy.

Damn it to hell, he was annoyed at how annoyed he was seeing her embrace another man.

He'd get an even better look at her later through his telescope on the top deck when she resurfaced. He didn't need 10X magnification to prove to himself that three days hadn't diminished his craving for the intoxicating fragrance of Casablanca lilies, the sweet taste of her mouth, or the way her lips curled into a delicious, kissable, contented smile after she came. And before she came again.

"It's the butt crack of dawn. What could you possibly be looking at? Zane Cutter came up behind him as Finn sat transfixed, long after his redhead disappeared under the water.

Blackstar, the closest ship to *Tesoro Mio*, probably blocked the new arrival from view from the Cutter ships. "You're here early." He pointed out the window, as the youngest Cutter sat across from him. Zane was an affable guy, with none of his three older brother's intensity. Britt, his chief steward appeared with a coffee pot and two mugs. The tall, Norwegian blond poured fresh coffee for both men. Finn smiled his thanks. "*Tesoro Mio*. Arrived during the night."

"No shit?" Zane swiveled his head to look out the window. "Crap, that son of a bitch always knows where we are? He's a god damned parasite with radar."

Finn shrugged. "No secrets when there's this big a salvage and this amount of money to be had."

"True. All we need now is for the *Sea Witch* to show up. Wait until you experience that redheaded little thief's antics. She's another pain in the ass."

"The only redhead I've seen is Miss Andersen. She's over there diving with Case as we speak."

"Holy crap. The ocean is littered with redheads." Zane added sugar to his mug, stirring it while watching *Tesoro Mio* as if it was about to rise from the water like a breaching whale. "Logan will have a fucking heart attack if we end up with Case *and* Sea Bitch at this salvage."

"No way to keep it under wraps. We knew people would come out of the woodwork." Finn sipped his coffee. "I've never understood why you guys haven't sicced the authorities on her and been shot of her. One theft would've been enough. The second time, I'd have had her taken away in cuffs."

Hands wrapped around his mug, Zane shrugged. "You'd have to ask Nick that question. He maintains she's harmless. She's a P.I.T.A., but so far, she hasn't stolen anything of enormous value. She's just a nuisance, and always around like a damned magpie."

"Last I checked, piracy is a crime in most jurisdictions. Perhaps the magpie should be prosecuted." There was more to this than met the eye. Finn wouldn't be so sanguine if the female pirate stole from him. Then all bets would be off.

"Who are we talking about?" Maggie Berland asked, as she and her husband Ben joined them. The couple were on Zane's dive team. Finn had met them several times over the years in his business dealings with Zane.

"Case showed up in the dead of night like the fucking bloodsucker he is. Just speculating if Sea Bitch will show as well," Zane responded, taking the binocs from Finn, and adjusting the central focusing ring to get a better look at the other ship.

"Our government oversight agent, Ariel Andersen's over there. *She* has red hair. . . " Finn hoped to hell they weren't one and the same.

Zane shook his head, glasses to his eyes. "That's not Sea Bitch, hair's the wrong red. Maggie?" He handed her the glasses.

"That's not her. We'd spot her *boat* before seeing her, anyway. She'll show. Sooner than later. Mark my words."

Zane glanced over at Finn. "I'm starving. Can I have a pre-breakfast breakfast?"

Finn smiled. "Ask Britt for whatever you like." His scheduled break was over. "I have work to do before the meeting." He got to his feet as Britt approached with menus. "Maggie? Ben? Pre-breakfast breakfast?"

"Lord, I don't know where you put all that food you eat. He's like a newborn, has to eat every two hours." Maggie gave Zane a look that showed Finn how much she loved the younger man. The Breland's were like family to Zane, and it showed.

Maggie smiled at Britt. "I'd just like a large cup of Finn's favorite brew. White and sweet, please. Ben will have his first breakfast now if that won't inconvenience the chef so early?"

"Enjoy your breakfast," Finn told them before Ben placed his order. "See you in a couple of hours."

He went straight to his office down the corridor, and opened the dossier his very efficient right-hand man, Walker, had compiled on Miss Ariel Andersen. He'd read through it yesterday. There was absolutely nothing he pretty much didn't know already in the two pages presented to him.

After studying at the Argentine Atlantis University in Buenos Aires, she'd worked for the Argentinian government for five years. She owned a piece of property atop a cliff, where she'd built a small, but innovative house.

Where she came from, and what she'd been doing prior to showing up in Argentina was still under investigation.

There was no mention of her owning a boat. No mention that she was a stunningly gorgeous, athletic redhead with the body of a goddess. Yet well-honed instincts told him she was hiding something. What, he had no idea. "What are you up to, Miss Andersen?"

Finn couldn't wait to find out. About to call Walker in, he retracted the hand he'd placed on the phone. He decided against hiring the private detective to dig deeper. He was going to enjoy uncovering all her secrets himself.

"Impressive first full day, huh?" Drysuit peeled down to her waist, Peri wrung out her hair, the sun warm on her cool skin. She, Ry, Momo and Dante, two members of her brother's dive crew, had just returned from their second dive of the day.

"You will make us a lot of money I think, *piccola Rosa.*" Dante Acura gave her his trademark charming smile. Tall and wiry, he was sex appeal on a stick. Peri wondered why he held zero attraction for her. Then acknowledged why when her gaze drifted across the water to Finn's obscenely large, black ship.

Momo Bergson gave her a thumb up as he towel dried his hairy chest. "We'll all make a killing here. Unfortunately, so will the Cutters, if their sites are anything like ours."

"Maybe, and believe me, I *wanted* to claim all four wrecks," Peri told him as she finished peeling off her suit. At mid-morning it was far too early to quit for the day, but Ariel Andersen needed to go to work

She still had to return home, switch runabouts, change clothes, and return to *Blackstar* before dark. "First, I couldn't afford the good faith payment required by the government, not to mention I figured a salvage of that magnitude would bring out all the vultures, not just the Cutters. There are about fifty nautical miles of wreckage from the four ships. Trying to tackle the entire area would take us about a hundred and fifty years. I had to prioritize which area to salvage first."

With plenty of time to grid and prep *Napolitano*, all the boring, arduous work had been done in anticipation of her brother's arrival. Now each artifact could be attributed to its exact location. Ry was a stickler for keeping all that info in his high-tech database.

Her brother held out his hands for the baby, and with a smile, Addison handed him over. The child wore the teeniest little blue Speedo Peri had ever seen over his diaper. Ry kissed the baby's head as he adjusted the child as if he were holding a football, his hand looking huge and dark against the baby's narrow back. "Phenomenal. Thanks for doing all the grunt work, Magma. Excellent job by the way."

Peri shrugged. "Makes a difference not having to waste time charting and setting up the grids." Glancing across the shimmering water in the general direction of the other ships, she shot her brother a grin. "We've had years head start on the Cutters. And *we* have the most promising wreck out of the four."

"Hey, you guys," Len Swanapoel, another of Ry's divers, yelled down from the deck above. "Check this out!"

They all climbed the ladder to see what the South African diver had to show them. The acidic smell of cleaning fluid hung in the still air, and water filled tubs lined the rails ready for coins and small artifacts. "Check this out. It came up in our last haul. Peri, this is one of the items you sent up from 178B. Interesting, ja?"

Peri took the item from him to get a closer look, then had to tighten her grip as her hands dipped with the weight of it. The artifact, a two-inch-thick slab, about twelve by eight inches, was a lot heavier than it had been underwater and it's covering of gold was as bright as it had been before it sank beneath the waves. "I thought it might be a plate of some kind, but it's too heavy for that. It looks like a whole piece. Not broken off from something larger, right?" Tilting it to catch the light she frowned. "It seems to have an allover print or design. What do you think it is?"

"It's gold for sure, probably covering some kind of stone. While I can't read it, I think this is writing. A shitton of it. Doesn't look like Spanish though."

"Hmm. *Could* be writing." Ry peered over Peri's shoulder. "Maybe. Probably just a linear design of some kind. Still, interesting."

"I think it's text of some sort." Peri quarter-turned the tablet. "Doesn't look like Italian either. Maybe I'm holding it upside down. Nope, that doesn't make it any more legible. Maybe after it's completely cleaned we'll be able to identify the language."

"Whatever it says, or whatever it depicts, this is an exciting find." Ry clasped his sister's shoulder. "Maybe this'll give us a clue as to why the armada headed south instead of north."

"And why there was an Italian ship sailing with three Spanish ships." As much as she was dying to stay, clean and X-ray the two-foot, almost square, slab, and see what it revealed, she couldn't hang around much longer. "Speaking of heading south- I need to go in. I have to report back to Theo about the Cutters, and I want to get *Sea Witch* stocked and ready." She smiled. "I think it's time for her to make her debut tomorrow." *If Finn and the Cutters don't do anything drastic to stop me.*

Ry gave her a stern look. "Report in tonight when you leave them. Will you go home, or come back to us?"

"It would eat up my day commuting between home, *Blackstar* and you. I'll just anchor *Sea Witch* tomorrow so I have more dive time. I can't wait to get an update on our slab."

"I'll do some research," Ry told her, taking the gold piece from her. "See if we can figure out what you have here. He clasped the back of her head and drew her in to plant a kiss on her forehead. "Stay on your toes in the enemy camp, Magma."

She loved her brother more than any other human on the planet. What she didn't adore was the warped reflection of herself he projected back at her without even trying. The uncomfortable swirl in the pit of her stomach was back. Peri didn't like feeling guilty. There was no way she could go through with her planned end game now that the conscience Ry had drummed into her for years had reared its ugly head.

Well hell.

Barefoot, drysuit peeled down to his waist, the hot, late afternoon sun evaporated droplets of water off Finn's skin as quickly as it dripped from his hair. He'd gotten the call from Security within seconds of returning from his first dive of the day off *Blackstar Two.* Working alongside his dive team, unearthing artifacts, was how he relaxed. The pressures of his life disappeared when he was sixty-feet under the water.

Or immersed in Ariel's sleek body.

About time she showed up. She'd come directly from *Tesoro Mio* where he'd observed her spending the better part of *her* morning diving with Rydell Case and *his* team. *Diving* wasn't part of her job description. She should've been here with him—

Shit. Was Case fucking her? Finn prodded the new emotion as one would a painful tooth as he jogged up the stairs. He didn't like the feeling. Didn't fucking like the *thought* of that kind of possessiveness crossing his mind. It was as annoying as it was distracting.

He valued the ninety-minutes a day he'd designated to dive, and being pulled out of the water early was annoying. But he'd been thinking about her nonstop for fucking *days*. Distracted by thoughts of her. Distracted by his own distraction.

He would discuss with her the windows of time he could open to accommodate their future trysts. Surely to God, the more time spent with her, the less diverting she'd be?

Finn reached the next deck. Located with easy access to the dive platform, this deck was designated to the processing, cleaning, cataloging and photographing of the artifacts as they were brought to the surface. Security was on high alert due to the treasure already salvaged. But then Finn always had tight security surrounding him. His K&R insurance policy demanded it.

The diver's and tech's cabins were on the same level as processing. The doors on all three sides of what had been the solarium were open wide to catch the breezes and dispense the chemical fumes.

The late afternoon was hot and still, perfect diving weather. Finn was in no mood to play referee, but he wanted- hell- needed- to see her.

Girding himself for an unpleasant confrontation, the sight of Ariel stole his breath and blew every other thought from his brain. She stood toe-to-toe with one of his techs, watched closely by his head of security, Seth McCoy.

A white tank top was tucked into bright yellow shorts which showcased long, shapely, freckled legs. Her glorious hair was pulled away from her face into in a long, fiery braid halfway down her back. He stopped, one hand on the rail to drink her in. Desire instantly overshadowed annoyance.

He strode across the aft deck, passed large seawater-filled tubs holding artifacts ready to be cleaned and entered into the database. On the foredeck, similar tubs held fresh seawater, and the objects already cleaned and processed.

Other than wavelets slapping at the hull, and the creak of wood, the sheltered second deck, usually a hive of activity and a blast of rock music, was suddenly unnaturally quiet. Music off, everyone had gone silent the moment Finn walked on deck.

Ariel turned her head at the sound of his approaching footsteps. Her expressive eyes lit up upon seeing him, and her slight smile did crazy things to Finn's heartbeat. She didn't look like a thief. But then thieves rarely did.

Hell. She hadn't lost a scintilla of her allure since last he'd seen her. In fact, Finn felt the draw more powerfully now, and he wasn't even in touching distance.

Aside from his acute physical attraction to her, he was shocked at the well of pleasure he experienced just *seeing* her. Christ. Not just sexual attraction, but genuinely happy to merely be in her orbit.

The two men parted to allow him into the tight grouping. He arched an inquiring brow as he held her gaze, but spoke to his head of security. "Summarize, would you, Seth?"

"Mike caught Miss Andersen here trying to remove the artifact from processing." He was careful with his wording. Smart move considering no one could miss the crackle of electricity between them unless they were completely oblivious. Which his head of security was not.

Finn ignored her soft murmur of disbelief, and the spark of flame lighting the cool depths of her eyes. "And take it where?"

"Off *Two* would be our guess."

"Indeed." The familiar, deep throbbing in his dick made him clench his teeth. "I'll take that," Finn addressed her, voice rough with lust.

The glow in Ariel's eyes dissipated and her brow wrinkled. She shot him a startled look when he plucked the artifact from her hands. It was roughly the size of a folded piece of foolscap paper, the gold glossy as if just freshly minted, its weight close to twenty pounds.

"Mike?" Finn handed the heavy item back to the nervously hovering cleaning tech who'd called security in a panic five minutes earlier. "Thanks, guys. I'll take it from here." With a curt nod, McCoy gave Ariel a hard parting look, then followed Mike across the deck and back inside the processing room.

The salty air held a tang of muriatic acid, yet he could also smell a faint trace of Casablanca lily.

She turned back from watching the two men. This time when she looked at him, the pleasure had been stripped from her gaze. "You *believe* them?" she said, incredulously. Clearly misinterpreting his taut expression, her spine straightened. "I see. Well, no matter what they implied, I *wasn't* stealing it." That high flush on her cheeks wasn't embarrassment. The small tremor in her voice and the oh-so-familiar flash of fire in her eyes indicated she was annoyed. "Which," she took a step forward and enunciated very carefully, "if any of you had bothered to *ask*, I would've *told* you."

The light breeze pressed the thin cotton of her top to cup her breasts. Finn wanted his hands there. Wanted to skim his hands up the long, lean swimmer's muscles in her shapely legs. Wanted to skim his fingers under the hem of her shorts to the juncture of her thighs to see if she was damp there. "They're aware of my zero tolerance for theft. They were merely doing their jobs."

Loose strands of fiery hair danced against her throat, and impatiently she shoved it away. Her skin was sensitive there, just under her ear. She'd shivered when he trailed his tongue down the sensitive cords, tilting her head to allow him easy access.

"Oh, for--I was *holding* it." Something moved behind her eyes. Disappointment? Guilt? Hurt? Taking a deep breath, she rubbed the tip of her nose, then shoved her fingertips into the back pockets of her shorts as she gave him a furious look.

She was pissed. Or guilty. Because she'd been caught? All he wanted right now was a dimly lit cabin and a horizontal surface. She had new freckles across her nose and on her upper arms. Stardust. He wanted to taste them. Now.

"That artifact might well be an epic find of significant historical value. It bore closer scrutiny." Her unusually colored eyes looked as if layers of transparent glass, blues and greens, were being pierced by the sun.

Finn shifted to ease the tightness of the drysuit across his dick, as he allowed his amusement to filter into his voice. "Your X-ray vision allowed you to deduce its value?" When she remained silent- discounting her murderous gaze, he said, "At around twelve hundred per ounce, American, even if it's gold *coated*- at guestimate about fifty grand. A hell of a lot more if it's made up entirely of gold."

"I'm not going to waste my breath talking to you if you're going to be a hardass. It's the largest piece retrieved so far," her words were clipped. "The appearance of even bumps indicates it might have some sort of writing under the gold covering. I was just-"

He didn't care what she was *just* about to do. All he could think about was that she was willing to fuck him one minute and steal from him the next. "You don't have jurisdiction to remove any artifacts from the salvage." Lust made his voice harsher than he intended.

Tilting her head, a tendril of red hair fell over her shoulder. "Jump to conclusions much?" Folding her arms beneath her breasts in a defensive stance, she jutted out her chin. "Holding and studying, don't equate to *stealing* or 'removal', Finn. Do you want me to take a damned *polygraph* test?"

Seth and Mike had done what he demanded of all his employees. Nip theft in the bud. But she was disarmingly indignant about the accusation. "Of course, not." He had a thought. "What were you looking for in the packing crates at the Bernardino Rivadavia Natural Sciences Museum in Buenos Aires?" If she'd planned to steal any of the artifacts, she hadn't done so, he knew first hand.

Her narrowed eyes glittered at the nonsequitur. "Are you implying that I was stealing then, too? You stripped me naked and kept me that way the entire freaking weekend. Where do you think I was hiding an artifact, you bastard? You knew every millimeter of my body intimately."

God. Yes, he sure as hell did. The tech and cleaning crew we're watching, so he couldn't do what he wanted to do right now which was intimately reacquaint himself with every millimeter of her body. "It's a simple question."

"It's a *loaded* damned question. And I resent like hell that *you* didn't *ask*, you *accused*. Just as I was doing at the museum, I was *looking*." She glared at him, a frown notched between her brows, her color high. "My only damned sin was trying to ascertain what today's new artifact was. I was too impatient to wait for it to be properly tested. It's unlike anything I've ever seen before. Obviously, I wouldn't have removed it from your ship."

He fought the curl of desire low in his belly. He wanted to shake her, because her actions had warranted inquiry. Her anger was over the top under the circumstances. Yet, he wanted to whisk her off this deck, find an empty cabin, and be done with the argument.

The violence of his desire for this woman, from the moment they'd met, was alien to him. A freshening breeze kicked up the water, making it sparkle like navy-blue sequins for as far as the eye could see. The wind plastered her skimpy tank top to her torso, showing the outline of a lace bra, and the soft plump of her breasts. Finn's tongue stuck to the roof of his mouth and his lust spiked, fogging his mind. Letting her off the hook might be the worst judgment call he'd made in years.

The errant coppery strand blew free again to unfurl, as if alive. dancing around her shoulders as if ignited by her temper. Her hair, as it always did, taunted Finn to touch, to linger on the glossy length. Tucking strands of silky hair behind her ear, he used the opportunity to brush his fingertips across her warm cheek.

He wanted to be done with this.

"I'm sorry for not giving you the benefit of the doubt." Finn didn't recall apologizing to anyone, about anyfuckingthing. *Ever.* She fried his brain cells. "I'll have a word with security and set them straight."

Closing her eyes briefly, she said, still annoyed, "Your life would be so much less stressful if you didn't jump to freaking conclusions."

SIX

I accept your apology," Peri told him crossly, distracted by his appeal. If she were a cat, her fur would be standing on end. "*Especially* since I suspect you don't hand them out very often."

He was wasting his time interrogating her. She wasn't going to break. And- color her shocked- she'd thought *he* wouldn't either until he'd murmured his apology.

She breathed him in. The scent of sea and citrus, probably some hideously expensive cologne from Paris, made her stomach quiver. Damn it, she was righteous in her anger and enjoying her mad. She wanted to hang on to it a little longer. It wasn't good for him to think an 'I'm sorry' was going to placate her that easily.

The more he maligned her character, the guiltier she felt, and the guiltier she *looked,* the madder she got.

Having Finn accuse her of the one thing she was already angsting about, made Peri's throat ache. She'd had no intention of stealing his damned artifact, but she couldn't say she wasn't a thief. She'd been excited because the heavy slab was *exactly* like the one she'd found that morning diving *Napolitano.* She'd just wanted to take a few pictures away from the watchful eyes of his people. That wasn't a damned crime.

He towered over her. Brow furrowed, silvery eyes glinting. She relaxed her tense shoulders. *Nice try. I have a brother who's got that attitude down pat. I teethed on intimidating and surly.* Unfortunately, it was exactly because of his coiled and dangerous attitude that she glared right back. She lived for danger, and holy shit, he was danger swathed in menace, wrapped in threat, double dipped in sex appeal. Six-foot-four inches of tawny skin and well-honed muscle. Finn Gallagher was a magnificent specimen of alpha manhood.

Peri knew every inch of that impressive hard body. As pissed off at him as she was, her girl parts were annoyingly ready to party and not in the least bit interested in the danger signals her intellect was reading loud and clear.

His drying hair, bitter-chocolate dark, fell in soft waves against his strong, tanned neck. Cupping her cheek, he stroked his thumb across her bottom lip. Eyes like molten steel, he said thickly, "We good now?"

Was he serious? Since his drysuit couldn't hide a damn thing, yes, he was serious. Peri took a step back. His hand dropped to his side. "*Absolutely.* Let me just switch off feeling like crap after three men accused me of being a felon. Give me a minute. . ."

He reached for her again. "Let me make it up to you."

She should *not* feel this much freaking attraction for a steamroller. Strongly resisting the temptation to fall into his arms, insist he carry her to his lair and have his wicked way with her, she stopped him with a narrow-eyed look. Putting the flat of her hand against his chest, she held him at bay. Oh, God. His chest. Hard slabs of toned muscle, and the steady beat of his heart, made her fingers curl and her own heart rate skyrocket. Damn it.

He was wickedly sexy, and even now, when he was throwing out accusations, the sizzle zinged between them. The most dangerous thing about Finn Gallagher was that no matter what, he made her want him.

If she wasn't careful, that want would become a need, just like air.

And then he'd walk away. Which was why she always ended affairs first. Not that there'd been many, but six months seemed to be her limit. She suspected it wouldn't last a tenth of that with Finn. Only because she found herself already mourning the loss of their relationship, and they didn't really have one.

Damn damn damn. Peri glanced up as a gull swooped overhead to land on the rail of the deck above them to give herself a moment to compose herself. The gull gave a plaintive cry that sounded like a kitten in distress. She returned her attention to Finn. “Stop manhandling me. You’re not a lion peeing on his mate to mark his territory."

It was annoying as hell when he laughed. “I promise, I won’t pee on you.”

Snatching her hand off his chest she narrowed her eyes at him. "You'd better not think this is funny, Phineas Gallagher. You can't accuse me of stealing and lying one minute and flirt with me the next," she said in a furious whisper.

"You liked being manhandled just fine the other day." His eyes glinted with amusement.

Irritation spiked. She needed no reminding. "I liked you three days ago." His touch burned her skin like a spark of electricity. It didn’t help that Peri wanted to lick him, all over. Right there. Outside. In public. Then she wanted to crawl all over his naked body and screw his brains out. "Before I realized your default-mode is caveman." Her words didn’t come out quite as emphatically as she would've liked.

"Know what I think?"

Her temper cooled, leaving behind simmering irritation. Not at Finn. At herself, damn it. For believing for even a nanosecond that he wouldn't think the worst of her with no damn proof. She'd been ready to tell him who she really was, and then she'd seen the tablet, and all her good intentions evaporated. So what if she'd held it a few minutes too damn long and made the twitchy tech guy feel uncomfortable?

"I have no idea, but I'm sure you're about to tell me. And for God's sake, lower your voice, everyone's watching us and avidly listening to our every freaking word."

Finn placed his hand on the small of her back and edged toward the rail. "Better?"

Why didn't the damn man put on a shirt? He was practically naked in the second skin of his drysuit, which hid very little. He was a big man. All over. His bare chest was tanned, and muscular, and an arrow of dark hair disappeared beneath the black neoprene. She knew precisely where it went. Prickly heat flushed her skin. Her body reflexively tightened, waiting for his touch.

She shivered in reaction when he placed a finger under her chin, tipping up her face so she was practically blinded by the sun. Of course, *his* face was shadowed. "I'm going to discover all your secrets, Ariel Andersen."

Ariel Andersen didn't have many. It was Persephone Case who had cause to be guarded. Her heart skipped several beats as she stepped out of his hold and used his shadow to block the spotlight of the sun. Folding her arms, she mimicked his eyebrow raise. Her brother had taught her how to do it to good effect. "It was your rule that we give each other false names and pretend lives, not mine," she reminded him, purposely misinterpreting his comment.

His eyes narrowed. He didn't like being reminded that he'd made the damned rules. "Rules change," he spoke through clenched teeth. "Like it or not, we're in the real world now. Stop hiding things."

"Hiding things? Me? How mysterious. What would I be hiding, I wonder? I believe you've seen me laid bare." Probably not something to remind him of when they were both pissed off.

"If I asked outright, I'm sure you wouldn't tell me."

"Give me a minute, I'm sure I can come up with something salacious and daringly spy-like."

"That's an interesting leap. Who are you spying *for*, Ariel?"

Shit. "Mr. Blofeld?"

His lips twitched. He got the James Bond supervillain reference. "You're quick, I'll give you that. How long have you worked for the Ministry?"

"Almost five years." She bet he'd checked. True. But her own salvage was the only thing she'd been supervising until the Bastard Cutters had shown up.

She didn't like Finn's cool smile, his questions, or the feeling that she was walking into a trap. A trap of her own making, but a trap nonetheless. She liked him more as a lover than an adversary. At least there the playing field was sorta, kinda even.

Most of her first-hand knowledge came from their pillow talk when they'd been too exhausted to move. The rest she'd discovered on the internet. Entrepreneur. Philanthropist. Inventor. Private. Brilliant. Reclusive. Sixth richest man in the world. All of which was a little terrifying if she really thought about it.

His bio confirmed that he *had* once been married. Peri had seen a picture of the exquisitely beautiful ex-wife, model, Erica Larson. Another Zagg search mentioned, briefly, that his ex-business partner, Derry Byrne, was in prison for embezzlement, and that Finn had testified against him in court, nailing his conviction. The business partner having an affair with Finn's wife had been tabloid fodder for months. And explained why he was so paranoid about people stealing from him.

She and Finn had been together for about thirty-something hours, and the only personal details she knew about him was where he liked to be touched. She knew where and how hard to caress him to make him shudder, knew exactly how he liked to be kissed. She knew his sexual expertise, and that he had incredible stamina and a large appetite for sex. And he'd told her she drove him bat-shit crazy with lust.

Everything else he'd told her could've been fabricated for that weekend persona. Truth couched as lies, lies couched as truth.

Peri's throat tightened. She'd allowed herself to fall a little in love that weekend because it hadn't come with any risk. She'd known she'd never see him again. But even with the confidences they'd shared, he still amounted to being a stranger. A stranger who had the authority to boss her around, tell her what to do, and how damn high to jump.

His ship. His rules. Her fingers itched to snatch back the tablet, now out of her sight, damn it. Hit him over the head with it, then make a run for it. How dare he treat her like a criminal. Serve him right if she *really* stole the damn thing.

That kind of impulsive behavior was her real-life *modus operandi*, but not in keeping with something Ariel Andersen would do. She wasn't ready to give up Ariel. Not just yet. Still, her heart raced, and her palms were sweaty with excitement. All she needed was a little time alone with the artifact to prove what she already suspected.

She pointed in the general direction of the cleaning room "Do you think I could just take a-"

"No."

"You don't even know what I was going to ask!"

"Take a closer look under the microscope at that artifact. The answer is still no. Once it's processed, you may get another look. Supervised. Until then, keep your hands to yourself."

“So that *sorry* was just paying me lip service?"

He arched an eyebrow. “Not used to being told no?”

She gave a mocking laugh. "Talk about the kettle calling the pot black. I bet no one has ever dared to tell *you* no."

"Many people- heads of State, high-level government official's, the lot. They've all tried to tell me no over the years. Those no's made me who I am today. Never underestimate the power of no."

"Double ass." Still, excitement fired her blood almost as well as a good argument. She couldn't wait to compare the two artifacts. Were they identical? Part of something larger? They appeared to weigh about the same, the sizes and shapes were similar, and both appeared to have the same markings. Would they fit together like a jigsaw puzzle? Why had they been discovered five miles apart? Debris field from *Napolitano*? Or had the two tablets been on different ships to protect them? She wanted to look at them side by side to compare. She had a million questions and couldn't freaking wait to get started on finding the answers.

"Thank you for the life lesson, I'll needlepoint it onto a -whatever people needlepoint on. *The power of no.* I'm sure it'll come in handy."

"Are you and Doctor Núñez lovers?" Finn asked in an annoyingly conversational tone considering he'd just reamed her out without anesthetic.

Seriously? One of the tech's nearby taking photographs of the day's finds, covered a gasp with a cough. *No shit.* Peri lowered her voice. "They can still hear us! And that's absolutely none of your business."

"After what we've shared, you bet your ass it is."

"One weekend where we gave each other fake stories-your rule, not mine, -doesn't entitle you to know a damn thing about me, my past, present or freaking future! I *liked* you." Peri pointedly used the past tense, and enjoyed the tension in his jaw at that flat out, blatant lie. "I don't think I do anymore. So, no more giving me hot looks, or playing with my hair, or staring at my mouth as though you intend kissing me senseless.

He rubbed a broad hand over his naked chest, silver eyes narrowed as he waited for her answer. Why was he squinting? The sun was at his back. She was the one in the spotlight. A muscle jerked in his jaw. He radiated heat and a heavy dose of testosterone. "Answer the question."

All she had to do was extend her arm and she could run her hand over all that lovely muscle on his chest. Proud of her willpower, heart hammering, she refrained. "I forgot what it was." Dear Lord, the man wreaked havoc just by looking at her.

"Núñez. You. Lovers."

"Would it bother you if..." One look at his thunderous expression and Peri reversed. "Doctor Núñez is my boss. He understands how impassioned I am about these wrecks, their history and what the discovery of their treasures will mean to Argentina."

Again, the eyebrow arch told her he was seeing through every lie she manufactured. He couldn't, could he? *Damn. Damn. Damn.* "Do you often sleep with people who work with *you*?"

"No."

There was that power of no again. Annoying as shit. *Your ex slept with your partner. Is that why you're so uncompromising?* "No, not often? Or no, you don't sleep with your employees?" Peri asked sweetly.

He gave a small shake of his head as though she was trying his patience. "Isn't work where most people meet their mates?" As he answered her throwaway question with a throwaway of his own, he glanced at the large black dive watch on his left wrist. To indicate his disinterest, to time her response? Or in a hurry to go? *I can only hope.*

Why did even his most benign question sound loaded? "I have no idea." She bet he'd slept with every one of the attractive women on board. Staff and crew. That thought ignited her temper all over again. A ripple of unease fluttered across her skin as he focused his gaze on her, as if he had x-ray vision and could see right through to her bones.

Other than the perpetual scruff on Finn's jaw, he looked like some manly GQ model selling sex and men's cologne as he stood there, tall and broad, drysuit around his hips. Cocky. Arrogant. His dark hair artlessly combed back off his elegant face, curled slightly at his nape.

Phineas Gallagher looked exactly like what he was. A self-assured, beyond-billionaire used to getting his own way. Someone who didn't take no for an answer, and didn't take shit from anyone he considered competition for something he wanted. She didn't for a second underestimate him. He hadn't become one of the richest men in the world by being a pushover. He wore the same air of danger and menace as her brother, Ry, did for people he didn't trust. Which was pretty much everyone.

She preferred the way his eyes softened when he'd looked at her while they were making love a hell of a lot better. Too bad this situation had them in opposite camps, him firmly with those bastard Cutters and her with Ry.

She made the foolish mistake of looking directly into eyes the thunderous, ominous gray of storm clouds. She'd probably turn to freaking stone as he gave her a stare down hot enough to melt... "What material has the highest melting point?"

"Tungsten has a melting point of 6192 °F," he answered readily, not in the least thrown by the non sequitur. "A material made with a combination of hafnium, nitrogen, and carbon has a melting point of more than 7460 °F. That's about two-thirds the temperature of the surface of the sun. Why, are you planning on melting something?"

She hoped he read something diabolical into her nonchalant shrug. "Just a question."

He just smiled.

He might look like a sportswear model, but he had more brainpower than the average half-naked man featured in advertisements. More brainpower than anyone, if internet reports were accurate. *Do not underestimate him.*

Peri tore her gaze from his and glanced over the rail to see three divers on the platform below. She gave Finn a saccharin sweet smile. "I see your divers down there waiting for you. They look impatient." Not at all, they were talking, and looked perfectly relaxed and in no hurry.

"Where did you go to school, Ariel?"

She suddenly hated him calling her Ariel. She wanted to taste her name on his mouth, damn it. "The Argentine Atlantis University in Buenos Aires." She really had attended a few classes there when the incessant high winds of the Patagonian summer made diving treacherous. But she bet he knew that, too. It was best to stick as close to the truth as possible.

"What do you do for fun, when you're not pilfering artifacts?"

She rolled her eyes. "I make spreadsheets and write reports."

His brow rose. "For fun?"

"You have no idea," she gave him something short of a dirty look. "Why all the questions? This isn't a date, remember. I'm here representing the interest of my government. Doing my job. If you have questions reference *that.*"

"Consider it a job interview."

"I have a job, thank you." *Down girl. Be Ariel Andersen.* His elegant, unreadable face appeared before her like the afterimage from staring into the sun for too long.

His probing questions were unnerving, and, despite sounding casual, put her on alert. The bright, burning intensity in his smoky eyes was in no way diluted by his casual tone.

Game on, Finn Gallagher.

Typically, she thrived on danger-when she chose the intensity, location, and who'd participate in said danger. "You've made your damn point loud and clear. No need to hit me over the head with a sledgehammer." She wanted to go inside and see what the techs were doing. And take another look at that slab under the pretense of cataloging the day's finds for the ministry. But it was as though some freaky forcefield bound them together and she couldn't pull apart from him. "How long ago did you leave Ireland? If she couldn't break away from him she might as well learn more about the notoriously reclusive multi-gazillionaire.

"I left in my teens."

In one of the rare moments when they hadn't been having sex, Finn had told her he'd been orphaned when he was a baby. His parents had died in a boating accident. He'd been in the foster system in Ireland for fifteen years. That would harden anyone. There was no reason for Peri to think he'd made that up, and she could certainly relate to the feeling of isolation and loneliness he must've felt.

There'd been no need to carry their charade to the point that they made up a fictitious past that weekend. She certainly hadn't.

Besides, once she'd realized who he was, she'd done her homework, too. He'd been born in Waterford, Ireland, made his fortune at seventeen by investing in the stock market, and parlayed that into the kind of wealth that could pay cash for this mega-gigayacht and anything else he so desired. Now he had his finger in hundreds of pies and had more money than God.

Peri didn't give a damn about his wealth, his power, or his good looks. The Cutters were her focus, Finn just happened to be in the same orbit.

It was a minor inconvenience that she was distracted by his sex appeal, annoyed by his autocratic ways, and lusting after his body all at the same time. The tightness of the neoprene wrapped around his lower body put all his assets on display and was *extremely* freaking distracting.

She kept her attention on his face. But his mouth was too diverting. Switching her focus three feet to the left of his head, she said sweetly, "If you have more questions feel free to email me."

He gave her a penetrating look that made her nervous as hell. "Will you answer?"

She hadn't even realized that, like iron filings to a powerful magnet, she was looking at the damn man again. "It depends on the question." She wished he wore sunglasses so she couldn't see his silvery eyes. They saw too much. Her breath caught at the well of feelings she really, really didn't want to feel as she struggled with conflicting emotions. There was a panicky excitement in her stomach being so near him, that said; Touch the flame, it won't burn too badly.

"Why are you blushing, *Persephone*?"

"In case you hadn't noticed, it's hot out here."

"Have I embarrassed you?" He splayed his hand on the small of her back and walked her into the shade. "Are you imagining me inside you, my mouth on your pretty breasts?" The words came out low and deep, somewhere between a growl and a rumbling, seductive whisper that rubbed across her skin. His Irish accent was more pronounced when he was thinking about sex, she realized.

Her hard nipples chafed the inside of her bra in response to his words. Just hearing them brought to mind the suck and pull of his mouth. That powerful mojo of his kept sneaking up on her. She should take note. "Of course not, you egotistical oaf. Hard for me to consider being full of you when you're already so full of yourself."

"Ah, then it's that redhead temper of yours."

"I don't have a temper," she said crossly.

Finn laughed.

Oh, God, Finn amused was almost as seductive as Finn in a dark pantry.

"Don't--" Peri's throat ached. She didn't want this. She had an agenda, and Finn Gallagher had never been part of it. He was ruining everything.

He stepped close enough to cup her jaw. "Don't what, *Persephone*?" he murmured, eyes now pewter.

"Don't make me want you when I'm mad at you, damn it."

Like a pirate, Finn wanted to scoop her up and carry her back to *Blackstar*. He suspected that would not go as well as he hoped. He'd never met a more infuriating woman, and yet everything about her drew him to her. As if they were destined to be together, which was fanciful bullshit. What it was, was painful lust. He found her amusing and entertaining. Charming. Nothing more. It was more than enough.

"Would you kindly issue a royal decree to your staff that I have permission to go into the cleaning area and do my job documenting the other items found this morning?"

"A word of warning, darling. I'm not someone you want to cross. I don't give second chances. Do your job. No sticky fingers."

"Yeah, yeah. Heard it before. I'll needlepoint it on a pillow." She scowled. Even that was adorable. "You drive me to violent thoughts, Phineas Gallagher, you really do. Why don't you let that *sorry* stand for an hour or two, so it feels sincere?"

"It's sincere." He smiled. "What you're sensing is suppressed sexual desire."

She rolled her eyes. "I'm going in there." She jerked her chin toward the cleaning room. "Unless you have a valid objection?"

"Come to dinner on board *Blackstar* tonight."

Turning her head, she made a rude noise of dismissal. "I've heard that one before. No thanks."

"I want you to meet the Cutters. I think you'll enjoy them. They're a colorful bunch."

God, her face was so expressive. A profusion of thoughts flittered across her features like the shadows of passing butterflies. She wasn't warring with him, she was warring with herself. Why and what was the field of battle? Work ethics? Something else?

"Okay."

That was easier than he expected. "Fifth deck. Seven." He'd told the others seven-thirty.

"Will you want to check my pockets before I eat?" she asked, sarcasm dripping off every word.

"After," he teased. "A full body search. Just in case you decide to pilfer the silverware."

Finn enjoyed the sway of her enticing arse and long legs as she marched through the double doors.

Dressed with studied casualness in wide-legged white linen pants, a matching, low-cut white linen tank top cinched with a thin black belt, and strappy sandals, Peri strolled through the solarium and out the French doors onto the fifth deck at precisely seven that night.

She'd spent the rest of the afternoon with the tech team, although Mike and the gold tablet were nowhere to be seen. At six o'clock she'd made her way to the cabin she'd been given onboard, *Blackstar*, a luxurious suite on the third deck. She wasn't surprised to see that her suitcase, the one she'd thrown into her motorboat before she left home earlier, had been unpacked and her clothes now hung in the closet in the bedroom.

She anticipated this first meeting with the Cutters with a roiling mixture of stomach-tightening dread and excitement. She'd waited so long for this to happen, that it was hard to believe the time was finally here. She'd rehearsed a dozen scenarios until she was sure she'd know what to say and do in any situation. She was ready.

The cool air felt good on her bare skin, and the expansive view from so high up on Finn's ship was nothing short of spectacular. The ocean spread out around them, for miles. But all Peri saw was Finn, his back to the rail, waiting for her. Behind him, dark purple clouds drifted across a rose-colored sky.

In her peripheral vision, she took in the swimming pool and hot tub, both of which mirrored the colors of the flamboyant dome overhead.

Even though it hadn't come loose, Peri pushed a hairpin more firmly into her casually messy updo. Her just-got-out-of-bed look had taken forever to get just right. She'd spent more than an hour doing her face, her nails were fire engine red, and she wore her highest heels. She was ready for battle.

Hesitating in the wide doorway, she casually glanced around. No one other than Finn and herself. The area looked suspiciously like a romantic setting with stringed lights and flickering candles in hurricane lamps in the center of the long table.

"Where's everybody?" she demanded suspiciously as he skirted the pool to come to her side. He looked handsome, urbane and altogether delicious in dark pants, and a slate gray, collared shirt. "If you lured me up here to have sex you've got another thing coming." The tinge of cranky in her voice was fake. Her temper usually flared hot but was short lived. And God help her, the idea of sex right now was tempting. But she wasn't ready to let him off the hook just yet. *Because that will keep him safely at arm's length while I deal with the Cutters.* She refused to admit, even to herself, that the powerful attraction she and Finn shared was almost too intense, even for a daredevil like herself.

She'd had sex on the brain pretty much since their weekend in Buenos Aires, almost two weeks ago. Revitalized by sex in the pantry three days ago. Hell, just looking at him turned her on. Her pheromones were hot for his pheromones all the freaking time. But he was her sexual kryptonite. And she couldn't- *shouldn't* get distracted by him. This promised to be the most important event in her life, and lusting for Finn might very well derail her from her long-term purpose.

Finn had the gall to laugh. As he got closer, the stringed lights surrounding the deck caused little stars to bounce off his shiny clean hair. The dark strands had a slight wave to them, and it made him look softer, more approachable as a stray breeze played with the strands. *Do not be deceived by his hair*, she cautioned herself. *There's nothing soft about him.*

Tonight she couldn't afford to be distracted by Finn's sex appeal. Tonight was all about the Cutters.

Brushing a loose skein of hair from her cheek, he traced his thumb along her jaw. No fair. A tremor went from point of contact to her toes. "You have a very suspicious mind, darling. Hold that thought. While sex with you right now has enormous appeal, it's not on the menu. At least not for another couple of hours. I told everyone seven-thirty because I wanted you to see something first."

When he held out an elegant hand, her nipples beaded, her body reacting as if he were stroking her skin. "Come look."

The man was painfully magnetic. Peri put her hand in his, then remembered her caution to herself too late as his fingers curled around hers. *Damn it. Holding his hand felt. . . Perfect.*

That "darling" stopped her heartbeat for a couple of seconds, it hiccupped in her chest before resuming a normal, if slightly elevated, beat. "What is it you want to show me?"

He led her to a side table where a large flat gold object stood propped on a table easel. Her eyes shot to him, and her fingers tightened around his as her gaze fixed on the artifact. "Oh!?"

"Had Mike put a rush on processing. Spectacular, isn't it?"

Understatement. That's why Mike and the tablet had been missing all afternoon.

Hidden beneath the sediment and dirt acquired over five hundred years, lay the gleaming sheen of gold. The lights reflected off the uneven surface, highlighting the almost straight horizontal lines, with a narrow border on two sides.

Mouth dry, she stared at the artifact, transfixed. "It's stunning." She wanted to call Ry, ask if his team had cleaned their tablet yet.

Way too close for comfort, Peri felt the heat radiating off Finn's body, and couldn't take a breath without inhaling that intoxicating mixture of grapefruit and sea air. She concentrated on the tablet. Letting her finger hover just over the surface, she took it all in. "This is writing." Unable to resist, she ran her finger along the uneven edge of the almost perfect oblong piece.

"Possibly some sort of text?" Finn captured a strand of her hair that had come loose from her updo and wound it around his finger as he spoke. Peri's insides contracted as if he were touching her bare skin. "But none of us have been able to read it. And between me and the techs, we cover about fifteen assorted languages. Did you pull your hair up to drive me mad?"

Yes. "I put it up so it's off my neck."

"I love it this way, too. I'd prefer you only wore it down for me."

She threw him a glance filled with amusement. "You're ridiculously Victorian, you know that?"

"I'm quite fond of your ankles as well," he teased, tugging her closer. "And everything in between." Finn's mouth hovered over hers. "Why is it you tie me into knots, Persephone?"

Every time he called her Persephone it did crazy things to her insides.

Torn between desperation for him to kiss her, and getting back to the artifact, Peri stood on her toes and pressed a chaste kiss to his mouth.

Wrapping his arm around her waist, Finn pulled her upand slanted his mouth over hers. The kiss was unlike any of his others. This one was achingly gentle, tender. No less passionate, but surprisingly restrained, all things considered. Too quickly he set her back on her feet, steadying her with a firm hand on her hip. "Rain check?"

Yes.

Every atom in her body was traveling at warp speed, colliding inside her in showers of sparks and small charges that had her heart racing. All her senses felt pumped up as if on steroids. Wordlessly, she nodded. There had never been any doubt that she'd end up in his bed tonight. She blinked him back into focus.

Amused, he said thickly, "Back to the artifact?"

"My God, this is epic." Thrilled beyond belief, she wanted to throw herself into his arms and take him up on his offer. Instead, she returned her attention to the gold piece on the table. "Thank you for having it cleaned so quickly."

His gorgeous smile reached his eyes, revealing straight, white teeth. "Pick it up if you like."

She didn't need a second invitation. Remembering the unexpected heft of it, she reached for the tablet with both hands, then slowly turned it this way and that to see the text. Whatever was written was quite clear, just indecipherable.

Both her brother and Theo were going to be blown away when she told him they'd discovered a second tablet. On her way from Ry's ship to her house on the bluff that afternoon, Peri had called Theo to fill him in on her intriguing find on her dive with her brother. Even though her tablet had yet to be cleaned, she'd sent him pictures of it from several angles.

She couldn't wait to see them side-by-side. Maybe they needed to be together to become legible. The thought was thrilling.

"This looks festive," a male voice came from behind them. "You picked a good night to be outside. No wind."

Her heart leaped, so hard she felt the knocks against her ribcage. Very carefully, with Finn's assistance, Peri placed the tablet back on the stand.

A Cutter.

Up close and very personal.

"Nick and Bria Cutter, Ariel Andersen." Finn drew her toward the couple and they met in the middle of the open space. Acutely aware of Finn's hand on her back, she felt the heat of each finger through the flimsy linen of her tank top. The newcomers couldn't miss Finn touching her, much less his body language which stated his claim on her. Even though he wasn't aware of it, Peri was grateful for Finn's display of emotion and physical support right then.

Nick was as tall as Finn, dark-haired and broad-shouldered in jeans and a dark t-shirt. She hadn't been able to see his eyes through her binoculars when he'd been aboard the *Scorpion*, when he'd been on her radar a couple of years ago. Wow. They were distinctive and gorgeous. She was struck by the penetrating ocean blue that seemed to see directly into her soul as if he knew exactly who she was and what she had been doing.

Wasn't this exactly what she'd wanted?

Yes, but now that the time had come, she wasn't as sanguine about the inevitable confrontation. She'd stolen a fortune from them. It was within their power to have her arrested for piracy and thrown in some godforsaken foreign jail where she'd spend the rest of her life futilely plotting her revenge.

The reality of her first meeting with them wasn't nearly as explosive as the fantasy had been.

One of Ry's favorite cautions was- Be careful what you wish for, you might get it.

"Nice to meet you, Ariel." Nick's smile reached his eyes. He looked genuinely happy to see her, which meant, despite the distinctive color and length of her hair, he didn't recognize her. Peri had not taken *that* into account.

Maybe he was biding his time? Waiting for his brothers to arrive so they could unmask her together? When she shivered, Finn rubbed her back with his warm hand. She took comfort in his touch.

"Finn's talked about you," Nick said easily. "We're looking forward to your visits to our ship, *Scorpion,* in the coming weeks."

She shot a quick glance at Finn. What had he said about her, and at which stage of their short relationship had he spoken of her?

"Yes." Bria's Italian accent was charming. Her blue-black hair shone in the light. Svelte, sophisticated and stunningly beautiful in a red, halter neck dress that bared her shoulders and long legs, and accented her body to perfection. Gold earrings, a dozen gold bracelets and a massive rock of a diamond wedding ring, made her look impossibly put together. Like Addison, Bria looked like a model in a glossy magazine.

Enveloping Peri in a soft, fragrant cloud of ripe peaches, she placed a kiss on each cheek. Very European. Bria was the Crown Princess of Merrezo, a small, Italian principality in the Mediterranean, but no one introduced her as such. "We look forward to getting to know you."

Peri very much doubted she'd say that if she knew who she was.

"And you, you charming man," Bria addressed Finn as she curled her hand into her husband's elbow. "This was a lovely idea to get the family together before the real work begins."

"Soon we'll be too busy to socialize."

Peri turned slowly as three men strolled through the solarium to emerge out on deck. The *other* Cutter brothers.

Even though she'd been waiting for this moment, the impact of their larger than life presence was like a blow to the chest. Heart galloping, palms slick with sweat she waited for them to join their group.

No one would mistake them for anything other than brothers. They all had a similar look. Tall, athletic, and dark haired. Having four pairs of identical, piercing blue eyes focused on her was the most terrifying experience of Peri's life.

"Ariel, my brothers Logan, Jonah and Zane." Nick pointed to each.

Since death or dismemberment was highly unlikely with this many witnesses, Peri held her hand out to Logan and tried to steady her breathing. Of course, croaking from anticipation was still a strong possibility.

"Nice to put faces to the names." Logan's hand was large, dry and strong. Peri extricated her hand as soon as was polite. She shoved it into the front pocket of her slacks, and surreptitiously wiped her damp palm. "I'm looking forward to an extraordinary salvage." This was a man who'd scuttled his own ship to defeat terrorists from getting their hands on millions of dollars' worth of diamonds. Clearly, he had no problem doing whatever was necessary to win.

Zane gave her a charming smile. The similarity between the brothers stopped at the youngest Cutter's piece of crap ship, the aptly named *Decrepit.* The decrepit look of his salvage boat indicated to Peri that Zane gave more weight to how *he* looked than the appearance of the ship he used to extricate millions of dollars worth of artifacts from the sea. "If the past few days are any indication I think your anticipation is well-founded."

Jonah was the dark horse. Peri knew absolutely nothing about him. He was the only brother she'd not stolen from only because she hadn't known of his existence until a few weeks ago. Why had they kept him a secret?

Did she care enough to find out now? Nope.

Braced for the moment they realized who she was, Peri's heart stopped and started like a malfunctioning outboard motor. The nasty oily swirl in her stomach returned. She hadn't expected them to be *nice* to her. Far from it.

She'd been braced for instant recognition, followed by hurled accusations, questions and drama. She'd been prepared with answers and accusations of her own. But so far no one had treated her as anything other than a representative of the Argentinian government. Which was damn disconcerting, not to mention *weird.*

This wasn't just waiting for the other shoe to drop, it was actually *seeing* its downward trajectory, only to find it halted an inch over her head.

"Let's drink to that." Finn went to the bar. "Wine? Beer?"

"I'd love a glass of red- Dios mio might be correct!" Bria whispered, hand to her throat as she caught sight of the artifact on the nearby table. Letting go of Nick's arm, she walked to it as if in a trance. "How does this come to be here?"

"We brought it to the surface this morning."

"Here?" Glancing at Finn, she pointed to the deck beneath their feet. "From *Nuestra Señora del Marco*?"

"Yes, this morning. We think those horizontal markings could possibly be text. Can you read it?"

"*No, non posso-*"

Walking up beside her, Nick put his arm around his wife's slender shoulders. His brothers crowded behind them to see what had snagged her attention. "English, love."

Peri pressed a hand to her stomach where nervous butterflies swarmed. The relic was suddenly out of sight behind a wall of males and she was on the outside looking in.

Selfishly, she wished Finn hadn't drawn attention to the artifact. She'd wanted time alone with it, and the one she'd discovered this morning, to see if she could crack the meaning of the text.

With a slight frown, Bria nodded to her husband, then turned large dark eyes to Finn. "We have one such as this. It looks the same as *la tavoletta d'oro Merrezo* in our little museum. In fact, I think *identico.* May I hold it?"

"Sure. It's heavy. . ." Finn cautioned, taking it from the stand. He placed it in Bria's hands, then, as he'd done for Peri that afternoon, braced it on the bottom edge when Bria's arms dipped with the weight.

"I'm aware." Bria smiled. "It is far heavier than it looks. It's just like ours. Same size and shape. Thickness. This exact shade of gold. A gold unlike any I've ever seen before."

"We've ascertained it's Peruvian gold," Finn told her. "Tests show the thin layer of sheet gold covers a chiseled marble tablet."

"If it is indeed the same as ours, it does," Bria indicated Finn take the tablet from her. "One corner of *La tavoletta d'oro Merrezo* is broken. Gold layered over marble." She looked around, face glowing, dark eyes bright with excitement. "It *is* the same."

"*Identical?*" Zane asked as their circle opened to include Peri.

Bria gave a very Italian shrug. "It certainly looks to be. You all know of our *Gold Tablet of Merrezo*, yes? How could this be here, off the coast of Patagonia, and its twin thousands of miles away on a small Italian island?"

Peri could barely contain her excitement. Holy crap.

Not a twin.

A triplet.

What were the odds?

Three tablets, worlds apart.

SEVEN

"I think almost everyone interested in archeology knows of the Gold Tablet of Merrezo." Peri's excitement rose. "It's almost as famous as the Shroud of Turin. I don't know much about it, other than the name and that every now and then there's new speculation when some expert or another attempts to read the text."

"They *can't* read it," Bria told her. "Still, Christians claim it, Jews claim it- Even various, off-the-wall, "religious" groups assert it to be theirs. None can provide provenance as Merrezo can, and so it remains with us."

Peri had never seen the famous and mysterious Merrezo tablet in person, nor had she researched it in any great depth, which was why it hadn't come immediately to mind when she'd first seen the artifacts from Finn's and her own sites. But as far as she knew, no one had ever claimed the Italian tablet had been salvaged from the *ocean*.

But now. . .

Damn it, if only Finn hadn't caught her this morning. She'd have photographs to compare this one with the one she'd found that morning. Then she'd do some research on the one in Italy. This was a thrilling turn of events, and she couldn't wait to see where her research led her. She was eager to get started.

And damn it, this freaking waiting on pins and needles for the Cutters to jump up and say, "Got you!" had her stomach churning. Foreboding was ruining her excitement about the tablets. Now she just wanted someone to say something. *Anything.*

Let's get it over with, people!

She'd watched them through binoculars- *often.* Had they not done the same when she was stealing right from under their freaking noses?

How many women salvagers did they know with long red hair? Admittedly when she dove to help herself to some of their choice artifacts, she wore a wet or dry suit, so her distinctive hair didn't always show. But when she was on her boat she left it loose. Intentionally.

It had never occurred to her that they wouldn't recognize her the second they saw it. Maybe they were waiting until dinner was over to rain Armageddon on her head? Maybe this was a clever trap to lull her into a false sense of security while they waited for the police to show up to drag her away in chains?

That would be embarrassing.

Was the tablet the bait? Had Finn told them about this morning? Did they believe she'd steal it from under their noses as she'd done hundreds of other artifacts? Then revel in catching her red-handed?

Shit. So many damned questions and no one answering. Maybe they all had that disorder where they couldn't recognize people's faces? What was it called? Ah. *Prosopagnosia.* Long nights alone at sea gave her plenty of time to read anything and everything, and bits and pieces of weird, random information stuck.

For instance; Finn's space race was public knowledge, but a little-known fact was that he quietly helped fund under-resourced students, college track, and nonprofit colleges' completion programs to the tune of fifty freaking *million* dollars. Peri bet that had a lot to do with him growing up in the Irish foster system. The dollar amount was either because he had money to spare, or because he'd not been given the same chances. She bet the latter.

When did the man sleep?

She'd love to watch him when he was oblivious to observation. Would the strength in his face soften in sleep? On their insane weekend together, she hadn't caught him sleeping. Not once. Probably because she'd been so exhausted by their sweaty calisthenics she'd dropped into the deep end of sleep herself whenever she couldn't keep going any longer.

She palmed her phone in her pants pocket, fumbled without looking at it, and allowed it to poke out so she could discreetly take a picture of the tablet. Either she'd get some decent pictures from pocket level- or she'd have everyone's butts to show for her subterfuge.

"This is absolutely fascinating." She didn't have to fake excitement. Angling to better face Bria, who had her back to the display, Peri clicked off another few photographs from her phone. She was pretty sure she wasn't going to have anything to show for the endeavor, but a girl had to try. "How did the museum come by it, do you know?"

Damn it. She wanted to *enjoy* this exchange. She was interested. Invested. The whole damned Cutter thing was distracting. Why were they dicking around? Waiting to see if she'd break first? For a nanosecond, Peri debated saying something herself. Surgical strike. Get it over with. After all, she had her own claim to work on. No matter what the Cutters decided to do, or not do, their actions wouldn't have any impact on her staked claim, or frankly, the rest of her life.

Maybe she should just jump up on the dinner table and yell, "Hey! Recognize me?" But no. Let them come to her. She'd delivered herself to their door. It was up to them to come the rest of the way.

"In 1484, our *profeta* - our seer, Foscari, was as famous in his time as France's Nostradamus became many years later," Bria told everyone as she accepted a glass of red wine from her husband. His hand lingered on hers, and Bria's gaze heated as she met Nick's eyes for an intimate, wordless exchange.

Finn's palm brushed the small of Peri's back, indicating he, too, had witnessed the heated glance. His touch accelerated her heartbeat, causing her to feel an intense yearning for something she couldn't name. Sex she could name. This wasn't that.

"According to legend," Bria continued after a sip of her drink, "*La tavoletta d'oro Merrezo* was sent to Signore Foscari as a gift 'from across the sea.' He died before it arrived, causing much speculation as to who, and *why*, he'd been gifted with such a thing. They asked; 'Is it important? What does it mean?'"

She took another sip of wine. "It has been in our small country since. Believers claim it to be some sort of religious text. Even though only our curator, Dr. Vadini, a linguist of some renown, has been able to read parts of the text after many, many years of study.

Scholars claim the script to be as profound as the ten commandments and hold the secret for true believers. Disciples. But no one knows who these believers *are*. Noted archaeologists, theologians and the curious flock to see it every year. Experts from all over the world have argued its meaning and tried to use other criteria to decipher the text.

No one else has, so far. All we know for sure about it is that its provenance is secure for over five hundred years."

"Across the sea?" Finn picked up the conversation as he indicated everyone to be seated as two stewards arrived with the main course. The smoky-perfumed, mouth-watering smell of *Cordero al Palo* filled the air. Peri had missed lunch and was starving.

"I think you'll enjoy this dish." Finn pulled out the chair beside him for her, then sat at the head of the table as everyone else found a seat. "It's spit-roasted lamb cooked over an open fire for several hours until the outside is crisp, and the meat falls off the bone."

Peri slid her chair closer to the table, glad to be sitting beside him and not surrounded by the Cutters. Perhaps then she'd have at least one escape route. That was if Finn were on her side, or too startled by the Cutters' reactions to pin her down before she could disappear.

Finn waited until they were all seated and settled before he picked up the conversation. His knee touched hers. When she shifted, so did he. "Getting back to the origin of the Merrezo Tablet, if my memory serves correctly, no one has pinpointed where 'across the sea' meant, or honestly, if that information was written on the tablet, right?"

"The language has been extinct for hundreds of years." Bria spread her napkin on her lap. "Our Dr. Vadini has been able to decipher some, but not all, of the text. There are theories, all of which are rigorously disputed by one group or the next. Dr. Vadini insists it's an ancient, long dead language from South America. Others say the South Seas or China."

"We're seven thousand miles from your country," Peri pointed out, as, with a smile, she accepted a warm crusty roll from the steward, then the butter dish from Nick beside her. "Could 'across the sea' mean over seven thousand miles?" She buttered the roll. Trying to swallow past the lump of anticipation in her throat to eat it was going to be some trick.

"Crossing the North *and* South Atlantic Oceans five hundred years ago?" Finn sliced off a thick piece of lamb, chewed, swallowed, then added, "I always thought the origins of the source of the Merrezo Tablet referred to the Mediterranean. But considering we've discovered a possible twin here, and with the wealth of gold, emeralds and silver we've already recovered on the wreck, it's feasible the Merrezo Tablet could've come from this region. Possible a *fifth* ship returning from here to Spain with its holds filled with treasures for the king, actually made the crossing."

Peri bit her tongue, so she didn't blurt out that *Napolitano* was of Italian registry. Finn's hypothesis made sense.

"Maybe our wrecks hold more than Finn's tablet." Jonah's suggestion mirrored Peri's thoughts, and her heart did a little happy dance. Holy crap. What if there *were* more tablets? What would that mean? What had they been made *for*? The possibilities were thrilling. She couldn't wait to get started on figuring it out. Ry would be as excited as she was, and Theo might be a big help, as well.

She had to get some good pictures of Finn's tablet before she was kicked off *Blackstar*.

If she was kicked off *Blackstar*. No. *When*. It was inevitable.

"Perhaps." Logan, eyes and voice intense, put down his fork, food forgotten. "This could be the reasoning why the small armada travelled five hundred miles *south* from the capital instead of north as charted. They'd already picked up gold, silver and emeralds up North, then travelled hundreds of miles south to pick up the tablets? They must've considered the tablet a damn sight more important than what they carried in their holds. Which, honestly, stretches the imagination."

"The reverse trip sounds logical to me. At least that explains the long detour. But logical or not, that doesn't mean it's the truth," Zane chimed in. "The armada could have traveled hundreds of miles south to pick up the two tablets. *Or* one of the captains had a girlfriend in Patagonia he wanted to see. Maybe we'll never know the truth."

Jonah's potato loaded fork was halfway to his mouth when he added his two cents. "The Merrezo tablet on an unnamed ship, made its way safely to Italy? And this second tablet sank with *Nuestra Señora del Marco?* Honestly? I'm with Logan on this one. Seems a bit of a stretch to me, too."

As everyone speculated on whether Finn's artifact could be a match for the Merrezo tablet, Peri glanced around the table. She sure as hell wasn't going to relax. Her big reveal was coming, anticipation thrumming in the air. Hungry as she was it was impossible to eat. She dropped the aromatic roll onto her plate and used her fork to move her food around as her stomach churned. *Get on with it!*

When she felt Finn's warm fingers on her knee, Peri jolted, her gaze meeting his. Narrowed-eyed, he gave her a small, are-you-okay-one-shouldered-hunch. Nodding, she stuck a forkful of roasted lamb into her mouth, hoping it would dissolve on its own because she was too tense to chew.

He made her long for things she'd denied herself most of her life. Worse, he reminded her how alone she was despite a fabulous boat and a spectacular house. She traveled too much to make lasting friendships, and she was never at her house long enough to make a home. It was a good thing she liked her own company because she realized, now, with the noise and laughter at the table, she was alone a lot. Now, with Finn beside her, the lively conversation and laughter, she realized she hadn't just been alone, she'd been freaking lonely.

And would be again, she reminded herself firmly, annoyed when her throat ached.

"Not to also be a skeptic, but a wide consensus believes that the Merrezo tablet is a hoax." Logan, who sat directly opposite her, frowned. "Many believe Foscari, to protect his legacy and sustain his followers, maintained that the tablet contained future prophecies. But since no one other than Vadini knows the language- and he's only been able to translate about ten percent of it so far, everyone keeps speculating what these words mean or could possibly mean. No one knows for *sure* what the tablet says."

Peri swallowed the cow-sized hunk of meat without chewing. Testosterone hung over the table, as thick as morning fog. Logan was clearly the oldest, but that didn't mean the others deferred to him. Everyone had an opinion, and they talked over each other like puppies at play. Debating the various merits of the origins of the Italian tablet.

"Or denied, *cognate,*" Bria corrected her brother-in-law. "The myth has preserved for over five hundred years, after all." She dabbed her mouth with her napkin. "*La tavoletta d'oro Merrezo* has been the subject of intense debate among theologians, historians and researchers for years. We could discuss various theories all night and still never know if one of them might be correct, yes?"

Nick smiled at his wife before glancing around to include everyone. "Diverse arguments have been made in scientific and popular publications claiming to prove that it holds the truth to the future. There must be at least a grain of truth, don't you think?"

"They could claim anything they want that might support their own worldview," Zane pointed out. He'd already cleaned his plate, and beckoned the steward, with a charming smile, to give him a second helping. "For all we know it's an ancient grocery list of no historical value. Thanks." He smiled, and the female steward smiled back.

Nick shot his brother a pointed glance. "You don't believe that."

"No," Zane admitted,"I don't. I just don't want to get too excited. Not yet. This tablet could be an ancient equivalent of a photocopy. Perhaps they - whoever *they* may be, produced a copy in case one didn't make it."

Ancient photocopy or not, Peri couldn't wait to tell Ry and Theo about the third tablet. "Does anyone know *who* sent the tablet to Merrezo? Perhaps if we start there it would be easier to unravel the mysterious text? For all we know it could be a really long letter in two parts."- *Three* parts. "If we can figure out who wrote it, maybe we can figure out what it says. Or perhaps w- one of you will find another piece which might reveal more."

The fact that she was loving this lively exchange hurt Peri's heart. She'd better enjoy every moment, because she seriously doubted this would ever happen with her there, again.

๑

His gorgeous redhead could certainly hold her own. Fascinated, Finn observed Ariel's interaction with the Cutters as they argued back and forth, each with their own theory. She didn't give an inch. Sitting beside her, he watched micro expressions drift across her features. It was fascinating to watch. Hell, admit it. Watching her was captivating.

She seemed to be as fascinated with the Cutters, as if she was observing wild animals in a zoo. Her jade gaze flitted from Zane, to Nick, to Logan and Jonah, then repeated as they talked across the table.

Her hair was swept up in a complicated pile on top of her head. He could nail down how to deliver over a million pounds of combined thrust, from his FG-200 engine, but he couldn't figure out how she'd gotten all that mass of hair corralled with no visible means of support. If he found just the right anchor, and pulled, would the whole shining mass tumble down her back and into his hands?

God, he wanted her.

In her white linen outfit, she looked cool, polished and sophisticated. Quite different from the wild cat he'd had spread-eagled on the pantry table a few days earlier. Or the indignant woman he'd challenged this afternoon on the deck of *Two.* He wanted her in his bed. Desperately. Repeatedly.

"Anyone want to lay odds we find more tablets in the coming months?" Jonah played with the stem of his wine glass.

Cheeks flushed from the wine, and Finn surmised, excitement, Ariel tilted her head. *Persephone.* His private name for her suited her.

"You think they were massed produced?" She didn't sound thrilled by the idea.

Jonah shrugged. "Maybe Zane's right. Why not? If we have two, there certainly might be more, right?"

"I've been thinking of that same likelihood." Under the table, Finn ran his palm up Peri's leg. Her fingers clamped down to stop his progress, but he was quite happy to rest with his hand nestled into the warm crease between her torso and thigh. "We'll give our divers the head's up to be on the lookout."

Would she inform Case of his finding and its relationship to the tablet in Italy? Would it matter one way or the other if she did? The two had seemed damn friendly this morning in Finn's observation. "Maybe we should hold onto this info until we know more? We don't want the public crawling all over the area, asking questions we have no answer to, right?"

They all agreed discretion was called for until they knew more.

Speculation on what might be on the tablets was shelved for now and Peri asked about the grids they were still installing, then listened intently to the answers. Every now and then her gaze would stray across the deck to the golden artifact, as though pondering the very same question he was asking himself. Could it be related to the Merrezo tablet? He could see her mind spinning at the possibilities as the conversation drifted to various dives, the eta of the Cutter wives, what else had been salvaged thus far.

"You lecture at MIT, don't you, Finn?" Zane asked as the plates were removed.

"Occasionally. I enjoy all those bright young minds. Generally, I find their ideas innovative and well thought out. In fact, I've hired several students over the years, and am always glad I did."

Bria smiled. "What do you give them as a take away?"

"Bend the rules. Think outside the box, and my God, they certainly do. Those kids are our future."

"Are you advocating people break the rules?" Arial asked, wide-eyed and a little too sweetly.

Little witch, she was referring to that afternoon. "Not just for the sake of breaking them," he shot her a speaking look. "I remind them that the greatest mysteries haven't been discovered yet. The future of mankind - if we're to advance and solve the mysteries presented by our changing world - lies with knowledge we don't have. Yet. We won't find our optimal future in rules that are already written."

"Maybe they're written on the tablets," she suggested, tongue in cheek. And, intriguingly, in perfect Italian.

"Maybe," Finn agreed, stroking her thigh with his thumb.

"Oh!" Bria clapped her hands in a jangle of gold bracelets, eyes alight. "You speak my language beautifully."

"Thank you." Ariel's cheeks bloomed pink. "Learning Italian was on my bucket list a few years ago and I lived there for about a year."

"You mastered it well." Finn wondered what else was on her bucket list and how he could help shorten that list. "Any other languages you're this proficient at?"

She shook her head, the candlelight flickering like fiery sparks in her hair. "Not proficiently, no. I speak French, okay. A little Afrikaans, enough German to get by. That's about it."

"You have a remarkable ear for language," Nick told her.

"Nick's the one with the amazing ear," Zane told her. "It's quite the parlor trick. Tell Ariel where's she from."

Ariel smiled. "I know where I'm from."

"London," Nick told her. "Then at a young age Boston. Time spent in. . .Rome? You pick up language well, your inflections in Italian are spot on."

"Wow, you *are* good." Ariel smiled back, causing Finn a rise of annoyance. Jealousy reared its ugly head again. And again, the unexpected emotion both bothered and surprised him. "If the artifacts are indeed the same, perhaps by comparing the two, we might get an insight to what language they are written in. How exciting it would be to finally be able to read what it says."

"Perhaps Dr. Núñez can help decipher what the artifact says." Color high in the flickering candlelight, Ariel glanced around the table. "And compare it to the Merrezo tablet. He might very well know what language was used, or possibly an ancient derivative of a local dialect."

"Promising idea." Finn felt the heat of her skin through a layer of linen. Damn it, he wanted the fabric gone so he could touch her skin. He wanted the freedom to touch every part of her body without barrier. Now he was damned sorry he'd invited the Cutters. He and his freckled darling could be in bed right now, exploring each other without restriction.

"Maybe Theo- Dr. Núñez, can take a look and give us his opinion. With the artifact staying aboard of course, because it isn't leaving and going to Buenos Aires." With no residual resentment or anger, she sent him a smile that shared the memory of this afternoon. Her annoyance had been like a summer storm, quick to blow up, and just as quickly over. "Should I call him after dinner and ask?"

"In the morning." Finn enjoyed the tide of pink in her cheeks as their eyes locked. He wanted to taste that rapid pulse at the base of her throat and marveled at his own restraint when his voice sounded almost normal. "*Late* morning."

"Good to maybe get some answers," Logan addressed him. "Hey, changing the subject here, I read about the success of your hotfire tests in the Scientific Journal last month. Fascinating reading."

"What's a hotfire test?" Ariel asked.

Candles, in the clear hurricane lamps down the middle of the table, cast a flickering light on her face. God, she was achingly pretty. Her cheeks were adorably rosy after one glass of wine, and her eyes sparkled with a fascinating glint that made Finn want to know what was going on in that clever brain of hers.

"One of a series of milestones for us," he responded, battling the familiar urge to whisk her away from his guests to somewhere more private. Somewhere he could give in to his desperate need to taste her freckled skin, and inhale the heady fragrance of lilies as he wrapped himself in the fire of her hair. "The first time we fire - hotfire - an engine is our first opportunity to operate it to test propellant inlet conditions." He *needed* to touch her bare skin, but settled for stroking her thigh over the thin linen of her pants as he worked to re-engage his brain and formulate words. "We evaluate the high amount of thrust generated by the engine, which is essential to achieving liftoff so we can travel beyond low-Earth orbit-"

Her eyes glazed. Finn smiled. "Too much?"

"Interesting actually." Studying him, she smiled. "To quote Captain James T. Kirk; 'To explore strange new worlds, to seek out new life and new civilizations, to boldly go where no man has gone before.'

Finn grinned. "My motto, exactly."

Logan took the basket of rolls when his brother passed it across the table. "You're getting close to passengers for a Mars flight, then?"

"Close is a relative term," Finn told him, handing him the butter with his free hand. "We've examined the tests to collect relevant data. We've made the down-selection based on those performance tests. We're well ahead of schedule, and far ahead of our main two competitors. I'm pleased." He was elated. No one knew about his manned rocket, Red Star, set to launch in less than half a year, with twelve people on board, who'd live on the planet for a year before returning to Earth.

"Hell, I bet you are," Nick said. "You have a space tug up there now, right? You've already taken up passengers. Hell, that must be thrilling."

"Sub-orbital. That advanced upper stage is capable of refueling and generating its own electricity with the on-board fuel cell. It's been up there for a couple of months, so yeah."

"Spendy." Nick grinned. "Upwards of a billion dollars to design, test, certify etc., right? That's a big damned nut, Rocketman."

Finn shrugged. "The U.S Air Force committed almost fifty mil in funding, which helped."

"Chump change." Logan's eyes rested briefly on Ariel before he returned his attention to Finn. "We're ready to throw in our change whenever you're ready to take in outside investors. Everyone likes your dedication to reusability." He took a pull from his beer.

"Thanks. We're always making engineering decisions leading to practical, operational reusability," Finn told them, always happy to talk shop, but also aware that no one at the table was as interested in the nitty-gritty details as he was. "Since two-thirds of the price of the booster is just the engine, we solved that problem. After using a giant parafoil to grab them out of the sky via helicopter, we've already successfully recovered three of our engines after launching."

"Hell," Jonah said admiringly, "that's a tremendous engineering accomplishment. No wonder you're ahead in your field. Broke a few rules developing that technology, I bet."

"We've done our homework," Finn told him, noticing Ariel's gaze returning to the tablet every now and then. "The idea of booster recovery has been around for a while, as well as single stage orbit. My people just pushed the envelope a bit further."

"A *lot* further," Bria smiled. "I'm so impressed with all you've accomplished, Finn. I wouldn't want to travel all that way to Mars, but I admire your ability to make it happen."

"Passenger Mars flights are a long, long, long way off." He returned Nick's wife's smile. "We'll be taking paying passengers into suborbital space, and to the Space Station, for the next few years. In the meantime, we've got three wrecks to salvage."

"Yeah. That'll keep us busy." Logan set aside his half-empty bottle. "You'll take people to visit the moon before we're done here. Maybe the end of our salvage will see your trip to Mars becoming viable."

Finn and his people were working on it. The trip was a lot closer than he'd told the press, but he was keeping that under wraps until they'd done more tests.

"How long will it take to get to Mars?" A skein of glossy hair escaped Ariel's untidy topknot to slowly unfurl, much to Finn's fascination. It fell to curl enticingly over her left breast.

While his mind was stuck on how the red of her hair, when the light caught it a certain way, matched the color of Mars, he murmured. "Years."

Unaware everything about her was a goddamn distraction for him, her eyes widened. "*Years*?"

"Mars is about 140 million miles away." Finn withdrew his hand from her leg. Aroused by the heat of her skin, and the unconscious - or conscious - flexing of her thigh muscle he couldn't take much more. He cleared his throat. "It'll take approximately nine months to get there depending on where it is in its orbit. A round trip could take up to three years."

"Only nine months one way? So, the passengers are awake the whole time?" She looked disappointed. "No pod people in stasis like in the movies?"

He smiled. He'd heard that question so many times, he expected it. "Unfortunately, not."

"Why do you say, 'round trip'? Wouldn't *everyone* want to come back?" she asked.

"Some people will stay to colonize Mars."

"That's *amazing*." She glanced around as if suddenly remembering that there were other people with them at the table. "Isn't that incredible?" Her attention returned to Finn. "They'll be the pioneers and settlers of their generation. I wonder what space *smells* like."

He smiled. "Human's can't smell anything out there. We'd die if we tried. It's a vacuum after all. Our solar system is particularly pungent, however, because it's rich in carbon and low in oxygen." Finn loved the way her entire focus was on his face as he spoke. "Astronauts returning to their crafts report space-born polycyclic aromatic hydrocarbons adhering to their suits. They say the smell is distinct; burnt meat. The smell of the moon is similar to spent gunpowder."

She wrinkled her nose. "How much would it set someone back to fly one way to Mars?"

"About thirty-five million."

"Say what?!" Zane, already on his third helping of lamb, paused to give him an incredulous look. "Each? Holy shit. Count me out."

"That's okay," Finn assured him with a smile. "We're fully booked for the first five Mars flights over the next fifteen years." Red Star One wasn't scheduled to take colonists when she launched in five months. That flight was scheduled to take scientists on an exploratory mission for a year- after that. . .

"Meanwhile," he told an avid audience. "We've done dozens of sub-orbital flights. About eight thousand people have already gone up."

"Have you?" Ariel asked, meal barely touched and apparently forgotten.

"Several times."

Her eyes shone. "I'd love to go."

He wanted to take her. Just her. What would it be like to make love while looking at the Earth from space? The thought fired his blood and made him even more impatient to be alone with her.

"How much does *that* trip cost?" she asked, clearly fascinated.

"The sub-orbital flights? Two hundred thousand for about two hours. At an altitude of about 50,000 feet, the plane climbs toward the edge of the atmosphere."

"Sounds wonderful," she said, eyes lighting up as she leaned forward.

Finn's gaze went from her bright eyes to her parted lips. God, he wanted to kiss her. His fingers tightened on the stem of his glass. "Passengers experience roughly five minutes of weightlessness before gliding back for landing." Finn contemplated what it would be like to make love while weightless. Couldn't wait to try it for himself. "Presently we're doing five trips a day with a massive waitlist." He'd add a sixth flight just for her. Them.

"I'm patient," she smiled.

Not, he thought, amused.

One of the Cutters cleared their throat. Finn had been lost in her for several minutes.

For now, though, the dinner plates had been cleared and they were waiting for dessert. Glancing quickly at the brothers, he realized that they were looking at him with assorted expressions. Logan curiously. Zane admiringly. Nick's expression, impossible to read, but he had a dangerous glint in his eyes that Finn had never noticed before. Jonah's Cutter-blue eyes were merely curious as he looked from Ariel and back to Finn.

"Are you based in Buenos Aires, Ariel?" Jonah asked as the flan was set before them and everyone dug in. It was startling to Finn how similar in looks all four Cutters were, considering Jonah's mother had been Daniel Cutter's mistress. The brothers' eyes were identical, piercing blue. The only other person he'd ever met with such distinctive eye color, was Ariel. In her case a clear blue-green.

Her shoulders straightened, and she blinked, clearly surprised the conversation had detoured to her. Finn suspected she preferred being a fly on the wall, rather than a participant. "I'm based at the Ministry of Antiquities, which is housed in the Government building there. But since this salvage could feasibly take months, if not years, I'll be based out of my home on the coast. It'll cut down on my commute time."

She didn't mention that she'd built the house. Or that she'd done so before she'd gone to work for Dr. Núñez. Information he'd received from his PI the moment he learned who she really was. That she'd omitted the timing was interesting. For Finn, details mattered. It was the difference between life and death with a million pounds of thrust under a live crew and passengers. So why omit this small detail? By doing so she unintentionally gave this info more weight. Made him even more curious.

"But you're staying on board *Blackstar*, aren't you?" Nick asked. Finn didn't like how intensely the other man observed her. Nor did he like the surges of jealousy he felt every time his friend looked at her with a little more goddamn warmth than was warranted by a perfect stranger.

He'd been a perfect stranger, and look how *that* had turned out.

"Yes." Peri kept steady eye contact. "I will need to go home periodically, and of course I'll start visiting your ships and cataloging your artifacts in a couple of days. I've already got plenty of work to do on board *Blackstar Two*."

"But you're bunking on Blackstar, right?" Zane had a wicked glint in his eyes, and Peri's cheeks flushed. "Why's that Rocketman?"

"I brought in extra divers for this salvage," Finn told the lie easily. "No available cabins there, plenty of room here."

"Buenos Aires is a long way away," Logan observed. "You didn't mind leaving your family and friends to work in such an isolated place?" He studied her over the bottle. Like his younger brother, Logan, too, watched her with a little more than polite interest. Finn wanted to remind both men they were happily married, and that their wives would be there in a few days. "Do you have family? In Argentina?"

"Not in Argentina, no. But I have a brother. We're really close, but he travels a lot, so we don't get together that often." She tucked the loose strand back up into the topknot, and within seconds it slithered free again. He preferred her a little disheveled. In fact, Finn liked her a lot disheveled. "The office is only five hundred miles away. I'll go back periodically."

Zane pushed aside his empty plate and accepted the untouched desert Bria slid in front of him all without taking his eyes off Ariel. "Dr. Núñez must value you highly to trust you on such a monumental salvage."

Her smile was a little tight. "He must. I'm here."

"He'll be pleased with today's find, will he not?" Bria asked from across the table.

"Without a doubt," Ariel agreed. "But there were other noteworthy finds retrieved in the past few days. A surprising number, since none of your grids are in place yet. The ocean floor must be rich with artifacts from the four ships."

"Spread out over fifty nautical miles," Zane pointed out.

"Right." She took a sip of her water. "It'll take time, but if what you've retrieved so far is an indication of what's down there, I think everyone will be very pleased with the outcome. I know Dr. Núñez will be thrilled with the variety of artifacts you've recovered so far. He's more into the historical value of the objects than the percentage eventually due the Ministry. I'm sure he'll be as excited by this artifact," she nodded in the direction of the table where the golden slab sat, "as we are."

Finn had no doubt Núñez was going to line his own pockets before the Ministry got their cut. Like pretty much anywhere in the world, government graft was a given.

Bria leaned her forearms on the table with a jangle of her gold bracelets. "I think we should send for our tablet and compare the two, don't you think, Nick?" Putting her arm across the table she waited for her husband, who sat directly opposite her, to take her hand.

Nick stroked his thumb across the back of his wife's hand. "I agree, my love. It would be worth seeing them together to determine if they are in any way related, or if they're two separate entities."

"That would be awesome, but will the museum lend you the tablet? To take halfway around the world?" Ariel asked Bria with a frown. "That seems unlikely, doesn't it?"

"Bria is the Crown Princess of Merrezo," Finn told her. "She started that museum, and owns it, right? "

Bria shrugged. "My *people* own it. But there will be no problem removing the tablet- *temporarily*, accompanied by my curator for safe keeping."

"Great. My plane is available," Finn offered. "My pilot, Kathleen will go to Merrezo and return with your tablet." He too was intrigued by the thought that both items might've come from the same time and place.

Bria smiled. "That would be most excellent, Finn. I think, if we may, we should have Ale Vadini accompany the tablet. I think he'd be an enormous help in comparing your artifact and *La tavoletta d'oro Merrezo*."

It was late. The sun had set, the black arc of the sky filled with stars. "Excellent idea," Finn told her easily, now impatient for everyone to go back to their respective ships.

He wanted to show his Persephone the stars so she could see them as he did. Beautiful and full of possibilities. Just as he saw *her*. He wasn't done exploring every freckle on her body. Stars first, followed by the rest of the night and well into the morning in his cabin. In his bed. The thought made him hot, eager for his friends to get the hell off *Blackstar*. He pushed back his chair and rose. "I'll have Kathleen file a flight plan. She'll leave first thing in the morning."

"All things considered," Nick said as he and the others rose, too, "we need to get security on this immediately, don't you think?"

"Hell, yes. I'll send some of my guys," Finn offered. "They'll see to the Merrezo tablet's safe transit."

"No need," Nick told him easily. "I have people in Italy. I'll take care of security from there."

Nick Cutter did black ops contract work for a counterterrorist group, utilizing his ear for dialect, and God only knew what other talents. He was a good man to know and seemed to have limitless resources. Yet, when Finn had asked him, casually, if he'd dig into Ariel's background, Nick had shut him down, saying unless Finn suspected her of terrorism, he didn't surveil innocent civilians.

"It's settled then." Finn started them walking toward the sunroom so they'd get the lead out and head back to their own ships. He was done socializing.

EIGHT

Can we go to the top deck to look through that fancy telescope of yours?" Peri asked as she observed the Cutters cross the solarium then disappear downstairs leaving her alone with Finn. Since, for some mysterious freaking reason, the shoe she'd been waiting to drop, had *not* dropped, she was filled with excess energy. She could think of a lot of ways to get rid of all that pent-up energy. All included Finn.

Excitement zinged through her veins, as her thoughts tumbled and spun. Between finally meeting the Cutters, the thrill of the tablets, and the host of freaking secrets she was holding onto, she was way too wired to sleep. Filled to the brim with questions she dare not ask, and exhilaration that buzzed and fizzed through her veins she needed something to distract her.

Finn would do nicely.

All through dinner he'd touched her. Her hand, her arm, her thigh. . . If his plan was to prime her for sex, she was ready, more than ready. As distracting as it was titillating, it hadn't been easy to concentrate on the conversation when he had his hand high on her thigh through most of the meal. He wasn't touching her now, but the electric current arcing between them was almost visible in the flickering candlelight.

Adrenaline seared through her veins in a heated rush, and her breath snagged in her lungs. Her lips tingled. *Kiss me.*

Tall, muscular and dangerous, he looked ridiculously sexy in dark slacks, and a pale blue dress shirt, open at his strong throat. His features were taut, and his eyes glittered as if he had a fever when she turned back to look at him. "Another time."

It took her a moment to recall the request she'd made. They were going up to the next deck, but she didn't think he was heading to his giant telescope. Peri fell into step beside him. He didn't touch her as he started walking, following the path through the solarium the others had just taken.

The black and white checkered marble floor reflected the ten-foot trees evenly spaced in front of tall windows running the length of the narrow room. Comfortable deep seating chairs, in small, intimate groupings were scattered about for private conversation. Enormous skylights, black with the night sky, would flood the room with sunlight in the day time. The air smelled faintly citrusy.

"What do you use this room for?"

Peri could hear the Cutters voices coming from below as they boarded their runabouts to head to their own ships. The splash and slap of the water and the murmur of voices drifted up as they took the stairs. To his cabin or hers?

"I work in here sometimes, mostly my office staff uses it in their off hours."

"If they live on board when do they get time off?"

"Ninety days on, thirty days off."

He walked so fast she had to double step to keep up with his speed and longer strides. "Your employees get a month off every three months? That's generous of you."

Finn shrugged. "They work hard. They're usually across an ocean from their families, it's the least I can do. My people come from every far-flung corner of the world. *Blackstar* is constantly in motion. Anything less than a month off wouldn't be worth such a long commute."

"You fly them home?"

He shrugged. "I have a plane." At the foot of the stairs, he stopped to back her against the paneled wall. "Take down your hair."

The man knew how to change the subject. Wordlessly, she reached up with both hands and slowly removed the pins, placing each in Finn's waiting hand. He stuck them in his back pocket. His eyes were all pupil as her hair slowly unfurled down her back in soft waves. The brush of his slightly roughened thumb over her mouth made her shiver in response.

She parted her lips, then flicked out her tongue to taste him. He shuddered. "I've never wanted a woman as much as I want you. I didn't give a damn about dinner, I just wanted to eat *you.*" His warm coffee-scented breath fanned over her damp lips as he sank his fingers into her hair to cup the back of her head, while his other hand slid between her tank top and the waistband of her slacks at the small of her back. His hand felt shockingly warm against her cool skin as he dipped a finger beneath the thin ribbon of her thong.

Her butt cheek flexed. His pupils flared, and a muscle clenched in his jaw.

"I hope you do." Legs weak, her knees buckled. Bracing her hand on his chest, she felt the thud of his heartbeat beneath her palm. It echoed the staccato beat of her own.

His voice, low and husky, stroked her frayed nerve endings. "Dinner seemed interminable."

God yes. On so many levels. She shot him a wicked glance under her lashes as he withdrew his wandering fingers to slide his other hand to the small of her back under her top. "I enjoyed it."

He lowered his head, lips almost touching hers. "It was too long to wait to do this."

Cupping his face, she lifted up to close the small gap between their mouths. The kiss was shockingly gentle considering the tension she felt in his jaw as his tongue stroked over hers.

He lifted his head, leaving her lips damp and aching for more. "Come and see my etchings."

There were paintings all over the ship, Peri knew they were all the real deal and must be worth immeasurable fortunes. Artwork was the last thing on her mind right now. "Are they in your bedroom?"

He smiled as he opened a nearby door. "Yeah."

The blood in her veins surged as she felt the heat of each of his fingers on the small of her back as he guided her into the middle of the room. "What kind of etchings?" She glanced around the large, private sitting area dominated by a plush dove-gray suede sofa. Comfortable-looking easy chairs flanked a dark stone coffee table with a lush green plant spilling over the surface. A sleek, modern mantleless slate fireplace soared to the coffered ceiling. Wide windows showed the black sky and moon tipped ocean framed by white drapes which fluttered in the breeze of the open window.

"Naked nymphs dancing through fields of flowers trailing diaphanous scarves?" she teased. Through double doors, a dimly lit room gave her a tantalizing glimpse of the corner of his big bed.

"Self-portraits of the artists mostly." Finn unbuckled the thin black belt at her waist.

Peri enjoyed the feel of his hands on her, the way the back of his fingers lingered on her stomach as he slid the belt from the loops with painstaking care. His eyes never left her face.

With sure hands, she started unbuttoning his crisp dress shirt. Pausing as he drew her top over her head, she continued until she got to the waistband of his slacks. As he tossed her top somewhere behind her, she tugged his shirt free and spread it open to expose the hard ridges of his abs, and the drift of dark hair arrowing down. She felt as though she'd been starving all her life and was suddenly being offered a banquet.

She didn't understand this overwhelming emotion she experienced when she was with him. More than great sex. More than- Hell, she had no idea. Whatever it was, it filled her with euphoria. He made her . . .*happy.*

Finn brushed his knuckles over the swell of her breasts. "I like seeing the artists the way they saw them. . .selves." Sliding his hands to hold her hips, he shuddered as she stroked both hands over his chest.

She couldn't keep her hands off him. Peri wanted her hands and mouth all over him. Wanted *his* hands and mouth all over *her*. That bed seemed a million miles away, and Finn seemed to be in no hurry. The hardness of her nipples pressing against the prison of the thin beige satin of her bra was driving her crazy. His hot touch, combined with the cool breeze coming off the water, made her nipples hard, painful peaks.

Reaching behind her, Finn pulled down the short zipper of her pants. *Slowly*. The man was a sadist. He walked her backwards. "That one there is van Dyck," he said thickly in passing. "This bad-tempered looking guy here is Nicola Poussin, early 1600's. Here's the Rembrandt van Rijn. Why did he look so surprised that he was drawing himself?"

How had they moved? Peri wasn't aware of her feet moving, but they suddenly seemed much closer to the bedroom than they'd been a few moments before. Kicking off her shoes, she let the pants drop to the floor leaving her wearing what amounted to a couple of strategically placed satin ribbons. Stepping out of the puddle of linen, she pushed his shirt off his broad shoulders.

She wanted to shake him, but Finn seemed to have a plan that involved taking his sweet time. He indicated another small portrait with a jerk of his chin. "Over there is John Constable done in the early 1800's. This is Jean Francois Millet painted in the 1800's. But he looks like a hippie with all that hair, doesn't he? Georges Seurat, moody and ominous. I rotate them now and then. There are more throughout the ship. Frida Kahlo, David Hockney..." He mentioned a few more artists, most of whom she'd never heard of.

Peri covered his mouth with her palm. "I don't freaking *care*," her voice hitched as the back of her legs hit the mattress. At last. Combing her fingers through his hair, she cupped the back of his head, drawing him closer to her mouth. "No more talking."

Finn placed a knee on the bed, then slid his hand to the small of her back, and lowered her carefully to the plush surface of his bed.

Bracing his elbows on either side of her shoulders, his gaze traveled over her face. "I forget to breathe when I look at you." His tone was dark with sexual promise. "You're as damned perfect as a painting, but warm, responsive, flesh and blood. I could barely keep my hands off you at dinner."

Peri stroked his hair out of his eyes. "You didn't try very hard."

"Any more," he said against her sensitized throat as he trailed his fingers down the curve of her hip, "and I'd have taken you right there on the table."

"Been there, done that." She angled her head so his lips could more easily reach the exact. . .right. . .spot that made her shiver. "What else do you have in your repertoire?" The warmth of his hand left her hip.

"We've never taken our time." Sliding his palms against hers, he drew both her hands over her head, anchoring her to the mattress with his weight. His erection pressed hard against her mound as he brushed a half-open kiss against her lips, his exhalation filling her mouth so she tasted the coffee he'd drunk after dinner. "Tonight there's no urgency."

He was holding most of his weight off her. Peri curved her legs around his hips and tried to pull him harder against where she ached. "Of course there's *urgency*, Phineas Gallagher! Your touchy shenanigans during our civilized dinner conversation was clearly foreplay," her voice was thick and sultry. Her fingers flexed impatiently in his grip, "I'm wet and aching for you. Fill me. Finish what you started."

She sucked in a shaky breath of need as he bent his head to trace the sensitive rim of her ear with the tip of his tongue. His teeth scraped, then nipped her lobe, as his breath tickled her ear. "Would it be torture if we took it slowly?"

Every time they'd made love in the hotel in Buenos Aires it had been in a rush, greedy. Even when they'd been satiated, exhausted, there was still an edge of urgency as if each time was the last time.

When they'd had sex in the pantry, she'd barely had time to drag in a breath because they were incapable of taking their hands and mouths off each other.

"Yes. It would be freaking torture to take it slowly. I want it hard and fast. And *often*."

"Often can be accommodated. Hard and fast will just have to wait." His mouth fastened on hers with restrained primal greed.

"What happened to your parents?" Finn asked, lazily using a strand of her hair to paint random designs on her bare shoulder. Replete after making love, skin still slick with sweat, she had one leg thrown over his thighs, the moist heat of her pressed against his skin. His dick stirred, but he was too content holding her like this to move. "You said your father left when you were what? Five?" His PIs had found bugger all about her. He told them to dig deeper.

"You have a good memory." She tasted his skin with a small flick of her tongue. The sensation tightened his balls. "Hmm. Salty. On my fifth birthday. He committed suicide a short time later."

The ache in her voice affected him deeply. He knew that ache. The painful need for family and the desire for a deep connection was a phantom, but very real feeling, of loss. A longing for what might've been. "I'm sorry."

"Me, too. We never had a chance to get to know each other. I only ever remember him as angry - My parents fought. A lot. I acted out. Got into trouble. At home. At school. "Her voice hardened, and her hand on his chest stilled. "Even then, I knew I never wanted to feel that weak and vulnerable again."

Oh, darling. He stroked his hand down her narrow back. *I would've wrapped that vulnerable little girl in cotton wool, and told her how she'd grow up to be a strong, secure and courageous woman.* "You were practically a baby."

"I grew up fast."

"What about your mother?" He brushed a kiss over the crown of her head. Her hair smelled like lilies.

Her nonchalant shrug, small as it was, told him more than her words could about her mother's support. Finn felt a small stir of pity and a surge of impotent anger at the woman.

"She had a lot on her plate. She packed us up and moved from England to America. New places, new people, no support system. And even though my middle brother had Leukemia, and was in and out of treatment as long as I can remember, she unofficially adopted our next door neighbor's daughter, who was about my age and in a bad situation at home. My older brother, who was fifteen when Dad left, became the man of the family. He was reckless and driven to make money to support the family. . .It was a lot for her."

Interesting how she never mentioned names. Was that intentional? To distance herself from an unhappy past? Now wasn't the time to ask, but he would. "Sounds like a lot for you, too."

"Everyone has a story. Was anyone in the foster system there for you? I read somewhere you made your first million at seventeen. True?"

"About that, yes." She stroked her palm through the hair on his chest as if she were petting a cat. Finn had never been touchy-feely before Ariel. He loved her hands on him. Hell, he loved any part of her touching any part of him.

"That's astonishing. Most kids that age are worrying about who to take to their prom."

"Apparently I had a twin who died at birth. So I always felt that something was. . .missing, I guess. I didn't have any other family, so I was moved around a lot. That was out of my control, but from when I was very young I knew I'd need money to get out of the system. I'd need *skills* to survive. Stealing and graft weren't out of the question. But I didn't want to end up indigent, or in jail at twelve. Selling drugs was always an option. But I was only with the Agan family two months before the lot of them were arrested for manufacturing and dealing. I knew nothing about the business and had no capital."

"You would've sold drugs?"

"I would've done anything to get out of my situation. At the time the drug trade didn't seem to me to be a longterm investment. I watched and learned from other families, wherever I was placed, waiting for something to spark, to get me going. I lived with the O'Brian's for seven months when I was twelvish. Jim, the father, was a computer repairman. He had anger management issues, and I learned to keep two arms lengths between us, but he let me watch him work, in his workshop in the garage. I was a fast learner. Because I knew that my time anywhere was unpredictable. I started doing computer repairs after school, whenever I could. I found I had a good technical brain, and I liked it. I got good. Made some money. He beat his wife to death, and I was shipped off to the next family." Right after he was released from the hospital after good old Jim whipped him within an inch of his life and left him for dead, too.

"Next were the Walsh's. Mrs. Walsh was an investment broker. A *crooked* broker, I might add. I was still repairing computers, but Eileen Walsh taught me about day trading and penny stocks. I'd found something I was even better at than computer repair." Eileen had also taken his virginity at fourteen. "I used my repair money to day trade, used that money for penny stocks. . .That's the long story to my first million."

"It's a fascinating story, and I'm sure you left out some of the best bits between then and now."

"I like your best bits between here..." He kissed her mouth. "And here…" He stroked his fingers through the silky tangle of damp curls at the juncture of her thighs and they stopped talking.

NINE

Twenty-five miles inland, on the wind-swept plains of Patagonia, the Supreme Leader of *el Elegidos,* the Chosen, was elated by the discovery of two *new* marble tablets.

At last.

He'd been staring at the photographs of all three gold tablets on his giant computer monitor for hours. The thrill of looking at them was profound. The one taken of the *La tavoletta d'oro Merrezo* was sharp and clear. *Indecipherable*, but the image was good. The other two pictures were not professionally staged, rather, photographed with a smartphone. The second so blurred that it could be any flat, gold object. Still, it was clear they were uncannily similar.

Stroking a finger across the cold glass, his heart actually leapt with elation. Now he'd have proof of the teachings of his forebears, and details of the work still to be done.

No coincidence that they'd been found mere weeks before the world as everyone knew it, ended, and the new world order began.

He would lead the Chosen. His position was ensured, passed down through the generations.

He knew the date his official rein would commence.

But what else did the tablet or tablets spell out?

What *details* had they kept hidden until now?

The Abipón language was ancient. Extinct. He knew but a handful of the obsolete words of his people. But not enough to read the Merrezo tablet which he, his father and his grandfather before him, had visited many times in the hope of learning something new. Those visits always proved fucking useless. He'd stopped going ten years ago. Waste of money and time.

It had become increasingly more difficult to retain his eleven thousand followers' attention over the years. It was hard, if not impossible to get them to maintain fervor for *el Elegidos'* promise, and keep the prophecy in the forefront of their minds. Sheep farming could no longer hold them to the land, and they were moving to big cities, with modern, big city ideas.

A five hundred-year-old prediction, by a child, with almost no proof, couldn't compete with sophisticated education, and access to the information highway. He knew he could only bullshit them with a scrap of paper and a promise for so long.

Even though he had not as yet seen them, he knew unequivocally that the discovery of the tablets, and *where* they'd been found, was the sign he'd waited for his entire life.

In the 1400's, a young boy was declared the village seer due to the accuracy of his visions. The specific content of those predictions and the identity of the child had long since been forgotten. The little they did know had been translated and interpreted multiple times over the next five hundred years, the true meanings of the seer's visions eventually lost. But, even based on so little, the belief and unshaken certainty of the seer's predictions had always, without exception, been believed by the followers of the Chosen.

Still, he, as Supreme Leader, had very little in the way of tangible proof to hold his people. A few scraps of worn parchment, the words, passed down from Leader to Leader. . . But now he'd have the tablets. And fuck it, if he *couldn't* read much more than a handful of words on them, he'd pretend to his people that he *could*. The Chosen sure as shit hadn't attempted to learn the ancient language as he had. Much good that had done him, but still- he'd made the effort.

His father had assured him, that when the time was right, all would be revealed. All would be clarified. The time was at hand.

The consequences, should these tablets *not* deliver as promised, was him being unseated, his legacy and leadership forgotten just like their language.

He was closer to learning the truth today than he'd been a week ago. Than any of his people had been for five fucking hundred years.

Things were looking up.

With a satisfied smile, he leaned back against the butter-soft leather of his chair. In his esteemed opinion, massive furniture, and a display of his wealth, showed his followers his power and importance. He inhaled deeply, relishing the familiar scents of his power; dusty paper, fine Cuban cigars, and the acrid smell of fear he instilled in his followers. The darkly paneled room was wrapped with ceiling-to-floor shelves filled with ancient manuscripts and old tomes.

He'd read almost every scrap of paper in the room, finding nothing of importance. All he had of any relevance to *el Elegidos* was a fragment of an ancient document. The worn, fragile piece of torn parchment had been given to him with great ceremony by his father on his deathbed, thirty years earlier.

Unlocking the top desk drawer, he opened a velvet-lined leather folder and lay it on the desk. The ancient parchment- this most holy of holy relics, was torn, worn thin, and stained. The rest of the prophecy he knew by faith alone.

Over hundreds of years, the writing was now faint, in most cases illegible. Worn away by hundreds of hands over time.

Heart pounding, he let his eyes scan down, hoping something would miraculously become clearer now that the time was so close at hand. The date of the End was unmarred and as clear as if it had been written that very morning. Ten days from now.

It seemed not only fortuitous, but divine providence, that the two tablets had been found *now.*

He scanned the words on the parchment, even though he knew them by heart.

The words High Altar and Holy Lake were slightly less faded than other words, not only recognizable, but quite legible.

His first name, the same as that of all his male ancestors, was as clear as day. *Nkaatek,* the Abipón word for fire, in the middle of a long, too-faint-to-read sentence had never made any sense. Possibly the means by which everyone would perish? "Warrior" was mentioned several times. Sometimes the two words were together, other times, not. *Aaloa,* meant Earth. "Star" could be anything. Possibly the date or time on which the seer had written the document.

Star *could* mean Gallagher's ship, Blackstar, but that was too much of a coincidence and stretched his credibility. Coincidence, that was all.

The words that put a chill in his heart were *el Ehnos.* The Protectors had not been seen, nor heard of, in *hundreds* of years. It was only on the rare occasions that he read their name, here on this parchment, did he think of them. If, as he knew, they'd died out hundreds of years ago, why was their name so prominently, and unmistakably written on this holy item?

Would the Protectors show up to thwart his plans?

They'd better the fuck not. He had a skilled army of true believers at his disposal. Five hundred strong, they'd been trained from childhood for this very moment. Should the Protectors still have any members, they would be annihilated, as would anyone who stood in the way of his divine path.

As stated in the prophecy, only eleven thousand Chosen would remain to populate the earth. Why were the Protectors mentioned, and what, if anything, would be their roll in the end of days?

Who were they? *Where* were they?

Was *eliminating* them part of the prophecy?

Frustrated that he couldn't read more, he looked forward to getting his hands on the two new tablets and was hopeful they'd aid in interpreting the mystery. He closed the leather folder and returned it to the drawer. Locked it, then sat back in his chair to wait.

Heavy, burgundy velvet drapes hung open at tall, leaded glass windows. Stark white moonlight washed across barren, open fields of scrub grass and hardy shrubs. The house had been built around an ancient temple that was on holy ground in the middle of fucking nowhere. Not a house, not a *human* for miles. He was surrounded by sheep.

With a deep sense of destiny pulsing through his veins he was ready, more than ready, for his next, even more exalted position; *el líder supremo del mundo.* Supreme leader of the *World.*

"*Adelante,*" he called at a soft rap on the ornately carved door to his private inner sanctum.

Like a timid mouse, his second in command peeked around the door. Thin graying hair stood up on the side of his head. A deep crease on his cheek indicated he'd rushed from his bed. "You wanted to see me, *su excelencia?*"

"Come in. Come in." He gestured impatiently for the other man to get his ass inside. "Do not hover, Jose Luis. Close the door. I have momentous news, the reason I summoned you in the middle of the night."

The late hour was unnecessary. He'd gotten word at noon about the first tablet. Mid-afternoon about the second. He just liked to fuck with his acolyte.

He'd positioned spies on each of the six ships anchored off the coast at the onset of the salvage. It was Divine Providence that he'd already had so many in place when the two tablets had been brought to the surface. He'd received the unexpected and astonishing news about them almost immediately.

If Jose Luis hadn't been specifically mentioned in the ancient document, he would have executed him years earlier. The man was a continuous pain, with his timorous approach to everything. He was tired of having the apprehensive man scuffling about.

Ah well, time enough to find a suitable replacement once he was *el Lidder Supremo del munfo.* He only had to suffer Jose Luis long enough to sacrifice him.

He waited with barely contained excitement for the man to approach and stand before his enormous, heavily carved antique mahogany desk. Jose Luis shuffled forward, but stopped near the center of the room.

The fear in the old man's eyes was palpable. And Jose Luis had reason to be afraid. As Supreme Leader, it fell to him to dole out punishment when necessary and with Jose Luis, it was frequently necessary.

Penance was an important part of life in the sect. Violence was the Supreme Leader's punishment method of choice.

"Two sacred tablets have been discovered on the salvage." His voice, sharp with excitement, rose. "They match *La tavoletta d'oro Merrezo.* A call twenty minutes ago gave me even *more* profound news. The Merrezo tablet will be on its way to Argentina within days."

He'd always known the date and time of the End. Ten days from today. That information had not varied over five hundred years. What was not known, but merely speculated was the *method* that the World, as everyone knew it, would dramatically change.

The Chosen would rule the world.

He would rule the Chosen.

"This is. . .*astonishing* news," his second in command whispered with awe as he stood before him, head bowed in deference. "Is it possible they contain the translation for the Merrezo tablet, *su excelencia*?" Jose Luis, a short, wiry man in his mid-seventies, looked up at him with anxious black eyes and a worried frown.

He didn't *need* fucking confirmation, and he resented a subordinate questioning him. "You doubt my conviction?' he asked in a cold, monotone that warned the other man that he was growing impatient with his negativity. "Our person on board Case's ship, *Tesoro Mio,* confirmed the first finding. As did our spy on board *Blackstar.* The main players have sent for *La tavoletta d'oro Merrezo.* It is expected to be delivered to Gallagher in a few days. Without a doubt, the joining of three tablets will have great significance. We retrieve the tablets from Gallagher, and we'll need to eliminate anyone and everyone who gets in our way. I don't want any loose ends."

Should I recall our army?"

Jesus, what a fucking moron. "You need ask?" His men were scattered to the fucking four corners of the Earth, continually honing their skills for what was to come. Not letting their training go to waste while they waited to be called, they were for hire to anyone who could afford a soldier with zero scruples and the best training Russia could provide. "Tell them to return home immediately. I expect them to be here by the end of the week. No exceptions."

"*Sí*, Excellency. It shall be done."

"We will, of course, intercept the tablet from Italy. And take possession of the other two before it even arrives. If anyone gets in our way, they'll be exterminated. A few weeks early won't make any difference in their lives, now will, it? "He chuckled, pleased with his gallows humor.

Unamused, Jose Luis shifted from foot to foot. "I suppose not, *su excelencia.* Even I have come to believe that the story of such, to be. . . honest-" He wrung thin, veined hands. "To be completely honest, Excellency, I oft wondered if additional tablets might be a myth."

"*Even you*, Jose Luis?" he challenged, his anger rising. "Five hundred years, thousands of believers, and you suddenly have doubt? You are vaulted in our Order, yet you question the message the seer foretold five hundred years ago?"

"*No*, Excellency. Of *course* not." He squinted his small black eyes, his face pinched with distress. "I believe in the Prophecy. It has ruled my life, just as it has yours, from birth. *That* has never been in question. My skepticism is about the written word of our directive - that is all. Now, knowing the writings have been found-"

"This manifestation of our teachings is the equivalent of the Rosetta Stone, that is all. The additional stones will merely be a clarification of our directive."

"One of the tablets will surely inform us of the locations of the High Altar and the Holy Lake, *su excelencia,*" the acolyte's voice rose, and his eyes shone with wonder. "*Sí*, that would be most- "

"Naturally the maps will be on the tablets, *imbécil*!" Or so he fervently hoped.

This massive house had been built on the land where the prophet's village had once stood. For hundreds of years, every inch of the land for miles around had been searched for the two holy locations. Nothing had been found.

For years, he'd sent acolytes to every far-flung corner of Argentina in search of anything that could, even loosely, be construed as a High Altar or a Holy Lake. Each had been rejected for various valid reasons.

Although he'd had great hope, all searches had been to no avail.

It didn't concern him that the Merrezo tablet had been indecipherable. There were only a few recognizable words there that were important. His name and el Elegidos.

"*The directives* we have followed for hundreds of years have not changed," he told the other man. "We *are,* have *always* been, *el Elegidos*. It is time the world discovered who the Chosen are, and the nature of our Divine purpose."

"Once we have the tablets in our possession," Jose Luis, spoke annoyingly softly. "Once we have them, and can *see* the writings with our own eyes- The *exact* words of the Prophet -"

"Jesus Christ!" Eyeballs throbbing from the pressure of his intense annoyance, he maintained his temper by a mere thread, only because he was in a good mood and didn't want to ruin what was a momentous day. He pictured shooting Jose Luis in the head. A close-up and personal shot between his beady little eyes. Or a hard blow to the back of the old man's head so it cracked like an egg. "We have no need of writings to instruct us what we must do," he said tightly. Killing Jose Luis was a daily fantasy, and one he'd fulfill once the man's usefulness was over. Hopefully, the tablets would tell him exactly how and when that would come to pass.

"We've always known. Do not falter, Jose Luis. A lifetime of worship, a lifetime of *planning,* is about to come to fruition."

Perhaps the writings of the Prophet indicated *how* all but eleven thousand people would die? Because he knew that to be true. It was preordained in the teachings. Did the *how* of it really matter? It was the result that was important.

He'd feared he would not live long enough to claim his destiny. He had no sons. No nephews. No blood relatives who bore his name. *Yet.* There was no assurance that his chosen mate would be fertile. God. Did he dare have personal doubts now? Of course, the seer wouldn't have foretold his lifemate if the woman couldn't bare him many strong sons.

He knew his future, but as the date of the apocalypse drew closer he'd become less sure. The prophecy was five hundred years old. Some of the Chosen worried that the verbal message could possibly have become diluted with the decades, like a game of telephone. One generation misinterpreting the words for the next.

No. As far as he was concerned, there was no room for interpretation. The details may have faded or become obscured over time, but the date had never changed. *This* specific date, *this* specific year. The world's population would perish. All but eleven thousand souls. The Chosen. They would rebuild the population. The world would once again become Paradise.

"I do not *need* proof of our purpose," he told his subordinate, who had been mentioned in the prophecy as a 'messenger'. Jose Luis' only purpose was to alert their followers when the time was right and bring together the eleven thousand people of *el Elegidos.*

"We will retrieve all three tablets and study them at length. Time may have diluted the message, but not our purpose or resolution. We will learn exactly what must be done now- in our time- to fulfill the rest of the prophecy for eternity." Pausing, he savored the next words as if they were manna from Heaven and he could taste their sweetness on his tongue. "And, as prophesied, my even more exalted role in the future of the world."

When Jose Luis didn't immediately respond, he said sharply, "What is it? Why do you scowl so?"

"Do you not fear the intervention of *el Ehnos* should *they* also discover that the tablets have been found?"

"The Protectors?" A vein throbbed in his neck. "*Who* are they?" He was at the end of his patience with the old man. "*Where* are they? Have you seen or heard anything about such a sect for the last hundred years? *Two* hundred years?" Anger made his voice deadly soft. Enough so that the other man tensed his narrow shoulders, and looked at him as a mongoose watched a snake.

"Has there been *any* indication *anywhere* that such a group even exists?" He answered his own question. "No."

With nothing to say, his subordinate just stood there, small and meek, sweating, like a frightened rat.

As usual, all answers were up to the Supreme Leader. Which was why he'd been so since birth. "Because they. Do. Not. Exist. Do not be naïve, Jose Luis. They were at one time fabricated by the first Chosen as a cautionary tale for those who strayed from the path of *el Elegidos.* Now we know our task. Retrieve all three tablets. Kill anyone who stands in the way. The clock is ticking. We have ten days to fulfill our destiny."

His heart thundered with anticipation. The time, so long ago foretold by the seer, was at hand. All would be explained, all would be clarified.

His position was preordained, written in the stars. *He* would not waver in his task.

TEN

The house is incredible, Magma, but this *view* is worth every dime you paid for the land. Rydell paused just inside the front door. "The pictures you texted didn't do this justice."

Peri loved her 280-degree views from her glass house. The only solid wall was the one at the back of the house, a nondescript gray expanse with few windows. It was all show once inside. Ceiling, walls and floors were crystal-clear reinforced glass, cantilevered over the edge of the rocky cliff.

Enormous, plushy upholstered furniture, in shades of palest blue-gray, blended with the sky, while cushions of various shades of muted blues, aquas and greens mimicked the changing colors of the ocean. The art was the ever-changing, expansive, view. Several large artifacts from her own salvages seemed to float in midair on the glass floor, while clear shelves held colorful books and objets d'art from her travels. Usually from a land base close to whichever Cutter she was tormenting.

Ry and Addy were her first visitors since Theo, who hadn't lingered for long. Terrified of heights, he hadn't enjoyed her house. Once had been more than enough for him. It was a little depressing to realize that she'd built the house five years ago, and had only had three visitors in all that time.

"Where do you want this?" Rydell asked, holding the duffel containing the tablet aloft while Addy walked to the edge of the large area rug to look at the view.

"Over on the counter, I'll get a stand for it." Peri got an easel from a cabinet and propped it up on the white counter between the kitchen and the living room. "Addy. The floor's perfectly safe. It's meant to be walked on." Personally, she found walking on the glass floor with a view of the eighty-foot drop to the rocks below, accelerating. But it wasn't for everyone.

Her sis-in-law shuddered. "I'm fine where I am, thanks."

"I'm not sure this is a good idea, Magma." Ry propped the newly cleaned gold tablet on the stand. "My security wouldn't have let any of them come on board, let alone take it."

Peri stroked a gentle hand over the horizontal lines. The gold felt smooth and warm to the touch. "I know, I just. . . I don't know. It just feels safer here, than there."

"Easy enough to find out where you live."

She shook her head. "Unless Theo tells someone who asks, no they can't. The property was purchased through a shell company of Koúkos Corporation."

"Still think it's a bad idea."

"Duly noted." Peri couldn't explain her compulsion to bring the tablet to her home, so she got that her brother was concerned. "Look around, this place is like Fort Knox. I have top of the line electronic security, and an eighty foot climb up a vertical rock face to sheer glass walls. Even if the Cutters found out where I live, no one is getting in here."

"Get good pictures of the other two tablets. I want my people to study them, too. I already have them researching the Italian tablet."

"I will. That's one of the reasons I want this one far away. Let them be excited about the two they have until we've had time with ours to do more research."

"You'll tell them you have it, though, won't you? This kind of momentous historical find shouldn't be kept secret. Not even from the Cutters. Not for long anyway."

"I just want a little more time alone with it." At his narrowed-eyed suspicious look, she smiled. "Yes. Eventually."

"Keep me in the loop. This some of the stuff from your China dive?" Ry asked, indicating a platter of exquisite blue and white porcelain on a stand beside several other smaller pieces on a glass shelf.

"Yeah. She was the 1405, giant, nine-masted junk I told you about. Part of the treasure fleet heading out of Taiwan. Four-hundred feet long, and a hundred and fifty wide."

Ry whistled. "So you said, but it's hard to believe a junk was bigger than Columbus's largest ship."

"She was, and quite a beauty." Her smile widened. "An extremely *lucrative* beauty. I sold most of it back to Chinese museums and private collectors. Just kept those pieces as souvenirs. That salvage alone paid for this house and pretty much everything in it." It had also funded her exploits as she followed one Cutter or another around for weeks on end for more than seven years.

"I'm proud of you, Magma. You've done well for yourself. The *Napolitano* will buy *twenty* houses like this."

"I already have a house. I can only live in one."

While she made a pot of coffee, she and Ry discussed the hiring of local divers for her salvage, something he wasn't too keen on. "Those Chinese divers were some of the best I've ever used," Peri told him. "I don't like having my divers underfoot like you do, not to mention *Sea Witch* isn't large enough to house a full dive team."

"You could buy a bigger dive boat." He said, as she showed him some of the other pieces she'd salvaged from her own, or their combined, dives.

"I don't *need* a bigger dive boat. My brother has one, I'll use *his* divers for *Napolitano*." She blew him a kiss, and he chuckled as he rubbed his knuckles on her head.

"Come on sweetheart," he said, crossing the room to his wife. "We'll brave my sister's terrifying floor together." He stepped cautiously, as if expecting the glass floor to give. Directly underfoot, an almost ten story drop showcased the rocks and crashing waves below. "How substantial *is* all this glass?"

"Heavy-duty enough to withstand two hundred mile an hour winds, and we're small potatoes, with just seventy-five mile an hour winds during the summer months, and plenty strong enough to hold a semi truck. I had them test it when the floor was put in. You're perfectly safe."

The couple left carpet for glass floor to get closer to the living room's expansive windows and the endless sky/ocean view. "Take a look, darling," Addy said, looking through the high-powered binoculars Peri had set up on a parallelogram mount nearby. "You can see the curvature of the earth through these. Wow. I can see forever," Addy said with awe. "Where. . ." Ry adjusted the direction for her. "Aw. Hi, baby." She waved.

Over her head, Peri shared a grin with her brother as Addy talked baby talk to Adam, who was on board *Tesoro Mio* with his nanny, over fifty miles away.

"This is the first time I've had ships to look at. I bought it to look at the sky," Peri told her brother. "You'll have to come back at night, it'll boggle your mind how close the stars are. I've seen four of Jupiter's moons and some surface color. The Orion nebula is visible too. These binocs are amazing, but if you want to look through top-of-the-line-money-is-no-object and *touch* the stars, you'd have to check out Finn's binoculars or telescopes. He has them everywhere."

"Pass," Ry told her. He frowned as he glanced behind her. "I thought no one knew where you lived. Someone's coming up the drive."

Through the narrow sidelight beside the front door, Peri observed a huge white truck slowly lumber across the bridge of land separating her from the mainland. The house, constructed on the edge of a small, rocky peninsula, with a narrow road from the mainland joining the two, was a veritable fortress. Not that that was what she'd planned. She'd bought the land, cheap, for the spectacular view, and direct access to the water from the caves below.

"Great, that's the equipment I was waiting for. Grab a cup of coffee, I'll have them unload into the garage. Be right back." Not *equipment.* The artifacts returned to her from Bernardino Rivadavia Natural Sciences Museum in Buenos Aires. The museum where she'd met Finn barely two weeks ago.

"Need help?" Ry followed as she headed to the front door. Far below, the surf foamed and sprayed the slick rocks, surrounding a well-hidden cave where she docked *Sea Witch* and several small runabouts. "No, I'm good, thanks. Enjoy the view."

Peri went through the kitchen into the garage to open the door. She'd wanted her brother and Addy to see her house for years. And since she had to return home to accept the shipment today, this was as good an opportunity as any. In a few weeks, they'd all be too busy with the salvage to return.

Why was she always freaking playing with fire? If her brother took one look inside any of the crates, he'd demand answers. Answers she wasn't ready to give.

After directing the four men into the garage, and showing them where she wanted the crates, Peri stood back to make sure everything was handled with care. The area where they were instructed to place the enormous crates, was a freight elevator. When the men left, she closed the garage door, then went back to shut the elevator door, concealing it from view. She'd just wait for the other two shipments to arrive before she had them delivered to the Cutters.

Before returning to the others, Peri pressed a hidden button, sending the enormous freight elevator down to the caves where it was cool and naturally climate controlled. It would be relatively easy, with the use of a compact forklift, to load the crates onto a boat and move them for shipping anywhere in the world.

Back in the house, she found Ry and Addy seated at the kitchen breakfast bar, drinking coffee. The kitchen/living room combo afforded a panoramic view that never ceased to blow Peri's mind.

"Where do you dock *Sea Witch*?" Ry topped off Addy's mug from the carafe beside him. "Do you have to drive down to the water?"

A logical question. "I have an elevator. Over there." She indicated the closed door of the pantry. Inside was a small elevator, much more convenient than the giant freight elevator in the garage which she only used when she had large artifacts she wanted to bring up to the house.

Addison had already slid off her stool, coffee forgotten. "I wanna see!"

Peri laughed. "I guess we could fit three in there. It'll be a tight squeeze."

"With two of the people I love most in the world? No problem. Show us," Addy demanded, already across the room. Opening the door, she frowned. "Wait. This is just a pantry. Were you teasing?"

"In back."

"Why do you even *need* a pantry?" Ry asked, following the two women inside. Narrow, ceiling-to-floor white shelves, held only small stacks of toilet paper and rolls of paper towels, and a couple of cans of tuna. "The shelves are bare."

"Resale?" Peri pushed the button and a door immediately slid open to reveal the aluminum interior. "I'm never here. If I'm hungry I raid my freezer."

"Secret elevators, glass floors- This is like Disneyland." Addy took the three steps to get to the back corner then turned around. "I love it."

Peri squeezed in next to Ry. "Press the button."

"Just one stop?" Ry asked. The elevator started to move.

"Where else do you want to go?" Peri poked him in the back. "Sideways?"

"This is so much fun- Oh, what's that?"

""Nothing alarming," Peri assured Addy as the elevator gave a human-sounding moan. "It always makes that noise about a quarter the way down."

"How deep are we going?" her brother asked.

"Eighty-seven feet."

Ry whistled. " That's impressive. How long did it take to bore through the granite?" He wrapped his arm around Addy as the small elevator descended.

"Just over a year." To drill and construct both shafts. "I hired a company from Norway. They brought the men and equipment and drilled before the house was built." While she'd been helping herself to treasure from Nick Cutter's Canary Island, *El Puerto* salvage.

"I want a cute elevator," Addison said.

"We have an elevator, sweetheart. We never use it."

"Resale," his wife reminded him.

"Never gonna happen."

Addison rested her head on his upper arm. "I love you, Rydell Case."

"Now and forever, sweetheart." He brushed a tender kiss on the crown of her glossy marmalade-colored hair. "Now and forever."

"Ah, geez, you guys, you're not alone!"

"If we *were*, we'd b-"

"Dear God." Peri covered her ears with both hands as the elevator gave its familiar bump when it reached the bottom. "Have mercy." As the door slid open, the small space filled with the musty, earthy scent of the caves, and the salty tang of the nearby ocean. Crashing surf could be faintly heard, but not seen. "Light switch on your right."

"Holy shit, Magma," Ry said as soon as they emerged into the illuminated corridor that ran vertically to the elevator. "How long did *this* take?"

"This is nothing. Just wait."

Peri smiled at her brother's appreciation for the spectacular space. The small chamber where the elevator stopped was about ten deep, twenty long, and thirty high. Caged lights illuminated the rough, gray-ish rock walls and floor.

"This section was pretty much as you see it. The channel for the elevator was blasted, and- keep walking straight- and a few of the other chambers had to be enlarged. Mostly, this was how I found it when I bought the land. All in all, it took about two years of explosives and excavation. Getting the dock built was a challenge." She grinned when her brother glanced at her over his shoulder. "I discovered, during construction, I really, really like things that go *boom*."

"God help us. Of course you do."

"Turn right here."

"It's really comfortable down here. I'm surprised it isn't cold," Addy, between Peri and Ry, observed, as they took the narrow right-hand corridor. Here, the jagged outcroppings of rocks had been smoothed, since the joining corridors were narrow, and the ceiling low. Bulbs in metal cages were strung on thick wire every ten feet.

"An even sixty-eight degrees all year round."

"Where do we end up if we go straight?" Ry's head almost brushed the low ceiling, and the walls were only three feet apart. It made carrying stuff down this way a pain in the ass. The larger elevator opened right beside the dock, and if Peri needed supplies for a long trip she used that one instead.

"An enormous natural chamber. I plan on climbing to the top one of these days."

"Not if you're here alone you won't."

She smiled- her *heart* smiled. God, she'd missed this. Him. Family. "What's the worst that can happen?" she teased. "I drop into the water below?"

"Peri- "

"Don't worry big brother, I'll bring an entire rescue and medical team with me. I won't do anything dangerous.

"Persephone Elizabeth-"

"*Fine*. Never alone. Got it." In one ear and out the other, but then her brother knew that about her. She loved that he still tried.

"There's no direct access to the ocean from there- Turn left here, then take the next right. Although the ocean has direct access to that cavern. It fills with water every high tide. Since I can't dock there, I haven't really spent too much time exploring. There are some cave paintings on the ceiling. I've taken a few pictures from ground level. I keep meaning to show the photos to Theo to see if he can date them. When he decided my house was too much for him, he missed out on seeing this, too."

The corridor lightened considerably as daylight started filtering in from the other end. The deep susurrus of the ocean amplified as they got closer. "Almost there." It was so much fun to show her brother and Addy everything she'd been laboring over for years. Proud of what she'd accomplished, she wanted Ry's stamp of approval, even though she didn't need it.

"Oh, Peri. This is magical," Addison marveled as they emerged into a long, wide chamber. The blue-green ocean, seen through an opening that was concealed on the other side by natural brush on the beach, sparkled in the distance. Sunlight sliced across the water, and dock.

Addy stopped dead in her tracks. Peri put out a hand to keep Addy from backing into her as a loud, aggressive bark echoed off the walls. "Oh, my, God, what the hell is *that*?"

Peri grinned. "That's Charlie. A four ton, southern elephant seal. He's taken up residence and is, apparently, too lazy to move south with his harem. He waits for them here, rested, and ready to mate, fifteen times a day when they return every September. Fortunately, most of the action happens on the beach out there."

"Fifteen times a day? Sounds like your brother."

Ry lifted an arm and flexed his biceps.

Peri rolled her eyes. "You two are incorrigible. Get your minds off your far too active love life and check out Charlie."

Perched on the end of the dock, the massive seal was ugly, fat and bad-tempered, his mustache -a la Charlie Chaplin- quivered with annoyance at their intrusion. He swiveled his head to watch them through one beady eye, then let out another bellow.

"Don't get too close,' Peri warned. "He's cranky."

"Not a problem." Ry and Charlie locked eyes. Amused, her brother shook his head. "Jesus, why not a kitten like a normal person, Magma?"

"He was here first." Charlie slipped gracefully off the dock as if he weighed pounds instead of tons. The wood vibrated with his weight. With barely a splash he disappeared under the water.

"*Damn* impressive. " Ry took in the well-built dock where her sleek, black-hulled *Sea Witch* and three runabouts of various sizes, bobbed gently on the water. Nearby, a storage shed held supplies and dive equipment. Beyond the shed, hidden behind a deep jog in the natural rock, the door of the industrial elevator was well hidden. Peri sometimes used it as storage for bigger, more valuable salvage items as well as to get things from the boat up to the house. Currently, it was up in the garage, filled with things she never wanted to explain to her brother.

"This is really something," Ry's voice was filled with admiration. "The scope of the herculean job it must've been to plan and construct this complex labyrinth beneath the house, and the house itself, shows your fantastic attention to detail. Next time, instead of coming by chopper, I'm coming by sea. This whole complex is amazing, honey. Spectacular job."

Her brother's pride, love, admiration, should be sweet, but wasn't. Peri knew damn well it was all going to be ripped away when he learned the truth.

Finn observed the rays of the mid-afternoon sun as it shone across the gleaming wood floor planks in stripes of shadow and sunlight. The strong rays were half blocked by the blinds on the wide windows wrapping Blackstar's salon. Nothing dimmed the satin-like gleam of the gold tablet, propped up on an easel on the black slate coffee table in the crook of the giant sofa.

The blue and white 'Diver Is Down Keep Clear' flag whipped in the high wind on the aft deck. *Blackstar's* stabilizers made the wildly choppy water feel almost pond-calm. Dangerous to land the chopper in this kind of wind, but Finn's pilot was top notch. If Kathleen couldn't do it, no one could.

The four Cutters, along with Bria and Zane's wife Teal waited, as did Finn, for his chopper to return with *la tavoletta d'oro Merrezo,* accompanied by four of Nick's counterterrorist friends. He'd enlisted their aid in securing the tablet from Italy, assuring Finn that there was no other group he trusted more than T-FLAC to keep the priceless tablet safe. As far as Finn knew, there wasn't a sign of a terrorist anywhere, but he kept his own counsel.

"Thought you and Callie were coming together," Logan addressed Zane's wife, Teal. Callie was Jonah's fiancé.

Anticipation for the arrival of *la tavoletta d'oro Merrezo* thrummed in the air, and small talk was the order of the day until the second tablet arrived.

"She was scheduled to come with me." Teal scratched a red insect bite on her arm beside a small smear of what looked like engine grease. "But the wedding prep is taking longer than planned. She's getting a bunch of stuff from God only knows where shipped in. She's sure going to a crazy amount of work. You guys should've done what Zane and I did. Go to the Justice of the Peace in St. Maarten. Thirty-five bucks and I didn't even have to wear a dress. No fuss. No muss. Win-win."

"Callie wants a white wedding, and she's going to get every bell, every whistle, her heart desires," Jonah told her. "I don't care if all the trouble is just for the two of us. Which it won't be because come hell or high water you *will* all be on Cutter Cay next month for this extravaganza. It's her day. She gets whatever she wants. All *I* care about is finally getting that ring on her finger."

"I'll drink to that." Logan raised his glass of tea, ice cubes clinking. "Happy wife, happy life, right? Got a call from *my* bride just before I came over. Dani will be here day after tomorrow. The sale of the building and her gallery in DC went through after a couple of hitches. She's doing last minute packing, and then she'll be on her way." Eyes gleaming, he shook his head. "She's bringing a *cat.* How does one cat-proof a ship?" he asked rhetorically.

"Did your Miss Andersen go back to Buenos Aires?" Nick asked casually as he absently stroked his wife's shoulder, bared by a red and white floral sundress.

I don't know where the fuck she went, and that's a problem. "Not that I know of."

Zane got up to get a couple of cold sodas from behind the bar. His t-shirt read: MY HEART BELONGS TO A MECHANIC. He held up a Coke. "Anyone?" When the others said no, he returned to the L-shaped couch to sit beside wife, handing her the second soda.

Teal, who'd arrived just that morning, was as far from Bria's sartorial beauty as a woman could be. Not that Zane's mechanic wife wasn't attractive. She was, in a quirky better-on-the-second-look way. Her shaggy dark brown hair looked self-barbered, a large bruise on her calf, probably caused by one of the engines she loved, was exposed by wrinkled cargo shorts. Her oversized black t-shirt read: IT'S DIVE 'O CLOCK.

Finn had always found Teal Cutter pithy, and amusing as hell, and, like himself, she had zero tolerance for bullshit. The woman preferred machines to people and made no bones about it. He could relate.

Zane pulled the tab on his drink and paused. "She came to *Decrepit* most of Tuesday. She was over on board *Scorpion*, yesterday, right, Jonah? I think she said something about going somewhere with Case today. I saw his chopper fly over earlier this morning." He made it sound as though she'd flown off on the back of the Devil himself.

"They were back in under three hours." Where had they gone and why? Even though Finn had been tempted to give chase when she'd gone over to *Tesoro Mio* early yesterday morning, he'd resisted.

If he didn't already have people's eyes on her almost every minute of the day, he'd have put a goddamned tracker on her. Even though she was staying on board *Blackstar*, Finn hadn't seen her *since she'd left his bed this morning, to go to her own cabin to shower and change. She hadn't said a word about working onboard* Tesoro Mio, *nor had she mentioned traveling to the coast with Case.*

"I left word for her to join us-" He'd identified the sound of the motor of her runabout arrive five minutes ago.

The whop-whop-whop of the *Blackstar* chopper landing on the helipad on the bridge deck, two decks above them, made speech impossible for several minutes. He glanced at his watch. "Right on time."

"This is so exciting!" Bria squeezed her husband's hand. "Aren't you excited, *amore mio?"*

"Yes, my love," Nick murmured, tone dry as he lifted her hand and pressed it to his lips. "I've been in a constant state of excitement-" His pause was long enough for his wife to give him a hard poke in the ribs and a mock scowl. "For *days*. Ah. Miss Andersen. *There* you are."

Finn knew the second she came into the room without even looking. His entire body stiffened at the electrical charge in the air. His heart knocked like some lovesick fool the second he'd heard her steps coming down the corridor.

Pheromones. Radar. An internal homing device. Lust unadulterated.

Crossing the wide expanse of wood floor, then the area rug, her steps were measured, as though she was approaching animals in the wild, and wasn't quite sure how they'd react when she got closer. Purple shorts exposed long, spectacular legs and the orange and purple striped t-shirt, which left a sliver of midriff bare, draped modestly over her breasts. In his mind's eye, Finn saw her naked, covered in nothing more than a galaxy of amber freckles and all that glorious hair. In a sleek knot at her nape, it caught every bit of stray sunlight and turned it to molten lava as she moved. Everything about her made Finn's mouth water.

Behind her was Dr. Thiago Núñez, preppy in chinos and a pink golf shirt. Finn's knee-jerk was, what the fuck was *he* doing here? Did their arrival together mean they'd spent the last few hours holed up somewhere? Together and not in a platonic, work-related way?

Their eyes met. Hers were clear, guilt free, but challenging. She knew what he'd been thinking, and wasn't having it. Their gazes lingered, stroked, challenged, invited.

They shared a small, intimate smile. No, she hadn't let any other man touch her.

Finn made introductions, and Núñez removed a pile of file folders from a straight-backed chair and sat down. As he moved them to a nearby table, Finn noticed a small round tattoo on the web of skin between the Minister's thumb and index finger. He didn't look the type of man to have a tattoo, but Finn wasn't interested in much about the man.

Ariel hesitated, looking around for a place to sit as Zane introduced her boss to everyone. The only available spot was beside Finn on the loveseat. "Over here, I saved you a seat." *Said the spider to the fly.*

The cushions dipped as she sat down, about as far away from him as the opposite sofa arm allowed. Which wasn't far. Finn's brain filled with the heady fragrance of Casablanca lilies. Close enough to feel the warmth of her skin, Finn stretched out his arm across the back pillows, then stroked a knuckle across her nape. Her skin felt warm. Smooth. She drew in a sharp breath, but didn't move of out of reach.

"I hope my unannounced arrival won't put you out," Núñez directed the question to a distracted Finn. "But when Ariel told me of the salvage of two new *Tabletas de oro*, and the original on its way from Merrezo, I find this discovery unprecedented, and deeply profound. *Three* such priceless antiquities. . .I had to come and see them with my own eyes."

"*Two*," Logan informed him.

Núñez gave him an inquiring look. "Two?"

"Two tablets. Not three. The one found by Finn, the other housed in the museum in Italy."

Dr. Núñez's brow furrowed as he gave Ariel a perplexed look. "But you are in possession of a *third.* Not so, *cariño*?"

ELEVEN

Shit. Peri realized she'd miscalculated by telling Theo about her find. She couldn't bluff her way out of this. She hadn't sworn him to secrecy because it hadn't occurred to her that a- he'd show up out of the blue, or b- he'd blurt out her discovery in front of everyone. And to make matters worse, by revealing that she had a tablet, he had divulged that she had her own dive site. He'd just aimed a blowtorch at a sky-high pile of kindling.

Her instinct to get her tablet away from the Cutters had been spot on.

"*What* third tablet?" Finn demanded with dangerous softness. A muscle tightened in his jaw. His eyes turned storm-cloud dark as he swiveled to look at her.

She hadn't even opened her mouth to respond when the oldest Cutter threw in his two cents. "There really *is* another tablet?" Logan inquired. Damn those deep blue eyes cut like lasers. "Where did it come from?"

No point prevaricating now. She'd never counted to three before diving off a cliff, and she didn't now. "I found it diving *Napolitano.*"

"*Diving-*" Finn bit the word off to demand, "Diving with whom? Case?"

"Yes."

"Is that part of your job description?"

"There's nothing in my job description that says I can't salvage in my spare time."

He had nothing to say to that. "So it's onboard *Tesoro Mio*, and accessible."

"No, it's not."

"Where is it?" It was chilling how a low voice could hold so much threat.

Cleaned, beautiful, and on her kitchen counter at home as of a few hours ago.

Lifting her chin, she responded calmly, despite the pterodactyls swooping en masse in her stomach. "Somewhere safe." And she didn't think for a freaking moment that Finn, or the Cutters, would let her end the conversation there. And honestly, in their place, neither would she, damn it.

"*That* wasn't the question." Each word seemed chipped out of granite. "Tell us where it is. Right now."

His tone put her back up. "You have no right to order me to do *anything*, Finn."

"Why? Don't you want the preeminent authority on the tablet to take a look at it?"

"Don't put words in my mouth. Of course I do."

"Why were *you* working a salvage?"

"Because I'm a diver and salvager, the same as the rest of you," she told him tartly. "*Napolitano* has been mine from the start." Finn was so close she imagined she saw angry little black dots darting around in his irises. "I was the one who discovered the wrecks. Five *years* ago."

"Is that so? So, you've had the tablet for *years*. Yet you didn't mention it the other night when it was the main focus of our conversation at dinner?" Not waiting for her response, he raised a brow. "*Napolitano* is registered to a shell company under the Koúkos Corporation umbrella."

She didn't correct the timing of her discovery. Peri shrugged while her heart pounded so hard she was sure it would jump right out of her chest and flee the scene. Holy hell. How had he found out who it was registered to?

Not that it surprised her. A man didn't get to be in Finn's position in business without knowing precisely who and what he was up against at the negotiation table.

"You named a corporation cuckoo." The lethal edge in Finn's voice could strip paint off a hull. "As in a bird that commandeers another bird's nest?"

He was too damned quick. "Huh. Is that what Koúkos means? I just liked the sound of the word." As if any intelligent person would name their company something without knowing what hell the name meant. She was the cuckoo. In the Cutter's nest.

She did a quick glance around the room to gauge if anyone else was connecting the dots. They were looking her way, but they hadn't become hostile. That, she knew, could change on a dime. Her entire body braced as if they were about to stone her. Rubbing her damp palm along the nubby arm of the sofa, she wished she had a drink to moisten her dry mouth.

Zane made a rude noise and shot a glare at Theo. "Isn't that a conflict of damned interest, Minister of Antiquities?"

"Miss Andersen was the one who brought the wrecks to my attention," Theo told him, voice stiff. He didn't like being questioned. "She already had her claim and was the logical choice to oversee the salvage. Especially one of *this* magnitude."

"In a fucking pig's eye," Jonah snarled. "It's a *major* conflict of interest to put the wolf in charge of the hens. I demand that she- "

"She's doing a fine job," Nick inserted smoothly. "I don't have a problem with it – her- at all. Naturally, we all want to see your tablet," he addressed Peri, his brilliant blue eyes kind. "Is it easily accessible? *Can* we get to it before Signore Vadini arrives?"

"As I said. I'll bring it in the morning."

Nick smiled. "Good enough."

"No," Finn said flatly. "We won't wait until tomorrow. Dr. Vadini will want to see all of the tablets when he arrives." Glancing at his watch, he stood. "We have two hours before then. Let's go."

"No need for you to leave your guests." Theo got to his feet. "It would be my honor to accompany Ariel to the location."

Peri didn't look at her ex-lover. Her entire focus was in trying to read Finn's stoic expression. "You don't know where that is, Theo."

"You'll tell me." Now Theo sounded mildly annoyed. He wasn't a man who showed his emotions on his sleeve, but boy, did he hate when people he dealt with didn't give him the deference he believed he was owed. Apparently, he'd taken a dislike to Finn for some reason. She suspected the feeling was mutual.

"It will take at least two hours for the round trip to the mainland wherever it is. At a guess I'd say it's at your glass house," he said stiffly. "And I think I should go alone. That way you'll be here when the other tablet arrives. If you'd give me the code to get into the house I'll leave immedi-"

"No," Finn repeated, cutting Theo off, his brusqueness verging on rudeness. "*You're* welcome to remain here. Or return to – wherever you came from, Dr. Núñez." His silvery eyes locked on Peri. "This is not a matter that's up for debate."

"One of you let me know when it's my turn to offer an opinion." Peri crossed her arms and legs and planted her butt more firmly on the loveseat.

"We'll take the chopper and make a quick round trip. I don't want Dr. Vadini to wait any longer than necessary to have all three tablets to study. *Up*," he told her.

She looked at him. "Try again."

A muscle ticked in his jaw as he gritted out, "Don't push me."

"Don't bully me." *Stand off.* Unfortunately, it was exhilarating sparring with him.

Did his lips twitch? Peri gave him a suspicious look, but he was still glaring, so obviously not. He held out his hand. "Please allow me to take you to your house so we can return with the bloody tablet before the turn of the century."

Placing her hand in his, she allowed him to pull her up beside him, and said sweetly, "Since you asked so nicely. . ."

In no time they were up on the bridge deck where two of his security people waited beside a sleek, black helicopter.

"Aw, do you need their protection to keep you safe from me?"

"They're here to prevent me from strangling you and dumping your body over the South Atlantic bloody Ocean. Get in."

With a snort of laughter, Peri climbed on board without his assistance. Finn went around and got in to sit at the controls. He motioned to the two men to stay onboard. They didn't look happy about it as they stepped away from the spinning rotors, but remained watching them.

Finn turned on the blades, and as they started to slowly rotate, handed her a headset. While she put it on, he leaned over to fasten her seat belt for her.

"I'm not a three-year-old. I can buckle myself in." She liked his hands on her. His warm breath fanned her mouth. His face was so close she could see individual eyelashes.

"Don't," she warned.

He didn't move. Not his eyes, nor the fingers curled around the webbed seatbelt across her chest. "I like touching you." His lips barely formed the words, yet the timber of his voice resonated through her bones like the vibrations of a tuning fork.

The heat of his fingers burned through her t-shirt. She didn't move either. But, God, she imagined his fingers stealing up the loose leg of her shorts to stroke her thigh, as he had the other day. She imagined him lifting her shirt to bare her breasts to the afternoon sun flooding the inside of the small space, nuzzling her breasts above the lace of her bra. Holding his gaze she imagined the roughness of his jaw scraping across her skin and the slick smooth heat of his tongue gliding across her nipple.

Squeezing her legs tightly together did the opposite of helping. Peri went hot, then cold, then hot again. "I like being touched by you," she pushed out, breath restricted. "But we have an audience."

Still leaning over her, he didn't straighten back into his own seat. "Do you give a damn?" Their mouths were barely touching, just enough that she could taste his coffee scented breath.

Peri licked the taste from her lips. "No. *Yes,*" she amended, mouth dry, heart trip-hammering as his eyes dilated into two black pools. "W-we're in a hurry, remember?"

The loud whop-whop-whop of the blades blocked out any other sound as he kissed her. Not a marauding pirate's kiss, but a soft, somehow more intimate brush of his lips against hers. Peri's insides melted into a puddle of mixed emotions too intense to describe.

She was in so, so much freaking trouble.

Lifting his head, he left her lips damp and bereft. Finn murmured, "To be continued."

"I'll be ready. Bring your A game, Gallagher."

֍

The gold tablet was propped on the center island counter at her glass house. Finn cast it a cursory glance as they walked past it to look at the jaw-dropping view, a spectacular, panoramic view of water and sky. As important as the artifact was, he was more interested in what he could learn about *her*. Here in her personal space, and in this truly private moment away from his ship, and the myriad people vying for his attention.

Her house, a five-sided-glass box, perched precariously on a wind-ravaged bluff. The mind-bending-275 degree-panoramic-view through fifteen-foot-high windows, was jaw-dropping, even for a man who'd seen spectacular architecture around the world. Miles of sparkling ocean and cloudless grey-blue sky stretched endlessly around him. Through the glass floor, waves thrashed soundlessly against the jagged gray rocks ten stories below his feet. Even the galley kitchen's floor was glass.

The open concept was approximately three thousand square feet. A white, Carrara marble, two-sided fireplace soared from glass floor to glass ceiling, bisecting the room, flanked by long, low, white bookcases, holding a display of ancient blue and white Chinese porcelain. Her large bed, covered in some soft fabric that mimicked the color of the palest blush found inside of a conch shell, appeared to float in space. A large, fluffy white area rug—an island—defining the L-shaped living room furniture, left plenty of room to walk across the gravity-defying floor.

She accompanied him diagonally across the room to the vast expanse of windows facing the ocean. "Incredible." Sunlight bounced off the water as far as the naked eye could see. The anchored ships from here were mere specks on the vast blue. "You really are fearless, aren't you?"

"Sometimes that's *not* such a good thing. Being afraid, and doing something anyway, isn't always the smartest choice."

She remained face forward, staring at the view. Finn took in the delicacy of her profile and the sweep of her dark lashes. He wondered what she was referring to, and how he could fix it. Damn. They had to hurry back. They needed time- he needed time. To learn everything about her. To discover what gave her joy and what made her beautiful eyes cloudy. "Being afraid, and doing it anyway is called bravery."

She smiled. "Some call it stupidity."

"I built my fortune on taking risks other people thought stupid. I did alright."

Her smile enchanted him as she turned up her face to look at him. "That you did."

Turning her in his arms, Finn kissed her. She immediately wound her arms around his neck, lifting up on her toes to position her mouth exactly right. She consumed him, filled his thoughts every fucking waking minute of every hour. Everything about her was music to him. A symphony of sounds and scents. The arousing play of her hands in his hair, the taste of the slick inside of her mouth, the assertive give and take of her tongue, were enough to drive him out of his mind. Lust on steroids.

His fingers dug into the taut muscles of her ass, pulling her firmly against his erection.

Tightening her arms around him, she moaned. Then pulled her mouth away from his. Her lips were kiss-swollen and pink, her cheeks flushed, her pupils huge. "Do you think we're unwittingly being given some sort of aphrodisiac?"

Finn laughed. "Whatever it is, let's package it and sell it. I think we'd make a fortune."

"Have you ever. . .?"

"Felt like this before? Never."

"Thank God, I'd hate to be alone in this. Whatever this is."

"Lust. Pheromones. Hunger."

Stepping out of his hold, she tugged down her t-shirt which had ridden up. "All of that. Do you think we'll burn out at some point?"

Wrapping his arm around her waist, Finn pulled her against his body and with his free hand gently pushed her hair over her shoulder so he had a clear view of her earnest face. "Not in the foreseeable future. You okay with that?"

She shot him a sassy smile. "As long as you can keep up with me, sure. As much as I'd like to take my bed for a test drive, we really can't stay here too long. But I'd like to take a rain check on that."

"A test drive should be slow and methodical, not taken in haste, I agree," he told her seriously, loving the way her eyes lit up, and lips curved. Turning around, he noticed some of her beautifully displayed pieces. "Are these artifacts you've salvaged over the years?" Sliding his palm against hers, Finn linked fingers with her as they walked.

"Yes, I keep the ones I can't bear to part with, the rest I sell. As you see, I don't like clutter, and having an ancient relic locked in some storeroom unseen would be a criminal waste. People need to see and enjoy them."

She motioned to the binoculars on a stand nearby, but he shook his head. He'd rather look at her. He'd like to come back and look through her telescope at the stars with her from her vantage point. But another time, "How did you get into salvaging?"

"My father had an interest, so it was a way to feel close to him. I worked as a freelance diver for a percentage of the salvage with various salvage crews for years. But I was looking for something to call my own. There's a small museum in the South of Spain that I've sold quite a few of my finds to over the years. They allowed me access to their underground storage facility, which contained storage drawers *filled* with, and was piled high with ship's manifests and log books from as far back as... "

She shook her head. "Probably the Crusades. Although I didn't get *that* far back. Every spare moment I had, if it was at all feasible- I went back there and continued my search, hoping to find that nugget. . . I must've combed through hundreds of thousands of documents before I discovered word of *Napolitano, Nuestra Señora del Marco, Santa Ana* and *El Crucifijo.* Then I followed that thread, reading hundreds and hundreds of other documents looking for another reference. It was a long and dusty road.

I finally found what I needed to locate the ships. Hundreds of miles from where they should've been. Then I did dive after dive until I had my hands on each one of them. Five years ago I moved here. Invested some of my earlier profits into the house, and the rest is history."

"You've done well with *Napolitano.* Is Rydell Case your partner?" *Your lover?*

"I've had several years to devote to salvaging her alone- or rather with the help of professional local divers. But it far exceeded my wildest expectations. I brought Case in a few years ago when I realized the scope of *Napolitano.* He was working another salvage, so it's only now he can devote his time to her. He brought his family with him. He's here for the long haul. With my job with the Ministry, and keeping track of everything you and the Cutters bring to the surface, I'm glad of his help and that of his divers. I'm pretty much sitting back, and will rake in the money while he and his team do all the work."

"There's no way you'd ever sit back, and I suspect you feel the same way about money as I do. It's just to keep score for achieving your personal best. But I know you love to dive."

"I do, and I will. But I'm just as fascinated at the history of everything that's being found. I'll dive *Napolitano* as I can. My priority right now is my job for the Ministry. It's a big responsibility, and one I take very seriously."

He looked around. "We must have the same decorator." Spare. Lots of white. Pops of color. Intriguing artifacts. Air and space. He could move in right now.

The idea, for a confirmed bachelor, wasn't repugnant.

Wrapping her arms around his neck, she spoke against his ear, "I noticed."

Finn slid his arms around her narrow waist, drawing her tightly against him. Her warm breath fanned his skin, setting up a domino effect of need.

Her smile barely curved her lips. "Everyone's waiting for us." She uncoupled herself from his light hold before he could steal a kiss. "Bria's expert is arriving any minute. We really should go," her voice was brisk as she headed to the all-white galley kitchen.

When he paused to admire a forty-inch-tall, intact, bronze statue of Aphrodite on a white marble plinth, she offered, "I found that on a small wreck off Cape San Vito, Taranto, in Southern Italy, six years ago. There wasn't much there, but she's one of my favorites."

"And this?" He indicated a deeply embossed gold box on a glass shelf nearby.

"I found that little tobacco box in an 1804- picked clean- Spanish galleon off the coast of Peru. One of my first salvages. All the treasure had been sold off by another salvager years earlier, and the wreck abandoned. But I hoped they'd missed a few things. And they did."

"How long did it take you to find this?"

"Five months. It was good practice. Ready?"

Finn picked up the small duffel bag, containing her tablet, off the Carrara marble countertop. "Brave and dogged. Admirable qualities."

The tip of her nose turned pink. "Some people don't think so."

"Who?" Finn asked, following her to the enormous swivel front door, set into the only wall in the place. The heavy metal door swung open with a touch of her finger. "Dr. Núñez?"

"Theo?" She huffed out a laugh as they walked outside into the sunshine. "He never knew me." She locked the door with her palm print on a nearby biometric pad. "I doubt he had an opinion either way."

Good to know.

The flight back was mercifully short, Finn held her hand from the helipad to the salon downstairs. They were all there waiting- an entire freaking room *filled* to the brim with Cutters. Taciturn Logan, boisterous Zane and his mechanic wife, Jonah looking distracted as he talked on the phone, and Nick and his Princess Bria, smiling, welcoming. The last two made Peri more nervous than Logan's non-verbal dislike. Of what she wasn't sure, but she steered a wide berth.

Finn handed the backpack to Nick, without releasing her hand. He made no bones about their relationship. Which both pleased and terrified her.

Urging her ahead of him, Finn drew her down beside him on the loveseat. The heat radiating from his body enveloped her as his arm brushed hers. Peri inhaled the sea-air/citrus smell of his skin and almost whimpered as it intensified the constant ache of awareness that electrified the fine hairs on her arms.

His eyes promised things that made her heart race even faster, and it was damn hard to catch her breath. What weird alchemy did they have that drew them together like two magnets? What was it about Finn that caused this reaction in her? Every. Single. Time. He was like fire, blazing hot, searing everything to ash that couldn't withstand the heat. She liked his brand of heat. Liked it a *lot.*

Liked it enough to love it.

In comparison to how wrong things were in the world she'd created, when they had sex everything felt so right. She didn't see how those two worlds could ever be reconciled.

Love would never be enough for the long term. That realization caused a fierce ache to fill her heart.

Does he know my connection to the Cutters?

He seems to know everything.

He can't.

"Behave." She gave him a little poke with her elbow. "I'm already on a razor's edge. Want me to come right here in front of your friends?"

"No, that's for my eyes only," Finn answered, not in the least repentant as she removed her hand and leaned forward away from him. Yeah, it was fine if she controlled the pace, the intensity, the seduction. To give him the power over her emotions was too freaking scary. Hah. Imagine that. She'd found the one thing that scared the shit out of her.

"You made good time," Nick smiled as he placed her tablet on the easel beside Finn's. Trying to convince herself that Nick Cutter was on her side in *any* of this was dangerous. No matter that she reluctantly *liked* them. These were the *Cutters*. Undeniably sneaky, underhanded, unprincipled. Always out for their own gain.

"Look at that. Same size, same shape." Nick said. "Thanks for sharing this with us, Ariel."

Damn it, Nick was so freaking. . .nice. And Finn was determined to embarrass her. He could try, but she was a hard woman to embarrass. "No matter who discovered the tablets, they're a remarkable find, and worth sharing. I'm grateful Finn was able to get me there and back so quickly." Wow, she was impressed by the even, *casualness* of her own voice.

"Was yours found beside what could've been a chest?" Zane looked over at her. Damn those Cutter-blue eyes were penetrating. Unnervingly so. "Bronze lock? Fist-sized emeralds?"

The thought occurred to her that maybe they knew *exactly* who she was and what she'd done. That they were toying with her like giant, devil-eyed cats, waiting to slam a heavy paw on her back and devour her in one gulp. *Bring it on. You have no idea what kind of trump cards I'm holding behind my back.* "Yes," she answered Zane. "The same circumstances as Finn's. I recorded everything, and of course, took pictures of the location before I brought it to the surface."

"Excellent." Zane hunkered down beside the enormous stone slab of the coffee table to get a better look. "Holy shit, look at them together. This is really something special."

Finn's hand brushed Peri's shoulder as he rested his arm along the seat cushion behind her head and played with her hair.

Theo whispered something, presumably to himself, in rapid Spanish so low Peri couldn't hear the words. Then said more loudly, "They are the same author, no doubt. But not identical as you see. A similar size and shape, comparable script and number of lines. But not identical."

Peri's heart skipped several beats. Was *this* an optimal time to tell them what she needed to tell them? They were all upbeat about the tablets. Distracted. . .

This confession would be much harder now with Finn in the mix. Once she told the Cutters who she was, and what she'd been doing all these years, she'd never see him again. *They* were his friends, *they* were the ones who had his loyalty.

It was a given that he wouldn't like what she'd done if he discovered even a small part of the truth. The thought hurt her heart. A physical pain.

But what if she *didn't* tell them?

Clearly, they still didn't recognize her. If they didn't recognize her as the thieving *Sea Witch* by now, there was no reason they ever would.

Or, when she least expected it, when she was defenseless, and even more deeply attached to Finn, would they pounce? That would be worse than this, surely? When she was lulled into a false sense of security and happiness?

"What's going on in this beautiful brain of yours?" Finn asked softly, stroking his thumb across the rapid pulse at her temple.

Peri turned her head. His face was inches from hers, a furrow of concern between his quick-silver eyes.

Euphoric happiness flooded every cell in her body, the joy bordering on pain.

Dear God. She was in *love* with him.

Back away.

No way was she in *love* with him.

She was in *lust* with him.

Yes. Of course. That was it. What red-blooded woman *wouldn't* be in lust with him?

Big difference between love and lust. She'd recover from lack of lust. The absence of lust wouldn't rip out her heart when he walked away as he inevitably would.

She'd never had a relationship that lasted longer than five months. She always made sure it didn't get emotional. And damn it, *she* was always the one who walked away first.

Stop. She dared not go there now. Not when her cover was about to be blown to shit. The first tender bloom unfurling in her heart was soon going to be stomped into oblivion. Unless she kept her mouth shut. .

Just a little longer, her aching heart begged. Just a little longer to feel like this. To hoard the memories to indulge in - afterwards.

She blinked back the foolish sting behind her lids.

Get over yourself. This isn't a freaking surprise. You knew- have always known that this would end. Sooner than later.

Not telling them really wasn't a viable option. Because come hell or high water, that other shoe *would* drop. They'd been in too close a proximity, for too many years, for that not to happen. Something or other would trigger a memory. No ands, ifs or buts. Back to Plan A.

But just a little longer. . .

"I was thinking about seeing all three tablets together, and what that means historically."

"We don't have long to wait," Finn told her, the slight frown between his brow smoothing. "The chopper is heading in. The curator will be here any minute now. "

"I always wanted to open my Christmas presents the moment they were placed under the tree. Waiting isn't my long suit."

His voice became low and smoky, "I've known you to be just fine with anticipation."

He touched her as if he couldn't keep his hands off her. Peri wasn't sure he realized how intimate it must look to the others seeing his hand resting on the back of her neck, absently winding a loose strand of her hair around his finger. "Everything with you is foreplay," she murmured softly, holding his gaze as if they were alone in the room. "I anticipate what's next with you, with every beat of my heart."

Don't tell them, her heart cried. Leave things as they are.

"*Macushla*, if you keep looking at me like that, I'm going to swoop you up, and carry you out of here like a Neanderthal," Finn whispered. "I don't give a damn *what* anyone thinks."

"And miss the arrival of Bria's tablet?"

"And miss anything and everything that keeps us fully clothed and upright."

"Anticipation," she teased, loving the flare of his pupils, and the feel of his breath on her lips.

He closed his eyes as if in pain. "Killing me."

"Me, too." She'd live in the now. And worry about the sense of dread growing inside her -later. "Want to see some pictures?" A change of subject should cool them off some. Lifting her butt off the cushion, she pulled her phone out of the back pocket of her shorts and entered in her password, then handed it to him.

"Naked selfies?" he asked hopefully.

"'Fraid not."

With a sigh, he took the phone from her and started to thumb through the images. "These are all your finds?" he asked as the sound of the rotors overhead suddenly became noticeable.

"So far. Those are of some of the more interesting pieces." Not many, because she'd been too occupied to dive her own site since *they'd* all shown up. "But it would be a good idea to compare the locations of the finds, don't you think?"

"Yeah. I do." He connected to his Bluetooth earpiece. "Walker, send these images to print. Yeah. Now please."

Before handing her back the phone he forwarded the images to his own phone.

Nick got up to pour his wife a cup of tea. Logan rose and strolled over to the window, tilting the blinds for a better view, letting in a flood of hot sunlight. It struck the tablets on the coffee table and made the gold glow.

"It's going to be awesome seeing all of them side-by-side." Teal, legs curled under her, leaned against Zane. "I can't wait to see if they're the same, or different."

"It would be presumed the tablets will show the exact same text," Theo told them with authority. "Surely that's why they have been found on different ships? To ensure at least one reached its destination? This would make sense since it was a long trip to Spain, and the waters along the coast of Patagonia can be treacherous. It would be a natural assumption that one or more of the ships would not make it back."

"*Napolitano* was *Italian*, not Spanish like the other three ships," Finn pointed out. "That raises more questions, doesn't it?"

Peri could tell it was a rhetorical question. But a question Finn would figure out like a dog with a bone. His hand tunneled under her hair, then his fingers closed on her nape. "You're very sensitive right here," he whispered wickedly, stroked his thumb up her nape, into her hairline, and then down again. "One of my favorite places to kiss you."

Peri elbowed him in the side. With a smile, he straightened, but kept his hand - now still - on the back of her neck.

"I will patiently drink another cup of this excellent tea." Bria took the fresh cup from her husband, her eyes smiling at him over the rim. "And wait to see what Signore Vadini, in his expert opinion, has to say."

Finn's warm breath fanned the hair at her temple, causing goosebumps to prickle her skin. He stroked his thumb gently behind Peri's left ear.

His unveiled affection made her skin grow hot with desire, while her breath caught with anxiety over the mountain of worries she'd created for herself. Not the least of which was his obvious decision to make their relationship, for want of a better word, public. Very public. Anyone looking at the two of them, his fingers on her nape, pushing her hair aside, certainly knew there was something between them.

He was in business with the Cutters, it wouldn't be fair to ask him to choose.

Scared he'll choose his friends over you?

Yes.

The heavy tread of booted feet moving down the corridor toward the salon had everyone turning to the doorway in anticipation.

Damn it. Falling in love with Finn was not in her freaking plans. In fact, it was the anti-plan.

"There's your curator."

"This is good news." Bria placed her cup on a nearby side table.

"Sorry about your floors." Nick got to his feet, holding out his hand to his wife. Bria rose gracefully to join him. They all stood as three men entered. The cause of the heavy treads on Finn's highly polished teak floor. They did nothing to hide the full arsenal of weapons strapped about their persons. It wasn't so much that the men were large and intimidating, pretty much every man in the room was of a similar height, and disposition, it was that they all looked. . .menacing. Not in a barroom brawl kinda way, but in an I-will-kill-you-with-my-bare-hands-if-you-make-a-wrong-move kinda way.

They stepped aside to reveal a slight, balding man with black, horn-rimmed glasses.

Given his deeply wrinkled skin, sunken dark eyes, and thin gray combover, Peri guesstimated the linguist/curator was a hundred and thirty years old. His shirt, even after the long flight, was neatly pressed, and blinding white. He wore it with a lizard green tie, a worn-shiny, three-piece brown suit circa 1950, and polished black dress shoes. His gaze went directly to the gold tablets propped up in pride of place on the coffee table.

Hands outstretched, Bria glided over to greet her curator, who'd managed to rip his gaze from the tablets to make nice with his benefactress. "Signore Vadini-" the two spoke in rapid, animated, Italian, accompanied by the requisite flourishing hand gestures. Bria asked if he needed to rest after his long trip. He said no, he wanted to study the tablets first.

Peri lost count of how many times the poor man gazed longingly at the tablets instead of Bria. Clearly, he was dying to get his hands on them.

Finn shifted. His bare arm brushed hers. Would it always be like this with Finn?

The sensation made her heart pound and her blood sing through her veins as if she'd just gulped down a giant glass of brandy.

When she moved, his fingers on her nape gently tightened, and the steely strength of his forearm pressed against her spine, from waist to shoulder blade.

Finn was a toucher, and Peri wasn't used to being touched, and certainly not so casually. And in public, no less. She'd become accustomed to being alone, doing without the physical contact most people took for granted.

There were several decisive moves she could make to put some space between them, but, damn it, she *liked* his hand on her. She liked the weight of his arm draped around her. To her, his possessiveness symbolized her control over him - a man whose reach extended beyond the solar system.

"You know you can only touch me like this in public because I allow it, don't you?" She knew her whispered words would be like a red, hot seduction to Finn.

He gave her a lazy smile, as he wrapped an arm about her waist and pulled her in more tightly. "Game on, Persephone. I see challenges where most people see problems. Looking forward to further discussion. In private."

Anticipation. She shivered with longing.

The princess clapped her hands. "Everyone," Bria said with an engaging smile. "This is my dear Ale Vadini. Signore Vadini not only secures the safety of our *el tavoletta d'oro Merrezo* and our other treasures as well, he is an expert linguist, and has managed to translate many of the words on our tablet."

"*Madre di Dio.* A t-*third* tablet has been discovered?" the curator's voice broke, as he addressed Bria in Italian. It was several moments before he was capable of speech again. His eyes glistened as he looked around at everyone gathered in the room. "This is truly-" his voice shook. "*Profound.* It is profound. And Divine providence to have *three* such tablets converge here where they began their arduous journey."

Theo, standing closest to the tablets, perked up, face flushed with excitement. Voice breathless, he demanded, "You are capable of reading the ancient text on *Tableta d oro, señor?"*

"*Sí.* Yes. Some. I, and many scholars, have had many decades to work on this project. May I sit?"

Nick went to talk in low tones to the men who'd brought the curator, then returned with a straight-backed chair for Dr. Vadini, which he placed next to the coffee table holding the tablet.

After several minutes, during which the curator was seated, served coffee, and given a slice of torta galesa cake, everyone returned to their respective seats. Without taking his eyes off the tablets, he said, "I will preface everything I say today with some caution. Yes, I have managed over a lifetime of work and study, to read a handful of the words on the tablet of Merrezo." Signore Vadini removed a pair of white cotton gloves from his breast pocket and drew them on like a surgeon before performing a heart transplant.

"May I?" He reached for Peri's tablet closest to him.

"Allow me." Zane stood, grabbed a throw pillow, then lifted the heavy tablet from the stand and set both on the old man's lap.

Eyes closed as if in prayer, the curator breathed in deeply, then looked down. With great reverence, his fingers hovered millimeters above the raised text. "It is the same author, and as hoped, the text is different." He pointed at Finn's tablet. "I wish to see all three together."

"Bring a small table," Bria ordered Jonah, who stood nearby. He went to find a small side table, and returned with it, placing it directly in front of the curator.

Peri leaned forward. She didn't want to miss a thing.

TWELVE

Both tablets were laid, side by side for the Curator to inspect. Which he did while the clock ticked off the minutes.

"Different?" Theo inserted after five minutes of absolute silence, leaning forward. "How so?"

"The tablets are not a single, identical, repeated message, signore. Rather, each tablet tells us something *new*." When he looked up his eyes gleamed with tears. "After all these years. I never thought..." He shook his head.

The old man glanced at one of the men in black, and the guy came forward to place a small metal case on the table. "Open her please."

The man opened the case, and the satin gleam of gold had everyone in the room riveted. Peri sucked in a breath and forgot to release it seeing the three tablets, side by side.

"Please, continue. Tell my friends what you know."

Vadini pushed his glasses up with a gloved finger. "I must tell the story to keep things in context, sí?"

For a moment Peri thought the old man was specifically addressing her, but it was at Finn that he was looking, and to Finn, he spoke.

"Five hundred and seven years ago, a young seer, living here, in what is now known as Patagonia, had a vision. He was a boy, just fourteen years old, but he'd been having visions since he was old enough to speak. All the boy's prophecies proved to be true.

"In our small country of Merrezo," he continued to his fascinated audience, "we, too, had a *profeta*- seer. His name was Foscari. He was, by then an old man, but like the child, Foscari correctly saw the future, and his prophecies were very famous. He was known all over Europe, and people- both high and low born-revered him. He was one of a kind, you understand?" Signore Vadini's black eyes twinkled.

Everyone was riveted to his words. "He heard of the boy's most profound predictions. Foscari had similar thoughts himself, but not as detailed as the boy's, not as certain. Foscari called for the young seer to be brought to him on one of the treasure ships so that he could validate his prediction."

The old man smiled. "I suspect, too, to convince his followers that the boy was, as you say, a charlatan."

"So, the tablets *did* originate here in Patagonia?" Finn asked, resting his arm on the back cushions of the sofa, and absently picking up the loose strand of Peri's hair.

"Oh, yes. According to legend, the boy's father, and those who venerated him, refused to allow the child to cross the ocean, even accompanied by a Protector. The boy had seen his own death, and knew he'd never reach Merrezo- "

"Please, tell us more, Signore Vadini," Bria urged."The prophecy was carved onto separate marble tablets. Then, because they were gifts to Foscari, they were coated in gold, before making their voyage across the sea. The tablet that became *la tavoletta d'oro Merrezo* was accompanied on the long voyage by my namesake, Ale Vadini, *el Ehnos*. The Protector, yes? It was the only ship to reach Italy."

"A protector?" Peri asked. "As in singular? Did a protector accompany the other ships?" She didn't add that, considering the other ships sank, they weren't very good at their jobs. A quick tug on her hair told her Finn was thinking the same thing.

"There has always been only *one* Protector. Perhaps the importance and value of the tablets required more than one at that time. We will never know. For over five hundred years the Protector, my ancestors in a direct line, have cared for *la tavoletta d'oro Merrezo*. My daughter will follow me, and her son will follow her as Protector. This is how we care for the legacy of the seer. The honor has been passed down from father to son or daughter through the generations."

"And *you* are this Protector, Signore Vadini?" Theo asked.

"It has been my great honor in life to care for *la tavoletta d'oro Merrezo*. And now these two tablets, as well."

"I do not wish to be rude," Theo continued with deference. "But how are we to know that you are this. . .*protector*, Signore? Is it an official title for the curator of a small museum?"

"Theo!" He might not think himself rude, but his words were confrontational.

Undaunted, Theo continued, "Are you thinking to remove the new tablets and keep them "under your protection"? No one here would permit such a thing. And I, as Minister of Antiquities, will not condone such a removal of what are three of Patagonia's national treasures. The tablets must stay here, where they all belong. *Together*."

"Of *course*, the tablets must remain *here*." The curator looked mildly affronted. "There is no dispute. It was prophesied by *Stellanera* tha-"

"*Stellanera?*" Finn sat up straight.

Clearly confused by the question, the curator frowned. "*Sí*. The seer, the child, his name was *Blackstar*."

Finn raised a brow, "*Blackstar?* Really?" He couldn't keep the skepticism out of his tone at the curator's purported "facts". He should just send Vadini on his way. But then he wasn't acting alone.

What kind of gullible idiot did they think he was? The more money Finn goddamn acquired, the more people presented complicated and parochial scams to him. All were meant to bilk him of his hard-earned money. It was fucking insulting, damn annoying, predictably boring, and a waste of his time.

Fools. If they'd done their homework, they'd know that everything he'd ever laid a dollar on-with the exception of his hobby of treasure hunting-was backed by cold, hard, scientific study.

Clearly thrown by the question, Vadini cast a puzzled glance at Bria, before addressing Finn again. "*Sí.* Is something wrong?"

Yeah, I'll play along another minute. Let everyone see the curator for the fraud he was. "You must be aware that *Blackstar* is the name of my ships," he kept his tone even. "It's also the name of my *company.*"

Goddamnit, he was not only *pissed* at this turn of events, Finn was *fucking* disappointed. The opportunity to learn more about the tablet had been exciting. Now he couldn't trust a word this guy said.

"*Sí.*" The curator gave him a slightly puzzled look. "I am aware of this. It is not a coincidence."

Finn waited a beat for the curator to say more, to make his case for the scam. He didn't.

"*Not* a coincidence? Come now, Dr. Vadini. Don't you think it seems farfetched in the extreme that a prophet from five hundred years ago just *happens* to have the same name as my ship and company?"

The old man smiled. "You do not believe in destiny, signore? There are many things beyond our understanding. We must take such things on faith, yes?"

"My faith is earned, Doctor, when there's logical reason. I've never heard of a prophet named Blackstar. I chose the name because I have business interests in space travel and the stars. Nothing more mystical."

Catching a glimpse of Bria's flushed cheeks, Finn softened his tone. "That said, although the romanticism of the tablets isn't lost on me, I need more. Do I believe this ancient story is really what happened? I suspect that, like the Bible, whatever story was written here, was a parable. Or passed down through time and distorted. A way to make whatever was happening at the time more palatable. We have to consider that the ancients were limited to the scope of legends and myths of their time, and were not *necessarily* a true account of the day. It's quite possible the tablets are works of fiction. Either as just that- fiction, or to explain away unexplainable phenomenon beyond their comprehension."

He loved the way Ariel nipped the corner of her full lower lip as she listened, the way her eyes lit up when she was fully engaging. Face alight, she said,. "A *parable.* Makes sense."

Or it was complete bullshit, and God only knew how much money this scammer had made off the Princess and her family over the years. Finn went with the latter. This old guy was trying to tie him to a so-called ancient prophecy in order to con him. Why, and what his long game was, he didn't know. Yet. But he wasn't willing to insult the Cutters by calling the guy out here and now.

He spared a glance at the others to see if they were buying any of this. The Cutters did 'poker face' extremely well.

Only Ariel seemed calm as she glanced at him with shining jade eyes. She was enjoying this. "Be nice," she whispered.

It wasn't as though he was being asked to write a check – yet. This was all a load of crap, and it annoyed the hell out of him that this fairytale of theirs was taking away from the very real historical significance of the tablet.

As a courtesy to Bria, Finn said, "Perhaps you confused the legacy with the name of my ship in some way?"

"No, signore. I did not," Vadini said, clearly affronted by the very suggestion. "Blackstar was the seer who wrote these prophecies on the tablets. His name has never been in dispute. Perhaps I should ask; -Why did you name your company after him?"

"I've never heard his name, and my company most definitely is not named after him. We have a room full of historians here, who spend their lives looking at ancient artifacts. Has anyone heard of an ancient prophet being identified as Blackstar? Anyone?"

"Can't say that I have," Logan said. "However, Doctor Vadini is a noted historian. The study of the legend, and the tablet, has been his life's work. If anyone would know, he's the one. It's worth considering."

Finn's bullshit barometer rose. He'd hold off accusing the Cutters of some sort of collusion until he knew more. Fuck. He liked them. Trusted them. Had called them friends for years. This was a turn of events he'd stopped considering many years ago. Now distrust was back on the fucking table, just as it had to be with almost everyone who crossed his path.

Vadini was *their* man, brought here by them.

Far-reaching conspiracy?

"I have indeed heard of this Blackstar. *Estrellanegra*, to Patagonians," Dr. Núñez said. "He was a prophet in ancient lore. It is said he was protected, not by a so-called *Protector*, but by a secret group named *el Elegidos.*"

"Not very secret if *you* know about it, Theo," Ariel said with a smile.. "So, we have the *Chosen* and the *Protectors*?" she continued, shifting so that her soft breasts brushed his arm. "It sounds like a superhero action movie."

"The Chosen were a small, dangerous, radical sect," the curator informed them. "It is said that they twisted Blackstar's predictions to suit their own nefarious purposes. Blackstar warned that the wheat harvest was tainted, and should not be eaten. These *Chosen* told the people of the village exactly the opposite, encouraging them to keep producing bread. They were told 'good people' would not suffer the afflictions. Because they were hungry, and gullible, they believed the interpretation of the self-proclaimed Chosen, and perished. Historians believe ergotism was the cause. Blackstar saw and predicted this."

"Ergot poisoning?" Nick asked.

Teal leaned forward to look around Zane. "What's ergot?"

"A fungus that infects cereals like rye and wheat. It's believed that long-term ergot poisoning occurred in Europe in the Middle Ages," Nick added. "Historians now believe ergot was responsible for the behavior of the so-called witches put to death in the Salem witch trials."

"I don't get it," Teal frowned. "If it was a poison, didn't they just die?"

"Not right away, unfortunately. It was also called Saint Anthony's Fire," Finn said. "I've heard of it. Pretty damn unpleasant way to die. An outbreak much more recently than the middle ages happened in the 50's. The French village of Pont-Saint-Esprit had half a dozen deaths from ergot poisoning, some claimed from eating bread made with infected rye."

"Blackstar predicted the people of his village would die from painful seizures, spasm, mania, psychosis. It affected people's nervous systems in these ways. Or the toxin caused dry gangrene. Black, dying skin, falling from the body." Vadini's fingers tightened on the arm of his chair as if he'd been there to witness such atrocities.

He was a good storyteller, Finn gave him that. He had everyone in the room riveted. Finn excluded. What was the end game to this elaborate hoax? Because there was one, he could practically smell it.

"He predicted another symptom of the ergot poisoning would be hallucinations followed by severe convulsions. . . It is said people went mad until they dropped dead in the streets."

Ariel shuddered. "Pretty graphic. Sounds like the plot to a particularly gruesome movie."

"Horrific," the curator said. "Because people refused to believe the predictions of a child, they died grotesque deaths. It wiped out three-quarters of the village. It was this fully realized prophesy that attracted the notice of our *profeta*, Foscari."

"Well, that's certainly an interesting story," Finn said. This was becoming more and more preposterous. An ancient prophecy. Two opposing factions. A child prophet. A slew of gruesome deaths? Ariel was right – it had the makings of a movie. But for him to believe any part of the high drama tale, there needed to be an explanation of the convenient coincidence of the seer's name being Blackstar.

"And you read all this on the Merrezo tablet? It's in Italian then?" It was hard to keep the skepticism from his voice.

"No, this is history passed down through many generations. The complete tablet has not yet been interpreted. It is in an ancient text long forgotten. Blackstar's people no longer exist. The group died out soon after the advent of the plague. A few men remained, protecting the seer. The story was lost after that. No one to carry it forward. The language died with them. I knew a few words only. I'm hoping that there are words or phrases on the other tablets that will help me interpret the first."

The old man looked up. The deep lines on his face more pronounced, his black eyes more deep-set and shadowed. "You do not have to believe for it to be a fact. It just is." Vadini seemed unconcerned by Finn's disbelief.

"It is indeed intriguing that you have named both your ships and your business by the seer's name." He leaned back in his seat and stared into Finn's eyes, much like he had stared at the tablet. "Perhaps you are part of the prophecy?"

Yeah, right. Here comes the crux of the scam. "I very much doubt that."

Vadini looked unperturbed. "I would like to rest before resuming this conversation, if I may? I would like to take these with me to study." He addressed the room in general, then looked at Finn for approval.

He knew which piper paid for the tune, smart man. Vadini smiled when Finn nodded his permission.

With a pointed look at Finn, Bria rose to her feet, clearly not happy with his skepticism toward her curator. "Of course. You must be absolutely exhausted after that long trip. Finn has a cabin prepared for you. Rest if you need. Darling, take the tablets please."

Nick waved over a couple of his T-FLAC buddies standing by the door. Two men broke off to take the tablets. The old man used Bria and Nick's arms to steady himself as he rose shakily to his feet.

"Now, with the three tablets together, I believe more will be revealed."

Yeah, I bet it will.

Finn was pleased he'd offered accommodation on board *Blackstar* to both the curator and the tablets. Here, he could keep them all under close scrutiny. The only reason he was permitting the removal of the tablets from the salon was because he had his own security on board. McCoy himself would be stationed outside the curator's cabin for the duration.

"I'll escort my guest to his cabin." Bria stroked a hand over her stomach as she got to her feet. "No, everyone stays here. These gentlemen will accompany us."

"That was an eye-opener," Logan said, after they took the tablets and left, escorted by the T-FLAC operatives.

"You think the seer's name was *really* Blackstar?" Zane asked his oldest brother. He sounded as dubious as Finn felt.

Logan shrugged. "Guess we'll find out tomorrow. We should put out word to see if any of the locals know this ancient language."

"I have studied this language," Dr. Núñez said. "There is not much written word about it, and of course it died out hundreds of years ago. But I have read what little there is. Many, many times," he offered. "I would be more than happy to lend my expertise. Perhaps I might spend some time with the tablets while the curator rests?"

"You're welcome to stay on board for a few days and work with Vadini," Finn offered. He didn't care for Núñez. Wasn't sure if that was because it was clear he and Ariel had a history, or if his gut was giving him a warning. He figured both.

"Vadini has the tablets for the night. The two of you can confer in the morning?" Finn phrased it as a question. Núñez, too, would have scrutiny for the duration. Rather the devils you know, than the devils you don't. Right now, Finn was calling bullshit on all of them.

"Sounds like a plan." Logan pushed off the sofa. "I'll put out a call for anyone familiar with this ancient language. See if we can find several people to work on the text with you, Dr. Núñez and with Dr. Vadini. Don't know about the rest of you, but I have diving to do before dark. Reconvene here tomorrow?"

Dark wasn't for at least another six hours. "Lunch. Noon." Finn agreed, also getting to his feet, and holding his hand out for Ariel. In the meantime, he'd set his entire team on researching Vadini, Ariel Andersen, the Cutters, and *la tavoletta d'oro Merrezo.*

Something stank in Denmark.

His expression hard and unreadable, Finn took Peri by the hand. "We have a thing," he addressed the room at large. "See you all tomorrow."

Peri kept up with his longer strides as he exited the salon and headed for the stairs at a fast clip. She tugged her wrist free of the shackle of his fingers. She would not be led around like a tug toy. If anything, she'd participate. "What thing?"

His fingers tightened between hers, not too tightly. He was pissed, but luckily for him, not aggressive. If the situation changed, she'd kick him in the balls and make a run for it. She hoped it wouldn't come to that because she still had things she wanted to do to those balls. And the rest of him for that matter.

"*Many* things."

They were heading to the interior of the ship, so she figured he wasn't planning to throw her overboard. At least not today. The chemistry between them arced and sizzled, so there was a pretty good chance she'd have sex with him any minute now.

The highly polished wood floors on *Blackstar* were a deep, rich black, African walnut. The walls a soft gray paper, on which hung his priceless, original paintings.

She'd never seen this part of the ship, but unfortunately, they were moving at the speed of sound so she couldn't appreciate it. She didn't have time to admire the large, colorful canvases, or the stunning artifacts and objets d'art, along the way as they moved down a long corridor. She had to lengthen her stride to match his since he wasn't allowing for her shorter legs. Apparently, he was on a mission and clearly wanted to get wherever they were going in a hurry.

She did mad like a volcano, a quick blow up, over quickly. Finn's mad was simmering water. It bubbled under the surface, and she didn't know him well enough to determine if or when it was in danger of boiling over.

Slanting a glance up at him, the grim set of his jaw and glittering eyes didn't bode well. She guessed she was about to discover his flashpoint.

"That was pretty abrupt." She tried uncoupling her fingers from his. "I don't think they finished their coffee."

Giving her a hard look, he tightened his fingers around hers. "Don't," he warned, urging her forward.

"Don't what? Escape? Make a run for it?"

"Push me."

"*What* thing?" She repeated the question she'd asked moments ago.

He maneuvered her up curved, beautifully polished stairs, his large hand engulfing hers. "You really need to ask?"

"I don't want to presume," she said with false meekness.

His lips twitched. "Jesus, you're a piece of work."

"Thank you."

He shook his head. "Hold your thoughts until we get to my cabin. Can you do that?"

Peri saluted.

The owner's cabin was one flight up, which took no time at the fast clip they were going. "Do we really need to travel at warp speed?" Her heart pounded as hard as if she'd just run a marathon.

"If I could perfect teleporting, we'd be there already."

"*Perfect*? You mean you-"

He used his thumbprint to open the door. "Inside," he bit off.

She went ahead of him into the sun-flooded cabin. He shut the door behind her with a portentous thud. Peri got a quick impression of blinding white before he swung her around to face him.

With a slitty-eyed look, she shook his hand free from her upper arm. The attitude was all for show. "We really need to have a serious conversation about your grabby han—" Her eyes went wide when she saw his taut expression and the tightness of his jaw.

When he raised his hand, Peri flinched, and shied away. "Hit me, and you'll have no balls. And just an FYI? I'm *not* having sex with you if you're angry about something. And especially if, for some reason, you're pissed off at *me* about something. Because your temper was crawling up to the red zone in there, and I want to know why."

"What?!" he looked appalled, which saved his future progeny. "I'm not pissed at *you*. I was digesting what the Italian was trying to sell." Taking a deep controlling breath, he ground out, "But for the moment, forget all that bullshit. I'm about to kiss you until neither of us can think straight, *macushla*."

She presumed that meant something like, sweetheart. Or possibly pain in the ass.

With one large hand cupping the back of her head, the other cupping her butt, he pulled her into a tight embrace, lifting her onto her toes. Their hips were in perfect alignment.

He had a hard-on. A *hard,* hard-on.

How could he be so hard all over and kiss her so softly? The temperature in the room spiked as Peri's body reacted instantly. Nipples tingling, she was already wet and ready for him. She was in a constant state of semi-arousal when he was near her.

The tension left her body, and she melted into him. Curling her arms around his neck, she was surrounded by his heat and the strength of his arms. Parting her lips, she kissed him with everything she had. Teeth, tongue, heat and heart. She didn't care about anything but the taste, the feel, the hot smell of his skin.

Hard hands gripped her butt, urging her impossibly closer.

The barest touch, a heated look, and she was turned on. Wet for him. She'd been aroused for *hours*.

He smelled of ocean breezes and sultry male and her broken heart. Illogically, he also smelled of hope and salvation. Maybe that was because she was desperate for a life-raft at this point.

Torn, she debated telling him everything now. To get it over with and take whatever happened next. But she reminded herself this man could crush her with a few simple words to the right people. Or a few simple words to the *wrong* people.

She was at the top of the highest diving board, and it was a long way down. Burying her face in his neck, she inhaled the unique scent of his skin. Memorized it.

He'd hear what she had to say when she told the Cutters. By then she'd be ready to leave anyway.

Liar. Angling his head, he took her mouth in another kiss that sucked every thought from Peri's brain. She was all shimmering sunlight through her lids, Finn's hot avid mouth, and his marauding tongue. His hands were all over her, stripping her out of her shorts-

"Bloody hell. You sat there that entire time with no goddamn *underwear* on?" The glitter in his eyes promised delicious retribution.

"I was in a hur-Oh!" She landed on her back, Finn between her legs. Warm sunlight bounced off the white comforter and made his tanned skin look lickable. He still wore his jeans, but his chest was bare. She looked up at him, committing his face to memory—the way his jaw clenched and his eyes turned pure silver when he was turned on. Peri curled her fingers around his biceps, with no idea when he'd stripped off his shirt. She was grateful she didn't have to rip it off with her teeth, because her mouth was otherwise engaged.

She stuck out her tongue to taste his shoulder. Ocean. Taking a little nip, she ran her hand up his chest, rough hair, smooth skin. Scoring his pecs lightly with her nails, she painted a path across his collarbone with her tongue. Her free hand was busily trying to pull down a zipper impeded by his erection and the fact that said erection was deliciously pressed between them. "A little help here."

With his hands on her hips, he rolled her over until she lay on top of him. Nothing soft about him. As a bed, he was the equivalent of sleeping on a cement floor. "That doesn't solve the problem-"

He lifted her over him with both hands, fingers digging into her waist. "Straddle me on your knees. Yeah, like that. Now lift up."

Bridging his body on her spread knees, Peri was very conscious that she still wore her t-shirt and bra, and that her lower half was bare and open to his gaze.

Sliding his hands up her sides, Finn eased her t-shirt up and over her head. It landed somewhere on the floor.

"Later, I'm going to spend time exploring every freckle," he murmured, his voice husky as he ran a finger up and over the swells of both breasts.

Reaching behind her with both hands, Peri slowly undid the clasp of her sheer, white El Beso bra. The gleam of appreciation in Finn's eyes made what she'd paid for the barely there scrap of silk and lace worth every penny.

Tossing the bra aside, Peri arched her back as he cupped both breasts. "Beautiful." Finn traced his finger-tips down the slope of each breast, then ran his thumbs over her aching nipples. She loved the feel of his big hands on her. Loved that he took his time to learn her.

"I love how your skin looks as if you've been dusted with cinnamon. An infinite cinnamon Galaxy worth deep, and lengthy exploration."

"Poetic." It was. She smiled. "But I'm naked."

"Something I'm incredibly grateful for. I'll remedy my being overdressed right now."

Bracing both hands on his taut abs, she admired the view as he shoved his jeans and underwear down. His penis sprang up.

Reaching between them, she wrapped her fingers around the thick length, using her thumb to spread the silky drop of liquid around the head.

A slow smile lit his features. Damn it, he had *the* best smile. And the best body. And the best- *Everything*. "Now who's being grabby?" he said, voice thick.

"I don't like leaving a job unfinished," she told him with gravity. "But I'll stop if you insist."

With a devilish gleam in his eyes, Finn stacked his hands under his head. "Have at it, or—?"

He moved faster than she could blink twice, and finished shoving his jeans all the way off, shifting in her hand.

Their faces were inches apart. His eyes glittered with lust as he reached up to weave his fingers in her hair, allowing it to spill over his naked chest.

She asked, "Or?"

"Or *now*. Either, later." Sunlight flooding the room through the large windows turned her hair to liquid fire as it pooled across his belly. Wrapping his hand in the long strands, he pulled her down for a kiss that melted her from the inside out. When he lifted his head, Peri's unfocused eyes couldn't quite read his expression.

"Now." Barely able to breathe, she clenched his hair in her fist, pulling his head down so she could kiss him with everything in her. *I love you I love you I love you.*

"I've waited for this for what seems a lifetime. You, a bed, *time*. Guide me home, darling." She positioned his penis at her damp entrance and he said, teeth clenched, "I can't get enough of you, Persephone."

His abs contracted as he pushed inside her, thick and hard. A moan tore from her throat as the walls of her vagina clenched around him. Their combined heartbeats throbbed deep inside her, as waves of intense pleasure flooded through every cell in her body. Arching, she surged and took him deeper.

Their hips moved in counterpoint. Digging her nails into his shoulders, she luxuriated in the power of every thrust. His arms tightened around her when she curled her legs around his hips and held on for a wild ride.

Tightening and flexing internal muscles she massaged him, pulled him deeper, made him groan against the side of her sweaty neck.

Heat shot through her, as he used his teeth to score the tender skin of her throat. Dear God, he was part of every nerve ending, every beat of her heart, the essential core that gave her life. The thick length of him penetrating to her very heart. Peri felt sharp, sweet pleasure that gripped her, quivering, on the edge. She held momentarily still and was rewarded with his shudders as he strained to hold back before pulling out slightly. Waiting for her?

Peri gave a little arch of her hips, and he resumed pumping into her.

Lifting his head to look down at their joined bodies, he murmured with pleasure. "You fulfil every one of my fantasies, Persephone."

"If. . .you. . . can talk. . .we're not doing this. . .right."

The warmth of his chuckle deep inside her body was pure sunlight.

The sound of their sweaty skin sticking and releasing, as their hips slapped, accompanied their muffled pants and groans in the quiet room.

This was everything.

He was everything.

She loved the feel of him inside her, hard and full, pulsing and alive as they strained together.

She wanted to store away the memory of each stroke, every touch, every look from his silvery eyes. But she was too caught up in the immediacy.

Their climax came in a series of never-ending tsunamis that left her shuddering, limp, and breathing heavily.

It was at least fifteen minutes before she was able to move. Finn's body wasn't that uncomfortable, after all. And what she thought had been a climax for him wasn't necessarily the end of this interlude. Not from the feel of him, deep inside. Hardening. Lengthening.

"I'm glued to you by my hair." Sweat stuck the strands to their skin, binding them together.

"Don't move," he murmured against her temple. "I like us just the way we are.

"So do I," she whispered.

"Tied together. Me. Inside of you. I could die like this. And die happy."

She smiled. "My thought. Exactly."

Hands on her hips, he started moving again, gently sliding in and out. He pushed a damp swath of hair off her face and gently kissed her swollen mouth, then began moving inside of her again. Each stroke heightened the already sensitive tissue. Peri tightened her crossed ankles in the small of his back. The slow, measured strokes were deceptive—their shared climax unraveled with the intensity of a tightly wound clock.

Gasping, shaking, sweaty and exhausted they lay together in the bright sunlight on his big white bed in a tangle of arms and legs. Finn was still semi-aroused inside her. He was a big man, and she should feel uncomfortable, but she liked the feel of him filling her.

He stroked her hip, a long, slow glide with his palm. "That should last us half an hour or so." Peri smiled. "That long? Didn't take your vitamins this morning?"

"I just did, darling." He pulled her tighter against him. "You're all the vitamins I need." He sucked on her bottom lip and hummed his satisfaction, closed his eyes and rested his forehead against the side of her cheek.

For several minutes, they lay there, not moving in the dreamy world of contentment. Not talking. Their breath syncopated as precisely as their heartbeats and, their thoughts. He was right- they could die like this... happy. She sighed, feeling sappy and perfectly content. She was not going to ruin this moment by spilling her guts.

"Now, tell me if you have anything to do with the *tavoletta d'oro Merrezo,* Signore Vadini and the Cutters and the bullshit story they're spinning?"

"Fuck you." Weren't the words she'd thought she'd say after making love.

THIRTEEN

Peri sat up, curling her legs beneath her butt, her hair covering her nakedness. "I have zero to do with either, and I freaking resent you making yet another unsubstantiated accusation." It hurt that he didn't know her by now. Then she realized how ridiculous that assumption was. He knew her body. Why couldn't that be enough?

"Why do you think the Cutters and Vadini are in cahoots and doing something nefarious? Is suspicion your default? It must be exhausting."

Finn reached over to arrange her hair to his liking. His liking had her nipples poking through the tangled strands. "You have no idea why Vadini is claiming that this seer had the same name as my business?"

He wasn't the least bit uncomfortable sitting there stark naked with the streaming sun burnishing his body. There was not a single damned freckle on all that toned, tanned, lickable skin. There was absolutely no point angsting over things she couldn't change, and she refused to spoil this time together by being hurt that he didn't trust her. He had every right to feel the way he felt. She was the freaking *last* person to try to convince him that not everyone had an ulterior motive.

"No. But it *was* weird and off the wall."

"More than." He played with her hair, running it over and around his hand, as if the strands were a string of worry beads.

Peri was fine with his seeming obsession with her hair. Any way he touched her was perfect. She'd happily have his hands on her 24/7.

"Can you look me in the eye and swear you're not in collusion with Vadini and the Cutters?" He gave her a piercing look, clearly gauging her sincerity.

"Geez, give it up already, Finn! I have nothing to hide." In that regard. But, her heart did a little flippy thing that reminded her there were other things she *was* hiding from the others, and by necessity, Finn too. She recognized her physical response was because she was growing more and more uncomfortable with keeping secrets from him – not so much the Cutters-although that was changing.

Damn it. She respected Finn. She trusted him. A lot. She liked him. A lot. Self-preservation had her falling back on what she'd always done – kept her own counsel. "I told you no, don't ask me again. Do you think that sweet little man and the Cutters are trying to con you?"

"Not sure." He'd find out, Peri knew, unnerved now that the time of reckoning had reached defcon two and a half for *her* situation. Finn suspecting the Cutters were also up to something nefarious was almost a relief. She felt crappy *liking* them. Now she could go back to hating them, because as sure as God made little fishes they were going to hate *her.*

And sue her ass, *and* probably make her walk the metaphorical freaking plank.

She shivered.

"Cold?"

She slid her palm up his thigh. "Hot."

"Are you now?" Finn's tone reflected the confidence that came with being a male who was dominant in all he surveyed and confident in his place in the world. He shoved her pillow under his back, then pulled her down, and against his side. His skin was warm. The strength of his arms alone was seductive. Peri buried her nose against his chest, inhaling the scent she was becoming addicted to. Storing it up for later.

"I'll get to the bottom of it." He picked up her hand and moved it to his chest. "Talk to me," he murmured against the top of her head. "Tell me what thirteen-year-old Ariel was like."

Thirteen-year-old Ariel had never existed. "Angry," she admitted, combing her fingers through the damp, wiry hair on his chest. "Lonely. But mostly angry."

"At your father?" Finn brushed his lips over her temple.

"Most definitely *him.* My mother. My middle brother for being sick, and for sucking up all the attention, which in turn made me feel like shit for being that selfish. My oldest brother because he was always preoccupied with money, and he travelled a lot. My friend from next door because she was sweet and even-tempered, and everyone loved *her.* I was angry at everyone around me. I had a hell of a temper, and unleashed it at the drop of a hat."

"What a surprise," he said dryly.

She pulled his hair. "I eventually learned to control it- somewhat. After my middle brother died, I really lost it. My oldest brother forced me into counseling for a while. It helped. Staying away from people who annoy me helps, too.

Finn laughed. "I'll take that under advisement."

"Salvaging turned out to be my salvation. I love it, and I was good at it, and I made a lot of money doing it. I was independent and self-sufficient."

"And no one can bug you underwater."

She smiled. "That too. Did working on computers have something to do with all the things you've invested in over the years?"

"Probably. But I always wanted to know how things worked, so I was forever taking something apart. Strangely enough," his lips tilted, "people didn't particularly like their televisions dismantled, or their refrigerator in pieces because I needed the cooling element for some invention I was working on. At least fixing computers kept me focused and productive. I was much of a handful. To say that I was hyperactive was an understatement.

And I was a bit of a smartass. Couldn't comprehend why people didn't understand me." He paused, then said quietly, "And it was because I knew people didn't give a damn to look, other than surface deep, I learned to control how my emotions appeared to other people."

"You don't have to hide them from me."

"You thought I was going to *strike* you."

"I wasn't going to make love if you were angry at me."

"I wasn't." Eyes tender, he brushed her cheek. "I'll never hurt you, Persephone. *Ever.* You can take that to the bank."

No, I'll hurt myself for loving you. "Good, then issue resolved," she said with a smile that hurt her heart. "Back to your life of demolition."

"My life of demolition and my "attitude" made me "difficult to place", is how they put it."

She knew better than to offer sympathy, but her heart pinched for him. "Were you close to anyone in foster care?"

"I stayed in one home for almost a year in my early teens. Their son, Derry and I were the same age and we became fast friends. We ran wild, I was sent packing after he was caught shoplifting and thrown into juvie, but we stayed in touch over the years. Old Derry was a con man of the first order. I was just too stupid to see it then. When I went to the States to make my fortune, Derry joined me after he got out. I was glad to see him. Considered him my brother. That boy-o had a sharp mind. He always had a wad of cash in his pocket and a ruddy smile on his face. I was working round the clock. Happy to have my best mate with me. I never asked where he got money or why he always looked smug."

Peri had a feeling she knew what was coming. "Did he cheat you?"

"We went into business together- investing in the stock market. We made good money."

"It wasn't 'good money'." With a smile, Peri nudged him in the ribs. "It was a *million dollars* and you were seventeen."

"Luck. Hard work. Determination to make my stamp."

"You did that and more. Is that why you got a divorce? You were a workaholic?"

"You know about that, do you?"

"I looked you up after we ran into each other again at the party," she admitted. "She was beautiful, in a cold, frosty way. You were sexy and enigmatic. Some fancy do in Monte Carlo, you looked amazing together." Finn tall and dark and serious, and the elegant blond smiling at the camera. His wife had a sneaky look – the smile in her red glossy lips hadn't made it to her eyes. "You were quite the catch."

"Money will do that," he said dryly. "I had Derry as my business partner and Erica on my arm. I was cock-a-hoop. It never occurred to me to have Derry's background checked when he showed up out of the blue. I'd discovered shortly after he arrived that he'd been arrested in Ireland for a bank scam. I warned him I wouldn't tolerate crooked business dealings. And he swore he was straight." His voice deepened. A muscle in his jaw twitched.

"Fast forward ten years, and I knew Derry was skimming money out of our company. Small amounts at first, and then he got bold and I couldn't ignore it anymore. He didn't have to steal it. I would've given it freely. I put the money back in, gave him another warning. He was contrite. Swore he'd never do it again."

I don't give second chances. "But he did?"

"Hell yeah. He went to the bank where we had our accounts, set out doctored deposit slips, and rerouted people's money into an offshore account just as he'd done back home." Finn lifted an arm behind his head. The action caused the tightly coiled muscles in his core to pull taut against his tanned skin. Peri couldn't resist, she began tracing her fingernail across the corded muscle.

"At the time my marriage was going downhill fast. I was never home. I was having Erica followed because I suspected she was having an affair. She was. With Derry. Lucky me, I got a two for one. I was one of many who prosecuted him for the bank fraud. He was put away for fifteen years. Erica didn't do as well in the divorce settlement as she'd hoped. Derry and Erica were the last two to successfully scam me."

His slate gray eyes showed his bitterness. "Though many have tried. I've not tolerated liars and cheats since. It isn't the money, it's the bloody principle of the thing. Moral integrity is everything. If the Cutters are trying to scam me, I'll prosecute to the full extent of the law."

And there you have it. No second chances. Peri got it. Loud and clear.

Mid-afternoon, after a quick call to his P.A to see if there was anything that urgently needed his attention, Finn cancelled everything on his crowded agenda and turned his phone off again.

He *never* turned off his phone. Only a few trusted business associates had his private number, and everything else went through his staff. But with his business interests Worldwide, he typically fielded calls at all hours of the day and night. If he got at least four hours sleep a night, he was good to go.

"Come on," she lightly slapped his stomach as she sat up. "Let's do something."

Sifting his fingers through her hair, tangled down her back, he smiled. "The last couple of hours of calisthenics didn't do it? Clearly, I need one of those awful energy drinks."

"You don't need an energy boost at all. Different kind of exercise."

"There's a fully equipped gym down the hall or a track for running if you're feeling that energetic."

"I want to *dive*." She patted his belly, then lingered, trailing her fingertips over his abs. 'There are four wrecks down there, and two of them have given up a tablet. Maybe we can find *more*. Rise and shine, buddy. With one from *Napolitano*, and yours from *Nuestra Señora del Marco*, aren't you even a little bit curious to see if the *Santa Ana* and *El Crucifijo* carried their own tablets? Wouldn't it be awesome if we found *more*?"

Yeah, it would. "Dr. Vadini might not be able to take much more much excitement." Finn sat up. "He and your Dr. Núñez, are in the salon working with the tablets we have. Let's leave them to it. Logan's diving now. Let's see if he'd like another pair of hands."

"Theo's not my anything." She slanted him a look under her lashes. "I can say, with great authority, that your pair are deft and dexterous."

He was rapidly learning her nonlinear thoughts. "Pair of hands?"

Her eyes lit up devilishly. "Those, too."

Seventy-two minutes later, after showering, making love again-several times, a second shower and getting dressed, they went down to the dive platform.

"I shouldn't be taking another day off, you know," Ariel said as they emerged into the sunshine. "I *do* have a job."

She wore a purple t-shirt over her bikini, and her long, bare legs went on for miles. She'd scooped up her hair, and pinned it haphazardly on top of her head, leaving the vulnerable nape of her neck exposed and begging to be kissed. Jesus. He had it bad. Finn couldn't figure out how it was possible to want her again, when muscles he didn't know he had, ached from their marathon love-making session.

When he was with her he was insatiable. "You can take inventory on Logan's ship while we're there," he said, somehow managing to keep his hands off her. If he didn't, they'd be back in his cabin, horizontal again. Since he wore just his black swim trunks, he shifted to rearrange his erection.

"I will-" Her eyes lit up. "Oh, yeah! *Now* we're talking."

Instead of the runabout, Finn had ordered a crew member to bring out two jet skis.

Finn grinned as she peeled out of her t-shirt to expose the white bikini he'd tried to remove the minute she'd put it on. She was all sleek muscles and golden skin. He loved the look of her in the sunlight. Even though she was lightly tanned, the cinnamon dusting of freckles all over her body looked as if he could sweep them up in his hands.

Four members of his dive team were just emerging from the water. "Give me a minute," he told her, glad to have something to distract him even for just a few minutes. "Want to go over there and get us a couple of suits? We can use Logan's tanks."

While she went to the nearby rack to find a drysuit, he caught up with what his team had found in the last few hours. Coins, a few small pieces, but nothing to write home about.

"All set?" Finn helped her stash their stuff in the jet ski, then showed her the controls before they set off.

The water had a bit of a chop, and the spray felt good on his warm skin. Hell, he felt damn good with her beside him. Her hair had unraveled and was whipping in the wind. She threw back her head and laughed at the wind, and Finn almost ran into her jet ski because his brain settled into his groin looking at her. No. His brain went directly to his heart and set it tripping.

They made good time to the *Sea Wolf.*

Several men were already suited up, and getting their tanks as they arrived. Logan and two other guys Finn recognized had clearly just returned from their dive.

Bobbing on the water, several dozen buoys, in various colors, marked datum points, and the locations of found artifacts.

Logan was peeling down the top of his drysuit as they pulled up to his platform, his dog stood beside him, hackles raised. The salt and pepper wolf/Alsatian was fiercely protective of his master and had the run of his ship. He gave a low warning growl that deepened as they got closer. One hand on the large dog's head, quieted him. Logan shaded his eyes as Finn and Peri tied off the skis to the stern. "Problem?"

"No." Finn held out his hand to help Ariel board. "We thought we could lend another pair of hands. See if we can help you find another tablet."

Logan shrugged. "You're more than welcome to go down with Galt and Earl here. But keep in mind, just because two have been found doesn't mean there are others."

"Nothing ventured nothing gained." Finn visually pinned Jed Jones in place as the diver slicked back his wet blond hair with both hands and watched Ariel like any red-blooded male would as she pulled on her drysuit. Bastard was preening for her, and he'd just seen them arrive. *Tofuckinggether.*

Finn nudged her hand out of the way and finished pulling up her zipper, lingering as he got to her breasts. *Mine.*

"The sidescan sonar and swath bathymetry have been completed, and we've already run the lines and set up a couple of grids. More as we go. I've reached my no- decompression limit for the morning, so I can't join you. Stay as long as you like. The viz is about seventy-five feet, so you'll have a good idea of the scope of the wreck. The pieces stayed relatively close together as you'll see. Check out Nick's grid, he'll be down later. Just an FYI," his eyes twinkled, but he didn't smile. "The face mask's mics are set to channel 2. If you want your convo private, switch to 4 right here." He showed Finn how to adjust the channel on the outside of the mask. "Have fun and stay out of trouble. Come on, Buoy."

Dog and man disappeared inside. Jones and the other diver settled into chairs, and what looked like an unfinished card game.

"Ready to rock and roll?" Earl asked, dropping down to sit on the edge of the platform, legs dangling as he adjusted a strap on his tank. He'd been on Logan's dive crew for years, Finn had met him several times. Nice guy, mid-fifties, didn't talk much.

He'd met the second guy, Steve Galt as well. Steve was a giant, towering over Finn's six four. He held out a ham-sized hand for Finn to shake, and grinned with big white teeth at Ariel, who eyed him warily as he said, "Let's go find us another tablet."

Due to the angle of the mid-afternoon sun, the water was the pale aqua of translucent jade, with visibility of about seventy-five feet. Perfect diving conditions. The integrated dive masks they all wore had 2nd stage regulators, and low-pressure hoses, which eliminated fogging and reduced CO and CO2 buildup. Adjustable head straps, attached to the face shield, made fit secure and comfortable. The built-in mics facilitated communication underwater.

Peri loved to dive, and sharing the experience with Finn made it that much sweeter. She loved the anticipation that had her blood racing pleasantly. Loved the sense of weightlessness and the rush of the water around her body, as much as she loved the endless aqua underwater and the thrill of new discoveries.

"This is what it must be like in space, huh?" she spoke into her mask mic as she followed Logan's divers, Finn beside her.

"Similar, but not really," his voice was pleasant in her ear and had the power to make her heart beat a little faster. She wondered if they should just switch to channel 4 now and avoid embarrassment. Cocking a brow, she held up four fingers to Finn.

He smiled as he shook his head. "Gravity comes into play under water. In space, there's zero gravity. But our astronauts train in deep water simulators to get used to weightlessness."

"I'll be ready for my flight to Mars, then," she told him, then jackknifed down to join the others. The idea of going into space, of being a pioneer, was appealing. Especially since space might be her final frontier if the Cutters decided to press charges. Charges in every country where she'd helped herself to their goodies. Might as well enjoy her freedom while it lasted.

"We do have some grids on the northeast sector behind the wreck- the debris fields over there are more contained," Steve The Giant's voice sounded like gravel in a cement mixer through the helmet mic. "But, since this field is so large, we used these chains, and the buoys on the datum points on the wreck, to form a triangle."

"I've never seen this done," Finn told him, eyeing the multiple links from the wreck to the surface. "I've only been on salvages where the grids were used. So, the artifacts are located by noting the compass bearing on the azimuth circle and measuring the datum point to the artifact?"

"You've done your homework." Steve grinned behind his mask. "More expedient doing it this way on a wreck of this size. Although we'll be laying more grids as well over the next few weeks. See that big grid down there on your right?" He pointed. "That area has proven artifact-rich. Nick's working that area personally, Logan's area is over there. He's diving with the *Decrepit* team with Zane and Jonah on the *Santa Ana* this afternoon. You do know that if you look up the word 'competitive' it shows a picture of the four Cutters, right? They've taken it to an art form." His laugh boomed through Peri's comm. "Man, it's a real pleasure to watch. Come on, we're over there-" He pointed to the remnants of the stern.

"No need to stick with us," Finn told the men. "We'll be happy looking around on our own."

"Sure?"

"Yeah. Forty minutes?"

They agreed and swam off. Finn set his dive watch, then held out his hand to her. "Let's take a look at this old girl."

Gliding through the water with him beside her, Peri had never felt more at peace. It was to be short lived she knew. But for right now, everything was right with her world.

The carrack, *El Crucifijo,* lay on her side, broken in two. They swam up and down her seventy-five-foot length, accompanied by a curious tarpon, trailing them like an inquisitive puppy.

In her mind's eye, she envisioned the four-masted ship, square sails puffed by the wind skimming across the water. The two high castles, bow and stern, hampered their sailing speed, but that was the design of the day for ships used for exploration and trade. It must've been quite a sight to see the four ships skimming over the water together.

They swam under a length of chain with several numbered markers on it. Went down low over the wreck, which had once sported a square sail rig mounted onto horizontal wooden spars perpendicular to the keel. Broken off like a twig, the main mast lay intact on the sandy bottom, fifty feet from the wreck.

"This would've been the aftcastle." Holding onto a chain, Peri pointed to a large pile of shattered wood, spread over a twenty-foot radius on the rocky sand. "They steered the ship from here. I wonder if they found the wheel?"

"How the hell do you know what that was?" Finn eyed the ragged pile of chunks of wood; broken planks, decking and the flotsam and jetsam of a shipwreck. "It's completely unrecognizable."

Not to her it wasn't, but then this was her life, not Finn's. His head was in space, not underwater. While she barely knew Andromeda from- "What's the name of a star starting with the letter Z?"

" Zubenelakrab? Zaniah? Are you doing a crossword puzzle in your head?"

"I know shipwrecks, you know stars." She paused to throw him a sassy glance through her mask. "I *presume* those are stars and not gibberish words you just made up?"

A small outcropping of rough rocks held algae and tufts of dark green seaweed, which swayed with their movement as they passed. Peri put her hand on a rocky formation covered with tractor bank mussels, letting a fearless sea cucumber crawl across her palm. "I can identify what's what because of the location, and those small cannons nearby. The aftcastle would've had a platform used to mount attacks on anyone trying to board."

She used her hands to draw a picture in the water, dislodging the sea cucumber, and scattering a few tiny brown fish nearby. Particulates swirled around her.

Tempted to stay and explore, she resumed swimming, eyes scanning the seabed. Looking for anything, everything of interest. Artifacts, pinpointed by numbered markers connected to the chains, protruded from the sand- a small cannon, more pieces of wood, but she didn't linger to see what else was in the area.

"She was really used as a long-range cargo ship, more than the warship the carracks would become later." The built-in headset was awesome, even though her voice sounded as if it was coming through an echo chamber. Still, better than not sharing this moment in real time with Finn. Hand gestures only went so far.

"Our four ships were fast and small. Still at least forty-fifty people must've died on each of them when they sank. There's no record of anyone making it to shore."

Finn lifted a chain so she could pass under it. "You really love this, don't you?"

"Diving? Ships? History? Yeah. I live for this stuff. I wonder if they knew what they came south for?" Peri swam down to run her hand along the length of a brass cannon, looked up, caught Finn's salacious grin, and shook her head. "One track mind, Gallaher. Do you think the captains of *Napolitano* and *Nuestra Señora del Marco knew* they carried the tablets? Or were they just ordered to come here, without knowing what it was they'd been sent to collect?"

"We'll never know. The hope is each of the four ships carried a tablet. Maybe together they'll tell us something."

Peri mentally crossed her fingers. "The hope is *we* find one right *here*."

"It'll still belong to the Cutters."

"It'll still be part of history, and connected to our tablets. No matter what they choose to do with it."

"Jesus." He stopped swimming to look at her. "You don't plan on *swiping* it, do you?"

Since he didn't sound too worried about it, Peri smiled and rocked her hand.

He shut his eyes behind his mask. "You'll be the death of me, woman."

She smiled. "But what a way to go."

The water was so clear, she could see the tiny crabs scurry along the white sand, and a pink starfish scaling a rock. "Come on, I see the forecastle over there." She indicated a slightly less broken section, where she could see the window opening, and a curve of deck still intact. "That's where they kept all their war toys. It made navigation a bit tricky because it caused the ship to be a bit top heavy- Oh, wow!" She saw another cannon on the sandy bottom and darted off.

Jack-knifing to dive low, she trusted Finn to follow. "I love finding the cannons. Look at this beauty."

Finn shook his head. "I'd appreciate it if you didn't stroke that thing like you mean it." He wrapped his arm around her waist and tugged her against his body. "You look sexy as hell in this drysuit. I'm so damned hot for you I'm surprised the water around us isn't boiling. You have no idea how badly I want you right now."

She didn't give a damn if the man in the Moon was listening in. "Do you think- "

"No," Finn laughed, taking her hand to twirl her around in the water as if she were a salsa dancer. "But later, when the probability of drowning in your arms is no longer an issue." He pulled her back into his arms. "Then not just yes, but hell yes."

Despite the cumbersome tanks, two drysuits, and the buoyancy of the water, she felt the same urgent need she saw in his silvery eyes. Peri gave a dramatic sigh. "Can't cross that off my bucket list then. Too bad. Okay." She kissed her fingers through her mask, then pressed them to his mask over his lips.

"Since there's no one working there right now," she said, indicating to the large grid on the port side of the wreck, "let's go play in Nick's sandbox."

On arriving at the edge of the grid they removed their fins, securing them on the post installed there for just that purpose. Then using the fixed position of the white, PVC pipes, spaced thirty inches apart, they pulled themselves hand-over-hand horizontally over the area.

"Be here. Be here. Be here," she whispered as she glided over the squares, the white sand rippling beneath them in their slipstream.

"It probably won't be," Finn cautioned, proving he had ears like a freaking bat. His attention was fixed, as was hers, on the area below him. "We have no indication that there might be more tablets, remember that."

"I'm going to find one here. *Today*," she said, determined. If this was to be her last hurrah, then damn it, she wanted to go out with a bang.

Seeing an intriguing bump in the sand, and keeping her movements slow and small, Peri sifted a finger through the shimmery grains. Even so, particles drifted up around her arm. Motionless she waited for them to settle. "And it mig- Holy crap! Finn. Look at *this*."

Coming alongside her, he closed the gap, hooking his ankles on the pipe to remain in place. "Could be anything- "

She withdrew her clenched fist. "Or it could be a giant, whopping freaking *emerald*." She opened her fingers to expose the apricot-sized green stone.

Finn was already sifting sand between his fingers. Looking for more. "Could just be part of the cargo- "

"*Could* indicate the chest holding the tablet. . ." She toed her way, hand-over-hand to the next opening, finger-combing the sand. "How close were the emeralds to your tablet? Mine on *Napolitano* were maybe a foot awa—"

Everything inside her stopped. Could it be? Was it. . .? The water around them became cloudy as she dug like a terrier after a juicy bone. "I found another one. Finn. . .I think- God, I *hope*- this is the corner of another tablet."

Finn put his hand on her wrist. "Slow down, you're stirring up the silt."

Her insides jumping around with excitement, Peri forced herself to freeze in place. "Damn I want to move fast, and I know we have to take this slow." The suspended particles seemed to take a lifetime as she waited for them to drift back to the seabed.

"Steady does it." His hands joined hers, and they moved in unison in slo-mo. "Yes. Just. Like. This."

Peri's heart went into overdrive, pounding frantically behind her eyeballs as, together, they slowly pulled a fourth tablet from its centuries-old burial place in the sand.

After marking the location and photographing their finds from every angle, they'd placed the emeralds and the tablet in a wire basket to haul to the surface. Finn and Ariel returned to Logan's ship, pulling themselves up onto the edge of the dive platform. The other two divers, ready to go down, stood nearby adjusting their masks.

Oblivious, Peri grinned as she ripped off her mask and drysuit hood. "Holy crap, holy crap, holy crap. Can you *believe* it?"

Even if he wasn't blown away by their discovery, Finn was excited just watching her.

Her glorious hair spilled free as she pulled the cap from her head. It tumbled down her back in a fiery fall. He wanted to lay her out, right there in the sunlight, strip off her drysuit, and take her as her body shivered with exhilaration and lust.

Settling for touching his thumb to her lower lip, he laughed. "Excited?" he teased. He wanted to capture that smile, that devilish look in eyes the color of water, that unbridled enthusiasm, to enjoy whenever she wasn't with him. Fuck it. He never wanted to *be* apart. "God. I wish I could bottle your energy and enthusiasm. I'd store it up and ration it so I'll always have it."

Her look of excitement dimmed, gone and back so fast he almost missed the subtle shadow that fell over her face. "Can't keep me in a bottle, Finn Gallagher," she said with a sassy grin. "When you leave, you'll go empty handed. Come on. Let's get this accumulated crap off it, and see what it looks l-"

"Did I hear that right? You guys found another tablet?" Steve Galt said as he removed mask and hood and joined them on deck. He was followed by Earl who also had a basket with a few artifacts in it.

"Over on G9-BH173," Peri told him, eyes glowing as she pulled the basket, heavy with its contents closer to her hip.

Since a blind man could've found the tablet, he wanted to talk to Nick and Logan before he highlighted that to Peri. Or perhaps he wouldn't ask the Cutters about this coincidence of whale-sized proportions. Finn didn't believe in coincidences, and finding a fourth tablet, in a location Nick had already searched, in less than an hour, smacked of conspiracy, not a genuine historical find.

"Do you have a way to contact Nick and Logan?" he asked the men in general, not taking his eyes off Peri who looked like a sleek, sexy mermaid with her sultry smile and loose red hair tumbling around her shoulders.

"Logan's on his way to the airport to pick up Daniella, and Nick's too far away to pick up the lip mics," Earl reminded him. "I imagine they'd want the tablets to stay together, don't you? Isn't that Italian museum guy on board *Blackstar* going to try and decipher what they say?"

Steve turned Peri's basket to get a better look at the tablet. The gold still gleamed, but once it was properly cleaned the true beauty would be even more evident. "Look, take it with you when you go back, I'm sure both Nick and Logan would say the same. Leave the stones, though."

"This tablet is probably a hundred times more valuable than any emeralds," Peri pointed out, twisting the length of her hair and feeling around for the pins that had held it in place when she dived. Found, she jabbed them into the coiled mass to anchor it on top of her head.

Suddenly Jones was there with an outstretched hand to haul her to her feet. "Thanks,' she said without so much as a glance his way. The guy didn't move once she was upright. He stood much too goddamn close. Finn started to get to his feet, but she *accidentally* elbowed Jones in the ribs as she unzipped her drysuit. He stepped back. Not far enough as far as Finn was concerned, but the diver took another couple of steps in retreat as Finn rose to his full height.

Ariel pulled one arm out of her suit. "I think that's a good call," she told Earl, freeing the other arm to expose her white bikini top and a freckled expanse of the upper curve of her breasts. "Finn's people have already cleaned his, they know their stuff." Tying the neoprene sleeves around her waist, she was ready to leave.

It was agreed that Logan's guys would notify the Cutters of their find, and let them know the tablet would be on *Blackstar* when they arrived there in the morning.

They jet skied back to his ship with the tablet safely secured on Finn's jet ski. "Want to see what our guys have discovered on *Nuestra Señora del Marco*?"

"Another tablet, maybe?" Wet, spiky lashes framed jade eyes that gleamed with avarice.

"Four tablets aren't enough for you?" Finn led the way across the deck to the processing area which smelled strongly of chemicals.

"For now. . ."

More tablets hadn't been discovered, but Mike and his team on *Blackstar Two* almost salivated as they took the new tablet from Finn.

Before Peri could insist on staying to help clean the new artifact, Finn took her hand. Walking back across the deck, he whispered, "I'm exhausted. I think I need a kip."

She glanced at her dive watch, before giving him a narrowed eyed look. "It's after seven at night, Gallagher. Almost dinner time."

He led her up the outside stairs. "Dinner in bed after our nap?"

Nap, of course, was a euphemism for wild monkey sex. He'd waited all day to get her naked, and they barely made it back to his cabin before he'd stripped her, stripped himself, and made it to the bed.

FOURTEEN

The next morning, at four-thirty on the dot, Finn opened his eyes, wide awake and as usual, rarin' to go. Beside him, Ariel stirred in her sleep. Her soft body snuggled bonelessly beside him, she tightened her arms across his belly without waking. She, on the other hand, would wake up later - slowly, surfacing as if doing a deep dive.

Finn was tempted to stay and make love to her again. He relished making love to her when she was soft and sleepy, their lovemaking languid and measured, with none of the heat and flash when they were wide awake and hot for each other. It took a ridiculously small amount of encouragement to get them both to boiling point.

Last night had been no exception.

Gritting his teeth, he resisted the temptation, great as it was. She'd gotten maybe two hours the night before, she needed a few more.

For Finn, this momentous salvage was a cog in a larger wheel of his business interests, not his entire world as it was for the Cutters. The fact that he smelled a con diminished his elation at finding his tablet. Ariel had found another, a fourth had been in the museum on Merrezo for years. It wasn't unique after all, worse, he suspected the Cutters had set up- Fuck. He didn't know what. But he'd sure as hell find out.

He slipped from their bed, then covered her with the sheet. Ariel was a delicious distraction, but he needed to grab whatever hours possible to work. He had something else going, that was even more momentous and potentially historical than the tablets.

The Mars launch was a mere five months away. No time at all, given the impact the momentous trip would have on interstellar travel. Leaving scientists on the surface of the planet for six months was as thrilling as it was groundbreaking. Those twelve men and women would eventually pave the way for more colonists to terraform Mars in the near future. There was already a waitlist of upwards of ten thousand families ready to go. Almost every aspect of the Blackstar Group was involved in some way on preparations for humans to inhabit the planet.

Finn's business interests wouldn't stop because he was distracted and perpetually hot for Ariel. While dressing as quietly as he could, he was amused by something he'd be an idiot not to acknowledge. This morning was the first time in memory he'd awoken to the idea of not immediately starting work. It was the first time something-or someone-excited him more than rocket blasters.

Two hours later, he observed her in the cleaning room on the monitor in his office. He'd been watching it with one eye, knowing she wouldn't sleep in for too long. Wearing white shorts and a lime green tank top which bared the gentle swell of her breasts, and her muscled arms, she looked fresh and vibrantly alive. Her hair was pulled back in a braid which swung between her shoulder blades as she moved.

She looked so pretty his chest hurt.

As he worked, his eyes drifted from time to time to the monitor, watching her with Mike on *Two*, as they painstakingly cleaned the tablet. After another three hours Finn took a call from his attorney before leaving his office for the salon one deck down.

Having cleared two hours in his back-to-back schedule, he was eager to hear what Dr. Vadini, and he supposed, Núñez, had to say about the tablets. They were going to shit themselves when they learned there was a fourth.

Sunlight, flooded the large room, bouncing off the pale grays and whites of furniture and walls. Beyond the windows, a strong gale had the waves frothing and peaking. Typical Patagonian weather, and not good conditions to dive in.

Zane and Teal were helping themselves to the buffet set up in the salon in anticipation of their meeting. They turned in unison as he entered. "Nick and Bria are on their way," Zane said by way of a greeting. "Water's rough and they wanted to see if it calmed a bit before they came over."

"They'll have a long wait. Wind is going to be like this most of the day," Finn told them.

"*Blackstar's* barely moving. Your gyro stabilizers are worth every penny you paid for them," Teal said, a note of admiration in her voice. "I'd like to take a look at them while I'm here. Since we'll be in this area for *years*, I plan on retrofitting *Decrepit* as soon as possible. Our stabilizers are crap. Don't help at all. Half our crew will be hanging over the side if we don't do something."

Absently she shoved up the unrolling cuff of what must be one of Zane's denim shirts. Her husband took her arm and effectively rolled it back while she poured a mug of steaming hot coffee with her free hand. "Bria's pregnant, that's why the rough seas are bothering her."

"You're welcome to check out any part of the ship. Talk to Dan Firth, my Chief Engineer, he'll be delighted to talk shop," Finn told her as he imagined Peri swollen with his child. His heart kicked in several extra beats. Other than the nebulous thought of, "one day" passing on his company, the idea of children had never really entered Finn's mind. Now it was firmly embedded there like an earworm of a song.

He imagined a fearless toddler with Peri's red hair roaming *Blackstar*, and his heart did a rapid dive of terror.

Dear God. He was afraid for the safety of a child he didn't have. He headed to the buffet for his own cup of coffee, thinking a drink would serve him better after that foreign, earth-shattering revelation.

Holy shit, who would'da thunk it? Phineas Gallagher, confirmed bachelor with an iron will and a focused agenda, actually thinking of himself as a father. Yeah. He saw it, no problem at all. Which begged the question of what did Ariel think of kids? He'd have to ask. Sometime. Maybe right after he offered her a ring big enough to cover one finger up to the first knuckle.

Logan walked in alone.

"I thought you went to pick up Dani from the airport yesterday? Where is she?" Zane asked, carrying two plates and following his wife with their coffee mugs to the table near the buffet. The dining room one deck down would be crowded with crew and staff. This meeting required quiet and no distraction. Other than what now seemed to be his favorite personal distraction ever – Ariel. When she eventually arrived.

Logan joined Finn where he was pouring himself a cup of coffee. "Long flight. She wanted to sleep in."

"She's pregnant," Teal announced, holding up her arm for her husband to roll up the other sleeve, and diving into her heaped plate of food like a starving lumberjack.

Logan narrowed his eyes. "Who- How do you know? We haven't told anyone yet."

"Everyone's pregnant," Teal said matter-of-factly around a mouthful of bacon as she tugged her arm free of her husband's ministrations.

Zane turned to his wife, his own food forgotten. "Specify *everyone*."

Finn smothered a sympathetic grin. The woman was diabolical.

"Since when has Daniella slept in? Never as far as I know."

"One person is not *everyone*, a*nd*?" Zane said dangerously, removing the loaded fork from his wife's hand and setting it on her plate.

Her brown eyes sparkled as she muttered, "And it's a birthday surprise."

"My damned birthday was five months ago!"

"*Next* birthday. By the time your next one rolls around, you'll be changing diapers between dives. Patience is a vir- Hey!"

Zane scooped his laughing wife from her chair. She wrapped her arms around his neck and rested her head on his chest as he strode from the room. Finn heard their laughter as they went down the corridor.

"Hope there's a free cabin somewhere close by," Logan said dryly, taking his coffee to his usual corner of the sofa. He set his phone on the table, in the center of which were four easel-type stands lined up in readiness to display the tablets.

"Better be a quickie," Finn told him. "The others are due any minute."

"The others are here," Nick announced, entering hand-in-hand with his wife. They both looked windblown and pink-cheeked. "It's getting worse out there." Nick combed his fingers through his dark hair. "We almost decided not to come, but we didn't want to miss this historic moment."

Bria said something to him in rapid Italian and he responded in kind. She left his side and headed for the buffet, smoothing strands of wayward hair back into the sleek bun at her nape.

After a moment, Nick glanced around, appearing perfectly relaxed unless an observant man happened to notice how alert his eyes were as he watched the door. "Where's Ariel?"

"For the last few hours working with my tech people cleaning your tablet . She barely slept last night, she was so excited." And because Finn had spoken briefly to both Nick and Logan the night before, to confirm removing the tablet was sanctioned, he now said, "It was generous of you to allow us to bring it to Blackstar's team for processing."

"It was going to end up here anyway for Dr. Vadini to look at. Might as well speed up the process where we can."

The grid where they'd found the tablet was Nick's pet project. The emeralds indicating the phantom presence of the chest that had once contained the tablet, and the tablet itself, had been ridiculously easy to find. Too easy.

Finn drank from his cup, then said, "I see your fine hand in yesterday's discovery.

Nick raised a brow. "That a question?"

"That your answer?"

Nick shrugged. "Luck of the draw. I would probably have found it myself if I'd been in that spot at that time."

"Uh-huh." The middle Cutter brother's response confirmed Finn's suspicion that Nick had either discovered the tablet himself at an earlier time and left it *in situ*, or unearthed it somewhere else, then planted it for them to find. But how and when? He hadn't known they'd be there today.

Either way- no coincidence. But why? What was his end game?

Nick went to join his wife, and Finn sat down on the loveseat near Logan. Leaning back, Logan stretched out his long legs and drank his coffee.

"*Buenos días*," Núñez said cheerfully as he strolled in, cutting off further exploration of the tablet's provenance.

The well-dressed Argentinian appeared to have walked straight out of a J. Crew catalogue. Wearing and open-collar royal blue polo, unstructured linen jacket, Chinos and trendy canvas deck shoes. He might have arrived "unexpectedly" yesterday, but apparently, he'd carried a change of clothes with him. Which meant he'd expected to be offered a berth last night.

Núñez glanced down the length of the room at the table where the food had been laid out. "Ah, breakfast, you are indeed a gracious host, Finn."

"Did you discover anything new this morning?" Finn asked. He didn't like the guy. It wasn't – *probably* wasn't, because he knew the Argentinian and Ariel had had a relationship. Although that certainly colored his view. Núñez was a little too slick, a little too unctuous. All in all, a man he didn't trust – not with business and certainly not with Ariel.

"This morning. Yes. But we should wait for him." He scooped eggs onto a plate and lifted the lid of one of the servers. "Vadini is an old man and wanted to rest. I look forward to spending time with the tablets in private today." Finding things to his liking, he filled his plate, then stood indecisively, clearly trying to decide if he should sit alone at the nearby table, or bring his food down the length of the room to eat off his lap. He chose the table.

"There'll be nothing private about the viewing," Finn told him shortly. "Look around. We have a full viewing audience." He glanced at his watch, still a few minutes before nine. His schedule demanded meetings start and end on time. But with the high winds, and the condition of the water, small craft would have a hard time crossing to *Blackstar.*

Zane and his pregnant wife were off somewhere celebrating. News junkie Jonah stood across the room reading the news on his phone. And his speckled darling would, no doubt arrive with the fourth tablet at any minute, or in the next hour. Or whenever she felt like the tablet was worthy of being viewed.

He took out his phone. He might as well drink his coffee and check his emails while he waited. Nothing was going to happen on time today.

He opened a report sent by his security people, labeled Doctor Thiago Núñez. Speed reading the lengthy document on the small screen revealed the Minister of Antiquities had hundreds of thousands of dollars worth of gambling debts, a mistress in Buenos Aires, and another, conveniently located in a condo near the airport in Rio Gallegos. Núñez was a frequent player at both the floating casinos in Buenos Aires where they held his notes. But horse racing seemed to be his thing. Wherever he bet he pretty much always lost his shirt. His salary as a government employee sure as shit couldn't pay for his excessive lifestyle. He enjoyed bribes and kickbacks. None of which surprised Finn.

"Good morning, all," Ariel said cheerfully, as she entered the room, clutching the cloth-wrapped tablet to her chest. Finn turned off his phone as he rose to take it from her.

He kissed her nose over the bundled tablet now in his arms. "Good morning," he whispered. "You look delicious."

"Should've stuck around to find out," she murmured low enough for only him to hear as several pairs of booted feet echoed down the corridor.

"You were snoring," he lied. "Didn't want to wake you."

"I was *awake*, didn't want to delay you going to work."

Finn pressed a kiss to her mouth.

Dr. Vadini entered the room, accompanied by three sharp-eyed T-FLAC operatives, each carrying a cloth-wrapped bundle. The next several minutes were spent with everyone getting settled.

Vadini's attention was riveted to the coffee table, as Finn set the recently discovered fourth tablet on its stand.

"*Santa madre di Dio*," he said breathlessly. "You found another?"

"We wanted to surprise you. Finn and I found it in the wreckage of *El Crucifijo* late yesterday," Ariel told him, a crease between her tawny brows as she watched the T-FLAC operatives place the other three tables on the waiting easels.

"Were you able to decipher the text?" Logan asked the curator, leaning forward, elbows on his knees.

"We now know *considerably* more than we knew before," Vadini informed them, gaze still riveted to the gleaming tablets lined up on the coffee table. "This morning, Dr. Núñez and I spoke to two of my colleagues who have had great interest in Merrezo' s tablet for many years. Dr. Hervé, professor at the University of Chicago, who's field of expertise is not limited to Egyptology, but ancient languages, texts, and religious writings. And Dr. Petra Schröder at the Smithsonian." He smiled at Finn. "Thank you for the use of your audiovisual equipment. It was almost as if the four of us were in the same room. Shall I – we start?" he asked eagerly.

"It's seven minutes after nine, we don't have to wait for everyone before we hear what Dr. Vadini has to say, do we?" Ariel asked as Finn returned to his seat and patted the cushion beside him knowing she wanted to pace. There was enough nervous energy and excitement in the air without her walking around the room. She sat but perched on the edge of her seat as if ready to jump up at any time.

"We're here." Zane and Teal strolled in, hand-in-hand, hair and clothing a little rumpled, faces flushed. Although on Teal this rumpled look was pretty much her natural state. Finn smiled. The love they had for each other glowed around them, and they clearly didn't give a damn who saw it.

"Present." Jonah glanced up from his phone as he brought up the rear. "Just an FYI on wife count," he grinned. "Callie Skyped before I left *Scorpion* to come over here. I've learned when dealing with a runaway bride to agree to absolutely everything, no matter how outrageous. I don't want her to get cold feet again. She wants to get married on Cutter Cay? Done. What Callie wants, Callie gets. All *I* want is Callie."

"Wise man," Logan told his brother.

"And I'll remind you all that the wedding is in *three weeks,"* Jonah told them, running a nervous hand around the back of his neck." I don't give a damn if you have to pause the salvage of- fuck- an *alien spaceship*- you *will* be there, no matter what."

"I'll make my plane available for the trip," Finn offered. His phone sounded a low, discreet beep. "My staff has accommodations available for all of you," he informed them after a glance at his phone. "These winds aren't going to die down until this evening, and while our ships have stabilizers and are large enough not to be impacted, crossing between them in a small craft with these high seas is unnecessary and dangerous."

Jonah's gaze slid to the fourth tablet. "Holy shit. One was profound enough- But four?" Jonah smiled at them. "Good for you."

"Good for *all* of us," Ariel told him. "Dr. Vadini – what do we know?"

Peri's first thought that morning when she'd opened her eyes, was that she could no longer live this lie. She'd carried it for so long, and it was a burden she desperately wanted to be rid of. Before Finn, the prospect of that task had been quick, if painful. Now she had a lot more to lose.

Her tumbling thoughts; the impending loss of Finn, the anticipation of the Cutters' response to her revelations, *and* the excitement of the tablets reveal, churned in her stomach. Those four tablets were going to be the best part of her day, probably the best part of her freaking *year*. She didn't want to ruin it by doing her big reveal and then being absent for the results. She'd wait...

She let her gaze sweep the room: Logan, stern and the patriarch of the group, Nick, impossible to read, Zane the charming jokester, Jonah the news junkie- Her throat closed. Damn it, she liked *them*.

Just a few more hours of inclusion, a few more hours of being welcome among them.

A gust buffeting the window made Bria jump. "It's so weird to see blue skies when we're in the middle of a wind storm. One expects to see low, dark ominous clouds and torrential rain in weather like this."

Finn's gray eyes, a little too penetrating, softened on her face briefly. He linked his warm fingers with hers. "Go ahead Doctor, we're all agog." There was an oddly challenging tone to his voice but his expression was impassive.

A glance outside showed the waves slapping against the hull, sending up fans of windswept spray. The flags on deck snapped and twisted around the poles in the high winds.

Externally, Peri reflected the excited stillness of the room. Internally, she felt the same savage winds seen beyond the windows. "High winds are common, and expected, at this time of the year," she told the princess. "You might've noticed the wind is always blowing. I've been in Patagonia when we've had winds of upwards of seventy miles an hour. It's about fifty right now."

Bria took a sip of tea. "Then I'm very pleased to be safely indoors."

"If I may--?" Dr. Vadini was almost quivering with excitement, and it was contagious. Peri's hand tightened in Finn's. After they'd made love last night, and he lay beside her, having fallen asleep mid-breath it seemed, she'd lain wide awake for hours.

Her eventual exhausted sleep was torn by dreams where she was once again alone. Alone onboard *Sea Witch*, and alone in her glass house on the bluff. She loved her house, but it didn't *feel* like home. There was no denying that she'd spent a hell of a lot of lonely nights there. She better get back to being used to it.

She'd been startled awake when, in the realism of a dream, she'd felt the sting of spray as the waves crashed around her, as she desperately searched the darkening sky for the light of a buoy to guide her home.

On waking, the Finn-less space beside her had reminded her of the inevitable and brought fresh pain to the fissures already starting to tear into her heart.

No more procrastination. She'd let everyone have their moments, and then she'd dive right in. Only adrenaline and steely determination, would see her through the next few hours.

"If I may have assistance to rearrange the tablets— Thank you, you are most kind," Dr. Vadini addressed two of the operatives who immediately stepped forward. "Lay them flat, if you please- This one and this one at the top, then this tablet here," he pointed. "And that one here beside it. A little closer together – about two centimeters apart. Yes, *precisamente*, just so. *Grazie mille*."

By the time the tablets were arranged precisely to his instructions, everyone was on their feet and gathered around the coffee table to get a better look.

The tablets formed a four-foot by four-foot square. The bumpy gold sheathing them gleamed dully in the sunlight flooding the room. One tablet had a chipped corner, and each had several greenish-white spots where sea creatures had once clung. But that didn't diminish their beauty or their historical importance.

"What are we looking at?" Zane tilted his head this way and that.

"First, the form of the tablets. Then see that the edges here and also here-between the tablets – and also this detail match as if cut from the same piece of stone, just like a jigsaw puzzle." Vadini indicated the space between the top two stones, then the same gap between the bottom two.

"But the edges don't match across the *middle* like a jigsaw puzzle pieces would, do they?" Teal pointed out, biting her thumbnail. "So how is this relevant?"

"I will explain. The tablets are chiseled by the same hand. See the upward stroke here and again here, the slope of this form, here, here and here? The cadence of the words, and syntax, probably dictated by someone else."

"This is written phonetically in the ancient Abipón language, extinct hundreds of years ago, as everyone knows. No one speaks it any more of course, but I and my colleagues have accumulated some knowledge over the years."

Peri looked from the curator to Theo beside him as if glued to the Italian's hip. Theo raised a brow, a move Peri knew he only did when he felt smug and knew something you didn't. His mouth curved into a subtle smile he tried to hide by rubbing his index finger over her bottom lip. Her direct gaze drilled into him and when the look in his eyes changed, going from lazy and smug to dark and intense, a small shock went through her. He was hiding something.

She frowned. "Theo, you're an ancient cultural expert. Did you study this tribe?"

"There is very little *to* study as the people have been extinct for hundreds of years, their language with them. Senor Vadini is correct, no one speaks it, and his two experts were of some help--but. . ." He paused for dramatic effect. She wanted to dash across the room to pull the words out of him but settled for glaring at him instead. "Like the good doctor, I have studied the culture. As he says, few written words survived the centuries. Most of what I know was passed verbally through third, fourth or fifth generation," he finished.

"Were you able to read them, too?" she asked on a rush of excited breath.

"I was able to contribute more words at our video conference call earlier," Theo said a little pompously, his eyes, not on Peri, but on Dr. Vadini beside him.

"This is good." Vadini smiled as he drew on a pair of white cotton gloves. "With those new words revealed to us- a few words here, a few words there, I believe between us we can accurately translate the words of Blackstar. I have spent a lifetime researching this ancient language. I have studied *la tavoletta d'oro Merrezo* my entire life, as did my father, and his father before him," he said with pride.

"While there is no written word of the language, just a handful of words and symbols passed down through the generations, interpretation has taken time and infinite patience. Even should I understand what they once meant, some of the words here are not legible at all, having been worn away. But with the brilliant brains of Dr's Hervé and Schröder. . .and Dr. Núñez of course, I believe we have the-" He glanced at Bria. "*La essenza?*"

"Just having the *gist* of them sounds fabulous," Bria encouraged him with a smile. "Please, tell us more."

Peri liked Bria's palpable excitement and the way her dark eyes danced with anticipation. In another life, in another dimension, she and Bria might've been friends.

"This is the order I believe, that the tablets should be read." Vadini waved a hand over the gold square. "From left to right across the top, then the same for the two on the bottom."

"Or perhaps there's no order at all?" Finn's hand rested on the small of Peri's back. She felt each individual finger as if it were attached to a specific nerve in her body. All of them erotic. More than sexual, she felt an intimate connection to him in a way she'd never imagined she'd feel for anyone. An integral part of her that was going to be severed without anesthetic.

I can't do this. Can't feel this way. In her head, a metronome ticked off the few remaining hours before all this heat, warmth and acceptance were blown to hell.

Peri broke away from Finn to get – something - *anything* from the buffet table across the room. She mourned the loss of his touch and called herself a fool for allowing herself to care so much when she of all people knew what the end result would be. It was inevitable.

After grabbing a bottle of water, she returned to stand between Teal and Nick. Finn gave her an inquiring look from his position on the other side of the table, a look she pretended not to see. She rubbed the icy bottle across the deep ache in her chest.

Did people die of a broken heart?

Of course not.

But considering how hot things smoldered between them, there could always be a first time.

"A simple explanation is the decorative border around two sides of each tablet, which, when matched together, form a perfect square."

"Do the things actually *tell* us anything?" Logan asked, sounding as skeptical as Finn.

"*Sí.* The first," Vadini pointed to the tablet top, left. "is the one discovered by you, Mr. Gallagher." He then glanced at Theo. "Please, feel free to step in to assist."

Theo was clearly delighted to be asked. He put on his serious face and leaned over to point at the second tablet, the one that had been in the museum in Merrezo. "This word is *chosen*."

"We're currently attempting to read tablet number *one*, Dr. Núñez. Let us keep our thoughts in order. We will get to the others in due course." Dr. Vadini told him. "Now that we have four tablets it's slightly easier to decrypt the text because we have now identified enough of the lost language to be able to interpret many words on *la tavoletta d'oro Merrezo*."

Sucking in a breath, Bria frowned and said something sharply in Italian.

The curator immediately looked contrite. "This information was not withheld from you, Principessa. I needed the words from the other tablets and the assistance of my esteemed colleagues. And they in turn needed to set their gaze upon the tablets to confirm what I hoped I knew. I have studied what we now have at length, and I will give you my educated opinion of what they say. The first states: '*Apocalypse preordained written in five parts-*'"

"*Apocalypse*?" Logan's tone dripped sarcasm. "Come on."

Peri knew when the apocalypse was happening. In about an hour. And oh, hell, Finn was casually strolling behind the others to reach her side. She couldn't handle his touch, or the smell of his skin, or the sound of his voice so near her when she was already on edge.

Vadini shrugged off Logan's incredulity. "'*One reaches landfall, three lie beneath the waves. The last remains in death's grip.*'"

"Wait. What?" Nick said sharply. "You're saying there are *five* tablets in all?"

The Curator nodded without removing his gaze from the tablets. "The numbers I know. See right here?" He pointed. "Five tablets."

This was so cool. Peri hung on every word. *Live in the moment. Remember every little detail. Stop projecting what's going to happen later.*

"One *did* reach us in Merrezo, and the other three *were* found under the sea! This is all true," Bria's voice rose with enthusiasm.

"*Two stars converge*," the curator read. "*One red, one black*."

"Which stars are black and red?" Nick looked around her to Finn.

"Red dwarfs are by far the most common type of star in the Milky Way." As he talked, Finn rested his hand on her upper back.

Same nerves, same damn reaction. Maybe if she didn't move she wouldn't feel. . .

"They're small, relatively cool stars on the main sequence, of either K or M spectral type. Low luminosity, so not easily observed. A *black* star is a gravitational object composed of matter. It's a theoretical alternative to a black hole. Neither of which sounds as if it has anything to do with an apocalypse. Unless we're talking that the ever-decreasing rate of collapse of a black star, leading to an infinite collapse of *time*, or asymptotically approaching a radius less than zero." He raised his eyebrow. "Is this where you think I'm the Blackstar reference? Because, just a reminder, your prophet's name was purportedly Blackstar, and he's probably referring to himself here."

"No, signore," Vadini stiffened further. "I believe the last line on tablet one is the reference to you: *Salvation delivered in Blackstar's powerful hand*."

Theo, who was practically leaning over the table, squinted at the words as he tried to read ahead.

Clearly not taking this seriously enough to argue, Finn's smile was a little shark-like. "I wonder if I'll be the one *causing* the apocalypse or the one destined to save the world?"

"It says, *'Salvation delivered in Blackstar's powerful hand.*'" Peri repeated, loving the entire drama-filled concept of stars, an apocalypse, dark holes and Finn. "You're just going to have to save the world, like it or not."

He shot her a warning glance. "Don't encourage this b.s."

"It's not clear what: *One reaches landfall, three lie beneath the waves, one is gripped by death,*' *means,"* Jonah said. "But are we going to have to find the fifth tablet in some graveyard somewhere?"

"I'm not digging in any graveyard, I'll tell you that right now!" Teal shuddered. "I'm sure Argentina has hundreds- *thousands* of graveyards. We wouldn't even know where to start."

"What's the powerful hand, then?" Logan asked. "Poseidon?"

Jonah rubbed the back of his neck. "The storm that knocked the ships off course and sank them? That seems like a mighty hand of fate to me."

"Makes more sense than Poseidon," Zane agreed. "But I suspect the waiting hand hasn't happened yet."

"I don't know." Teal pointed to the flapping flags and wild surf beyond the windows.

"Remember, these were the supposed words of a *child."* Finn took the bottle of water from Peri and drank. "Five *hundred* years ago. This sounds like a story the kid's mother made up to keep him out of the surf, for God's sake."

"No *signore*," Vadini assured him, his lined face set. "This was Blackstar's prophecy. I have no doubt."

Theo gave Finn the stink-eye, then shared it around the room as if daring anyone else to doubt Blackstar's prophecy. "I, too believe this to be Blackstar's prophecy."

Peri was surprised. Theo was such a down to earth, not a woo woo, kind of guy. "You do, Theo?" she asked, plucking her almost drained water bottle from Finn. When she drank she imagined she tasted him and held the bottle to her lips for a moment longer.

"Believe Blackstar's prophecy?" Theo's eyes went dark and serious. "Of course. Ask any sheepherder in Patagonia the story of the seer, and they will tell you of his remarkable prophecies. He was legend long after he died. Every one of his predictions came to pass. This is not a fabrication. Blackstar's prophecy is very very real."

FIFTEEN

Vadini might be sincere as hell, but as a scientist, a number cruncher and a no bullshit visionary, Finn didn't believe one word of this so called 'prophecy.' There was a hard sell coming. He just hadn't figured what it was, or who was behind it. and what the fuck their end game was. Yet.

"I will paraphrase the inscription on *la tavoletta d'oro Merrezo,* tablet number two, as follows," Bria's linguist rubbed his papery hands together before leaning closer to the second tablet. He spoke haltingly, clearly reading in the language the texts were written in, thinking in Italian, and then translating again in English.

Or he'd memorized a script.

"*Warring factions distort the truth,*" Vadini intoned. "*The chosen are not protectors. Blackstar's words must be heard or humanity will be lost. Goddess and stargazer unite. If message goes unheeded, fiery death.*"

Nicely done in suitably reverent and hushed tones. Finn wondered if the Cutters had found the guy at Central Casting. He was good, really good.

Not once in the decade he'd known the brothers, had they ever given him any indication that they'd been playing the long game. But some cons were worth a longer, long game.

"Again with the apocalypse," Logan shook his head, sending Finn a sardonic glance. "Better get out your cape and tights, buddy, sounds like you'll be busy."

"No. No. No." Núñez's mouth pinched in disapproval. He jabbed the tablet with his finger, causing Bria and Dr. Vadini to gasp. "This section says, *'The chosen are the protectors.'*"

Nick put a hand on Núñez's shoulder, drawing him away from the tablet. "No touching."

"I do not think so, Dr. Núñez," Vadini's censure was mild. "My studies of the Abipón language tell me there is a negative in this line. Are *not.*"

"I, too have studied and I most strongly beg to differ."

Vadini shrugged his narrow shoulders. "It is of no consequence that we disagree. Let us continue on."

"Okay, so we're listening to Blackstar's words," Zane said as he absently, and tenderly ran his palm over his wife's bedhead hair. All it did was make the dark strands spring up untidily in another direction. "But he doesn't seem to be telling us much of anything. Other than that people are going to war. Something us humanoids have done since time immemorial."

Teal laughed at her husband's quip. A little bit plain, a lot rumpled, she was a marked contrast to her sister-in-law

Bria, whose dark hair was in a sophisticated coil behind her head, her clothes stylish and immaculate. And to Ariel, who'd bared her gorgeous legs in white shorts, and her arms in a lime green tank top, her crowning glory in a fat fiery braid that was already starting to unravel. Just the way he liked it. The three women couldn't be more different.

"I *love* this stuff," Ariel held the empty water bottle to her cheek. Finn wanted to be the bottle. He wanted to be the thin fabric of her shirt cupping her breasts, he wanted to be her damned shorts clinging to her heart-shaped ass.

Dear God, he had it bad. He was so distracted by her, he was only half paying attention to the revelation of the century about an apocalypse that was going to destroy their world – if he had the script right.

"The tablets are like a Shakespearean play," Ariel said with relish. "History and dark, ominous predictions. I wonder if he was foretelling the atomic bombing of Hiroshima and Nagasaki."

"No, *signorina*, I will show you in a minute that he has pinpointed the precise date."

"Really? Okay." she smiled. "In the cast of characters who are today's world leaders and influencers, who did boy seer cast as the goddess and the stargazer?"

As far as Finn was concerned, he had a red-headed goddess right beside him.

"You're certainly standing next to a major influencer now," Jonah told her, shooting a grin to Finn.

Unamused Finn said, "And this influencer has a pretty astute nose for hoaxes. Let's finish up with the 'reading' and get real. Then we can carry on with the business we're here to do, which is dive and find treasure, right? Not engage in a myth designed to waste our time."

"The next is the tablet retrieved by you, s*ignorina*." Vadini pointed bottom left. "*Centuries of benevolent light becomes a swiftly moving force of evil," he read. "Appearing as bleeding wound in the Eastern Sky. Proceed with all haste. The lance must be propelled with all speed. Hesitate and all will be lost.*"

Oh, for crapsake. "A comet? A meteorite? An alien spacecraft coming in for a landing?" *How fucking coincidental was it that space travel was coming up? Not.* Finn tried to read the faces of his friends and colleagues to look for collusion in this con game. Ariel? Shit, he hoped like hell she wasn't involved in whatever this was.

He had no idea where it was going. Pretty soon he'd shut the bullshit down and demand answers, but for now he was willing to bide his time and see where it went.

Logan grinned. "Don't get a run in those superhero tights, Rocketman."

In response, Finn shot him the finger. "I'll get right on that." He took out his phone.

"What are you doing? Calling the Batmobile?" Ariel asked, with a cheeky smile.

"This 'apocalypse' is supposed to happen in three days according to this thing, right?" he addressed the group, now wanting this to draw to its conclusion. "Eastern sky? Let's see what's coming to kill us off." He tapped the screen on his smarter-than-most phone.

Finn logged into one of his encrypted databases which was connected- thanks to his many hefty donations- to NASA's Near Earth Object Program. The coordinated efforts detected, tracked and characterized potentially hazardous asteroids and comets on a collision course with Earth. At his *Blackstar* space facility, this proprietary data was being coordinated with months of intricate calculations. Accumulated, tabulated, and studied on a minute-by-minute vigil. Every aspect of space was being assessed in readiness for the Mars launch in five months. Nothing could possibly be a surprise.

The debate continued around him in a hum of voices. As everyone added their two cents, whether their theory made logical, scientific sense or not, Finn scanned through calculations. He put up his hand when he'd run through several options. None of them panned out. No surprise.

"Unless the alien's ship is traveling faster than the speed of sound, we're safe," he told the gathering, tone dry. No point going into Near Earth Orbit Asteroids, or any other pesky details. There was fucking nothing out there for the foreseeable future, and everyone in the know knew it.

Science. Fact. Black and white. No bullshit. A kid getting attention by drawing shit on rocks wasn't that interesting.

Since they claimed their prophecy had something to do with space travel and the threat of NEO, he presumed the scam, when it came, would have something to do with Blackstar Galactic.

"Aw, that's disappointing," Ariel said. "I was kinda hoping to meet a little gray man."

Teal shook her head. "You are one weird, chick, you know that?"

"Don't want to rush you," Finn said, hearing the testy in his voice. "As enlightening as this is, I have a business to run and an international meeting in forty-eight minutes. Can we finish this up?"

"The tablet discovered yesterday on the *El Crucifijo, sí.*" Vadini seemed eager to get back to what they were all doing there. "*In the twelfth month when Mercury, Venus, Saturn, Mars, and Jupiter align- Oceans will rise, mountains will topple, the mighty and innocent alike will perish. Seek the High Altar to discover the answers written in the stars. Raise the map to divine the truth.*"

Well, at least they'd put some thought into this con. "A metapuzzle."

Bria asked, "What's a metapuzzle?"

"A puzzle that unites several puzzles feeding into it to obtain one answer." *The answer: either money, power or control.*

"The technique is called backsolving. The metapuzzle is structured to make it possible to guess, with a greater or lesser degree of certainty, the solutions to the puzzles that feed into it without actually solving them."

"May I-?" Vadini said quietly. "There is more. In all my years studying *la tavoletta d'oro Merrezo,* I did not put as much attention to detail into this intricate border surrounding the whole, as I should have. I was more focused on learning the ancient language as best I could than to concern myself with what I considered basically a decorative border."

"Jesus." Logan shoved his hands through his hair. "What does *it* have to say?"

He didn't sound any more interested in this 'new' revelation than Finn did. But then one "dissenter" with the same views as the mark was classic misdirection.

"Instructions to build an ark?" Finn suggested dryly. Ariel jabbed him sharply in the rib with her elbow.

Vadini removed a jeweler's loop from his saggy back pocket. "Going up this left edge of tablet one, and continuing across the top edge- It appears to be a date, November 12th, followed by a string of numbers- eleven thousand, I believe. Will die."

"That's exact. And not the date the four ships sank," Nick pointed out. "That happened in *June*. You think we'll have this disaster in a few days?"

"Or *last* November 12th," Finn's voice dripped with sarcasm. "Or November 12th five hundred years ago."

"Or three days from now." Ariel slipped her arm around his waist, hooking her fingers into his waistband.

"Maybe we have to be on the lookout for Santa's sleigh?" Finn inhaled her unique scent of warm Casablanca lilies, and thought of a cool room, rumpled sheets, and the two of them alone, with all the time in the world to explore each other.

"*Perpetual life will flow.* And here, down the right-hand edge, it looks like a long string of numbers. . .Then; *Will be lost.* Presumably, the number of souls lost if the warnings are not heeded."

"Eleven thousand *saved,*" Núñez informed him, his tone unequivocal, his features set like a bulldog with a bone.

"Saved?" The Italian linguist gave him a skeptical glance. "Where do you see that? The text is barely legible, and in some areas- like there and there – non-existent. We can't be sure-"

"Eleven thousand *saved. The other* numbers are those who will perish."

Vadini acquiesced without a fight. "*If message is unheeded, apocalypse.*"

"That's cheerful," Logan said, "And annoyingly repetitious."

Undaunted, Vadini walked around the table, bent double, and read through the magnifier, the tiny text that looked, to Finn, exactly like a not very well drawn decorative border. "*Warring factions distort the truth. Blackstar, the transformer, must be heard, or humanity will be lost.*"

"My head is starting to hurt with all these doom and gloom allegories." Jonah went to the buffet to grab a drink.

To Finn he looked as guilty as sin. And as jumpy as he'd ever seen such a laid-back guy.

"Seems simple to me." Nick and Bria headed to two easy chairs, then ended up squeezing into one together. "Someone better listen to this message or all hell will break loose and humanity will be wiped off the face of the Earth. That about sum it up?" he glanced at Vadini. "Pretty standard for your end of the world apocalypse."

"All but eleven thousand people," Núñez repeated with authority. "The transformer will lead the people into a New World order."

"I didn't hear anything close to that interpretation, maybe Dr. Núñez is Blackstar reincarnated," Finn couldn't keep the sarcasm out of his voice. Ariel nudged him again.

"Here-" Vadini hunched, and read- "*Do not believe the sages who discount mysticism.*" Then: "*Trust goddess*– I believe this word is *fire."*

Zane took Teal's hand and pulled her to one of the sofas to sit down. "What does that even *mean*? Did they have a goddess of fire in their theology, Dr. Núñez? Dr. Vadini?"

Finn slid his hand up Ariel's back, to urge a return to the loveseat they'd vacated earlier.

"Not as far as I know."

"*Bria* was known as *Fiammetta*, fiery one, as a child. . ." Nick's lips twitched. "Is it possible that *she's* the goddess of fire?"

"Maybe it's *Ariel*," Finn offered, tongue in cheek.

"Anything is, of course, possible," Vadini told them absently.

"This does not refer to the sinking of the ships," Núñez stated unequivocally, clearly not interested in either woman present being part of the prediction. He was the only person still standing other than the Italian. "But rather that, on a specified date, the world will end, and only a designated number of people will survive,"

"Wow, that's pretty sad." Ariel sat as close to Finn as she could, without being on his lap. Fine with him. "Why did Blackstar bother with four tablets if November is the end of the world? He could've said that in the first tablet. One and done. And on that cheerful note," she said with a slight tremor in her voice, "I have a slightly less apocalyptic announcement to make."

"Oh, dear God," Teal blurted, staring at Ariel wide-eyed. "Are you pregnant, too?"

"*What?*" Peri, too stressed to be amused, said, "*No!*" a little too loudly. Damn it to hell. She should've retrieved her tablet *before* doing this. The four tablets lay, side-by-side, gleaming on the table in the middle of the room. Just an arm's length from her grasp. Once the Cutters knew who she was and what she'd done, they'd think it was their damn right to keep her property. Too late to make a run for it now.

Finn's fingers tightened around hers, even though he had no idea that she was about to blow their friendly gathering apart. His show of solidarity and support gave her that extra spurt of courage to face this head on. Grateful to have his strong hand linked with hers, she realized how much she needed him there, but it scared her, too. Would he be supportive when he figured out exactly how many times she'd freely chosen deceit as a course of action?

How had this dependency crept under her usual defenses so quickly?

Drawing comfort from being anchored to him, in anticipation of a potential shitnami, was simply another thing that was wrong in her life. Dragging him blindly into the middle of her complicated revenge plot, she realized too late, was unfair.

His lifestyle made it clear that he wasn't permanently affixed to anything, except his goals of reaching the most distant horizon of space. And even that horizon constantly shifted, farther and farther away, as he accomplished each lofty objective. Without a deep breath, or counting to three, she took the dive. Probably into a pool with no water. "I'm the captain of *Sea Witch.*"

Dead silence.

Numb with anticipation, it took a moment to realize that Finn had actually *released* her hand, not squeezed it in solidarity. It had simply been a figment of wishful thinking.

He knew about the thieving pirate on board *Sea Witch* then. Of *course* his best buddies the Cutters had told him about her stealing from them over the years.

Even though she knew Finn would distance himself, her heart sank. It hurt, damn it. He didn't say a word as her gaze roamed the room; from Cutter blue eyes, to Cutter blue eyes, to gauge *their* reactions. Finn's defection hurt so much it made whatever the Cutters threw her way seem trivial.

Although she'd expected it, the condemnation from the Cutters stung.

Screw them. She didn't care. She'd expected it after all. Defiantly, she held up a hank of her bright hair. For God's sake, they didn't "see" her, even with the brightest red hair this side of the freaking Equator. "I said, "I'm *Sea W-*"

Logan scowled. Figured. He seemed like a guy who liked everything by the book, and this was definitely not by the book. He glanced at his brother. "Nick?"

Middle brother Nick's expression was inscrutable. Peri had held onto the lifeline in the last few days that he'd seemed friendly toward her. Now she wasn't so sure that wouldn't turn on a dime. He could, like his threatening-looking spy friends, be picturing gleefully how to break her neck and toss her body overboard. Zane frowned as he exchanged a long look with Nick, then his eyes drifted back to her with a marked frown. Jonah looked annoyed. He had the least reason to hate her, since she'd never stolen from, nor lied to *him*. Probably just didn't like that she'd pissed off his brothers.

Teal and Bria gave her sympathetic looks. But perhaps they felt compassion because they knew the hell the Cutters were capable of raining down on a person when they felt threatened and formed a united front.

The three T-FLAC operatives still blocked the door. Perching on the edge of a chair as if waiting for the right moment to leave, Dr. Vadini looked uncomfortable. Theo looked intrigued. Neither left the room. Peri figured she was the floor show as long as the storm raged outside.

"We know who you are," Nick's voice was gentle, his scrutiny far too penetrating. It was as if he knew something no one else in the room knew. "We were waiting for you to tell us."

"Took you long enough to come clean," Zane groused.

Logan leaned forward. "Hope you made a shitload of money selling your ill-gotten gains. It should pay for a decent attorney." He shot the words out like bullets he'd chambered for years. *Bam. Bam. Bam.*

Beside her Finn stiffened, but he made no move to touch her again. The few inches between them seemed as deep and wide as the Mariana Trench. "You knew who I was all along?" Holy crap. On one hand, she was almost relieved that they had at least recognized her, and on the other, mildly insulted that they hadn't confronted her from the moment they'd met.

Which indicated in flashing, neon lights just how disinterested they were.

She turned to a silent Finn. "Did *you* know?"

Finn's poker face chilled her anew. "I should've listened to my instincts when you tried to steal my tablet. Once a thief, always a thief." He turned to address the Cutters. "I'm stunned you haven't put legal proceedings into motion before now. It would be well within your rights to have her arrested on multiple counts." He got to his feet, his absence leaving a cold spot next to her on the loveseat.

"I haven't sold *any* of it," Peri told the others as Finn walked away. "I'll return every last *reale* and artifact in better condition than before."

"And when will that be?" Logan demanded as Finn reached the double doors leading out of the salon.

"Logan—" Nick shot him a stern glance.

Peri dragged her attention away from Finn just as he turned to face the room, back to the wall, eyes, flat and cold. "As soon as you tell me where you want it delivered."

Logan flexed his fingers. "Cutter Cay and immediately."

The other side of the world and out of their hair? "Consider it done." When she responded, her voice was toneless. Finn had already cut her heart out with a blunt knife.

"You won't be taking that tablet anywhere until we've established exactly how and where it was found," Finn said from his position across the room. Expression unreadable, he leaned one broad shoulder against the door jamb, his face half in shadow. With his fingertips shoved into the front pockets of his jeans, one ankle crossed over the other, he looked the picture of relaxed.

Relaxed wasn't in Phineas Gallagher's vocabulary in any language. The animus radiating from him was marked. His temper was tightly, chillingly, leashed. If he were a panther his tail would be flicking from side to side, eyes fixed on his prey. Unlike her own quick blow up/quick recovery, Finn's anger, once ignited, was of the slow smolder variety. Far more lethal. Far more lasting.

No second chances.

Pulling her eyes away from him with difficulty, Peri said. "I'm also Rydell Case's sister."

Zane dramatically fell back into the cushions of the couch like he'd been struck, his hands cupping the back of his head. "Fuck."

Logan shook his head. "Ah, Shit. Nick, you might've mentioned *that* bit of pertinent information."

"Explains everything in a fucking nutshell, doesn't it?" Jonah snapped, rhetorically, folding his arms across his broad chest.

"Actually," Teal said, "it *doesn't.* Just because Case is a dishonest shit, doesn't mean *you* have to be. We all know that's not a gene passed from generation to generation." She moved closer to Zane and laid a hand on his shoulder. The Cutter ranks were closing fast.

Peri looked Teal in the eye. This was not a time to back down. She'd laid her cards out, face up on the table for all to see. "My brother doesn't have a single dishonest bone in *his* body. That ball belongs squarely in your family's court."

Zane leaned forward, his wife's hand on his shoulder. "So, ripping us off all these years was a show of solidarity with your brother?" he snapped. "He must be so proud."

"He doesn't know about my activities. When he finds out, he'll kill me."

"If we don't do it first," Logan echoed her thought. "He's so honorable he knows you work for the Ministry of Antiquity and sent you over here to fucking spy on us. How convenient." He turned to Theo, then back to her. "Wait- You *don't* work for them, do you?"

"Of course, she does," Theo spluttered, obviously having no idea what the hell was going on, nor how to benefit from it. "Ariel's worked for me for *years*."

"Buddy, you shouldn't even be in the room. In fact, I don't know what the fuck you're doing on board in the first place." Jonah cast him a withering look, then turned those Cutter eyes on her like sharp knives. "Why's your last name Andersen and you're brother's Case?"

"Don't badger her, *cognati,"* Bria said quietly, the tea cup poised at her lips before she set it gently in the saucer she held in her other hand. "Let her speak. There are many reasons a woman changes her name, are there not?"

"My last name *is* Case." Hearing how rapid her breathing was, Peri tried to slow it. "*Persephone* Case."

"*Not* Ariel Andersen?" Zane said tightly. "Not just a thief, but a liar as well. Nice."

Zane's wife punched his shoulder none too gently. "I *told* you her name was the same as that cartoon mermaid. And I *told* you it was weird that her last name was Andersen as in Hans Christian- Didn't I *tell* you that it was odd?"

Zane captured Teal's fist, then brushed his lips across her knuckles. "Several times, sweetheart. You were right as usual."

Jonah scowled as he typed on his phone with his thumb. "Calling the police."

Peri glanced briefly at the windswept waves beyond the water splattered windows. They wouldn't come anytime soon.

"Then you'll want to contact the Prefectura Naval Argentina directly," she informed Jonah, proud at how calm she sounded. "They're the ones charged with protecting the country's maritime territory. Unfortunately, since none of the artifacts were stolen from their jurisdiction, and I'm legally employed by their government, you'd have a hard time getting them to arrest me. Technically, you'd really have to contact the police in every location globally where the recovery operations were held."

"Difficult, but not fucking impossible." Logan started to get up, then thought better of it, and sank back into his chair.

"I'm a thief, not stupid. Call the local police to get the ball rolling if that's what you want. I'm not going anywhere."

"No one is calling anyone. Cool your jets," Nick told them as he and Bria shared a brief silent conversation in a shared glance which spoke volumes about their close bond. "Let's all take a deep breath here. No one died, no one lost a limb. Persephone was just doing what any one of us would do when faced with our brother's enemy."

"Her brother *is* your brothers' enemy, dickhead," Logan reminded him. "Do you see any of us stealing Case blind?"

"Yes," Peri told him with asperity. "You did. You *do. Consistently.*"

"Bullshit. Is your brother too chicken to come over here and say that to my face?" Logan demanded, his voice curt. "Because I'd be more than fucking happy-"

"I'm sure Finn doesn't want any bloodshed onboard Blackstar," Nick said, tone cool. "Bullying Persephone isn't productive. She's confessing voluntarily. Trying to make amends. Seeking a peaceful resolution."

"Jesus." Logan ran his fingers through his dark hair, clearly exasperated. "Other than spying on us, what the hell are you *doing* here?"

"If by *here* you mean Patagonia?" she spoke to the oldest Cutter. "You don't own the damned entire *world*, Logan. Over seventy percent of the Earth is covered by ocean. You could've gone any damn where else in the Universe other than here. I freaking *live* here. If you mean on this fifty-plus miles of Patagonian coast, then I have as much right- more right even, than any of you."

She hesitated. Should she spill it all? But…she couldn't make herself say the words that would reveal the truth that no one else knew. Obviously, not the Cutters. Not Finn. And not even Rydell, the brother who had loved her all her life. Her real motivation made her seem. . . pathetic. Needy.

"Dangerous and pretty damned brazen of you to beard us on our own ships to spy for your brother." Zane tucked Teal against his side, linking his fingers with hers on his knee.

The gesture made Peri's eyes sting. She looked at the ceiling for a second to center herself. She was damned if she'd cry in front of these people. Damned if she'd show even a sliver of a chink in her armor.

Yet they deserved their pound of flesh. They'd get it, then she'd be done with them once and for all. "Rydell had no idea I was doing this, so don't blame him. This was all my idea. Besides, I was here first. I discovered the wrecks almost six years ago. *All* of them-"

She eyed each man one at a time. "The references were so obscure, so badly documented that I sincerely doubt you would've found them on your own. The only reason you're here now is because you saw the notice of my multi-ship salvage claim, and like bloodsuckers glommed onto the location. As usual, just as you've done year after year with my brother's claims."

"How could we possibly know you were the Koúkos Corporation?" The penny dropped for Jonah. "The cuckoo stealing another bird's nest. How appropriate. Sneak in, steal our shit, and run. If, as you say, you were here first, why didn't you stake claim to all four ships?"

"First of all," she snapped. "I never stole a damn thing from *you.* So you don't get to pick up a pitchfork."

"You stole from my family," Jonah informed her, eyes blazing. "Which means you stole from *me.*"

"Can we get on with this?" Logan demanded.

"Guess I'm not as greedy as you." Peri tucked a strand of loose hair back into the braid hanging down her back. "I couldn't afford the good faith payment required by the Argentinian government," she admitted. "Not to mention, trying to tackle the entire area alone would take me about a hundred and fifty years. I had to prioritize which area to salvage first. I partnered with my brother. You showed up like your usual bad penny selves. Bottom line; if I'd had the funds at the time, none of you would be here at all." Not strictly true. If not the Cutters then another salvager would've followed her trail.

"You would've *had* the funds if you'd sold all the artifacts you stole from us over the years," Logan pointed out.

"True." Chin high, she crossed her arms trapping her braid against her chest. "Money wasn't my motivation." Never. "It was just-" Payback. Petty. Hollow now. "Freaking stupid," she admitted, releasing her hair and shoving the long plait over her shoulder.

"But you're not a stupid woman." Nick scrubbed the back of his neck. "Ballsy, impulsive, yeah. Stupid, no. So why *have* you been stealing from us for years?"

Looking for a touchstone, her gaze went to the doorway to gauge Finn's reaction. Peri wished she hadn't. Quick-silver eyes like stone, lips pressed into a hard line, he looked furious.

No second chances.

Spinning away, Finn strode out of the room without a backward glance.

SIXTEEN

When Finn left, Peri felt as though all the oxygen had been sucked out of the room. As though her lifeline had been ripped away, she was overcome with an acute sense of loss. Swallowing against a tight, dry throat, the sensation of sinking deep underwater and drowning, enveloped her.

Damn it to hell. She'd *planned*, *anticipated* this confrontation for *years*. And somewhere in the back of her mind, she'd hoped for a glimmer of support from Finn. Hell, a little freaking *compassion* would've been nice. Instead, he'd walked out.

Surprised? her mind jeered. *Really*?

This was why *she* always walked away first.

She'd waited too long, become too attached to him, making the cut deeper. She'd ignored every mental caution to herself. Damn it, she *knew* better. People she cared about never stuck around.

None of this was unfolding as planned, and with Finn's complete withdrawal, every molecule in her body wanted to jump up and say fuck you all. Instead of being impetuous, Peri drew in a breath. No one could go anywhere because of the high seas. She had a captive audience, and things to say. Like it or lump it, they'd hear it. "Do you really have to ask, considering the way you guys have treated Rydell over the years? You screwed him over time and again." There was also that other pesky detail that was none of their damned business.

"I grew up hating you which made stealing from you easy. You had every freaking opportunity to confront and stop me. You didn't."

Retribution for Rydell was the motivation. Besting them, and taunting them with her presence, had kept her going. But getting zero freaking *acknowledgement* was what had driven her to dangerous extremes.

Because the Cutters had ignored her as if she didn't exist. For years. They hadn't given a hoot who she was, or bothered to find out why she'd appropriated their salvaged treasure. In the long run, the only pleasure she had derived from swiping stuff from right under their noses was the thrill of being caught.

Peri loved living on the edge. Knowing she could be caught in the act at any moment. It was like amazingly good sexual foreplay. The anticipation, the adrenaline rush—exactly like when she and Finn had made love behind an unlocked door, mere feet away from a hundred party guests.

Even now, when she'd revealed her identity, presented herself for who she was and what she'd done, the damn Cutters still had no interest in acknowledging her.

Maybe this was her punishment after all. Total disinterest. To be ignored as if she weren't more than a pesky fly. "I never planned to *keep* anything."

"Keeping what you *stole* you mean," Logan said. "Finn's right. It's well within our rights to charge you with piracy and grand theft."

"Why do you hate the guys so much?" Teal asked, her brow furrowed.

"Let me put it more bluntly; What the fuck did we ever do to you to warrant you stealing from us?" Logan demanded.

Zane looked grim. "*Nothing* warrants her stealing from us."

God, Peri desperately wanted to get up and pace, but the room was littered with Cutters like a damn physical minefield. She stayed put, chin high. "It's complicated."

Jonah snapped, "Simplify. You're damn quiet over there, Nick. What's your two cents on this?"

"I'll jump in when necessary. Right now, I'm listening."

"Your family started screwing over my family for years before I was even born."

"So, nothing to you personally?" Jonah rose to go to the other side of the room, poured another cup of coffee, and returned to his seat. He placed the steaming mug on the table next to him without drinking.

So they could close ranks, but she couldn't? "Anything you've done to my family is done to me by extension." What was sauce for the gander. . .

Nick scanned her features. What was he looking for? "Tell us about your brother."

"Rydell knows nothing about my actions and, believe me, he wouldn't condone what I've done. *He's* an exemplary human being. Honest. Honorable. *Ethical,"* she said pointedly. "And a damn good brother."

"Did this damn good brother tell you to *steal* from us?"

"She just said he didn't. Let her talk, Logan," Nick said. More gently, to Peri, he added with a nod, "Go on."

"Did you know that your father and mine were once partners?"

"Not until last year," Nick admitted, his gaze intense as he leaned forward to listen to her. "It was a long time ago."

"Yes," Peri acknowledged. "But with long reaching repercussions. Our fathers had a falling out around the time I was born and their financial agreement fell apart. Or so Rydell was led to believe. My father had another partner/investor, a Frenchman named Antoine Baillargeon. What Rydell didn't discover until a couple of years ago, was that Baillargeon had been subsidizing our father for years, pouring multi-millions of pounds into the failing salvage company. The Euro had gone up in value, interest compounded, and Rydell was unaware of the loan until after old man Baillargeon died and his heirs demanded repayment.

"It didn't matter that the debt belonged to our father. Case Enterprises is Rydell's company, and he takes his responsibilities as seriously as a heart attack. While all that was happening, you guys kept trying to horn in on his salvages, or taking him to court, or- pissed him off in some way.

Intentionally, I might add. If he defaulted on that balloon payment, you had the right of first refusal. If my brother lost, *you'd* conveniently own Case Enterprises."

Teal looked from brother to brother. "That didn't happen."

"No," Peri said. "Because Ry and Addison got back together, and they actually got a finder's fee for discovering stolen artwork, so they were able to make that payment." They'd been divorced, mourning the death of their first child, Rydell's ship had been hijacked. She snapped her mouth shut. They didn't need to know any of his personal business.

Nick's gentle smile confused her. Maybe it was just a trick of the light. "I remember reading about that. The thief tried to smuggle stolen paintings on his ship, right? Quite the finder's fee as I recall. Sounds like your brother's a sensible, responsible guy."

"He's always been my rock."

"Where are your parents?" Bria asked gently.

"Dead."

"So you only have the one brother?" Bria seemed to have forgotten her tea as she cast Peri a sympathetic look. "No other family?"

"I had another brother. Adam."

"He died of leukemia six years ago," Jonah told them.

"And you know this *how*?" Logan demanded, swiveling his head to look at his brother.

"My Callie was married to Adam Case."

"Fucking hell," Logan muttered. "Are you all keeping damned secrets? You didn't mention Callie was a Case. I thought her last name was West?"

"Maiden name." Jonah shrugged. "Not my secret to share."

Logan glared at Nick. "What's your excuse?"

"Same answer."

"Hell. I'm not done with either of you." He turned his attention to her, annoyance clear in his expression. "Question to you is; How the hell is this tale of woe *our* fault?"

Peri scowled right back at him. "Ry faced adversity from the moment Dad walked out on us. He emotionally supported our mother, practically raised Adam and myself, brought in Callie from her abusive parents who lived next door, financially and emotionally supported Adam after he was diagnosed, and supported Callie after Adam died."

"Jonah's Callie?" Zane looked from Peri to Jonah.

"*Our* Callie," she said tightly.

Jonah's lips tightened. "The same Callie sent by your conniving brother to spy on *me*, you mean?"

Nick shot him an amused glance. "The woman you forgave, and love with all your heart, right, bro?"

"Fuck you."

"Then what happened, Persephone?" Nick asked.

"In all that time, your father did nothing to help his partner and best friend. Not. A. Damn. Thing. He let him sink like a rock."

"Tell us about Rydell." Nick leaned forward, elbows propped on his knees.

"When he got the business back in the black, when he'd found a little freaking happiness, Ry's baby daughter *died.* His wife *divorced* him, and she took his brand-new ship in the settlement. On top of all that, his ship *Sea Dragon* was *hijacked* and eventually destroyed."

Zane shrugged. "A crap hand, but nothing to do with us."

Shut up. Shut up. Shut up. None of this was *any* of their business, they didn't need to know ninety-nine percent of any of this. They were the last people on the planet who needed to know how badly loneliness had strangled her as a child and well into her teens. How this vendetta had given her the strength to keep going.

People. Walked. Away.

Always.

She'd figured that one out early and well.

She was always prepared to walk first, and she handled it just fine.

"Tell us about your father," Nick said.

There'd been a lot of yelling and slamming of doors. Peri shrugged. "When he split, and left us behind in London, he ran Case Enterprises from an apartment in Boston. *Your* father cleaned him out financially, screwed him over a big salvage in the Sea of Japan, leaving him with nothing but his ship."

"News to me," Logan said. "We heard it was the other way around."

Acid burned her stomach. "Daniel Cutter was a liar, a thief, a drunk and a womanizer!"

"No shit," Jonah muttered under his breath.

"Whoa! All true. Yeah, he was. No secret." Nick addressed Zane, who'd half risen from his chair, his face flushed, his eyes flashing blue fire. "Two sides to every story, right? Let's hear Persephone out, and we can take it from there."

"Dad took his dive boat, what was left in the joint bank account, and my Mom's broken heart with him. A year later he committed suicide without leaving so much as a note." She shook her head on an exhale. "None of this is relevant, this has nothing to do with anything."

"No. We're interested. Aren't we?" Nick demanded of his brothers. "Keep going, Persephone. This is all relevant. Hearing about your family, your life, helps us get to know you."

Too damn late to get to know her now. The only thing holding her hostage was the weather. She was a captive confessor now. What had she expected? That they'd take her at face value? Of course not. "My Mom fell apart." There was no need to tell them that her mother had pretty much ignored her for as long as Peri could remember. It was Ry and Adam who'd stroked her back when she was bullied at school. It was Callie who'd helped pick out her first school clothes, with Ry and Adam tagging along to supervise.

It was Ry who'd gone to PTA meetings, Ry who'd bought all her Girl Scout cookies- Adam who'd run her paper route- the year she'd fallen off her skateboard and broken her leg. "At fifteen Ry held all of us together." By taking the ship left to him, and going out to look for a freaking wreck to salvage. At sixteen! What had the Cutters been doing at sixteen? Been tucked into their nice safe, warm beds by their loving mother? "With all that responsibility, he had to grow up fast-"

Feeling uncharacteristically fragile, Peri couldn't prevent skimming a glance toward the door, searching for one more glimpse of Finn. He was long gone. The dreadful weight of his absence was so heavy she was almost incapable of interacting with these people who didn't care for her either. The heaviness on her chest felt unbearable and made breathing difficult.

Lacing her cold fingers together in her lap, she no longer felt invincible. It was as though finally acknowledging her lies had stripped her of her hard outer shell leaving nothing but a soft squishy center for others to stomp on. Without Finn there, she was dying a death of a thousand cuts, with nowhere to run and no one to turn to.

Squaring her shoulders Peri sat up straighter, locking her spine. She had to get a grip. But right now she was incapable of doing much more than take whatever they threw at her. Desperation to be alone ate at her hard-won composure. She was damned if she'd cry, but she needed not to be 'on'.

"You've seen for yourself who we are," Nick told her. "I think if your brother sat down and had a real conversation with us, he'd discover we have a lot more in common than our mutual hatred for each other's father-"

"I have no plans to sit down with that bastard," Zane interrupted. "He's as culpable as she i-"

"Surprise!"

As one, everyone turned to face the door.

"Callie!" Sister of her heart. After a stunned pause—the taking of a step that wasn't there—Peri jumped up and flew across the room and into her sisters-in-law's arms. She buried her face against Callie's dark hair for a moment as her closed throat tightened even more, and her eyes smarted.

Looking puzzled, dark hair whipped by the wind and sea spray, Callie took Peri's face between her hands. "Peri what are you *doing* h-"

"Calista West, soon to be Cutter, love of my life!" Jonah closed the gap, took Peri's shoulder and moved her out of the way so he could engulf his fiancé in his arms. Callie wrapped her arms around his neck and kissed him.

After several moments while everyone looked their way, Jonah broke the kiss and cupped her cheek. The way he looked at her friend made Peri's heartache and the tears she'd been struggling to hold at bay burned her lids like acid.

"I just spoke to you an hour ago," Jonah told Callie, his face showing his love for her. He brushed her cheek with his fingertips, as if to convince himself she was really here and not a figment of his imagination. "All that wedding talk, and you forgot to mention that you're *here*!"

"I wanted to surprise you." Her face glowed. She released him to hug everyone else in turn, as they elbowed their way to get to her, laughing and talking over each other. "I decided I didn't *want* to wait three weeks. I called to fake you out as I was about to board the rental chopper at the airport. The pilot required a ginormous bribe to fly me in this weather. I think he prayed with his eyes closed most of the way. I risked life and limb to get here, and I want to get married *today*. I brought a priest. . . I think he's somewhere puking right now." Her smile lit up the room as she waved in the general direction of the interior of the ship.

Nick said, "I'm not sure this is the best—"

Jonah shot his brother a none too subtle shut-the-hell-up-glare, then turned back to his bride-to-be. "Sweetheart, to get that ring on your finger, at last, I'd marry you anywhere, anyhow, anytime. Hell yes, let's do it now. Here or *Stormchaser*?"

"The storm isn't abating, I'm afraid." A tall man in his mid-fifties stood in the background. "For those of you I haven't met, I'm Walker Goodman, Mr. Gallagher's PA. He had to take a call and asked me to relay several messages. You're all welcome to remain on board until the weather clears tomorrow at approximately three a.am. We'll be pulling up anchor on *Blackstar* soon thereafter, as Mr. Gallagher has a business meeting scheduled in Hong Kong regarding a merger and has decided to take *Blackstar*. Any discussions you might have concerning the salvage should be made through Hachirō Okabe in our New York office, as Mr. Gallagher will be tied up with merger negotiations for quite some time." He paused to let that sink in.

"Since congratulations are in order, I offer mine, and, because I couldn't help but hear the conversation as I approached, I'd like to offer the services of Mr. Gallaher's staff to facilitate a wedding while you wait for the winds to die down?"

Was there a message for her? Finn's guy didn't- not once- make eye contact with her. That *was* his message. Loud and clear.

"Perfect." Callie spread her arms. "Ladies?" Bria and Teal linked arms with her as she turned her head. "Peri? Come on."

Peri forced a smile. Everywhere from her hair follicles, to her toenails, hurt. "Right behind you," she told Callie, infusing the words with as much excitement and happiness as humanly possible, when she'd never felt more like crawling into a hole and pulling it in after herself. Before following Callie out of the room, she glanced at Logan, Nick, Jonah and Zane.

Their ice blue eyes cut through her with looks of disapproval. She was tempted to stay and take her conversation with the Cutters to some sort of conclusion, but Nick gave her a solid headshake. "We've heard enough for now. This is Jonah and Callie's time. We'll finish our business after the wedding."

Peri wondered exactly where he thought that meeting was going to happen. They were all being evicted from Finn's ship at three the next morning.

Bright late-afternoon sunlight streamed into Peri's cabin, where Callie was changing for her impromptu wedding. While her sister-in-law's joy was apparent in her smile, Peri couldn't help but wonder if it was selfish of her to be sad that Callie was only going to be a Case for another hour. Heavy-hearted, she also realized this would be the last time she'd be in this room. Onboard this ship.

Teal had opted to go back to "help" the guys. Doing what, Peri didn't really care. She suspected the mechanic wasn't much of a girl's girl. *Blackstar* was sure to be a madhouse as everyone raced around prepping for the unexpected wedding while the weather tethered them all inside for the duration. The high winds buffeted the wave-splattered windows, and foaming water sluiced over the decks.

Peri would've loved some time alone with Callie, but Bria was there as her sister-in-law got ready. All three women squeezed into the small bathroom while Callie did her make-up.

This was Callie's day, and Peri wasn't going to ruin her happiness by allowing her own unhappiness to show.

Finn was clearly furious if he was willing to literally pull up anchor and leave just to avoid her. Hard to reconcile that cold-eyed man with the human furnace who'd had his tongue in her mouth, and his hand on her breast just hours ago.

The house phone rang in the other room.

No second chances. She didn't need to be hit over the head with a freaking anchor. She got it. Loud and clear. Happy for the distraction, she went into the bedroom to answer it. After a moment, she poked her head back into the bathroom. Since Bria was handing Callie brushes as if she was a surgical nurse and Callie the surgeon, Peri remained in the doorway. "That was Finn's P.A. He says it's still too windy to be outside. Solarium okay?"

"Sure. Wherever. I'd get married right here in the bathroom if that's what it takes."

"Where's your dress, Callie?" Bria asked as she handed a big fluffy brush to the bride-to-be. "I'm sure it needs to be pressed."

Callie glanced from Bria to Peri and back again. "Probably. Would you mind? I left my carryall on the sofa in the living room. Thanks, Bria."

When Bria left, Peri slipped back into the bathroom. There were no more makeup brushes to pass. She propped a hip on the other end of the sink. Callie, an accomplished Marine Archaeologist, would be a big help to the Cutters, Peri knew. She'd been a big help to Ry who'd paid for that fancy degree.

Damn it, Persephone, stop being a bitch. Look at that shining, happy, in-love face. How could you possibly be mad at Callie just because your *heart's been ripped out?*

Throat burning with everything she wanted to share, she touched a finger to Callie's dark curls. "This reminds me of when you helped me dress for my junior prom, remember?"

"Fourteen and already a knockout." Callie said. "And that dress. . ." Her smile grew wider at the memory of Peri's skintight, strapless black evening gown.

"I thought I was so cool and sophisticated with my updo, Juicy Tube ultra-shiny lip gloss and smoky eyes. I looked like a hooker, didn't I?"

"Not at all." Callie smoothed a strand of hair behind Peri's ear. "Your brothers just didn't recognize a goth fairy princess when they saw one. I knew you'd grow into a rare beauty, Persephone. You've far surpassed the dreams we had for you. Your amazing house- which I'm determined to see *soon.* This mind-boggling salvage which will keep all of us busy 24/7, and make us all very, very rich, for the rest of our natural lives. You've done so well. And all on your own. You're a remarkable woman. I'm *so* proud of you, Magma."

Not if you knew what I've been doing. Peri closed her eyes. 'Thank you, but today is all about *you.* You'll have plenty of time to come to my house. We're going to remain anchored right here for the foreseeable future."

"I'd better bone up on my Spanish, then."

"You speaking Italian will help with that. Your hair looks cute shorter. Are you happy, Cal? No doubts or second thoughts this time?"

"Not a one." Callie took her hand and brought it to her cheek. "I don't even understand why I balked before. Jonah is the only m-"

"Man you've ever loved. I understand. Adam was a boy. You were a nurse, not a wife. I think he'd be pleased to see you this happy, Callie." Callie had been more nurse than wife for the six years she'd been married to Adam, and she'd done it without complaint. Adam had been dead for more than six years. It was time she found happiness.

Callie's eyes swam with tears. "You think?"

Her friend had had a shitty childhood, been accepted by the Case family, and married Adam knowing he was dying from leukemia. She was a freaking saint. "Without a doubt." Peri blinked the sting from her dry eyes. God, her chest hurt as if she'd been punched in the heart. "Did you call Ry?" she asked quietly. "Do he and Addy know about this?"

"Of course. Called right before I left the airport. He said they'd try their best to get here."

Peri's eyes went wide. "Seriously? Does he know all the Cutters are here?"

Callie shrugged. "*I* didn't know they were here when I called him. All I cared about was that Jonah was here."

Bria came to the door, a white dress draped over her arm. "There must be an iron somewhere."

Peri though a moment. "Closet, I think."

"Eccellente." She disappeared. A door opened and closed, the latch on the built-in ironing board snapped and Bria raised her voice to be heard from the other room. "I would love to do your hair, Callie. Let me iron this while you finish your makeup, and we'll do something simple and elegant and knock Jonah's socks off. Not that he'll care if you come out with your head shaved. I've never seen a man more besotted."

Callie smiled. "That focused passion is a Cutter family trait. That's part of the reason we love them so much, right?"

Had Callie already forgotten the boy who'd taken care of her, treated her as family, paid for her education and loved her unconditionally? "Rydell is like that, too."

Callie smiled. "God, he is that. Wouldn't it be-" She shook her head. "Yeah, no."

Peri almost snorted. Yeah, no was right. There'd be no happily blended families. Tough on Callie to be in the middle of the feud.

The Cutters were taking Callie away from her. Her friend wasn't going to get cold feet this time.

Rydell and Addy and baby Adam were a closed unit.

Peri was on the outside looking in, no matter where she turned.

Oh, get over yourself. She played a mental violin and told herself to snap the hell out of her funk. Everyone was happy. How could she begrudge Callie, or Ry and Addy, every scrap of happiness they deserved?

In the bathroom mirror, Peri saw Bria behind her, arranging the garment over the ironing board, then testing the heat of the iron. "You should see how Finn looks at Persephone."

Peri fought to drag a sip of air into her constricted lungs. "Then you didn't see his face when he walked out earlier."

"Perhaps he had an emergency?"

He had a million people on board at his beck and call who could handle any freaking emergency thrown at him. "Perhaps."

What Bria thought was passion was disgust. Peri would have to have been blind not to see his cold, deadly anger just before he stalked out. It was as though a door, ajar to show a sliver of warmth, had been slammed shut in her face.

Whatever physical attraction Finn had felt for her, had been wiped away when he'd learned who she really was deep down. Someone who sure as hell didn't deserve his love. The room blurred. Her heart, shriveled to dust, was too dry for tears. Tilting her head back, she blinked rapidly to bring the bathroom back into focus.

"Are you okay?" Callie asked softly, wrapping her arms around Peri's waist from behind. Resting her cheek on Peri's shoulder, their eyes met in the mirror. "You look like you're about to cry."

"Have you ever seen me cry?" Peri asked with a smile that felt forced and brittle. Callie didn't seem to notice.

"No. But- *Are* you all right?"

Enveloped in a cloud of coconut-scented lotion, and memories, Peri hugged Callie's arms against her. "*Absolutely*. I'm happy for you."

"I love Jonah, Peri. More than I ever thought possible. But I'll never forget Adam."

"I know." It annoyed the hell out of her that Callie's words made her throat ache even more.

Behind them the iron let out a burst, bringing with it the sweet smell of steam, and the crisp scent of hot linen. The elegant Principessa was industriously ironing the white sundress Callie would wear for the ceremony.

Letting her friend go, Peri stepped back and turned around to face this woman who was as much an older sister to her as Ry was her brother. "You deserve this happiness, Cal. You do."

Callie reached to cup her cheek with a cool hand. "I know you're happy for me, please don't look so sad."

She'd feel a hell of a lot better, and be able to think strategy, as soon as she was home and away from all this excessive emotion swirling around her. "Sad? Silly bride-to-be," she teased. "I'm not sad at all. I'm thrilled you're getting the man you love."

She really, really, really needed her old self to kick her butt so she could get back to normal. A new normal. Without Finn.

"I have to go and find more distilled water for the iron," Bria raised her voice. "I'll be right back to finish with your dress, then I can help you with your hair if you like, Callie." The cabin door opened and closed.

"She didn't need to go." Peri tried to smile, but her lips felt tight. "She's already heard everything I had to say. It wasn't pretty."

Callie's brow knit with concern. "What wasn't pretty? I'll repeat and would like an answer this time. Are. You. Okay?"

"I- Yes. I'm still alive. Not sure how long that's going to last. Your arrival was either fortuitous, or inconvenient, depending on who you ask. I was right in the middle of a confession."

"What on earth were you confessing *to*? That you're Ry's sister? Who cares?"

"That, and I've been stealing from your future in-laws for years."

Callie frowned. "Stealing what?"

Peri told Callie everything she'd told the Cutters.

"Oh, Peri-" Callie turned to hug her. "Does Ry know?"

"Not yet." Peri dreaded *that* conversation.

"I won't even go into the danger of diving alone. When you were God only knows where, and no one knew who you were. Anything could've happened to you, and we would never have kno- Damn it. Do *not* make me cry on my wedding day. No one was watching out for you Peri. That was really crazy dangerous. Why did you do it?"

"Honestly? Now that the cat's been let out of the bag, it doesn't make sense to me either." It did in her own convoluted way, but the explanation she'd given wasn't enough to satisfy them. Which was too damn bad, because it was all they'd get, the rest was none of their damn business.

"Rydell asked me to spy on Jonah, remember? *I* met him under false pretenses and lied my ass off when we first met. In spite of which, he fell in love with me." She gave Peri another hug before disengaging to lean over the sink to draw a cat eye. "He loves me. I love *you.* He'll convince his brothers not to prosecute. Besides, *Rydell* will insist on making it right, you know that."

"It's not *Ry's* job to make this right, Cal." Ry was going to be furious. He'd forgive her, after some time, but she'd have to face his wrath first. Jonah, on the other hand, was disgusted with what she'd done and was more likely to add to the lawsuit his brothers would bring.

Rydell would be bitterly disappointed in her. She'd rather the Cutters threw her in jail before she saw that look on her brother's face. She stiffened her shoulders, turning away to watch the wind whipping up the waves beyond the large, uncurtained window.

She turned to face her friend. "I don't need anyone to fight my battles for me, Callie. I've been fighting my own battles for years. *I'll* make it right. I'll have all the stolen artifacts delivered to Cutter Cay in a couple of weeks, and I'll make whatever restitution a court finds reasonable. It'll be a relief really, I've been waiting years for this confrontation. I'll deal with whatever they throw at me."

"I'll always stand by you, you know that."

"You'll stand beside your husband, Callie. As you should. And if the rumor of a baby is true-"

Callie laughed. "According to Teal, right? That's because *she* is, and she thinks we should all have babies together. Nope. Jonah and I haven't changed our minds about going kidless for the foreseeable future. If that ever changes, which we both doubt, we'll adopt. In the meantime, I'm pretty sure the rest of the family will breed like bunnies, so we can be the doting aunt and uncle. I want us to spoil *your* kids rotten, Magma, so you *can't* be in jail."

Another piece of Peri's heart shattered as she realized the possibility of someday having Finn's child, was one more thing she'd lost.

Peri's chest ached and her eyes felt scorched and dry. "What I did was wrong, and I deserve whatever the Cutters dish out."

The door opened. Bria came into the cabin followed by a steward bearing a tray. "I brought tea and a few sandwiches to hold you over for a while, Callie. Right over there. Thanks, Sandro."

The steward gave the Princess a smitten smile, deposited the tray and left.

Not a sign of the distilled water she'd gone to find.

"Things are humming along nicely," Bria told Callie. "I think you'll be pleased, *sorella*." She pulled the desk chair over to the small seating area, then sat down and started to pour the tea into the three waiting cups. "Your future husband can wait a few more minutes to claim you. Let's sit and have a nice cup of tea and a little protein to keep up your strength." Bria smiled wickedly. "Then I'll finish ironing your pretty dress and help you with your hair, so you can go off to start the rest of your life."

Sorella. Sister.

And she'd thought she couldn't feel any worse...

Everything inside Peri now felt freezer-burnt.

SEVENTEEN

Sitting behind his large desk in his office one deck above the festivities, Finn's heart clenched like a tight fist as he observed Ariel's- no, *Persephone's* beautiful face, fixed and pale, in his monitor.

"Prosecute the son of a bitch to the fullest extent of the law," he told his lawyer in New York, eyes on the feed from the surveillance cameras in the solarium where Jonah and Callie were getting married.

Mentally he swore, unable to look away. She'd thrown him off balance from day one. Turned him on. Infuriated him. Driven him out of his fucking mind to possess her every second of every fucking day.

He knew damn well he should've indicated to her he had to leave the salon to take an urgent call and felt like shit for not doing so. Maybe not excusing himself was a subconscious way of punishing her. Fuck. Was he that small?

No. He was *that* fucking furious. Disappointed.

His anger had been directed at Derry, but hadn't it also been directed at *her*?

He felt betrayed. "Asshole."

"Yeah, he is," his lawyer agreed.

Finn didn't correct him.

Flailed by lashes of guilt, and in spite of how he felt about her lies and subterfuge, he couldn't take his eyes off her. Watching her now ripped a small jagged hole in his heart. Her hair rippled down her back in molten splendor. Had she worn it loose to torment him?

She'd changed into a purple dress that hugged her curves and made him aware of what he was missing by sitting in his office talking to his damned lawyer.

"Hell no, I don't give a flying fuck if he's thrown back in jail for *another* fifteen years. He's had all the chances I'm willing to give him, and then some. Throw the book at him, then fire Chamberlain for not paying attention. We knew the date of Derry's release, Chamberlin should've anticipated that Derry would try something."

Chamberlain, one of Finn's fleet of lawyers had been tasked with keeping an eagle eye on all of Derry's doings. Inside the joint and outside. He hadn't done his job.

His dick for brains foster brother slash ex-business partner, three weeks out of prison for embezzlement, had forged Finn's signature on several of his bank accounts, yesterfuckingday. To the tune of several million dollars. Redirecting the funds into an offshore account. Stupid mick to think Finn didn't watch his every dime like a fucking hawk. He'd been caught red-handed.

Derry business concluded, and annoyed this call had pulled him out of the salon earlier, Finn wanted to wrap things up. Impatience clear, he demanded brusquely, "Anything else?"

Of course there was. He suffered through another seventeen minutes of urgent business. He wouldn't've had to be playing catch up if he hadn't been so distracted, and busy with Ariel- no Persephone. She hadn't lied about that.

He disconnected the call.

On his big screen monitor, he could see every freckle, every micro-expression as if she stood right there in the room with him. But reality was, he didn't need the high- resolution camera to tell him where the freckles were. He'd memorized every goddamn one, paying as much attention to every inch of her as though he'd been charting a course to Mars.

Standing well back from everyone gathered around the happy couple, she looked starkly alone and, damn it, *vulnerable*. She*wasn't* vulnerable, he reminded himself. She'd spent years plotting and scheming to rob the Cutters, with the thinnest of excuses. Nor was she alone in the back of the room. Thiago Núñez stood beside her.

Núñez said something to her, and she lifted her chin and looked straight ahead. Finn had seen that pugnacious chin lift before. When she was put in the hot seat. When she felt judged. Finn's chest ached, and he rubbed his fist over it. God damn it, when she had to defend herself against being hurt. How often had *that* happened in her life?

His harsh words before he left the salon had been knee jerk A first for him. He was usually meticulous and precise in his words and actions. For that alone, he needed to apologize...

Even though he knew damn well he had a valid reason for leaving, he felt as though he'd made the biggest mistake of his life by doing so at that particular moment. The lawyer had texted him in the middle of Peri's big reveal with an urgent message, and Finn was torn about not signaling to let her know that she hadn't been the cause of his abrupt departure. But that wasn't strictly true.

It wasn't his modus operandi to walk away from a problem. But Persephone Case tied him in knots and skewed his judgement. Two valid reasons for putting her behind him. He hadn't gotten where he was today by being a sucker. He'd learned quickly when to fight, when to hold the course, and when to walk away. With Derry and Erica, he'd done all three. They'd each had multiple opportunities to course correct. Both had chosen poorly.

He'd divorced Erica, and felt zero compunction being instrumental in putting his business partner into the prison system for another fifteen years.

He wasn't about to compromise his principles for a sexy, freckled, redhead, with more bravado than integrity. Persephone Case aka Ariel Andersen was the least defenseless woman he'd ever met.

He knew her to be foolishly fearless, and seemingly invincible.

She'd tried to steal his tablet, withheld that she was already in possession of another, all while holding back the truth about her real motive for being on board *Blackstar*. Were the words true at all, or had she specifically wormed her way into his heart to take advantage of her position as his lover?

He'd given her more than enough opportunities to tell him what the fuck was going on before she presented it to them. All the hours they'd spent alone and she hadn't confided in him. That rankled and he added that to his list of warring emotions. She'd opted to be secretive, effectively shutting him out, and rendering any help he might've given her, moot.

He was used to making calculated, incisive decisions and acting on them immediately. He *trusted* his own goddamn instincts.

How many times had he granted someone a second chance only to get kicked in the head for it? Twice.

So why the hell would he allow a pretty redhead to kick him in the heart?

Because she held him firmly by the balls?

Fuckshitdamn.

When the priest indicated the groom should kiss the bride, Peri slipped from the room unnoticed, leaving Núñez behind. With zero interest in the wedding which was winding down, Finn turned off the monitor. There was no reason to watch the Cutters celebrating a private, family moment.

Honest to God, with the tablets and legend of Blackstar, he still wasn't sure if they were building the con to out-con even Derry. Or were they what he'd believed them to be for all the years he'd known them? Like a Rubik's Cube, he tried various scenarios to see if any of them lined up. Thus far nothing did.

Zane *must've* recognized her as the owner of *Sea Witch* when he'd checked her out with Finn's binoculars the other morning before breakfast. What was the reason for *that* lie? Unless he'd been looking at the *other* redhead on the dive platform on Case's ship?

Leaning back in his swivel chair, he knew it wasn't the Cutters actions that had him absently rubbing his palm across his aching chest. If he lived to be a hundred, he'd never forget the stark expression on Peri's face just before he walked out.

Damn it. He couldn't support her on this. Refused to bring into his well-ordered life a liar. A thief. A con artist. Been there, fucking done that. His reputation had been hard won. His personal code of ethics *worked* because he'd learned the hard way that to give an inch compromised everything he believed in and lived by.

His expensive divorce, and the dissolution with his business partner, didn't come close to the kick in his gut when he heard Peri blithely confess.

Fucking hell. Fucking, fucking hell.

It seemed that everything she did was calculated, planned. Had 'accidentally' bumping into her at Natural Sciences Museum in Buenos Aires really been a chance meeting? Hell, he didn't know anymore. Where Persephone was concerned, he'd clearly lost his judgment.

He closed his eyes, then had to quickly open them when, in his mind's eye, her face appeared before him as a tactile after-image. Damn. He couldn't even escape her in his thoughts.

It was one thing to crush a business rival, quite another to crush the spirit of a woman he'd allowed himself to care about.

"Fool me once- My judgement was skewed the second I saw that hair. Those lying eyes tasted that soft mouth- Damn it to hell." Shoving the chair away from his sleek glass desk, Finn rose. "I warned her. Didn't I goddamn *warn* her? No second chances. Don't screw me. Don't lie. Don't steal."

The Cutters had known *exactly* who she was. Known from the get-go. Which made it all the worse. He felt betrayed by *them* as well as Peri. The Cutters should've clued him in from the start. The fact that they hadn't indicated that they were inexorably entwined with her in *something*. And why had they let her swing in the wind like that without confronting her days ago?

Never mind. He now didn't give a flying fuck what or why. None of them had been straight with him. That's all he asked. Transparency. Honesty. Was that too fucking much?

His captain had orders to pull up anchor the moment it was feasible for *Blackstar* to depart. Maybe once he put distance between himself and the woman who drove him to the point of madness, Finn would get used to sleeping without her by his side.

How the hell long would it be before he stopped thinking of stripping her naked? Before craving the scent and feel of her skin against his was in the past? How fucking long was it going to take to forget the silky glide of her fiery hair over his body and the taste of her mouth under his?

It had only been a couple of hours since he'd stalked out of the salon and he craved touching her like an addict needed a fix. He paced to erase the visceral memory of her ankles over his shoulders, and the dig of her sharp nails scoring his back. He remembered the feel of being deeply embedded in her slick sheath and her small breathy gasps of pleasure against his ear as he surged inside her.

Yeah. An addict. Only there was no cure. Nothing that could wipe the scent or taste or touch or her from his memory.

He wasn't any more of a drinker than the Cutters, but he was tempted to get blind drunk and stay that way until he could forget every tactile and visual cue.

No second chances.

Finn was a hardass about it. He'd learned that any other way was detrimental to his life, his business, and his heart.

"If I think feeling this way is bad, how would I feel when she lies again?" Because she *would*. Someone with her track record would lie and steal again. Because that was inevitable, too. What would he do if he'd let himself believe for even a second? When there'd be no fucking hope in hell of getting out the other end alive?

And yet – why *had* she stolen from the Cutters? There was more she hadn't told them, Finn was sure. Had she done it for attention? A need to be one up on those she perceived had taken advantage of her family? But why?

More than the bitter family rivalry and dissolution of their fathers' partnership. He remembered her telling him - with a smile that broke his heart, that her mother had claimed to have postpartum depression for twelve years, until her death when Peri was in her mid-teens.

She'd lost her father when she was barely five.

Her brother had a slew of his own shit to deal with while raising his siblings, and taking care of business. He'd married. Her other brother had died. Callie was leaving her family and becoming a Cutter.

"Bloody hell." He imagined Peri in a filthy prison-God only knew where. Imagined what they'd do to her there.

He'd buy off the Cutters tomorrow. Save her at least from the horror of prison. Maybe that would rid him of this sick feeling. It would do nothing for the craving ache in his gut.

"Fucking hell." A lightbulb moment had him dropped back into his chair, as he pieced together snippets of information she'd told him. "Her entire life has been filled with unmet expectations by the very people who should love her unconditionally."

She'd told him her background in the barest terms, but seeing that look of abandonment on her face, for that split second, said it all.

She *expected* people to leave her.

Mother. Father. Brother. Whatever it was she wanted from the Cutters. Himself. *None* of them had given her what she needed – to belong, to feel like she was included and part of something. "Did we all fail you, Persephone?"

He'd fucked up. Royally.

She masked the need with a cheerful and upbeat exterior, the chip on her slender shoulder just waiting to be knocked off so she could come out fighting.

"And I call myself an astute judge of character? How was I so damned wrong here?"

He hadn't heard if she'd explained more to the Cutters or if what he'd heard was it. What he did know was he needed to hear her out before making a judgment call that would change the course of his life forever.

His private line rang. It was the call he'd been waiting for, but he needed to wrap it up quickly. "Zak," he answered on the second ring.

The call took six more minutes of precious time.

Tapping his earpiece, Finn left instructions for his assistant, "I'll be incommunicado for the rest of the evening. Don't allow Persephone to leave with the others. Text when everyone else has disembarked and we're underway."

He'd put some mileage between himself and the Cutters until he found a resolution.

Every minute that passed that he didn't talk to her, was another minute she'd think he'd walked out on her intentionally, deepening her wound.

If he were going to make this right, he had to know everything his business partners and Peri were hiding. The truth.

Persephone Case may well be the one person who deserved that second chance.

But first, he went in search of answers.

The wedding was simple and moving. Finn's staff had pulled in greenery and orchids from all over the ship in lieu of traditional wedding flowers, and the solarium had looked festive and pretty. Callie, incandescent with happiness caused a lump to form in Peri's throat. She was happy for her sister, who'd gone through so much to end up with the man of her dreams and an instant big family.

Yeah, the Cutters were one big, happy, freaking family.

Finn hadn't been in attendance, no matter how she willed him to walk into the solarium to stand beside her. No matter how many times she rehearsed what she'd say to him if he did. To hell with it. She didn't owe him a goodbye or any explanation. And she sure as hell wasn't going to beg him for anydamnthing.

Dr. Vadini had gone to his cabin earlier, and Finn hadn't joined them again. Not even for his friend's wedding. That left her and Theo to stand, like extra appendages, in the back of the room. Two outsiders watching happiness and love swirling around the Cutters, at arm's length. She felt like a gatecrasher.

Numb, as if she were watching something sad on T.V. and she couldn't change the channel, Peri was torn between resentment and jealousy of their close-knit family. She missed Ry.

Her chest hurt. They were so freaking *happy*. They'd already forgotten her and her big confession. For *years* she'd been blatant and in their faces in the hope of forcing a confrontation. What the hell was wrong with them anyway? She'd moved from being covert to being in the open - face to face. She'd admitted what she'd done, yet, they still didn't freaking *see* her as important enough to give a damn. All her mental hand- wringing and angst had been for nothing. She was no more interesting to the Cutters than a pesky mosquito.

Insignificant.

The next step was up to them. It was going to be damned hard to prosecute her when all the pilfering had taken place in international freaking waters. Given the lack of attention they were paying to her, they probably wouldn't even bother. She was *that*insignificant.

She was tough and resilient. Not a moper, she wasn't usually this damned introspective. It sucked. She inhaled deeply and breathed out slowly. She was over it. Done.

She was damn sick of them. And God, she was *so* sick and tired of her *own* vulnerability *around* them. It was exhausting. Useless. Now that she'd said her piece, it was over and done with. She could walk away with a clear conscious and concentrate on her own salvage.

Peri took in the fading light, and froth of whitecaps beyond the windows. "The winds are dying down enough to leave," she told Theo in a low voice as Callie, at the far end of the room, kissed her groom to much applause. The seas *were* down, but really too high to safely go out in her twenty-foot runabout.

But, when had she ever backed down and done what was safe? Hell, she was an excellent sailor, and her need to put space between everyone on board *Blackstar* and herself was more urgent than a few second thoughts about the danger of traveling from*Blackstar* to home. *Tesoro Mio* was closer, but right now she couldn't handle one more confession, followed by more recriminations. She just couldn't.

"Good," he whispered back. "I'll come with you."

"Fine. But I'm in a mood, so stay out of my way and don't talk to me." *Or bring up Finn's name*. "I'm going to slip out, you stay for a bit. Don't make a big deal about leaving. Get your things and meet me down in the garage in about ten minutes."

Peri left. No one stopped her. Hell, she doubted anyone even noticed her absence. *Stop it. You don't care, remember?*

Callie's arrival had put a full stop to whatever whoop-ass the brothers Grimm had been about to deliver. Finn's closed expression, followed by his blatant absence, told her all she needed to know about how *he* felt. So be it. She'd had her say.

She'd let all sleeping dogs lie.

She went down to her cabin to get her things. Chest tight, eyes hot and dry, she just wanted to crawl into a dark hole and stay there. But since that wasn't an option, she grabbed her suitcase and started throwing in the few things she'd brought on board with her.

She needed to talk to someone who loved her no matter what. She took out her phone and called her brother. Not to tell him about what she'd done to his arch enemies, just to hear his voice.

Ry's phone rang and rang. He must be hunkered down with Addy and the baby riding out the high seas. Chest tight, she disconnected before it went to voicemail.

Hell, even the freaking animals went into the ark in pairs.

She wanted Finn with an intensity so deep she could barely breathe.

"The farther I'm away from him, the easier this will be," she said out loud to reassure herself. "I'll miss him for twenty-four hours. Max." She didn't need some guy to "complete" her. She was complete just the way she was.

Rolling up the white linen pants and tank top she'd worn to dinner the other night she stuffed the balled-up fabric into the case.

Whether she was on board *Sea Witch*, in the middle of an ocean, or in her glass house on the bluff, she'd never felt this alone. Isolated. Hell, she always prided herself on liking her own company and the feeling of self-sufficiency. It really ticked her off that, because of them, the brothers and Finn, she didn't feel that now.

The exclusion she'd felt as she'd watched the Cutters tease and laugh, and damn it- love each other- hurt. It shouldn't because she hated them, but it did, which made her hate them even more.

It hurt that Finn hadn't cared enough to stay with her.

It hurt because she'd wanted him to care about her as much as she cared about him.

It hurt because she'd anticipated the end of their relationship barely before they'd started. She'd *known* it would happen. Eventually. But on her terms, not his. And not yet, damn it. She'd made this mistake of lowering her defenses. He'd snuck into her heart before she could raise her usual barricades, damn it.

Peri much preferred being the dumper than the freaking dumpee.

His expression would now be indelibly marked in her brain, and she'd never forget it. His features had been hard and fierce, his eyes pewter as they bored into her for that split second before he'd turned his back.

She pressed her palms over her burning eyes, breathing through the ache in her chest. "Alone is good," she reminded herself, dropping her hands. "I like being alone." *Liked* not reporting to anyone. Liked being unentangled emotionally. She reminded herself that she'd done what she'd come for. Finn had never been part of the plan. Just an extremely attractive distraction. Time to move on.

After changing from the purple sundress she'd worn to the wedding into jeans, and a long-sleeved black t-shirt, she stood in the middle of the well-appointed cabin. "To hell with *all* of them."

Her phone rang, and her stupid heart leapt.

"Is it done?" her brother demanded.

"I'm absolutely *awesome*, thanks for asking. How are *you*?" Peri said tartly, tossing a lone sandal into the case with enough force it bounced onto the floor. "It was a lovely wedding, Ry. Callie's very happy." She didn't want to make him feel bad by pointing out that he hadn't walked the bride down the aisle.

"Despite my misgivings, and loathing of the Cutters, I *did* try to get there to walk her down the aisle," he said gruffly, echoing her thoughts, as he frequently did. "I just want my sisters to be happy."

One of them was, and the other would be as soon as her freaking pity party was over.

"She understood." She tossed her makeup bag into the suitcase. "Maybe you guys could have them over sometime so you can welcome Jonah to the family," she said tongue in cheek. It would take Dr. Vadini's apocalypse before Ry consented to breaking bread with the Cutters.

"Jesus, Magma-" A lengthy pause, before he said with resignation. "Yeah. We'll do that for Callie-Hell, gotta go. Does this fucking wind ever stop?"

"Eventually. . ." she said to a dead line. "Love you, Ry," she added, knowing he wasn't there to hear it.

She sighed. "I'll go over and tell him everything tomorrow. He'll get over being pissed at me- relatively soon. As for these damned Cutters-What did I expect? An open-armed welcome after I told them I robbed them blind for years? Grow up, Persephone." Her wobbly voice sounded tinny, and the pep talk just depressed her further.

As for Finn. . .He'd torn through the emotional protective shield she'd armored herself in as if it were wet tissue paper. Destroying what had taken her years to build. He didn't know her at all. Hell, she didn't know *him* either, apparently. Because his walking out, when she needed him, had come as a shock. Although she'd three-quarters expected it all along. Peri had no freaking idea why the hell she was so affected by it. They'd known each other for a minute, and fifty-nine seconds of that had been spent having wild monkey sex.

She padded barefoot to the window to assess the wind and the water. Not that it mattered. She was going. High seas or not. Dusk was falling, darkening the sky. She'd been on the seas in inclement weather, loved it when the waves frothed over the bow of her runabout, loved the feel of the wind in her face, and the danger. But never when the waves were this high, or the wind this fierce.

"Scared of a little wind, or go?" she asked herself. "*Go*," was the only answer.

Finn had decreed the wind would stop at three am. She had no doubt he would be obeyed. By then she'd be safely asleep in her own bed. When she was back in her house, her boat, her dive, then this shaky, uncertain, emotional person she was right now, would be gone. Finn or no Finn.

Best of all, there was no need to interact with him or the Cutters ever again. Her lawyer could talk to their lawyer. She had her own claim, and salvage to fill every waking hour. She'd barely be aware of the larger ships anchored miles and miles away.

Screw them. Screw them all.

"*My* fault for having illogical expectations. So- screw me."

Resolution made, and backbone restored, she pulled on her waterproof windbreaker and looked around for her cap. Someone knocked on her cabin door. Hope leapt into her heart. Finn. The first and last person she wanted to see right now.

Yanking open the heavy door, her hopes sank. "Theo."

"Ready?"

She found her cap in the jacket's pocket. "We were supposed to meet down at the garage." Twisting her hair on top of her head, she pulled on the knit cap.

He shrugged. "Didn't have much to pack."

Crossing the room, she slid her bare feet into the tennis shoes she'd left out of the suitcase. As she tied the laces, she said over her shoulder, "Did anyone say anything before you left?"

"No." He shook his head, smiled, and held up a duffel bag. "But I *did* get this." Tilting it so she could see inside, he chuckled. "It is yours, after all."

He'd taken her tablet from the salon while everyone was upstairs. Peri hugged him. "Thank you. I was thinking it might end up as the spoils of war." Actually, she hadn't given the gold tablet a second's thought in the last couple of hours, which showed how distracted she'd been. "Weren't those security guys on duty?"

"They were, and I informed them that Dr. Vadini and I had been granted permission from you to study your tablet further, and you would be joining us. I merely recovered your property."

"And I appreciate it." She indicated he go ahead, then closed the door to her cabin behind her. The corridor was empty and quiet. Everyone on board was fully engaged in the wedding reception above decks.

"I don't know those people well enough to celebrate the marriage of two people I don't give a damn about," Theo said ruefully. "And honestly, neither should you. None of those people like you, Ariel. And that's an understatement. You shouldn't trust any of them to have your back. I'm glad you weren't there to hear how they talked about you after you left with the other girls."

As they took the elevator down to the hull garage, Peri didn't ask him why her enemies would talk about her in front of him, knowing she and Theo were friends, nor did she correct the 'girls' comment.

"Holy crap!" She paused in the open doorway of the elevator and took in *Blackstar*'s garage. It was a jaw-dropping space, filled with water toys on either side of what looked like an indoor swimming pool. First, the space was *enormous*. Second, there were not just three of the Cutter's runabouts moored near Finn's sleek black speedboat, but there was also a shiny black pickup truck parked beside a-of course -black convertible, and two massive motorbikes.

"Apparently when not in use, the internal basin is used as an indoor swimming pool. A stupid waste of space if you ask me." Theo told her, indicating she go right along one of two docks. "Your boat is first in line, in position for departure."

The scent of salt water mixed with a faint trace of diesel permeated the fresh air flooding the expanse from the open doors at the far end where they were headed. A warm wind made her loose hair dance around her face, and she pushed it under her cap.

The garage door was open, and she saw that the sky wasn't quite black yet. The rimi on the horizon, a thick stripe of pale gray and tangerine, bled into a deep charcoal blue, scattered with pinpricks of pure white stars.

Witchcraft was already in position on the automatic slide mechanism, ready to drop with a push of the button.

Finn's sleek space-age-looking runabout was stored on a rack to the side of Peri's much smaller boat. She paused to give it an admiring glance. "And Finn's crew was okay with this?" Tossing her small suitcase on board first, she jumped from dock to deck.*Witchcraft*, snug in the rollers of the slide, rocked only slightly with her weight as she untied the bowline, then stood at the helm.

"Theo, I'll need you on the stern." Noting the key that she'd left in the ignition what seemed like a lifetime ago, she continued with directions. "We've got to hit the water before starting the engine. The controls for the slide are on the starboard side of the garage door. Given the rough seas, I'll start right away, which means I'll need you on board, and fending off until we're away from the boat."

Remembering the procedure from the last time she'd departed in her own boat, she added, "The slide automatically retracts, and the garage door auto shuts, so we don't need to worry about that." Adjusting her cap so it didn't blow off, she zipped her jacket up to her chin, then pulled the hood up over her cap and cinched it at her throat. The best she could do to keep dry. Having no peripheral vision, she had to turn her whole body to see if Theo needed help with the slide mechanism, but two men were there to help. She hadn't seen them when they'd entered the garage, and with the sound of the wind and waves beating just beyond the open garage doors, she hadn't heard them on their soft-soled shoes.

"Senor Gallagher authorized us to assist you in whatever way necessary," the shorter, younger of the two men shouted as he threw the untied rope onto the deck near her feet. He spoke with a Spanish accent, with a strong hint of Patagonian.

Yeah, she bet Finn authorized her speedy departure. He wanted her gone. She'd made the right freaking decision. "Thanks for your help." She removed her waterproof Pelican case from the console, and placed her turned-off phone inside, then returned the case to the cubby, snapping shut the small door.

The three men spoke in rapid Spanish, their words barely audible over the slap of waves. The second man was older, mid-fifties, with a shock of black hair, which matched his black eyes. Without comment, he stepped on board and went to tie off the rope nearby.

"I've asked Santi and Eneas to accompany us back," Theo told her. "I know you're an excellent sailor, Ariel, but I won't be much help. I feel much safer knowing we have back-up should we need it.

"Theo, we can't take Mr. Gallagher's crew with us." Peri frowned, as Theo got in the boat with her. The other man took over at the garage's control panel. "No offense," she told the two men. "They'll have no way back for one thing, and for another the water's settling, and I certainly don't need help."

"They have tomorrow off," Theo told her dismissively, as the boat started sliding toward the garage door. "Both have family in Puerto Mahón. They can find their way back to *Blackstar* on their own."

As *Witchcraft* glided from the shelter of the garage, the first man jumped aboard, and Peri no longer had time to argue, as the wind swept away her words, and she had to aim the bow into the waves. She started the boat as it hit the choppy water, then immediately maneuvered away from the yacht.

"As long as the Blackstar people know where they are, I suppose it's okay. Theo, grab life jackets for everyone from below. It's going to be a rough ride."

Pushing the throttle forward, she eyed her instrument panel, and pressed a button on the electronic guidance so she'd stay on track. She had about an hour of light left, and she'd need radar after the sun went down. "We should reach Puerto Mahón in two hours give or take."

The rough trip would require every scrap of her concentration. Perfect. The last damn thing she wanted was time to think about Finn.

EIGHTEEN

Finn headed to the salon. He needed to see Persephone, touch her, breathe her in. Knowing he'd hurt her broke his goddamned heart. He had to make it right.

It had taken extraordinary courage for her to remain in that room filled with her perceived enemies- alone- and tell them what she'd done. To his knowledge, her friend Dr. Núñez hadn't offered her any support while Finn had been in the room. Maybe he had after Finn left?

In her own inimitable way, she'd sat there daring the Cutters to knock that chip off her shoulder. If they had, they'd done it after he'd left. If she hadn't finished due to Jonah's fiancée showing up, then she'd go back to them for more. She was tenacious as hell. She'd had something important to say, and he knew she wouldn't stop until she'd said whatever it was she wanted to say.

Even though they'd all - and that fucking included himself, insulted everything from her veracity to her honesty, she'd taken it, head held high. Her quiet dignity when she'd spoken, despite their judgement, showed her inner strength and resolve.

She wasn't a woman to back down, and she wasn't a woman who'd take no for an answer. She'd been a winter storm pounding against a sea wall, as she bared her soul to the Cutters. She'd held her own.

He should've fucking stayed, but all he'd thought about when he got the text, was dealing with Derry once and for all. Knowing Derry had fucked him over yet again, pissed Finn off royally.

He'd dealt with the situation. Now he needed Persephone like a touchstone. If she forgave him for being an asshat, that was.

He took the stairs.

He knew the way she liked her breasts touched, and the way she was drawn to adventure. He knew she didn't shy away from confrontation. He knew she protected her brother like a mother lioness, but he had no idea how she dealt with disappointment. Would she be somewhere licking her wounds? Punching a hole in the wall? God, would she cry? His heart pinched.

He'd sit her down and let her tell him anything she damn well pleased without comment. Then he'd explain about the call. About Derry's betrayal. She was a reasonable, intelligent woman, she'd understand.

He also wanted to clear the air with the Cutters before they went their separate ways. Ensure there was no misunderstanding his position. He wanted to look them in the eyes and hear from their mouths, what the hell was really going on with them and that cock 'n bull story about the tablets.

Now that the winds had died down earlier than predicted, his guests didn't have to wait another six hours to leave, they could bugger off at any time.

When he strolled into the salon it was to find his guests enjoying the hospitality his staff had provided. Damn nice of Britt, his chief steward, to break open a couple of bottles of Cristal for them.

"We need to talk." Finn strode into the middle of the room. He'd half expected Peri to be there, and when she wasn't, his heart hitched.

Still, his Persephone was a fierce warrior, and Finn's other half had expected her to come at him, guns blazing.

Unless the wound he'd inadvertently delivered was deeper than anger.

Callie, an attractive woman with dark hair, and intelligent green eyes, came over to him. "Thank you for opening your home and for allowing us to have a beautiful wedding."

Jonah joined his new wife and shook his hand. "Thanks, Rocketman," he said stiffly. "Appreciate you accommodating us. We were just about to call to let you know we're heading out early since the wind's down."

He felt the tension in the air, but all Finn cared about was a long-legged, redhead. "Where's Persephone?"

Nick gave him a dark look. "Clearly not here. We haven't seen her since the wedding. Did you really think she'd come back for more?"

"She's not a woman who backs down," Finn informed him coldly. "She had things to say to all of you. Was she done? If not, I expected her to wait out the festivities, and come back to confront you."

"Well, she *didn't*." Bria scowled at him. "I think she was done talking. She was devastated when you walked out right in the middle of what must've been a very difficult conversation. It was clear she needed your support."

"I had an urgent call." Christ. He sounded defensive. He already felt like a shit without being scolded, and god damn it, he *was* defensive.

"You spent the preceding hour practically stripping her naked in front of us, and making love to her on the goddamned sofa, Gallagher." Nick's eyes blazed. His wife placed a hand on his arm. Nick sucked in a furious breath. "You staked your claim, but as soon as things got tough you bailed."

"Who are you?" Finn asked coldly. "Her father?"

"We know you're a workaholic, pal." Zane glared at him over a full champagne glass. "But that was a tough shitshow for her. You should've stuck around in a show of solidarity. It was six against one."

Finn raised a brow. "You certainly changed your tune."

The youngest Cutter shot a brief glance at his brothers. "We had a meeting of the minds."

"Bully for you. I'm going to go and get her, let her finish what she had to say if necessary. You'll listen, and you'll remain fucking civil. When that's done, you can tell me what all that bullshit was with the tablets. Then you can all bugger off and give Peri and me some privacy."

He turned to go, but Logan grabbed his upper arm, stopping him. "You've known us for ten fucking years, Rocketman. After all this time, do you *really* believe we had anything to do with what was written on the tablets?"

Finn looked at him over his shoulder as he turned to leave. The urgency he felt to find Peri was overwhelming. Right now he didn't give a flying fuck if or what the Cutters had up their sleeves. "I don't know. Did you?"

Logan released his arm, jaw set, deep blue eyes glinting with challenge. "Will you take our word?"

Finn searched his friend's face. He'd already proved to himself recently that his judgement was skewed. *Trust your instincts.* "Yeah."

"Then you have it," Logan assured him. "We were as surprised and puzzled as you were."

"You see how bringing up the name Blackstar would spark my disbelief?" The urgency Finn felt to find Peri throbbed behind his eyeballs.

"Yeah. We figured." Jonah wrapped his arm around his new bride's waist and tugged her against his side as he addressed Finn. "But no matter. That's what Vadini and Núñez assure us the tablets say. Nothing to do with us. And talking about tablets- one's missing. I'm guessing it's no coincidence that Peri's isn't here."

Blood pressure rising at the flat-out accusation, Finn glanced behind Jonah to see that only three tablets gleamed on the coffee table. The fourth easel stood empty. "Before you cast aspersions, legally it's hers to take. I'll go and tal-" His phone buzzed. "Talk to her." His phone buzzed again and he glanced at it briefly to see if Persephone was calling him to read him the riot act in private. Fair enough.

It wasn't Persephone. "It's the Captain. Hang on, I'd better take this." Everyone stopped talking as Finn listened for a few minutes. "What the fuck?! How did that happen with no one seeing it? Fire whoever was on surveillance, effectively immediately. A glitch like that is unacceptable."

Finn stared unseeing at the slowly darkening sky after he disconnected. Nothing but open water. Damn it to hell, Persephone. . . He turned to the Cutters standing in a group as if – waiting. "Did you lot have anything to do with her leaving?"

"You know what, Gallagher? Fuck you," Logan told him. "We're not even going to dignify that with an answer. She was absolutely *fine* after we all spoke to her right here before the wedding." He turned to Callie. "She was okay when she went to change, right?"

Callie shared a look with Bria. "She was. . .subdued."

"Introspective." Bria looked worried.

"She knows the seas here." Zane too shot a look at the diminishing waves, visible through the ceiling to floor windows across the room. "Hell, she knows the *weather* here. Going out on the water in a runabout doesn't make sense. She's not that stupid."

"She's not any kind of stupid," Finn snapped. "She wouldn't leave." *Leave me.*

"*Caro.* Dark eyes distressed, Bria rested a slim hand on Finn's arm. "She was deeply hurt after you left, I think."

"The wind's have died down earlier than predicted. Núñez and her boat are gone." Finn told them, curtly, his annoyance- no fucking *fear*- making his voice gruff. "I can assure you, Persephone wouldn't retreat. She'll storm in here any minute now, tell all of us to sit the hell down and shut up, and she's going to finish what she started. Núñez was with her in the solarium watching the wedding. He's idiot enough to steal the tablet and her boat. I'm sure she's in her cabin."

He was sure of no such thing.

He touched his earbud. "Page Dr. Núñez. Have him report to the salon asap if he's still on board." Núñez was long fucking gone. Bastard had taken a tablet and Peri's boat and pissed off before anyone could stop him.

He *would* be found, and suffer the consequences for his fucking actions.

Finn strode from the salon, taking the stairs down to the lower deck three at a time, passkey in hand. Sliding the key into the lock without knocking, he pushed open her cabin door.

Immediately he was engulfed in her soft fragrance. "Persephone?"

When there was no response, he went into the empty bathroom. The fragrance of lilies was stronger here, mingled with the womanly smells of cosmetics and lotions.

Going back into the bedroom he opened the doors to the large closet. "Fuck it." *Empty.*

"Shit." *Blackstar* was the size of a football field. She could be anywhere. He hoped to hell she *hadn't* taken out a twenty-five-foot boat, on the open water, in these winds.

Acid burned his stomach as a bad feeling surged through him. What if something had happened to her to *prevent* her leaving with Núñez?

Finn picked up the house phone on the bedside table and called the Captain. "Use the P.A. to call Miss Andersen- No, make that Miss *Case*, to come to the salon immediately. Hell, use both names, and keep repeating until I tell you to stop. Alert the crew. I want her found. I'm returning to the salon. Send me any surveillance footage of the garage and of her for the past two hours. Have the T-FLAC operatives, and our full security team, meet me in the salon in three minutes. And ready my runabout with emergency equipment.

Please God, don't let it be necessary.

It was fully dark by the time Peri saw the lights of the Puerto Mahón marina in the distance. No one knew about the entrance to the caves in the cliff under her house other than her brother. She planned to keep it that way. Currently, the service elevator was filled to bursting with stolen Cutter artifacts. She didn't want anyone else to know about that either. And she certainly didn't want Theo to have unrestricted access to her house from the caves below.

The marina it is then.

Her bright green slicker had kept her body comparatively warm and dry, but everything else- from top to toe- was cold and soaking wet. She looked forward to a long hot shower and her own bed. She was too tired to think, feel, or have a rational conversation with anyone. Given everything that had happened today, that was both a blessing and a curse. Good thing she lived alone. She didn't even want to talk to herself tonight.

It seemed like a lifetime ago that she'd driven the ten miles from her house to the marina to meet Theo to take him with her to *Blackstar*. He'd parked beside her, and together they'd walked down the dock to where *Witchcraft* was moored.

Then, she'd felt energized sailing to Finn's ship, knowing she'd be with him, and would soon confront the Cutters. Anticipating the confrontation had filled her with a mix of excitement and dread. The anticipation of spending time with Finn had filled her with pure joy. Now, she just felt hollow about both.

Fortunately, the wind and slap of the waves had precluded conversation with Theo and his friends the entire trip. She'd left *Blackstar*, too numb to make polite conversation with anyone. Pretty soon that wall of nothing was going to crumble, and she damn well wanted to be alone for that.

Theo sat beside her, the older guy sat on the small seat in the bow, and the younger one was on the stern seat behind her. Needing every advantage possible in the rough water, she'd directed the men on where to sit so their weight would be evenly spread in the small boat.

The swells had decreased throughout the trip, but the random high crests and low troughs were as jarring as skating up and down a cement skateboard ramp. She'd bitten the inside of her mouth several times as they bounced along and her jaw ached from gritting her teeth. The muscles in her neck and shoulders were stiff and sore from fighting the wheel for two hours.

She'd stood for most of the journey. Now, her legs felt rubbery and weak, as though she'd run a marathon.

"*Querido Dios,"* Theo said fervently, seeing the lights of the marina approaching through the water drops streaking across the windshield. He perked up, loosening his death grip on the edge of the plexiglass. "I am *very* grateful *that* is over. You are an excellent sailor, Ariel."

Peri dredged up a smile. "You might as well call me Peri, Theo."

"I'm not sure I can. I have called you such ever since I've known you. After five years it would be hard to call you something else now."

"Ariel is fine."

"To be honest," Theo told her, using both hands to comb through his wet hair. He staggered, putting out his hand to hold on again. The swirly tattoo on the web of his right thumb glowed in the dark. She'd never noticed its luminosity before. "I had no understanding of what was going on with you and the Cutters this evening. You know I hate drama of any kind, and the tension in the room was thick enough to cut with a knife. I was focused on the beauty of the tablets, and tuned out most of the conversation. Was it important?"

They passed the rock breakwater, and the water was relatively calm. Peri took one hand off the wheel to shove her drenched hair over her shoulder. She'd sacrificed her cap to Poseidon an hour ago. "No. Not at all. You didn't miss a thing," she said, inhaling deeply of the fresh smell of the day's catch and a hint of cigarette smoke as they passed a fishing trawler with a light on.

You didn't miss a thing other than my life imploding. Nice to know you cared as little as everyone else. Most of the craft in the marina were small fishing boats and sailboats, well-secured against the high winds. Patagonians knew their weather well. No one went out when the winds were as high as they'd been when they left *Blackstar*. There'd been some dicey moments.

Peri pulled into the wide bay of the marina and glanced back at the other two passengers. "You know how to tie up a boat, right?"

She knew from past experience Theo didn't have a clue.

"*Sí, señorita*," the older guy said, standing, steady on his sea legs.

Peri returned her attention to reversing into her slip. "Of course, you do, sorry. You work on *Blackstar*, you must've tied up dozens of craft." She twisted her shoulders to get the kink out. It didn't help. "I left lines on the dock when I left," she said looking between the two men, since she didn't know which was which. "Would you crisscross two on the stern, use a spring line, and another on the forward piling for the bow? We'll do a port side tie."

"Santi," Theo ordered, and the older man stepped easily onto the dock to grab the lines. His friend, Eneas went with him.

After throwing the bow line to Eneas, Santi handed the spring line to Theo, then walked over to grab the stern lines.

After checking her position, Peri caught the lines and secured the boat. Normally, after being in the open water, she'd take care of the boat by either cleaning it herself or hiring someone to do it. But not tonight. The marina was closed, and although well lit, only the security guard was around. The light was on in his little hut, and she could hear the bass on his radio faintly on the wind.

She didn't have the energy to give *Witchcraft* the TLC she deserved. But tomorrow was another day. She'd come over and take the runabout to her place and give her a good scrub down.

Theo, holding the heavy bag with her tablet in it, handed her onto the dock. With a concerned frown he scanned her face. "You look exhausted."

No shit. "Not something any woman wants to hear, Theo."

Peri adroitly sidestepped him to check on one of the cleated lines. Unwinding it, she re-cleated it more securely before turning back to him.

"Why don't you let me take you home? I'll bring you back tomorrow for your car," he offered as they started walking in the direction of the parking lot. Forty-foot-tall cypress trees formed a windbreak in a semicircle around the perimeter of the marina, and their smoky, pungent, piney, scent mingled pleasantly with salt water and fish on the night air.

There was no sign of his friends. "Nice try. And you no longer have sleepover rights, Dr. Núñez," she said, trying to add a teasing tone to her voice.

"You're fucking the millionaire," his voice was flat with a tinge of censure.

"*Billionaire.* And not anymore."

He gave a bitter laugh, and Peri glanced at him, as he said, "Then you never looked at him when he watched you. His eyes fuck you every time you're in the same room, and when you leave, he watches the door. And I'll tell you something else. You never looked at me the way you look at Gallagher. Even if you didn't keep your hands off each other in public, the heat between the two of you was obvious to everyone."

Was he jealous? After all this time? She had no intention of fanning those dead embers with him. She'd better make that clear. "Theo-"

"I don't care, Ariel. I really don't."

She touched his arm. His slicker felt wet and cold. "I'm glad. I still want to be friends." Which she couldn't imagine any man wanted to hear, so they were even, she supposed.

"Well, as your *friend*, I insist on driving you home. You're too tired to do it on your own safely. Don't argue."

Tall, utilitarian metal lamp posts lit the way as they passed a shack that sold hot coffee and the fresh catch of the day in the early mornings. Theo's friends were almost at the parking lot, as they wandered down the length of the dock, apparently in no hurry. One lit a cigarette, and the red tip glowed, bobbing in the dark as he walked.

It was impossible to think she'd *ever* had sex with Theo. Their relationship had barely lasted the five months she usually allotted to lovers. There was nothing at all she found attractive about him now, certainly not in comparison to Finn.

Both lights on the tall poles in the gravel parking lot were burned out, and they stepped into the deep shadows under the trees.

"You should report the lights," Theo told her, taking her hand to wrap it over his forearm when she stumbled over an unseen rock. "It's dangerous out here in the dark, you could fall and hurt yourself, and that guard is probably old and drunk and useless, so no one would find you until morning."

Peri withdrew her hand, as she walked. *No touchy-feely.* "What a cheerful thought." She *would* report the lights, but it was rare that she came into the marina, although she kept a slip there.

The smell of the cypress overhead was much stronger under the trees. The pungent piney smell thick in the now still air. Their shoes crunched as they walked across the gravel parking lot. Damn, it was dark enough that she might *need* Theo's strong arm after all. She'd rather not.

His black truck was still parked beside her electric blue SUV. When Theo wasn't in Buenos Aires doing his job as Minister of Antiquities, he ran a sheep farm twenty-five miles inland, so he didn't have that far to go.

They got to their vehicles. Thank God. She had about enough energy to make it back home. Skip the shower, she'd just fall, nose first, onto the bed and deal with everything in the morning.

She reached for the bag he carried. "Thanks for the offer, Theo, but I want my own car in the morning." He handed the heavy bag to her, and waited until she was inside her car, the tablet on the passenger seat beside her.

"I'll follow you."

"Go home, Theo." Peri pulled the door closed. He stood beside watching her. Peri smiled and shook her head, waving as she started the car. The engine clicked. She tried again. Damn. Had she left the lights on the other day and run down her battery? She tried again, and again the engine refused to turn over. Not even a hopeful click. Damn it to hell, she was too tired, cold and freaking wet to deal with this.

Cracking the door, because she couldn't lower the window without power, she said, "Do you have jumper cables in that fancy truck of yours?"

"I do. I'll turn the heater up, and you can sit in it and at least warm up while we jump start your car."

Sounded good to Peri. Grateful he didn't push driving her home again, especially now that her car didn't work, she got out and started walking around the back to his truck.

Something painfully hard struck her on the temple. Her head seemed to implode from the blow. Peri's eyes rolled back in her head as she slumped to the ground. Confused, she blinked back the pain and dizziness. The dark canopy of the trees swirled sickeningly, and nausea rose in the back of her throat as pain radiated from the point of contact. Had she been hit by a falling branch?

Her vision dimmed. Don't lose consciousness. *Do. Not.* There wasn't a hospital for mil. . .

Time seemed to pass in lightning fast slices, as if she was inside a strobe light. Theo. Her car. Trees. Men's voices.

She hung on by a thread, the intense pain seemed to surround her. Eyes blurry, she focused on Theo's feet and legs to orientate herself as everything around her spun. "Theo-"

"*¡por Dios!* What are you doing? I almost had her in the truck, you fool."

Another voice so close, it was practically in her ear, responded in angry, rapid-fire Spanish. The man loomed over her. *Think. Breathe.*

Think, damn it.

Move!

Struggling weakly to twist free, she was jerked onto her back by rough hands. A man leaned over her, a dark shape against the darkness behind him. She caught a glimpse of his feral black eyes and rough unshaven jaw before the sudden, alarming, heavy weight of a knee compressed her chest, stealing her breath.

His hand smelled of nicotine and sweat, as he covered her mouth and nose, to wrench her head to the side.

Swallowing bile, Peri broke her fear-induced paralysis and fought for her life. Kicking out proved useless, and trying to punch and buck her hips garnered her nothing more than him almost breaking her ribs with the full weight of his body pressed down in the middle of her chest.

Someone else held her legs, stopping their useless flailing. The sharp sting of a needle piercing a vein in her neck had her fighting manically, as full-fledged panic and terror flooded her body. A surge of adrenaline gave her strength to do whatever it took to get the man off her. Thrashing and bucking, she fought him with everything in her. But an insidious fire and lassitude melted her veins like hot syrup, slowing her movements.

Her world faded to black.

NINETEEN

Wired, adrenaline surging, Finn returned to the salon. "Peri was last seen entering the elevator going down to the garage well over an hour ago," he told them, sick in his gut. No matter how good a sailor, the high winds and large waves were nothing to mess with. And it had been *more* dangerous an hour earlier than it was at present.

"Left for *where*?" Logan demanded. "Don't you have video surveillance on this big, fucking fancy ship of yours, Gallagher? For god's sake. . ."

"Hang on-" Finn looked at his phone, watching a very chummy Núñez and his Peri leave her cabin. Surveillance followed them into the elevator until the doors opened. He swore. "Security cams in the garage were dark."

Nick frowned. "Are you saying we don't know if she was coerced, or went on her own?"

"Didn't look like coercion to me," Finn admitted, still feeling an urgent need to go after her. He stabbed her number on his speed dial. "Either she went directly to her brother on *Tesoro Mio,* which would've taken thirty minutes give or take, or she headed back to the mainland, which means she's still out there."

"Hi, I can't find my phone," Peri said cheerfully in the message recording. "Call back sometime." The beep was as annoying as hell because he wanted to hang onto the sound of her voice a few seconds longer. No 'leave a message' no 'sorry I missed your call'. Trust her to be different.

Ah, Jesus. I am sorry. So fucking sorry, sweetheart.

Don't panic. Her boat was out of range, or her phone turned off, that was all. Every fiber of his being demanded he race out and find her. His pounding heart and dry mouth showed Finn he *was* fucking panicking.

Blackstar's security cameras covered every inch of the ship. Not only because it was his home, but because it was also his corporate office. The fact that every single fucking camera in the garage had been dark for six and a half minutes while she and Núñez departed scared the living crap out of him.

Teal frowned. "Alone?"

"Dr. Núñez was with her." Finn scrubbed a hand over the stubble on his jaw, not feeling comforted by the knowledge at all. He punched in her number again. "But he's no sailor, and won't be any help if she's in trouble. I'm going to go look for her." Voicemail. The sound of her cheerful voice gripped him by the throat and wouldn't let go even when he disconnected.

Peri where are you?

"I'll go with you," Nick told him, zipping up his jacket, and indicating the three T-FLAC operatives standing silently nearby, accompany them.

"Wait." Callie removed her phone from the tote bag slung over her shoulder. "Let me call Ry first to make sure she arrived there safely."

"Good idea." Just because he was thinking the worst didn't mean the worst had happened. She'd gone to her brother, of course she had. Right now she was thirty minutes away, enjoying a cocktail with her family.

For some reason, thinking she was safe with her brother didn't lessen the tight knot in Finn's belly. He watched Callie's face as she talked to Rydell Case, and used the time to alert his crew to ready both the runabout and his chopper immediately. If she was with her brother, Finn still wanted to hold her, touch her, *see* her, to ensure she was all right. If she wasn't he'd fly to her goddamn house and make his apology.

"Call me back right away when she does show up," Callie demanded. "Okay. Thanks-"

"Give him my number." Finn held up his phone.

"Yes," Callie said, reading out his private number to Case. "I don't think so. Not yet. Yes, I will." After disconnecting, she looked first to Jonah, then to Finn. "She didn't go to Rydell and Addy. Ry wanted to know if he should go looking for her or come here. I told him- Well you heard."

"Jesus." Logan closed his eyes, then opened them again. "The water's calming down some. She must be almost to the mainland by now, right? She's fine."

Finn didn't know any such thing. He started for the door, Nick beside him. "I'm going to look for her to make sure of it."

His phone rang. A quick glance told him it was Persephone.

Ripping out his earpiece, he slammed the phone to his ear, so angry, so fucking *scared*, he lost it. "Are you out of your goddamned mind going out alone in this weather? What the *hell* were you thinking-"

Bria touched his arm and shook her head.

Finn closed his eyes and breathed deeply. Only then was he able to modulate his tone. "Darling, tell me you made it home safely."

෴

Dizzy and disoriented, Peri tried to breathe away her nausea through slightly parted lips. She lay on a soft surface, and everydamnthing hurt. No. It was just the pain radiating from the base of her skull where some asshole had hit her.

Her clothes stuck to her skin, cold and clammy. Her rain slicker was now trapping the moisture *inside* it. Strands of wet hair clung to her face and neck like annoying seaweed, indicating she hadn't been unconscious that long.

Voices penetrated the fog, and nausea ebbed and flowed in sickening waves. How long she'd been wherever she was, she had no idea. But she hadn't been out long enough for things to dry. So she was close to the marina.

The last thing she remembered was the blow, followed by a few seconds of fear before someone stuck her with a freaking needle.

She didn't want whoever knocked her out to know she was awake, but, God, she wanted to puke. It was as if she was *inside* her nausea and dizziness with no end.

Where was poor Theo?

"How much of that tranq did you give her, for God's sake?" Sounded like Theo? Well, shit. He was *in* on this? That didn't make any sense at all. "We need her alive to convince Gallagher to come. Without her, we have no bargaining chip."

"She's fine." A deep, unidentified male voice said. "I estimated she was about the same weight as a sheep. I gave her the appropriate dose."

"There was no need to drug her at *all*. I almost had her in the truck. With her car disabled, she would've come willingly."

"We weren't prepared to risk it. You know her better than any of us. Do you really think once she knew what we had planned she would've come willingly?"

"She *wouldn't* have known until we got here."

"She had no intention of inviting you in, and you know it. This was the most expedient way to get into the house."

"Why isn't she waking up?" Deep Voice, said as his booted foot struck Peri's ribs.

Pain radiated from the sharp kick, jarring her teeth. It took everything in her to remain limp and unresponsive.

Sheep tranq? Peri played possum as she fought her way out of a thick, mind-numbing daze. Succumbing to new waves of nausea, her mouth filled with saliva, but she didn't dare swallow too overtly. She was aware enough to know she was in grave danger. A few minutes might clear her brain and enable her to think while she listened to their conversation to get a clue as to who they were and what they wanted.

The police would want descriptions of the kidnappers. If she was alive to give them descriptions. Think this through, clear your mind, and focus. What do I know?

She pictured in her mind's eye the few moments between being struck and being injected. She'd caught a quick flash of fluorescence on the man's descending hand. Why did that strike a cord?

Dear God. Did it match Theo's tattoo? Were they some kind of gang? No. She couldn't picture Theo in a gang, tattoo or no tattoo.

What then?

"She should be coming around soon." A third man said in Spanish.

Theo and at least two others, then. She didn't recognize their voices. Were the two men she'd brought to the mainland here with them? That would mean five men in total.

Peri slitted her eyes to look through the shield of her lashes. Everything was a blur. She was so tired. It was much easier to shut her eyes. Take a little nap. She'd deal with- No! God, no. Wake the hell up!

"I still dispute bringing her here."

"He'll come to her. You know we can't reveal the citadel's location. Gallagher already knows she's a thief. He'll believe that she wants the other tablets for herself. Trust me on this. . ." Theo's voice faded as Peri struggled to clear the cobwebs.

Moving incrementally, and as silently as possible, her eyes gradually focused as she got some feeling back into her extremities, albeit with painful pins and needles.

Lying on her side, she recognized the annoying tickle on the side of her nose was the white flokati rug in her living room. She was in her own house.

She had the home team advantage, if having the advantage was being bound hand and foot, and surrounded by men with guns.

All the lights were on, even the pendants over the island in the kitchen. The sky beyond the enormous windows was pitch black, reflecting the three arguing men, and more shadowy figures across the room. Her sluggish heart started skipping beats. There were *more* than three of them. She heard fabric rustling and the slide of a shoe on the floor behind her. *More* people unseen. Other black-clad men, not participating in the conversation, ranged around the room. A giant Peri party, apparently, with her as the trussed-up guest of honor. All she was missing was the damn apple in her mouth.

Time to see which of her body parts would cooperate. The arm she was lying on was numb, and she tried to wiggle her fingers behind her back to encourage circulation. Sweat beaded her brow. Her heart skipped several beats before resuming a faster rate. Her wrists were bound tightly behind her. A slight shift of her legs told her what she'd dreaded. Her ankles were bound, too.

"She's awake."

Shit. Her heart sank, and she instinctively recoiled, even though she couldn't get far. Theo glanced at the two men she'd transported from *Blackstar,* reflected where they stood behind the sofa.

"Ahh," her tongue felt thick and useless. She wet her lips before managing to spit out, "You two went ahead and were waiting in the parking lot so you could ambush me." When she moved her head, the room took a few twirls which almost made her throw up. "So much for no g-good deed goes unpunished."

Now that she got a better look at them, she remembered the younger one as the waiter she and Finn had almost flattened the night they'd had wild monkey sex in the pantry on *Blackstar*.

"What's going on, Theo?" Her voice slurred and sounded terrifyingly weak to her own ears. Peri struggled to sit up. Her head swam as she flopped down weakly on the rug. How long would the drug take to dissipate? "Who are these men, and what do you all want?"

"Bring her phone over here," Theo ordered someone behind him as he crouched beside her. "You're to tell Gallagher that you want the other three tablets. He has an hour to get here. Alone."

Theo held an ivory-hilted curved-bladed knife in front of her nose. It seemed enormous, sharp and deadly. She heard the fast pulsing of her heart in her ears and kept her expression as impassive as she could. "No."

Theo grabbed her chin in his palm and squeezed her jaw.

"Do not doubt for a minute my intention, Ariel. One swing of this blade has sliced off a sheep's leg. Think what it will do to the fragile bones in your wrist. Or this pretty face."

"You're going to kill me? What have I ever done to you, Theo?" His behavior was so bizarre and out of context that her drugged brain couldn't figure out what the hell was going on. " You want my tablet? Have it. I don't care."

"Kill? No, I have great plans for you, Ariel. That doesn't mean I won't hurt you. I *have* your tablet. I want the other three."

Her cheeks flared hot with anger. This was a crappy end to a really lousy day. "Go. To. Hell."

Her stomach swooped sickeningly as Theo dug the tip of the knife into her cheek. It took a second for the pain to hit, and another second for the heat of her own blood trickling down her chin to register.

"If Gallagher doesn't deliver them, *alone*, within an hour, I will cut off your hand."

Her vision swam, and her throat worked as she swallowed nausea. "Theo, for God's sake- Finn doesn't give a damn about me. You were there when he made that abundantly clear this afternoon, remember? He. Won't. Come. " Aw, shit. She shouldn't have admitted that. Every second she was alive was a second she could find a way out of this freaking terrifying situation.

"Yes. He will. No man would imperil the woman he loves if he thinks he can save her life."

That sounded really good to her. Too bad that wasn't the case. "You mistake sex for love, Theo. Why ask for Finn? The Cutters found the other two tablets. Ask them to come."

"They don't give a shit what happens to you, Ariel. Gallagher *does*. You'll call your lover, and this is what you will say. Don't deviate from the script, or I warn you, it will be most unpleasant. Repeat this; 'Finn, I want the other three tablets. Bring them to my house. You have one hour to get here.' That's it, Ariel. No improvisation. Do you understand?"

"Sure." Even if Finn *himself* decided to come, which he wouldn't, it would take someone at least how long? Ten - twenty - minutes to get the helicopter ready? And that was if a helicopter could fly if the wind was still up. Then at *least* the thirty-five, forty to fly to the mainland. So, bottom line. Even if Finn *wanted* to come, he'd never get here in time. Peri knew no matter how he'd left things, he wouldn't want her dead. So he *might* send those counterterrorist guys to retrieve her tablet and make sure she stayed alive. Surely they wouldn't allow Theo and his thugs to dismember her?

Nice thought, but unless they had super powers, *they* couldn't arrive in time either.

Even if all that were logistically possible, the biggest thing to quash Theo's grand theft plan was – Finn and the Cutters would never relinquish those tablets.

Theo was right. They all knew her to be a thief. No one would be coming to her rescue.

She was going to have to freaking rescue herself.

Twisting her wrists behind her back, she kept her face expressionless even though whatever was binding her cut into her skin and she felt the slick warmth of blood with each painful twist. "You have my tablet, why isn't that enough for you?"

"They are *not* Blackstar's prophecy for *El Elegido-"*

When she tried to lever her upper body upright, her head swam and saliva pooled in her mouth. It was no point trying to free herself until she was sure- pretty sure- she could stand. "Then why do you want them?"

"They must be destroyed."

"Whoa." Peri frowned, then wished she hadn't when her jaw pulsed painfully. "You want to *destroy* the tablets? Priceless windows into antiquity, worth who knows how many millions of dollars?"

"What is written is blasphemous and incorrect," Theo snapped, eyes blazing with a feral gleam. "We have anticipated a sign from Blackstar for five hundred years. But this is not it."

"*We*?"

"The Chosen. *El Elegidos*. The tablets must be destroyed so that our followers are not confused. Our prophecy must be found elsewhere and quickly. We are running out of time."

"You believe there *is* a prophecy?" Feeling was coming into her bound hands with a vengeance, tears of pain stung her eyes.

"The world will die a fiery death, leaving eleven thousand true and faithful *Elegidos* to repopulate the Earth."

"And *you* guys are the Chosen?" Peri scoffed, glancing around as much as she was able. The men looked through her. "Seriously?"

"*El Ehnos* knows of this false prophecy. The gold tablets confirm everything they hold holy, Excellency." A man out of her range of sight said, "Dr. Vadini will not permit the tablets to leave the ship."

"I sent word to kill him. But now he is no longer an impediment." Theo held Peri's gaze.

Peri rolled her eyes. "The *Chosen* and the *Protectors*? Is this some kind of joke? Let me see if I have this straight." Every second they didn't kill her, was a plus. "*You* are the Chosen, Theo? Really? And you're saying sweet, ancient Dr. Vadini is the Protector?" If any of this was true, Dr. Vadini seemed more likely to be the real thing. "Why don't you just work *together*?"

"The four tablets found," Theo told her, taking her phone from someone out of her line of sight, "have imprecise information on them."

"So the prophecy *isn't* true?"

"It's true," Theo told her impatiently, "but not the way described in the tablets. They are wrong. My people would be confused. They must be destroyed before they do any harm."

"There must be *other, accurate,* tablets," the older man who'd accompanied them to the mainland said with authority as he stood behind Theo.

"According to the first tablet, there are *five*." Peri tried flexing her sore fingers to get more life into them. "So even if you get your grubby hands on the four we have, or destroy them, there will still be a tablet out there that you *can't* find. It'll haunt you forever, Theo. Or until the apocalypse, I suppose."

"It is more likely that we will find the correct tablets at either the High Altar or the Holy Lake. Then the prophecy will take place unimpeded."

The man who was beyond her line of sight said flatly, "We don't *know* where the Holy L-"

Theo held up his hand. The man stopped talking.

None of this made any sense to Peri, and having her head throb, and her eyes trying to roll back in her head wasn't helping. "If all three of you have been on board *Blackstar* all this time," she said impatiently, "why didn't you just destroy the tablets *there* instead of going to all this trouble?"

"The bomb we planted on board *Blackstar* will destroy all records and transcripts. Your Mr. Gallagher, or one of his people, will deliver them to us here, or we will personally see to destroying every trace of the tablets where they are."

A bomb? Dear God. "You placed a freaking *bomb* on board *Blackstar*?" Her vision swam as she lifted her head. "Are you *insane*? There are hundreds of innocent people on board!" Finn was onboard. Dear God. . .

"It is set to detonate in," Theo glanced at his watch, "sixty-five minutes."

"What if they don't send someone here with the other three tablets?" Why would they?"

Theo smiled. "They will."

"You're insane! Why are you demanding the tablets be brought *here* when you're going to blow up Finn's ship and kill all those people and destroy the tablets?"

"Quite simple, really," Theo told her, as he tried to figure out how to turn on her phone. "Either they will be destroyed in the bomb blast, or if I have the tablets in hand I can 'read' them to our people. And since none of them can read the Abipón language, they will believe everything I say as gospel. I will assure them that the tablets verify the prophecy while we look for the real tablet."

"You're crazy, Theo. Please-" Thinking he was going to hit her, Peri flinched as he sliced his hand down. Instead, he squeezed her jaw again, grinding her teeth together.

"Repeat what you will tell Gallagher."

Probably shouldn't tell a crazy man he was crazy. "I don't remember."

On her side, and bound wrists behind her, she felt the coolness of the leg of the heavy stone coffee table. No way to lift it as a weapon. The kitchen, spare on cooking gadgets, was twenty-five feet away. She didn't think a spatula was going to do much anyway. While Sea Witch, down below in the caves, was loaded for bear, or pirates, she had no weapons in the house. Her gaze flickered over the white marble plinth beneath the forty-inch-tall, bronze of Aphrodite.

Her head was starting to clear, the nausea, manageable. All she had to do was free her bound arms and legs, make it unimpeded across the room, pick up about eighty pounds of bronze statue, hold it aloft long enough to take down at least ten determined men, and run like hell.

Piece of cake.

Theo repeated what he wanted her to say.

"Finn," Peri parroted obediently, "I want the other three tablets. Bring them to my house or Theo will amputate my hand. How's that?"

"If you think we'll permit Gallagher or his people to come, guns blazing, to rescue you, think again. He won't get away with anything," the man behind Theo told her. "The house is surrounded by our men. No one will be able to come in without our express permission."

"Surrounded? Really? You have people hanging off the sheer cliff-face like geckoes, Theo?" Unlikely, but not impossible, that he had men perched on the hundred foot drop down to the water. There was only one way in – that they knew about- and that was across the narrow spit of land that joined the mainland to her small peninsula. Her house was a fortress. They must have used her hand on the biometric pad while she was unconscious to get in. Now every sick and crazy could just freaking waltz in and threaten her.

Or unless Theo and his crazy friends knew about the cave access.

"And snipers on this side of your little peninsula," Santi, the other guy told her, joining the other two men standing over her. "No one will be able to cross from the mainland, no one can reach you from the sea. Gallagher is your only hope."

"Like Obi-wan Kenobi?"

"Say the words, Ariel." Without waiting for her response, Theo speed dialed Finn from her phone. He'd used the speaker, so everyone could hear the conversation. It was answered on the second ring.

"Are you out of your goddamned mind going out alone in this weather? What the *hell* were you thinking-" Finn dragged a deep breath, then said in an achingly tender voice, "Darling, tell me that you're home and safe."

She had one shot at this. "Bomb on *Blackst*--" Theo backhanded her across her bleeding cheek, snapping her head against the leg of the coffee table directly behind her before she could relay more information. Yelling in shock and outrage, Peri saw a galaxy of stars as Theo snatched the phone out of reach.

"You have one hour from now, Gallagher," he told Finn. "Send someone to Ariel's house with the other three tablets. He comes alone or she dies. Take longer than an hour, she dies. More than the pilot, she dies."

There was no hesitation before Finn responded through the speaker, the venom in his voice as clear as his fury. "Do you think one lying, cheating, little thief has more value to me than these tablets, Núñez?" Frost dripped off his voice. "Think again. She has zero value to me. The tablets are priceless. If she's dead or injured you have bugger-all bargaining power." The phone went to dead air.

"And there you have it." Dizzy as hell, Peri pushed herself half upright against the side of the table. Had Finn heard her warning before Theo snatched the phone away? Her jaw throbbed where Theo had hit her, and stung where he'd stuck her with his knife, and the back of her head, where she'd bounced against the table smarted. "Finn doesn't care what you do to me. So, no tablets for you."

Theo's smile chilled Peri to the marrow as he said confidently, "He'll come for you."

"Trust me. He won't. But since you gave him a time limit, let's wait and see, why don't we?" *Give me time to get my sea legs under me, and my brain time to clear.* Out of the corner of her eye, she counted seven other men, all well armed and silent. Ten men inside that she was aware of. How many outside?

No way to outrun a bullet or brute strength, she'd have to use her brain if there was a snowball's hope in hell of getting out of this alive.

TWENTY

"Code Red. Initiate bomb protocols onboard both *Blackstars*, we have a credible threat." Finn instructed his head of security, via his smartphone's earpiece. Voice calm, heart thundering, he pushed out words that scared the shit out of him. "Persephone's being held hostage on the mainland."

He turned to Walker, his assistant, standing beside him, phone to his ear, relaying instructions to key personnel in a low, urgent undertone. "See who'll give us access to any strategically positioned satellites," Finn instructed. "Pinpoint on our location, then have them focus on the coordinates for Persephone's' house. Infrared and 30-centimeter resolution. I want a head count. Need to know how many Bad Guys I'm dealing with." Jesus, couldn't be that many, could it? Núñez was a government agent, for God's sake. None of this made any sense.

"On it." Walker took his laptop and sat down, tapping keys even as he made the call to one of *Blackstar* Corp's telecommunications partners.

McCoy, his chief of security came up beside him, and Finn said, "I'll take the chopper in alone. Assemble a small away team to rendezvous with me there. Take the cigarette boat, it's the fastest we have. I'll send detail as I go."

"Bad idea, sir. I can bring-"

"Alone."

"I'll bring your clothes."

"Good man. Hurry."

Logan frowned. "You don't think you're suitably dressed for the occasion?"

"These clothes are specially constructed in case of a kidnapping."

"Hell. Didn't know there *was* such a thing," Teal said with curiosity.

"NASA has a satellite in position," Walker said, phone to his ear even as his fingers hovered over the keyboard. "They're reading- Please confirm?" He looked over at Finn as whoever he was speaking to confirmed the number of people on location at Peri's house. "Twenty-seven and counting. Heavily armed- Yes, thank you, please do keep us updated." He rose to come to Finn. "You heard? Take a look." He tilted the screen for Finn.

Impossible. Improbable. Persephone kidnapped and surrounded by more than two dozen armed men? What the fuck was going on? None of this made any goddamn sense. Finn addressed the room at large. "Satellite imagery- both infrared and also 30-centimeter resolution, indicates two dozen armed men on the grounds surrounding the house on three sides. Snipers here, here and here." He showed the others as they closed in to look at Walker's screen. "Nine inside the house."

Bria put a hand to her throat. "Dear God, is that *Peri* lying on the floor?"

"Jesus. They're expecting a full out fucking *war*." Zane, standing between Jonah and Logan took a closer look at the infrared image on the left of Walker's screen.

It was quite clear that Núñez's men were patrolling the narrow peninsula and the road leading to it and the house.

"Over thirty men holding one woman?" Zane looked at Finn. "Why? I don't get it. Clearly, this isn't a straight kidnapping in exchange for the tablets. They're expecting a full-scale assault."

Nick, talking quietly to the three T-FLAC operatives, who'd been guarding the tablets, dispatched them to head for the mainland as well.

"What's your plan?"

"Get there," Finn told him, voice grim as he coldly sorted facts and variables. A strategy needed to be put in place, but right now he was trying to assimilate as much information as possible. It took precious time, but it was necessary before he allowed his fear to take hold. Going in with the guns blazing, while appealing as hell, would get him killed. And if he died, Núñez would probably kill Peri as well.

More haste, less speed.

Fuck.

McCoy returned with his change of clothes. Finn yanked his t-shirt over his head, tossing it aside to pull on a black shirt

"Wait." Nick motioned to one of the T-FLAC guys over at the door. "Let one of my guys give you a LockOut suit-"

"How long?" Doing up his shirt buttons, Finn already knew there wasn't time. The impervious garment, invented by the counterterrorist organization Nick frequently worked for, LockOut was a fabric that was almost indestructible, with many features suitable for the task at hand.

"Twenty minutes to Scorpion, twe- Fuck. Sorry. No time."

"What I have should do the trick." Finn undid his zipper. "Ladies-" Without waiting to see if stripping would offend them, and he doubted it would, Finn toed off his shoes, pulled off his jeans, and took the black pants McCoy held out, then added the belt before shoving his feet into lightweight boots.

"How will you go in?" Nick pulled up a closeup image of Peri's glass house and the cliff on his smartphone. Why he had such an image was a question for Finn to address later. "This way?" He drew a line from the water at the base of the cliff, straight up the rock face to the house. A hundred feet of sheer granite.

"Hell no." Finn did up the laces on the boots. " I'll fly in and land on their fucking doorstep."

"You're insane." Teal's eyes were troubled. "They'll shoot you on the spot."

"Not until they have the tablets. And since they'll believe *Blackstar* will be destroyed in their bomb blast, they'll know I have them. *Where,* they won't be told. Not until I have Persephone."

"You *are* crazy," Zane told him flatly. "There's got to be a better way. Nick? Talk some sense into him."

"A full frontal attack has its merits. They won't know you have back up. Might work."

"*Might*?!" Callie's voice shook, and her eyes glistened with tears. "That's my sister in there! You have to-" Her voice choked off.

Jonah wrapped his arm around her shoulders as he drew her aside. "We're not without our own considerable resources, sweetheart."

Ignoring the urgency of the clarion sound of a countdown clock syncing with his heartbeat, Finn fired off instructions to his security people, and both his ship's captains.

The four Cutters broke off to alert their own people on *their* ships. He knew Nick had ties to the black ops of T-FLAC, but hearing the brothers' concise instructions to their people, made him realize what excellent allies he had in his friends. He knew he was going to have to apologize to infinity for accusing them of collusion about the damned tablets.

Cold as ice, he kept his fear and urgency tamped down so he could construct, analyze, dismiss, and put into action plans even as he mobilized his people. As much as he wanted to haul ass out of there, show up at Persephone's house sooner than expected, Finn knew the advantage of a well thought out game plan.

He couldn't afford to fuck up. Not with her life at stake. He'd automatically set the timer on his watch the moment Núñez had come on the phone. A quick glance showed him too many minutes had passed.

McCoy handed him a micro-sized comm that fit over his back molar. "They'll check you for weapons and phone. They won't see this, and we'll be in contact for the duration. I'll coordinate efforts from here, and keep everyone in the loop. I'm guessing that trying to convince you to let us handle this is out of the question? Yeah, thought so. I have your six. The away team is heading to the motorboats now. We'll also utilize the Cutter choppers and men. They'll meet us as we instruct. Rodriquez is boobytrapping our chopper, he's waiting for us on the flight deck with an arsenal."

"Good man."

"How long do you think we have?" Logan demanded, phone to his ear.

"You heard Núñez. Sixty minutes to get to her house. We've already eaten up nine getting our shit together. So, that, or less, to detonation would be my guess." Finn strode over to the tablets as he fitted the tiny comm over a molar, biting down gently to seat it. A glance at his own pale face, reflected in the night black windows, showed just how fucking scared he was. He might be able to control his voice, and expression, but not his physical, involuntary responses. Not when it came to Persephone.

When he got his hands on Núñez, the sick fuck was going to wish he'd never been born.

"Find the bomb," he told his people remaining onboard. "When you do, toss it onto one of the runabouts and send it, full bore, out into the middle of the ocean." If they didn't find it, they could kiss their asses goodbye. "Evacuate *everyone* on board both ships in exactly twenty-four minutes if it's not found. Nobody be a hero. Ships can be replaced. This isn't your fight," Finn told the group, voice grim as he hefted the first tablet.

"A stupid fucking statement. Doesn't deserve a response," Zane said, jaw tight, eyes hot.

"Fair enough. I need that," Finn told Callie, who had her large duffel bag at her feet as she readied to depart.

"Of course." She immediately opened the bag and dumped her clothing and cosmetics on the floor without hesitation. "Pad them. Here."

"Thanks." Finn, quickly and efficiently, loaded the tablets into the case, placing whatever clothing Callie handed him, as padding between them. As he worked, he touched his earpiece to alert the crew readying the chopper. "On my way."

"We're *all* going," Nick informed him, offering him a Sig. Saur from the small of his back.

"I have my own, but thanks." His people would have an entire arsenal waiting for him at the chopper, but he figured the more firepower he had, the better.

"Take this at least," Jonah braced his foot on the coffee table, lifting the leg of his jeans to expose an ankle holster. Withdrawing the gun, he handed it to Finn, then unbuckled the holster, and handed that to him, too. "Glock 27. Pearce extension. Ten rounds. If they're professionals, they'll find these. You need deep conceal. I'll get a neck holster for you. Hands up, hands behind your head. You'll be covered." He indicated what he wanted to one of his counterterrorist guys nearby.

"Appreciate this, but you know they won't let me do anydamnedthing until they've disarmed me."

"You can shoot plenty of the fuckers before that happens," Logan said. "Always be prepared is my motto."

"Oh, I plan to be," Finn said grimly.

"Where do you want us?" Bria asked Nick.

"I'll accompany you back to *Scorpion,*" Nick told his wife. "I think the safest place for you is the mainland. You, Callie, Teal and Dani, head directly to the marina, I'll send a couple of armed men with you. Stay there until we clear things. I'll follow Finn in our chopper."

"First, we don't know that this psycho isn't patrolling the marina waiting for us. Second, there's no damned time," Callie pointed out. "We'll go to the *Tesoro Mio.* Ry's got plenty of security. Don't worry about us. Every minute counts."

"I'll talk to Case," Finn told her, as he fastened the ankle holster, dropped the Glock into it, then rose to zip Callie's bag. He hefted it onto his shoulder. He'd gladly hand over the fucking tablets to Núñez to save Peri. Nobody present suggested anything different.

Callie shook her head. "Better not. I know him. He's going to want to be right in the middle of the action to save his sister."

Finn held out his hand. "It should be me telling him." Callie slapped the phone into his palm like a surgical nurse a scalpel.

Hell of an introduction, but it had to be done. "Phineas Gallagher," Finn said without preamble when Case answered. "Dr. Thiago Núñez is holding Persephone against her will at her home."

"What the fuck? Why?"

"In exchange for the tablets. I have..." He glanced at his watch. "Forty-eight minutes to make the exchange."

"How many people holding her?"

Finn appreciated the way Case went directly to the crux of the matter.

"Thirty men for a *kidnapping*?" Case's voice was incredulous. "That doesn't make any fucking sense- I'm going with you."

"Appreciate it. But no time. The Cutters will be right behind me in their choppers, security's taking boats in."

"Know about the caves?"

Finn turned the phone on speaker as he and the Cutter men strode down the length of the corridor. "*What* caves?"

"The entire bluff under Peri's house is a *labyrinth* of caves," Case told him shortly. "Her *Sea Witch* is anchored there. She has an elevator from her private dock up to the house. I'll bring my people and come in that way. Do you have enough firepower?"

"We do."

"Gallagher?"

"Yeah?"

"If one hair on my sister's head is harmed, I'll hunt your ass to the ends of the earth, and I'll kill you. Got it?"

Before he could respond, Case cut him off.

Finn did a quick practice draw. Reaching behind his head for the semi-automatic .380. It cleared the holster between his shoulder blades with ease, and fit, with room to spare, in his palm.

"Eleven ounces," he told Nick. "Six .380 ACP rounds in the magazine, one in the pipe. He listened to McCoy via his comm. "Yeah, I remember. Trigger's a little stiff, but it can fire sixty feet."

"Make them count."

Finn nodded. "Let's get this shitshow on the road." He was heading to the door, now at a run. "You'll have to land at a distance," he addressed everyone behind him without slowing or turning his head. "There's only room in front of her house for one chopper. A narrow road connects the mainland to her peninsula. One way. Hundred foot drop. We don't know the capabilities of the men holding her. Be prepared for every eventuality. Let me make myself crystal clear. The *only* thing I care about is *Persephone*."

"Agreed," Logan said, his voice flat.

The tablets were just a bargaining chip. Peri's life was everything.

Everyone left the salon at a run.

"Keep me advised," Finn told the others, just as Dr. Vadini came toward the women who were yards ahead at the other end of the corridor.

Frowning with concern, the curator spoke rapidly in Italian to Bria, backing up as the men barreled toward him en masse.

Nick's wife responded in equally rapid Italian, without slowing her pace, eyes fierce.

Vadini turned terrified eyes to Finn as he fell into step with them. "I was most afraid of this. It's *imperative* you not allow El Elegidos to get possession of the tablets! Dr. Núñez's interpretation of the meaning of the tablets was completely erroneous! I *must* accompany you." The curator grabbed Finn's forearm.

Finn shook him off. "Too dangerous. Go with the women to the Case's ship. The men at Persephone's house are armed, and her house is a fucking fortress," he told the Cutters, who had no problem keeping pace with him. "Which they now hold."

"Please," Vadini's voice broke as he tried to keep up.

"You sure you don't want me to-*Go*." Nick urged when Finn shook his head. Nick put his phone to his ear shooting out rapid-fire orders to his own people on board his ship *Scorpion*. "Prep the chopper for immediate departure, and ready all the runabouts," Nick said into his own phone, running beside Finn. "Have security arm themselves and be ready to be wheels up the minute I get there." To Finn, "The others are doing likewise. Don't worry, you'll have plenty of back up for this assfuckery."

Callie reached up to kiss Jonah on the mouth. "Don't get any damned holes in you, Jonah Cutter, or I'll kill you. I still want that honeymoon you promised me."

"Always keep my promises."

"We have a veritable army," Finn said dryly. "These fuckers won't know what hit them. Núñez is mine. Let's go."

The Cutters headed to their runabouts in the garage. Finn took the stairs to the upper deck, and the helipad, two at a time

The metronome ticked at a furious rate as he climbed into the waiting Augusta Westland AW139. "Everything set?" he demanded of his men waiting for him beside the chopper, their hair blowing in the whir of the rotor.

"Yes, sir," Caplan yelled, climbing in after him, followed by Rodriquez. Both ex-NAVY SEAL's had been with Finn for over ten years. He trusted them with his life. *Peri's* life.

"Get in. Keep low when we go in for the approach. The house is made up primarily of glass. Don't want them to see you until we need them to see you."

Finn put on his headset. Blades already spinning, they lifted off the helipad.

Other than the dash lights, the interior was dim. His eyes adjusted to the night sky pressing down on the water. The wind had died down as if it had never been, and other than a few clouds, the sky was black and bright with stars. Using his left hand, Finn gripped the collective and increased the pitch of the blades to hover briefly over the deck as he opened the twist-grip throttle to produce more engine power as he pressed the yaw pedals.

Right hand on the cyclic, he pushed sideways, making a curving turn over Blackstar's stern before straightening out and heading inland at top speed. At almost two hundred MPH, they'd be there in minutes. "Show me you're worth your fourteen million dollar price tag," he said under his breath, pushing the machine to its limit.

The whirl of the rotors overhead matched the rapid beat of Finn's heart as he flew low over the star-speckled blackness of the ocean. His earpiece came on and Nick Cutter seemed to speak directly into his brain. "Finn?"

"Yeah."

"Vadini just admitted that *he* is the Protector mentioned in the tablets. Part of a group called *el Ehnos*- the Protectors of Blackstar's prophesy. Given what has transpired this evening, he believes Núñez is the head of the opposing radical religious group called the Chosen, *el Elegidos*. The Chosen believe they've been selected by God to fulfill the prophecy. Vadini claims the two groups are in direct opposition. The Protectors are just that, protectors of the tablets, certain that the prophecy he read on our tablets is gospel and the direct words from the seer."

Listening with half an ear, Finn snapped, "And I give a fuck-why?"

"Núñez *doesn't* believe the interpretation at all. His cult's belief is that the end of the world is coming, and he'll be the one to lead the remaining eleven thousand people to the Chosen's version of Nirvana. Vadini believes Núñez will stop at nothing to get his hands on those tablets. He has five fucking hundred years of indoctrination behind him.

"Vadini believes Núñez intends to kill anyone who knows the truth about the prophecy on the tablets. He'll lie to his disciples flat out since no one but Núñez and Vadini can read the ancient text. Núñez needs to keep the real meaning of the tablets a secret to maintain his hold on his followers. From the images, it looks as if he has his followers who are militarized and willing to kill, or die, for what he believes in. We don't know how far reaching the Chosen are. But Vadini claims they are dogmatic, violent and will stop at nothing to achieve their goal. Oh, yeah and another thing. . .The end of the world *is* in three days. Just sayin'. "

This was all so much bullshit.

All Finn knew was that some fuckhead had his filthy hands on Peri.

If it was a choice between the end of the fucking world and Peri, there was no contest.

Peri *was* his world.

"He won't need to destroy the tablets or anything else if I kill him first."

"Works for me," Nick responded. Under Nick's voice was the sound of the motor on his runabout, and the faint slap of water as the Cutters made their way to their own ships.

The green dash lights shone eerily on the slight chop of water below as the rotors churned up the surface. Finn made a small adjustment to change course slightly when the lights of the small town of Puerto Mahon appeared in the distance.

"As ludicrous as it seems, goes to motive." So much for the story he'd considered a bullshit scam to part him from his money. Considering these nut jobs held Peri's life in their hands, he'd swallow his disbelief and go along with it. "We need to know more about these 'Chosen'. How many people are part of this cult? Are they prone to acts of violence? Do they have more assets at their disposal? Can you have T-FLAC delve deeply into what we're dealing with here? Walker will give them the access info to the NASA satellite contact person."

"Excellent, already working that angle. I should have more soon."

"Sooner would be better," Finn said, voice grim.

"I hear ya. I'll let you know, the second I know," Nick told him. "Our ETA is fifteen minutes behind you." He disconnected.

The lights of the small coastal town became brighter, and Finn swooped the helicopter low over the marina, heading south.

Sick to his stomach, he realized that what he'd dismissed so readily might just be something that would cost Peri her life.

All the lights were on in the house as the helicopter rose up the rock face. He counted at least half a dozen heads inside. He did *not* see Peri's bright hair. Mouth dry, he skimmed the chopper above the glass roof to hover briefly over the gravel driveway. Finn brought the chopper down lightly in a hail of gravel that sounded like buckshot against the metal body.

"Stay down," he instructed his men. "Sit tight. The only way I want you to leave this chopper is if you see Peri coming through that door. Once she's secure, take off."

"But, sir-"

"No variations. Your prime goal is to make sure Peri leaves here alive."

A triangle of light flooded the driveway when the front door pivoted open. Finn stepped down from the helicopter as four men emerged, each pointing an assault weapon at his chest.

her heartbeat sounded deafening in her ears as Peri calculated that it would take about twenty-*running-flat-out*-steps to reach the open pantry door.

Bound, and in full view of the armed men surrounding her? That was going to be some trick.

Hopeless.

No. Hopeless was accepting whatever Theo had in store for her. To hell with that.

Think.

Every inch of her body protested painfully as the sheep tranq wore off. Her stomach roiled in reaction, and it was hard to fight her way through the mental fog and lassitude.

Think harder, damn it.

She'd been scared before. She *loved* scared, she reminded herself. Scared and doing shit anyway, was her crack.

But this was a whole other level.

A faint and distant whop-whop-whop of rotors caused her heart to gallop.

Nobody was crazy enough to fall for Theo's ransom demands, she was pretty damn sure. The tablets had historical significance and were worth an untold fortune. They might show up to try to bargain with Theo for her release. But whoever was out there, was coming empty-handed.

Which was exactly something Rydell would do. If, somehow, Ry had gotten wind of this and broken the sound barrier to get here this quickly.

The sound of the helicopter got closer, and Peri worked harder to liberate her numb hands. Her bloody wrists made her skin slippery, and the cord bindings were stronger now that they were wet.

"Someone's here," Santi cupped his hands to peer out of the blackness behind the window.

She renewed her fight against the fastenings while everyone was distracted. There was no give in whatever was tying her ankles together, and instead of expending useless energy trying to free them, she'd worked her wrists for what seemed like hours. She almost didn't notice the pain any longer as she twisted and pulled. Backed up against the coffee table as she was, whoever stood behind her couldn't see what she was doing. If they had, they would've stopped her long before now.

The cut on her cheek stung like fire ants, her jaw ached where Theo had backhanded her, and her wrists were an agonizing, bloody mess. The son of a bitch was a sadist, and she had no intention of waiting to see what he had planned for his freaking finale.

Theo and the two men who seemed to be running this kidnapping with him, had retreated to the window where they'd been talking quietly for some time. Every now and then one of them would look through the telescope to see if anyone was approaching from the water.

Someone *was* coming. By air. The throbbing sound grew louder and louder.

The group of three, eight-inch marble fertility statues from a long ago dive with Ry, rattled on the coffee table, seconds before the entire house vibrated. The men at the window backed up in a hurry as a helicopter rose up the cliff face out of the darkness, like Kong peering into the windows of the Empire State Building. For a few seconds, the bubble of light hovered, a blade's-width away from the thick windows.

Finn.

For a second she saw his set face through the glass, then the helicopter rose overhead, blocking him from view.

It looked as though he was alone. Oh, God. He had no idea how many armed men he was about to face, and there was no way to warn him before it was too late. The instant burst of hope was crushed by fear for Finn's safety. He had no idea he was walking into a trap.

The sound of the descending rotors so close to the house was deafening. It drowned out the crackle and pop of the two-way radios that the men outside had been using to report in every five minutes with 'No intruders.'

The intruder was here.

"Time to go," Theo shouted to be heard as he walked cautiously across the glass floor to her side. It was impossible to miss the gun he held loosely against his leg. His smile instilled the fear of God in her. It was unnerving seeing him in this new, scary light. He'd always been respectful, always gentle when they'd been together. A fact that had frequently got on her nerves. Now that calm stillness had a whole new meaning.

It was merciless, sterile, psychotic, like someone picking apart a biology specimen just to see how it ticked, only the specimen was still alive. When he'd used that knife on her face earlier there hadn't been one shred of empathy in his eyes. She was merely a means to an end.

He motioned impatiently to a soldier standing nearby. "Get her up."

A pair of black military-style boots came into view. A rough hand grabbed her upper arm, and beefy fingers dug into her bicep like a vice. The guy hauled her unceremoniously to her feet. Pins and needles sent shards of agony through her legs as the blood rushed to her extremities. Peri couldn't help sucking in a gasp of pain as her knees seemed to melt. It was only the man's grip that kept her upright.

"She's our bargaining chip, Excellency," the new voice was elderly, respectful, but determined. The man was right behind her, which gave Peri the creeps. "They must not know how important she is. We do not want to show our hand until we have the tablets."

"That's Gallagher." Theo brought the gun up to Peri's face, stroking the barrel under her left eye, then sliding it down her hot cheek, smearing the blood in a wet trail across her skin.

His eyes were snake-dead and creepy as hell. Peri went hot then cold, then hot again.

"He came alone, willing to die." Theo motioned someone behind her to come forward. "Get the tablets and then grant him his wish. I'll take my lady below. We'll be long gone before anyone else shows up."

Several years ago, dogging Logan's salvage off the coast of Peru, she'd thought he was coming after her underwater. She'd ascended too rapidly and almost given herself a pulmonary embolism. Peri felt like that now. Restricted lungs made it impossible to drag in a breath, pressure on her chest, heart beating too fast.

Panic attack. Breathe. Just breathe.

Why didn't he kill her now that Finn had arrived, presumably with the tablets? Not that she *wanted* to be dead, but wasn't she redundant now? Why take her down to the caves? And how and *when* had Theo discovered the caverns below her house? What else had he found? The freight elevator filled with Cutter artifacts? Had he disabled *Sea Witch*? If so, she was really screwed. The only way out of the caverns was by water. Deep water. Dead of night black water. She was an excellent swimmer, but still. . .

Never allow yourself to be taken to a second location rang in her head. First rule to remember if you're kidnapped. She'd read that somewhere. But *below* meant Theo knew about the elevator and the caves. That was the bad news. The good news was she knew her way around down there, and, hopefully, he didn't.

"You won't get away with th- Omph!" The man Theo had motioned forward materialized to grab her around the waist without warning, then sling her over his massive shoulder like a bag of flour. The movement jarred her wrists and caused black dots to swarm in her vision. She turned her head so she didn't have her face smashed into his back, it was hard enough breathing, let alone upside down. "If Finn doesn't shoot you on the spot, he'll beat your ass, put you in jail and throw away the key."

No. Finn would be summarily shot. If he'd brought the tablets, the men would take them, then kill him. If he hadn't, they'd kill him, then contact one of the Cutters or her brother. They wouldn't stop until they got what they wanted.

"Your lover won't find you, *querida*," Theo told her, in the creepiest, most gentle tone. He motioned the man to get going with her. Every step the guy took jarred her wrists, and made the compression on her lungs worse as blood drained to her head.

Theo entered the pantry ahead of them. "You are an important key in the narrative of the Chosen, Ariel." He pressed the button to open the narrow door of the elevator. "Once I explain the *true* meaning of Blackstar's prophecy, it will all be made clear to you."

That sounded ominous. "Give me the Cliff's Notes."

"You will rule at my side, and bear me fine, strong sons in the New World."

Oh, hell no. "You had your chance. We broke up way back, remember?" She listened for gunshots, but only heard her own rapid heartbeat. The shirt of the guy carrying her was damp with sweat, and he reeked of what she imagined dirty socks would smell like. She braced her bound hands on the man's belt at the small of his back so she could lift her swimming head. "You didn't seem that devastated about us breaking up at the time. I thought you were fine with us being friends."

"I allowed you freedom of choice. All women like to sow some wild oats before they settle down. I have always known you would be my goddess, and help me lead my people. Gallagher was a misstep, I must admit. I wasn't prepared for you to fuck another man."

"Yeah, that must've been a tough one," she said dryly while her heart ached.

"Untenable. But I knew you would be mine in the end. Blackstar ordained it."

"If so, Blackstar was a freaking moron. Never going to happen. Believe me, I'm no goddess, far from it. Which you would've noticed if you'd been listening to my confession this afternoon. And news flash, this is not how you win a woman's heart."

"I don't give a fuck about your heart. It's your womb I want."

"My wo- Are you *listening* to yourself, Theo? You're nuts."

"I've never been more sane, more focused. I've waited my entire life for this moment. In this the tablets were *correct. You* are my Fire Warrior, Ariel. "

"If that part was true, why isn't the *rest* of Blackstar's prediction, Theo? I didn't hear anything from Dr. Vadini that indicated you could pick and choose what to believe and what not to believe."

The man's shoulder dug into her belly. Her blood pounded in her head, and it was hard to draw air into her lungs. Theo didn't answer. "We won't fit in the elevator with me slung over this guy' shoulder like this, nor will we fit in the tunnels."

The narrow elevator door slid open emitting a faint blue light. Theo pulled her head up by the untidy braid dangling over her face. She'd never noticed that he had the eyes of a reptile.

He must've given the other man a signal because she was flipped onto her feet. "Don't do anything foolish." Taking out his curved bladed knife, Theo sliced between her ankles, then made a sharp upward stroke. "In three days I will become Supreme Leader of the World."

Peri snorted out a laugh, even though the action hurt her ribs. "Supreme leader of the *World*? Not just Argentina, but the entire *world*? Theo, you're delusional." Probably not a wise thing to say to a man who was delusional.

"You are my lifemate. Blackstar ordained it. There is no other." He shoved her into the tiny elevator first, then he and the other man got in.

"Either you can stand beside me proudly, bear my children, and reap the benefits of being by my side. Or I will hold you by force, put a child in you, and make your life extremely unpleasant. The choice is yours."

"My choice is none of the above."

His black eyes flashed, and his mouth tightened, but he didn't respond. The elevator barely contained the three of them and she did her best to put space between them by crowding the back corner. The elevator moved slowly; less than five minutes to get to the caverns below. Did Theo have more men waiting there? Did he have a fast boat? Oh, hell. Was he planning on kidnapping her in her *own* damned boat? "How did you know about the elevator?"

"I followed your runabout into the cave last year. I've been exploring every time you left the house."

Which was often, as she'd been diving *Napolitano* every day. "Snooping." Her brain was like a gerbil on a wheel while she strategized her escape. It beat worrying about Finn, possibly already lying dead on her flokati rug in her living room.

"You are too stubborn, Ariel. Too opinionated. Too independent. When we were together I thought you an unworthy vessel to accept the planting of my seed."

"Thank God. My vessel would repel your seed so fast your head would spin. You really are delusional, Theo. I'm not *your anything.* I never *will* be your anything.

"Blackstar's prophecy is clear. Not the false prophecy of the tablets you found, but the prophecy passed down to me for hundreds of years. You are my lifemate," he repeated. "We *will* be joined before the apocalypse."

"If the tablets aren't the prophecy you think they should be, why the hell do you want them, Theo?" They were speaking in English and she wondered if the expressionless man with them understood what they were saying.

"Because *I* am the only person who can read them. Because they will fucking say whatever I want them to say when I show them to my people. They will confirm what I know. There will be eleven thousand people left after the apocalypse, and I will have you ruling by my side, Ariel."

The elevator door opened. Heart pounding with dread she Breathed in the familiar scent of sea air and the unfamiliar stink of old sweat coming from several shady figures of Theo's men waiting for them. "My name is Persephone Case, dickhead!"

TWENTY-ONE

Finn found himself looking down the business end of four H&K G36 assault rifles. The four men, standing in the wedge of light in front of Peri's ten-foot pivoting front door, wore flak vests and held the weapons with sure knowledge. Their hair and clothing fluttered in the draft from the slowly spinning rotors of his chopper.

The guy in the middle seemed to be in charge as he ordered, "Link your fingers behind your head, Gallagher."

Lifting his arms, Finn quickly plucked the small gun from it's concealed holster between his shoulder-blades, palmed it, then linked his fingers loosely behind his head. The gun pressed between his scalp and his palm. Gravel crunched loudly underfoot as he crossed the wide driveway. "I have the tablets. You have two minutes to bring out Miss Case. If not, I take the tablets and leave. "

"You don't fucking get to give orders, Gallagher. Where are they?"

"Núñez. No one else. One minute-forty, tell him to hurry.."

Keeping the men in his line of sight, Finn changed focus to glance through the open door behind them. No one visible in the triangle of light coming from inside. But in his peripheral vision, he saw five or six men at three o'clock, motionless in the dark, black against black, another handful at eight.

Where are you, Peri? His thumping heart had to believe she was still alive.

"Stay where you are," the man ordered. A two-way radio crackled, and he spoke into it quietly, then demanded, "Where are your men?"

McCoy, coordinating everyone with the help of the satellite imagery, was Finn's point of contact via the tiny comm transmitting through bone resonance. "Ten on the ridge, on your six. Closing in," McCoy told him. "Five snipers on the roof."

Yeah, Finn saw them silhouetted against the night sky. "I came alone as instructed. You were a steward onboard *Blackstar*," he said, recognizing the guy. "Eneas, is it?" *Second steward. Local hire.* McCoy would have someone on his team look into this guy. "How many people inside?"

"Tablets."

The question had been for McCoy. Not Eneas. McCoy said, "Nine."

"Secure," Finn responded tersely to Eneas. "Nobody gets them until I see for myself that Miss Case is unharmed." And the longer they stood out here fucking chatting, the longer she was in there with a dangerous psychopath.

"She is with his Excellency. No harm will befall her." Eneas signaled his men, who fell into step with him, eyes watchful, weapons ready.

Finn felt rock-steady and calm. Focus had pushed out fear the moment he landed. "Befall her. . . *if*?

"She cooperates."

"Then we have a standoff. No negotiation."

"You're not going to offer us more money to help you?"

Finn calculated how far apart the four men were. "Would it work?"

"Can you offer us salvation?" Eneas scoffed. "The way to fulfill our destiny?"

In a fairly smooth movement, Finn whipped the small gun into position and fired off four rapid shots. *Bam bam bam bam.* McCoy was right, the trigger was a bit stiff, but it got the job done. Two men dropped almost at his feet. The next bullet hit Eneas between the eyes and the fourth man in the back of his head as he started to turn away. "There. You've fulfilled your fucking destiny, assholes."

He replaced the .380 in the holster, retrieved the Sig. from the small of his back. Pausing before removing his Glock from the ankle holster, he took the two way radio from Eneas' body, clipped it to his own belt then continued into the house.

"Lautaro Eneas and his buddies were military trained in Yavoriv, Ukraine. Don't underestimate them," McCoy said via the comm as Finn strode across the gravel. "Vadini's theory of an organized and dedicated army appears to be correct. Wait for backup, for God's sake. . ."

"Not waiting." Walking into a confined space with nine armed men, alone, was a calculated risk. Finn was banking on Núñez's determination to get his hands on the tablets to keep both Peri and himself alive. Peri because she was bait, and himself because he was in possession of what "Núñez wanted most.

"I have the tablets, and I'm unarmed," Finn yelled, closing and securing the heavy front door before he stepped into view. No one could come in behind him.

Backed by the night sky, the windows in the house became giant mirrors reflecting the bright lights, and men clustered in the middle of the room.

Finn took in the black-garbed men, same Flak vests, same 5.56X45 mm assault rifles. Same steely looks.

Weapons were immediately raised, and several men took aggressive steps forward.

He aimed the gun at the glass floor as he looked beyond the fireplace to the bedroom area to see if Peri was still in the house. She wasn't. "If the glass breaks, we all plummet to the rocks below." He knew he was aiming at bulletproof glass, but judging by the way the men were clustered on the area rug, they probably weren't so sure. "Where did he take her?"

An older man cast rheumy eyes toward the open pantry door. "Please. The tablets?"

Finn recalled Case's words; The entire bluff under Peri's house was a labyrinth of caves." Shit. He had no idea of the layout. Or how he'd even manage to get past these goons and down there. "Call Núñez. Have him bring her back to the house."

There was no doubt in Finn's mind that the red stain on the rug was Peri's blood. He touched it with the toe of his boot, and when he moved, left a wet, red streak on the white fibers.

Seeing three, glossy, reale-sized splats of blood on the glass floor between where he stood and a door near the kitchen, gave Finn hope. The fresh drops indicated she'd been moved within minutes of his arrival. Most likely alive.

Striding to the pantry door, he yanked it open.

"*Wait*- You can't-"

"Stay right where you are." The man kept walking, Finn fired off a shot. He staggered backwards, then fell to his knees, a startled look on his face. "The next one goes into the floor."

McCoy was talking rapidly in his earpiece as Finn strode into the pantry, and slammed the door. Leaning his full weight against it, he slipped his belt from the loops. Doubling the thick leather, he made a loop, slipped the tongue end under the door, and cinched up the buckle. One of its many intended uses. Someone banged against the door. It opened a quarter of an inch, no more. The force from the other side made the makeshift wedge fit even more tightly. The wedge held.

Raised voices, and the sharp retort of several shots being fired at the door, made him cross to the metal door at the other end of the long, narrow, shelf-lined room. Wedge or not, that door wasn't going to hold under the onslaught of bullets for long.

"Found the bomb," McCoy told him. "Sent it out to sea on your cigarette boat. Three choppers coming in hot, Case approaching from the water."

"On my way down to the caverns. What's their eta?"

"Eleven minutes. I have you on tracker."

The elevator was tiny, barely large enough for two or three people who really liked one another. Finn stabbed the down button.

His comm crackled, then died, just as he heard the ping of a bullet ricocheting off the metal door of the elevator, now above him. "I'm coming, Núñez. You better not have harmed a hair on Peri's head."

The narrowness of the small elevator made it simple for Finn to use his arms and legs to monkey up the metal walls. Braced near the ceiling, above anyone's expected line of sight, he waited for the lift to reach the bottom.

The minute the door slid open, he was greeted with a hail of bullets, and the welcome sound of Peri's seconds-too-late warning shout.

Dropping down from his elevated position, gave Finn the element of surprise. Grabbing the shooter by the forearm. Using the guy's arm as a fulcrum, he slammed the soldier against the wall before he could fire off another shot. Together, they tumbled, rolled, crashed against the rough rock surface, then staggered to their feet.

There were several other people crammed into the narrow space, but they had to wait. Using both hands, Finn grabbed the man by the neck of his flak vest and head-butted him. His opponent screamed. Seeing stars, Finn brought his knee up and drove the man's balls up his throat. Sobbing and screaming, the guy dropped to the ground in the fetal position, hands between his legs.

Finn had a quick view of Peri's red hair before he sprang at the second man waiting in the shadows. Surprised the shit out of the guy enough that he dropped his weapon. Finn slammed him hard against the rock wall, grunting with satisfaction when the man's skull cracked against the rough surface.

The guy staggered, disoriented, his meaty fist swinging too fast for Finn to avoid. It connected with Finn's jaw, snapping his head back. He tasted blood and came back with a roundhouse punch that had the guy's head bouncing off the wall even harder the second time.

Without hesitation, he spun, grabbed the barrel of the gun out of the first man's hand, brought it up hard, and used the stock to strike him on the bridge of his nose. Even though there was literally no room to swing a cat in the narrow tunnel, he hit the guy with everything he had and heard the satisfying crunch of bone and cartilage. The guy dropped like a rock.

Vaulting over the body, Finn rushed the next man. It was darker than a witch's heart, but he already had the G36 assault rifle raised like a bat. Turning sideways, he struck down using his full body weight as he pivoted. The man staggered back, making a garbled noise as if to yell for help. Finn swung again, and this time was rewarded by what sounded like a watermelon hitting cement. The guy dropped at his feet. Finn leapt over him and came in fast for the next guy in line. Finn went in with a rabbit punch to the kidneys. The man gagged. Came at him again. Hit a glancing blow to his temple. Shaking his head, Finn connected a volley of solid punches to the man's stomach as he danced out of reach.

Finn felt a rush of air and saw a sharp movement out of the corner of his eye. Spun around. Right into the barrel of an assault rifle. Dazed, he raised his fist, and took a step back to get some bite behind the punch. But his foot came down on the rifle one of the other men had dropped, and he stumbled. The man hit him again. Down on one knee, Finn slapped a bracing hand on the wall, pushed to his feet.

The butt of the rifle struck him across the forehead and his knees buckled as he went down, seeing a galaxy of stars. "Finn!"

"Get him on his feet, secure him well. We have to go."

Two men grabbed him under the arms and hauled him upright. Finn's head swam and saliva gathered in his mouth as they wrenched his wrists behind him, and secured them with a zip tie.

"Don't hurt him - Damn you, Theo. What's *wrong* with you?"

Núñez grabbed her by the upper arm to prevent her from getting too close. "Do not harm her. Use this if it becomes necessary." He threw something over her head, and it was caught by one of his men."

Finn blinked all of them into focus. Peri's eyes said it all as she looked at him with stark fear and a false bravado that ripped at his heart. The dull scrape and creak of the elevator returning to the top floor warned Finn that reinforcements would be on their way down at any minute.

Needing a visual wellness check, he took her in at a glance. Her hair was partly in a braid, the rest a loose tangle around her shoulders. Her cheek was swollen and had a runnel of partially dried blood on it. Her arms were secured behind her back. His eyes met hers. An encyclopedia of silent messages went back and forth between them.

She might be afraid, but clearly, she was damned if she'd show that to Núñez. She was stubborn, infuriating, and brave. He intended to keep her.

"If he tries anything," Núñez ordered as he grabbed her arm, "go ahead and shoot him somewhere that won't kill him, but that will inflict maximum pain. He's leverage. Shoot him. Either *she'll* get us the tablets, or they'll be blown out of existence soon enough. We'll keep him until he tells us where they are." Turning on his heel, he led the group deeper into the cave. The bright beam of his flashlight illuminated the uneven roughness of the walls in patches of light and shadow ahead of him.

"Asshat." Peri, directly behind Núñez, aimed a kick in his general direction. It didn't connect, but Finn gave her props for trying. They continued in single file, two men behind him. The rocky area echoed their footsteps and amped their voices.

The man behind him, who'd been given a taste of power, prodded him every few feet with a hard, fucking unnecessary slam of his weapon. Finn tolerated it because it kept the guy too busy to look down to see what his hands were doing.

It took some maneuvering, but as he walked, Finn pushed up a thin blade hidden in a double layer of fabric sewn imperceptibly inside the waistband of his pants. It had been designed and placed there with just this kind of scenario in mind – hands tied behind his back by a kidnapper.

He'd never needed any of the life-saving tools designed to go undetected inside his clothing. But he and McCoy had weekly practice runs to make sure that he could extricate himself in most situations. He was grateful for the proficiency now.

Finn's shoulders almost brushed the walls of the narrow corridor as he sawed at his bonds only a few feet from the man following in his footsteps. It was a slow, frustrating process. Especially since he was racing against time.

Right now he only had the two guys behind him to deal with. He had no idea what awaited them when the cavern opened up to where Case had told him *Sea Witch* was docked. They were unlikely to kill him. Not until he told them how to access the tablets. But there was a risk he'd be shot. Worse, Núñez could use Peri to leverage the information out of him. The fucker had already proved he was unscrupulous and sadistic.

He palmed the four inch, mini, carbide hacksaw. While narrow, the blade was flexible, and razor sharp. It was made to cut through metal. A plastic tie was nothing. After nicking himself several times, he sliced through the zip tie. The binding dropped way.

Finn's rage was ice cold as he whipped around, and stabbed the small blade into the jugular of the man directly behind him. He put his weight into it, felt the hot spill of blood over his hand. The guy gurgled, then dropped.

The second man started to shout out, but Finn slashed out blindly at about throat height. Without a sound, the guy dropped, falling over his friend. Finn wiped the bloody blade on the guy's shirt, then did the same for his hand.

Strike two.

He kept an ear open for the creak of the elevator indicating more of the Bad Guys coming down. "How badly are you hurt?" Finn eased up behind her as she limped a few feet ahead of him. Her bleeding wrists were still strapped behind her back. She'd worked at that plastic they'd used to control her until her wrists bled. Red-hot fury, knowing the pain she'd endured, almost derailed the calm he needed to maintain.

"My ribs where the son of a bitch kicked me, and my neck where they shot me with an animal freaking tranquilizer," she said softly. "And my pride for falling for Theo's bullshit. Other than that I'm peachy." She looked at him over her shoulder, her eyes widening, as he sliced her hands free.

"I'll kiss every inch of you better when we get out of here." There was a hitch in her step, but she didn't cry out to alert the others. "Any other way out?" Case hadn't known of one, but Peri had built the house, the elevator shaft, and the tunnels leading to the ocean.

"Main entrance. But they're sure to be watching that."

If there was no other way out, it had to be through. So be it. Through it was.

Núñez's flashlight bobbed, casting long, weird shadows up ahead as he yelled, "Keep them the fuck quiet back there."

"You know something, Theo?" Peri's voice echoed eerily. "You're not only a psycho, you're a complete dick. How the hell do you think you can possibly get away with this? We have friends. Family. They'll alert the authorities."

"They'll never find us. After you provide my heirs, they'll never find your body."

Peri raised her voice. "I'll kill you before I let you touch me."

"*I'll* kill you before you touch her again," Finn assured him at the same time.

"There are ways to make you compliant, Ariel. Drugs are just one method." He paused. "Imagine being paralyzed but completely aware the entire time. As for you, Gallagher, once I have the tablets your usefulness will be at an end."

"Don't hold your breath. Unless I deactivate that electrical charge and defuse the bomb on the chopper, no one is getting their hands on those tablets. Impasse, dick for brains." The charge would kill anyone who touched the doors of the chopper.

"You'll change your mind about giving me the tablets when Ariel has my cock in her. I'll make you watch, Gallagher. She likes it rough, don't you, *cariño*? She'll beg me for more, and you'll beg me to stop. You'll give them up to me quickly enough." Núñez resumed walking. "Hurry up," he told his non existent men in Spanish. "My destiny is waiting."

"You aren't the only person in the world who can read those tablets, Núñez." Finn sped up. "You know Dr. Vadini read them, too."

"He bought into the shit he *pretended* to read," Núñez scoffed. "He can no more read all that text than I can. I, as Supreme Leader of the Chosen, have thousands of devout followers. Followers who will kill for me. Die for me. These followers have expectations. I'll show them the tablets, and "read" Blackstar's words to them. They have no idea what the tablets say. The Chosen know what Blackstar's prophecy is. The tablets just confirm what the seer predicted.

"Eleven thousand of the Chosen will be saved from Armageddon. We will populate the Earth with fresh ideas and innovative technologies. It will be a new era of enlightenment."

"You can't create a legend that doesn't exist. You can't change the language on the tablets to suit your myth."

"Read the news, watch television," Núñez sneered, clearly talking with his hands as the beam from his flashlight jerked across the rough-hewn walls with his movements. "Our world has gone mad. The Chosen will bring it back into the light. Purify it. Vadini claims to be a Protector, even though we know there are no longer any living Protectors. And *he* isn't living either,"

Núñez laughed. "By now the ship and all hands on board are nothing more than a large oil slick."

Núñez wasn't aware that the bomb had been found and sent out into the middle of the ocean. But even Blackstar's safety paled in comparison to Peri's safety. *She* was everything. Anything else could be replaced. His staff and crew were trained for all emergencies, notwithstanding a bomb. Even though it had been discovered in time, everyone would've evacuated the ships by now.

Núñez turned a corner. The light of his flashlight dimmed, faded and then plunged them into complete darkness.

The dull creak of the elevator descending spurred Finn to move even faster. He touched her shoulder, and at the same time cupped his hand across her mouth before she could cry out in surprise.

"Elevator's on the way down. More of Núñez's men. And he'll realize we've dropped back in a minute. Other tunnels? Anywhere to hide?"

She felt for his hand in the dark, and when she connected, wove her fingers with his. Her hand felt ridiculously fragile for a warrior. "This way."

"It's here somewhere. . ." Peri ran her hand lightly along the wall, searching for the narrow opening into another tunnel. The tunnels connecting the caves were riddled with branches and offshoots. Some leading to other caverns, some dead-ending into a solid wall of granite.

"What are we looking for?"

"There's a huge cavern somewhere around here where we can hide out for a while. He'll never find it. Hell, I only discovered it when I was exploring down here during construction of the house." But that had been with the lights on. Now it was pitch dark, she was under duress, and she had no idea if it was back the way they'd come, or forward and closer to Theo and more of his gun-wielding henchmen.

Her heart throbbed in her throat. How long would it take Theo to realize that his entourage was no longer behind him?

"Stop for a sec and orientate yourself. We're heading back toward the elevator, right?" His warm breath lifted loose hair around her face to tickle her check. Peri wanted to bury her face against his chest. Wanted to wrap her arms around his waist, hold on, and never let go. She made do with finding his hand in the darkness, linking her fingers with his.

"There's a split, about two feet wide, just big enough to slip through down one of the branches. Most are dead ends and I don't want to get stuck with no way out." Her heart knocked against her ribs so loudly she was sure it was echoing like a drumbeat through the entire length of the tunnel and someone would hear it. With every thrum of her heart, she expected Theo and/or his men to come charging back to find them.

Hurryhurryhurry. "It *should* be here-"

The familiar creak of the small elevator descending caused a jolt of panic, making her stomach flop. "Oh, damn, the elevator is about quarter the way down. Where the hell is it?"

Finn clasped her shoulder and gave it a gentle squeeze. "We'll find it."

"I've never been down here in the pitch freaking dark before. Damn, I think it might be back the way we came a bit."

Finn turned around. "Be careful where you walk, there are bodies and assorted debris scattered about."

With her left hand in his, Peri felt her way along the right-hand wall. But every second, she anticipated the men who'd come down, to round a corner and see them. Or for Theo to backtrack with his bright flashlight. More men, more guns.

Her foot bumped one of the downed men, and she shuddered as she cautiously stepped over him.

About six, agonizing feet later, she felt a narrow opening which would lead- hopefully- to the right branching tunnel. "This way. Duck!" She led him in. This smaller tunnel was narrower, the ceiling barely over their heads. With the walls and low ceiling so tight, it was claustrophobic. The air here felt cold against her warm skin, and it smelled danker than the main tunnel.

"Is this-?"

Please don't let this be a dead end. "We'll soon find out." The rough granite abraded her hand as she brushed her palm along the walls, searching for the opening. "Yes!"

Another ten feet and she felt the narrow, angled gap in the granite. Peri sucked in a shaky breath of relief. "Here." *Thank God.* "Think of this as the eye of the needle, and we're the thread. It's extremely narrow. You'll have to slip through sideways. Be careful once you're on the other side. There are a couple of feet just inside the opening that are flat, then there's a sharp slope down to the water. It's slick, and hard to get a decent foothold because it's always wet. I'll go first."

"No, I'll-"

"I know what to expect," she assured him." Trust me."

"I do," he said, voice low, as he caressed her cheek. God, she wished she could see his face. She knew he rarely said that to anyone. There was more in those two simple words than most men ever said in a lifetime. "Be careful." His fingers dropped away, his warmth gone. Turning, she slipped between the rough walls into the large cavern. Pausing inside, she was met with the same stygian darkness as was in the outside passageway. The air here felt heavy, and smelled musty and strongly of salt. Unlike the corridor, there was no feeling that the outside was nearby. No fresh air. Just stale, still, cool air.

She squeezed his hand before releasing it. "It's about ten-ish feet down to a wide flat area. Then a narrow 'path' goes about a quarter the way around a lake on the right-hand side. From there it's sheer rock face. Go down on your butt, it's easiest. Ready?"

Finn made his way through, and together they sat, legs extended. Side by side, they hip-walked down the slope. At the bottom, he pushed to his feet and gave her a hand up. "It seems to be a bit lighter in here." Even his whispered voice echoed.

Her wrists and ankles burned like fire ants were eating her abraded skin, but adrenaline had fortunately wiped out the last of the tranquilizer. Now her rapid heart rate began to slow as she put distance between herself and the imminent danger.

Peri barely moved her lips when she responded. "Maybe, but I still can't see much of anything." As her eyes adjusted she realized that she *could* see darker shapes. Rocks, high walls, and the extremely faint glint of light on the vast area of the black water of the indoor lake.

"I explored in here -as far as I could at least, a couple of times over the years. I had no reason to want to climb and had plenty of excitement with my salvage. Not to mention I didn't fancy doing that alone. The lake fills with water at high tide and the rocks pretty much stay wet and slippery. This flat part goes about a quarter the way around to the right before it drops off. But there are a few deep depressions in the rock about fifteen or twenty feet down that way, that'll keep us out of sight if necessary. Keep your hand on the slope on the right, it changes to a sheer face a couple of hundred feet in. Not sure how to get around the other side of the lake other than swim across. Don't fall in. The water is icy cold, and at least fifty feet deep."

"Ocean's got to come in somewhere. That means there's a way out."

"I presumed there's an aquifer feeding the lake. I didn't *see* any opening the last time I was here, and I had a strong flashlight. But that doesn't mean there isn't one somewhere." Finn grabbed her arm to steady her as her foot slipped.

He made sure she was steady before he let go. "Let's get away from the entrance, out of view until Núñez gives up looking for us. There's some kind of light coming in, we just have to find the opening."

"Núñez won't give up, you know. He sees me as a vessel for his future progeny. I'm apparently part of his twisted destiny."

"Like hell."

"Yeah, well," she smiled at his vehemence. "I'm not thrilled about the prospect either." When she fell silent, the barely perceptible sounds of yelling and the pop-pop-pop of gunfire carried inside the cavern. "Hear that?"

"Yeah." He cocked his head. "No idea of distance or direction. Let's presume they're on their way. If there's no way out to the beach from here, we shouldn't have long to wait. We sit tight until your brother and the Cutters get here. They're either en route or already here. They have enough firepower to keep Núñez's people busy."

Peri stopped walking. "How—You contacted my brother?"

"You were kidnapped. Of *course,* I called your brother."

"I'd love to have been a fly on the wall for *that* conversation." Peri flattened her hand on the wall beside her as her foot slipped on the slick rock again. "I'll take all the help I can get right now. I don't normally *need* rescuing, but this is over and above crazy."

"Kidnapping was one thing, but your psycho ex-boyfriend brought a fucking *army* with him. We're talking several dozen or more heavily armed, trained soldiers. He's not dicking around. Hell, we'll both take all the help we can get."

"Thanks for reminding me what poor judgement I had. Be careful here, the footing gets narrower." The slope on the left became a sharper drop. The good news was her eyes were adjusting, and unlike the tunnel, this area had some source of light. Her heart leapt at the prospect of getting out of the caverns before Theo found them.

The flat area abruptly narrowed to nothing. "I think this is about as far as we can go without swimmi—" Again, Peri's feet skated on the smooth, slick rock and it was only Finn's quick reflexes that stopped her from falling. He held her tightly against his chest and rested his chin on top of her head.

The achingly familiar scent of his skin was comforting. His strong arms encircling her made her feel invincible. Closing her eyes, she rested the back of her head on his chest, and clasped her arms around his to pull them more tightly around her.

"This is neither the time, not the place, but I have to tell you-I was an ass," he whispered, turning her in his arms, holding her securely. "And sorrier than I can ever say."

"Which time?" she smiled up at him as she wrapped her arms around his waist.

"All times you deem appropriate," he said wryly. "But specifically this afternoon. I was insensitive, and reactionary when I heard what you told to the Cutters. I reacted from emotion, not rationale. Then while I was processing that, I got a text from my attorney telling me my ex partner, Derry had been released from prison- I was so pissed, I forgot the most important person. *You.*"

Heart knocking, Peri realized she'd misinterpreted the reason for his departure. From there, she'd assumed he was proving himself to be just like everyone else in her life, treating her as if others were more important than herself. "I'm sorry too. I should've told you before I told them."

"No. You told them first because it was what you were there to do. I got it. I might've behaved like an ass, got distracted when I should've stayed by your side. But I get what you were doing and why. I know how hard that was for you. I failed you, and I swear, never again will I be so distracted by business that I fuck up my priorities."

The time for prevaricating had long since passed. Her throat ached as she admitted, "When you walked out, I realized even good swimmers can drown."

Finn closed his eyes briefly as if in pain. "Jesus, it kills me that I hurt you. However unintentionally. I'll make it up to you, I swear."

"You have a habit of not believing in me, Finn. That's damned hard to look past."

"I'll work on it."

Peri knew, when this was over- if this was ever over- he'd sail into the sunset as fast as his ship could go. "Great," she said with faux cheer, and the returning ache in her heart. "In the meantime, I've made a mess of things—"

He tilted her face up and stroked his mouth over hers in a sweetly poignant kiss that left her craving more. "Darling," he murmured against her damp mouth, "I *fix* messes. And you had bugger-all to do with whatever Núñez is up to. He's delusional. I swear, I'll make him pay heavily for what he's done to y-- Shhh."

She heard it too. Voices. Faint. Indistinct. But coming closer now.

"No way they'll find the entrance," she whispered, stiffening in his arms.

From the entrance, the brilliant white beam of a powerful flashlight sliced through the darkness to shoot a broad swath of white across the water.*Damn.*

TWENTY-TWO

"There's no way out," Núñez shouted, his voice echoing and re echoing against the vaulted ceiling and rock walls. More lights flashed, each staffing its own section.

"Fuck."

"Ditto. But at least now we can see what we're up against. Do not even *suggest* we try to fight our way through them." Eyes blazing, Peri unzipped her slicker, tossing it onto a nearby rock. Her t-shirt clung damply to her body, revealing nipples erect from the cold.

Showed just how fucking besotted with her he was, that even threatened with death, Finn still wanted her. He raised both hands. "No argument here." Of more importance to note, he saw the determined jut of her jaw, and the squaring of her slender shoulders. "The situation is dire, no doubt. But we have to keep our heads and think smart here, right?"

Appearing both calm and focused, Peri said, "Right." Quickly and efficiently she raked her fingers through the tangled skeins of her hair, braided, twisted and somehow anchored it securely at her nape without pins. "I'm not damn well going *anywhere* with them." She pushed up her sleeves. "And I don't want you anywhere near Theo, either. Where are the tablets? Far away, I hope?" The bright beam slowly stroked the surface of the water, missing their position by a dozen feet.

"Landed on your driveway." Finn kept an eye on the shadowy figures near the entrance. It was hard to tell in the dark, but each pass of the flashlight showed him that there was a large group of men positioned around Núñez blocking the only exit.

"Oh, my God! Finn! Why on Earth did you bring them *here*? You should've left them-"

"I wasn't going to fuck around if your life was on the line, Persephone. If it was you or the tablets, I chose *you*."

She pressed two fingers against his lips. "Aw, thanks."

At what point would Núñez decide he wasn't worth keeping alive? It would be like shooting fish in a barrel to kill him here with no retreat and no cover. And if he was dead, Núñez would get his filthy hands on Peri.

"I have two men in the chopper waiting for you, if we can get you topside again. The chopper is boobytrapped and rigged with explosives." Finn blocked her body with his in case those damned beams got any closer. "It's wired to deliver a four hundred volt charge to discourage anyone attempting to break in."

"As soon as he gets what he wants, he's going to kill you, you know that. That's unacceptable."

"No one is getting into that chopper other than *you*. And the cavalry will be here soon." Finn tightened his arms around her as an arc of light crawled across the craggy domed ceiling, inch by inch. Bits of mica made the dark rock look like a night sky as the light glinted off it.

She gripped the front of his shirt. "Don't you damn well *dare* imply that you're not going to make it, too. Whatever happens we're in this *together*, got it?"

He'd protect her- until he couldn't. "We'll wait Núñez out. But not right here." Hundreds of years ago, this cavern had been abraded by the tides to form a natural amphitheater. Dark water lines striated the cliff-face indicating how the water levels had dropped over the years. The last, sixty or so feet overhead.

"Can't see it from here, but there's a hole right at the very top of the ceiling," Peri said. "Probably a blowhole at some point. I always wanted to rappel down to explore. But first I have to learn to rappel." She smiled. "If we can reach it, I think we can exit that way."

Possibly. He could certainly take out a few of Núñez's men, but there were a couple dozen right behind those. The tunnels were easy for the soldiers to defend, and there'd be no getting past them. Finn's backup would have a Herculean task breaking through. It would get done, he had no doubt. But there was a good chance that a prick like Núñez would use Peri as a bargaining chip or, at the very least, a shield if they *were* caught.

"We are not going to die," she said firmly. "We're smart and capable with mad skills. There's got to be something we can do to get the hell up there. Swim? Climb? Fly? Something."

Finn gauged the distance to the ceiling. He saw no hole, but he trusted she knew what was on her own property. If she claimed there was a blowhole, there was one. They were out of options.

"Right now they need you alive to give them access to the tablets," she said when he didn't immediately respond. "But if they think they won't get them no matter what, they might just kill you or worse--" Her lips tightened. "If they capture you, they'll hurt you. I'd do *anything* to make them stop. Theo knows that. Hell, anyone who's seen us together knows it."

"Think a little thing like the fear of dying would stop me from protecting you?"

Every year he went on an extreme climbing trip with his friends the Starks. But it wasn't a sport for everyone, and this sure as hell wasn't going to be a practice run. "*Can* you climb?" Finn whispered, stroking the back of his fingers across her smooth cheek because he couldn't not touch her. Her soft breasts pressed against his chest, and his heartbeat sped up to syncopate with hers.

"I can, but I haven't had much practice since I've been here." Peri took his hand and kissed his palm. "Water's our best bet."

Understandable for a water baby, but from what he saw, as the flashlight staffed the water, there was nothing on the other side of the lake but the same sheer cliffs they were faced with here. Swimming, *or* climbing, they'd be sitting ducks.

"We have to get to that opening up top."

"I've seen it from the outside. Great plan, except it's a million feet up!"

Six or seven stories vertical. Yeah, a million feet. But on the last pass of Núñez's flashlight, Finn saw a deep ledge about halfway up. "Use these strong, swimmer muscles to climb, love. Take the challenge. I'll give you a boost. Plenty of handholds. There's one about seven feet up. And a foothold right here. We'll sit tight, and let our army take down Núñez's army."

As much as Finn wanted to be more proactive, the only cause of action in this situation was to do whatever the hell they could do to get out of reach. He patted the rock just above her head. "Ready?" He cupped his hands for her to step up.

"No." But she placed one foot on his hands. Finn lifted her, and a second later, her weight was gone as she found a toe hold. He used both hands to cup her butt in support. "Feel around for another, I'm right behind you, I won't let you fall."

From the entrance, the sound of voices and the squeak of a dozen rubber-soled boots on rock, echoed in the vast space, ricocheting off the hard surfaces. The flashlight beam continually strafed the water, climbing now and then up the rock face.

They climbed silently. Not nearly as quickly as Finn wanted to go, but at an impressive rate thanks to Peri's courage, and athleticism. Her competitive nature, coupled with the very real fear of being caught, or trapped, gave her strong motivation.

A man shouted in Spanish, and suddenly they were spot-lit as they clung like lizards to the sheer face of the cliff twenty feet up.

Brilliant light suddenly illuminated the cavern. Done with puny flashlights, Núñez had brought out the big guns.

"Shit." Peri paused. "Looks like the bastard found my night diving light."

The light was so bright that, other than a few deep pockets, there were virtually no shadows. The illumination flattened the bumpy rock face making it hard to see handholds. "Keep moving." Finn wrapped his hand around hers so she could better grip a too small handhold. He was practically supporting them both on his one decent foothold.

"There is nowhere for you to go," Núñez yelled. "Come down."

"Keep going." Small pebbles rained down on his face, and Finn had to blink dust out of his eyes. "Stay focused."

As more distance was put between them and Núñez and his men, Finn relaxed into the climb. His recent summit climb of *Siula Grande*, had been more dangerous, and more technically challenging. But it hadn't scared the crap out of him like climbing this sheer rock face with Peri.

One slip and she'd plummet twenty feet. Yeah, there was a vast lake below, but there were also outcroppings of rocks. And hitting water from this height would be like hitting concrete. She'd die, or at the least break every bone in her body.

Since he had no rope, couldn't harness her, or put a helmet on her, Finn did his best to cage her body with his. Matching her hold for hold, he made sure he was ready . for her slightest misstep.

"Why are you right on top of me?" she groused when he guided her hand up to the next hold. "I have the hang of this. In fact I think I might even like it if I wasn't acutely aware that people are trying to kill us."

"They won't shoot you."

"No. But they *will* shoot you."

"Focus on the climb. No matter what happens." Every second they were exposed like this, Finn anticipated a bullet slamming into his back.

"Bring them down," Núñez shouted to his men. Half a dozen started to climb. Some, clearly not climbers, made a hell of a racket as they slipped, fell, yelling at each other in Spanish. Every now and then a large splash indicated someone had lost their grip.

He eased to Peri's side, but kept to her slower pace. "There's a ledge about ten feet above us."

"How could you *possibly* know that?" she demanded, her breath ragged as she resumed finding hand- and footholds and kept ascending.

Heart in his throat, he caught her foot as it dislodged a loose rock. The fist-sized stone skipped down the cliff below them. A man shouted as he was struck, and several seconds later there was a splash. Finn placed Peri's dangling foot on a narrow jut and waited until she was steady before he said, "I see stars."

She gave a small, breathless laugh. "You always see stars."

"The ones I'm looking forward to seeing again, and soon, is that galaxy of starry freckles on your naked body." Finn grinned at her huff of laughter, then turned serious. "Just a few more feet and you can rest." He had a solid perch, and was able to free a hand.

"Here, I'll give you a boost." Placing it on her butt, he pushed her up onto the ledge.

She landed with an "Oomff!"

Leveraging himself up and over, Finn landed beside her. As his eyes adjusted to the shadows behind them, he realized the outcropping was more than a ledge. Behind the three feet that extended from the wall, there was a shallow cave carved out of the granite over millennia of water rising and falling.

He rested his palm on Peri's back, while he liberated the Glock 27 strapped to his calf.

Nine bullets. He'd make them count.

Under his hand, Peri's t-shirt was damp with sweat, her breathing erratic. Plucking long strands of hair off her sweating skin, he asked softly, "Okay?" He kept his focus over the edge, counting the shadowy figures of the men tracing the path upwards that he and Peri had just navigated. Climbing like fucking spider monkeys, Núñez's people swarmed the cliff wall. "Núñez is sending up more men."

"To do what?" She rolled over, sucking air. "Carry us down on their backs? Frankly I'm too tired to give a rat's ass." She blew out a breath. "Next time I'll insist we *swim* to safety."

"There won't *be* a next time." Getting to his feet, he extended his hand to pull her up beside him. The cave was at least twelve feet deep, and twenty-or so feet wide. It was about forty feet above the water, and the dark line of the most recent waterline was visible just below where they were standing, indicating the depth of the lake at some long ago high tide. The back of the cave was steeped in deep shadow, but the front half was washed with lights from below.

Starlight came from a jagged hole some thirty feet overhead. Dark runnels on the rocks indicated centuries of rain coming through the opening that had formed a curtained barrier between the cave and the rest of the cavern.

"People have been in here." Peri pointed up. "Look. There are paintings on the dome. Judging from the water lines on the walls, this cave was once full. They could have painted the ceiling from boats, I imagine."

"They probably used a mix of kaolin and some kind of mica to get that glittering effect." As Finn talked, he kept an eye on the progress of the climbers. Noting the closest men were thirty or more feet down, he looked up at the ceiling.

"Whoever they were, they went to a lot of trouble to replicate an accurate starry sky. . ." he trailed off, turning more fully to take in the pattern, illuminated by Núñez's lights

"Jesus. These aren't random dabs of paint. It's our fucking *solar system*. The hole in the center represents the sun." He pointed. "Mercury, Earth, Venus, Mars. The grouping over there is the Asteroid Belt. See that roughly triangular formation? Those are the Hilda asteroids. Those the Trojans. There; the Greeks, and that's Mars, right where it's supposed to be. The accuracy and detail is astonishing."

"I'm more interested in those *real* stars I see through that hole you say is the sun. But unless you have a super power and can fly, I don't see how we'd th- -

With a loud *crack,* a bullet ricocheted off the lip of the ledge, scattering rocks and grit in a stinging spray. As stones and rocks rumbled and bounced down the side, Peri grabbed his arm to yank him back, but Finn was quicker. Slamming his arm across her chest caused her to stagger back.

As adrenaline kicked in, his vision narrowed and his heart rate increased. Crouching, he adjusted his grip on the Glock. A volley of shots followed, this time hitting the wall behind them.

"Stay back." Hyper-focused, Finn dropped down flat, then belly-crawled to peer over the edge. Half a dozen or so men were climbing, some more proficient than others. To his left, three men lined up perfectly. He squeezed off his first shot.

The bullet drilled into the closest guy's eye and he fell back soundlessly. Whether the bullet went through and through, striking the second and third man, Finn had no idea, but he got the result he wanted. The lead guy took out the other two on his way down the sheer rock wall.

The three men twisted and turned as they tumbled down. They slammed into outcroppings, banged against the smooth sections of the cliff, and scattered rocks, stones, and clouds of dust in passing.

The first guy's body slammed into a fourth climber, taking him down, too. The four men fell the forty feet in a matter of seconds. No one screamed as the bodies hit the water hard enough to make Finn wince.

Four down.

Dakkadakkadakka. A hail of bullets sent up debris. Gritty sand and small rocks peppered the surrounding area.

Dakkadakkadakka "Stay down," he shouted to Peri over the resonating pings of ejected spent cartridge cases interspersed with semi-auto fire and the *crack* of shattering rock.

"Let my men come for Ariel, Gallagher," Núñez yelled up. He hadn't budged from the entrance, choosing instead to send his men as sacrificial lambs. "They'll spare your li-"

Lifting his head, Finn aimed at Núñez, and squeezed off a shot. But the son of a bitch shifted, and the bullet struck the soldier next to him, who fell against Núñez, taking him down. The soldier was dead, but the impact sent Núñez plunging down the slope towards the water. A couple of his men darted after him, and hefted him back to level ground.

Another short burst of gunfire. Finn held tough. Law of averages forced him to bide his time. Two men were still doggedly climbing, and more on the flat surface near the entrance. He had only seven more chances to level the playing field.

Not great odds. His biggest fear was failing Peri. If anything happened to her- Fuck. Nothing was going to happen to her on his watch. To his right, the two climbers, some thirty feet below his position, inched closer, clinging to the sheer granite face. They didn't move like experienced climbers, they were slow and cautious. Finn calculated the angles. Not yet. He scanned the area from right to left. He had the advantage of higher ground, he just had to be patient.

He spared a glance over his shoulder. "I'd feel a hell of a lot better if you'd move your ass as far back as possible out of the range of fire. One of these fuckers is eventually going to get lucky."

Using her elbows to move forward, Peri slid up beside him. Her cheek brushed his arm. "You don't seriously think I'd cower in the dark while those asshats take potshots at you? Think again, Rocketman. We're in this together."

Almost giving Finn a fucking heart attack, she suddenly jumped to her feet. The brilliant lights below picked up the orange flame in her hair, and the stark freckles on her pale skin. "Hey, Theo?" she yelled down, wildly waving her arms. "If you want my womb, you better not shoot me. And by me, I mean Finn. He's as close to me as white on rice. If one of your men kills him, they'll kill me, too."

Finn, who was up, and trying to place his body in front of hers, grabbed her arm, to pull her down. "Are you fucking *insane*?"

She locked her knees, and refused his urgent pull to get down. "Hear me, Theo? You said you need me by your side to fulfill your destiny. Shoot Finn, and you kill any hope of your future heir. What will your followers think about *that?"*

"Come down, and we'll spare him." Fucker didn't pretend to be sincere.

"Go away first."

"Peri, I swear to God," Finn said through his teeth. "I'll knock you out and put you back there myself."

"Take your men and leave," she yelled. "I'll come to you willingly if you give Finn safe passa-"

Dakkadakkadakka. Too fucking close for comfort. The rain of bullets strafed the edge of the platform, causing six inches of granite in front of him to break away.

"Hold your fire!" Núñez yelled in Spanish, sounding apoplectic.

"Get. To. The. Back. *Now*!" Finn ordered Peri through clenched teeth. "Not because I'm telling you to do so, but because you're an intelligent, courageous and rational woman. If you're here, I'm distracted. Go." He glanced at her set face. "Please, darling, move the fuck to the back and give me room to shoot these assholes."

"Don't *you* get shot."

As Peri disappeared into the deep shadow behind him, Finn shifted his gaze from one climber to the next. Yeah. These guys were in the right spot. He shot them both. Didn't hear any splashing, but the bodies landed with a gratifying *thump thump* on the rocks.

Núñez yelled. "—ly Lake!" Finn missed part of it since Peri was back there muttering to herself, and Núñez had sent up three more men.

"Holy shit! Finn-"

He fired off another shot, which echoed off the granite as if they were in an auditorium, but missed his target by inches. Fuck.

"You okay back there?"

"I think you'd better come and take a look."

His heart leapt into his throat. He jumped to his feet, Glock aimed into the darkness. How the hell had someone managed to climb onto the platform without being seen?

"Come out or I'll shoot." Not blind he wouldn't. Not taking the risk he'd hit Peri. He advanced into the wall of darkness the lights below didn't quite reach.

"No one's here. Not alive, at least." Peri sounded strange. Shaky. She came to meet him, taking his hand to lead him to the wall in back. "You need to see this."

As long as *this* wasn't a semi-automatic wielding Núñez follower, Finn was prepared for just about anything. Except. . .

"A skeleton?"

The unexpected, incongruous sight of bleached bones was shocking enough, but the seated body was fully intact. Knees upraised, skeletal hands clasping something against its chest. Sightless eyes stared out of the small skull.

"It's a *child*. Look at her small feet and han-" Peri hunker down beside the small form. For a moment she said nothing, then tilted her head to look up at him. "Do you believe in fate, Finn?"

A frisson ran up his spine, and his heart began to pound. "From the second I laid eyes on you, my darling."

Peri rose from her crouched position to come to his side. Sliding her arm around his waist, she held on tightly. "It's not a *her*. It's a *him*. Check out what's in his hands, Finn. That's the fifth tablet." A tremor of excitement shook her voice. "I think we just found Blackstar."

A single gunshot echoed throughout the cavern. Peri flinched. The loud, sharp *bang*, sounded extremely close as it bounced around the small space where they stood.

"Ariel. Your obstinacy is annoying," Núñez shouted. "Come down immediately. You know Blackstar's master plan for the world is dependent on *us*. *Together*. Enough is enough. Accept your part in the prophecy. This is a holy place. I cannot permit the death of more of my supplicants. If you remain up there with Gallagher, I cannot vouch for your safety. Without food or water, how long can you survive? Your willful disobedience will be punished if you keep resisting your god-given future by my side. It has been ordained. Stop this stupidity right now."

"What now?" she asked Finn, as she shot Theo the finger in response, which he, of course, couldn't see, but made her feel marginally better.

Like Finn, she was torn by the mesmerizing sight of the small skeleton and what he held, but also acutely aware that the men climbing toward them were getting closer by the minute. It scared her to death that those crazed religious fanatics were willing to kill Finn given the chance. Finn's bullets wouldn't last forever.

He narrowed his eyes, assessing the massive wall they had yet to climb. "Now we get up to that opening and get the hell out of Dod--."

Dakkadakkadakka. A chunk of granite exploded near their feet. Finn grabbed her arm and shoved her back.

"Ariel! Got your attention now? I'm not playing games. Listen and obey."

Peri's heartbeat skittered. "Leave Blackstar and the tablet here?"

"I can't carry him on my back. He's been here for five hundred years, he can wait a little while longer."

"Agreed. But we have to take the tablet with us. We *can't* allow Theo to get his hands on it."

"I'll carry it."

Peri winced as he gently lifted the gold tablet from Blackstar's two-handed grip. The movement didn't make the small, bony hands fall apart, they remained exactly the same, almost as if lifted in supplication. She rubbed the chill on her arms. "I feel like I should say a prayer or something."

"Make it quick." Finn started undoing the buttons on his shirt with one hand, then undid the top button on his pants. He pressed the tablet to his chest, then did up the buttons and tucked his shirt tightly into his waistband.

"Will that hold? Can you climb like that?"

"It'll hold." The tablet, held against his body, made for hands-free climbing. "Let's do this."

It looked uncomfortable as hell. "Even though it's a bit smaller than the others, it still weighs a ton." Peri frowned. "It'll change your center of gravity."

"I'll adjust for it. Come on, let's haul ass before anyone gets up here."

"Where they'll shoot you in the back, for god's sake. Hang on, I have an idea- Theo?" she called as she stepped out of the shadows and walked to a few feet from the edge. "The more I think about this prophecy, the more

I'm coming to like the idea. Tell me again, what your plan is? You'll be Supreme Leader, right? Is that like a king? Will I be the queen to the Chosen?"

"What the fuck are you doing?" Finn whispered furiously. "Get the hell back here."

"Yes," Theo shouted. "But your most important job will be to produce my heirs."

"I want that, too." She wondered how the hell she'd ever let this man touch her. Gag. "I like bossing people around. I'll be a good queen." She let that disgusting thought penetrate. "Theo, I know *exactly* where the High Altar, *and* the fifth tablet, are. I'll take you there. I'm coming down. Take all your men, and wait for me at the house."

"Persephone," Finn said from the shadows. "Get your ass away from the edge, and for crapsake stop goading him."

Finn wasn't happy, but there was method in her madness. She hoped her raised voice sounded just as creepy with the echo as Theo's did for her. "This *isn't* the Holy Lake, Theo. Trust me. There are writings up here on the cave walls showing a detailed map of all the caverns. It spells out precisely where the Holy Lake and High Altar are. It says *that's* where Blackstar placed the tablet."

"Tell me," Theo called up, voice reverberating. "I'll send my men to retrieve it."

"I want to place it in your hands myself. I want my place in history, Theo. I want to ensure a direct link from Blackstar, through me, to you."

"What about Gallagher?"

"Gallagher is going to *kill* your skeevy ass," Finn said behind her.

"Shh." Peri knew for Theo to believe her, she had to use just the right tone. He believed she was in love with Finn and would only accept words that indicated to the contrary. "I thought Finn was the love of my life. I was wrong, Theo. We must be pre-ordained to be together since Finn was shot. I doubt he'll survive this injury. Especially if we leave him up here without medical help." She extended her arms, palms up in surrender.

"He's weak. Dying. He's going to bleed out. So clearly he wasn't my destiny after all. I see where my future lies. With you. You know I am not a fool. I'm pragmatic, logical. Smart. But to Finn, I'm a liar and a thief. Remember? He didn't want me, not the way you do." She paused again, to make sure he was taking all of that in. "He told me how to get the tablets out of his helicopter. I have the password for that electrical shock device he rigged it with. Once we have all five tablets secured, your men can leave him up here to rot."

"Thanks," Finn muttered.

"Why would you do that?" Theo yelled, not sounding convinced. "The man's richer than Croesus."

"True, but we aren't married, so his wealth won't mean shit to me when he's dead. More importantly, you and I are going to *rule the world.* No contest. Power trumps great wealth. But we'll be wealthy, too, won't we, Theo?"

She didn't pause for his answer. "The tide's starting to come in. You see where the watermark is on the rocks to your right? You have to go. Wait for me upstairs. You won't be disappointed, I promise. We'll have Blackstar's entire prophecy to show our people. We can take Finn's helicopter and fly wherever we want to go."

"How will you get down on your own?"

"I told you. I know a shortcut. Trust me. Go. I'll see you in twenty minutes or less."

"I'll wait-"

"You'll *go.* And no. Your men don't get to stay either. Until you and I are married, I don't want anyone to know the secrets of these caverns."

"I have your word?"

Peri shot Finn a grin. "Absolutely."

Silence throbbed like a living thing, then Theo shouted. "All right. Twenty minutes?"

"See you in the house."

Theo shouted in Spanish for his men to come down. "I'll leave the light for you."

"Thanks, you're so thoughtful, Theo."

Finn, standing well back, shook his head and said quietly, "He can't *possibly* be this stupid."

"He's actually brilliant. But his obsession with Blackstar, and his absolute certainty that he and I will rule the Chosen, have clearly made him dangerously unbalanced. He's convinced I'm the redheaded warrior from the texts. That without me, he can't rule and pass down that rule to his children."

"Hopefully I baffled him with all that bullshit." Peri walked over and planted a kiss smack on his mouth. Then shifted to smile up at him. "I think I might've bought us a little time, while he tries to figure out what the hell I'm up to. But he won't buy into it for long. Let's go before he realizes he's been had." She peered over the edge. "Whether he bought it, or was just humoring me, to see what I'll do next, his men *are* climbing down."

"Then let's get cracking. Head that way-" he indicated the vertical path they should take. Large patches of glass-smooth rock would have to be bypassed, craggy rocks would have to be navigated. All presenting a long circuitous route to the very top. And freedom.

Peri's raw fingertips throbbed just looking at the distance, and her body balked at dredging up the wherewithal this portion of the climb presented. "Awesome. I love a challenge."

He grinned, and she knew he read her like a book. "I'll be right behind you. Move fast and move smart."

TWENTY-THREE

Peri wasn't confident about moving either fast or smart. She was physically spent, her brain mush after the day she'd put in *before* this fiasco. Sweat rolled down her temples even though the cavern, she knew, maintained a sixty-eight degree temperature year round. Her sore fingertips bled, the hole in her cheek where Theo had poked his damn knife throbbed in unison to her heartbeat, and her wrists felt as raw and painful as they looked.

"I've seen the aperture from the water," she said breath harsh and- damn it- a little shaky as she had to blow long strands of hair away from in front of her nose. The plait hadn't stayed braided, and her hair hung annoyingly loose down her back. And her front. Hampering her movements. "I didn't realize it was the ceiling of this cavern. I thought it- Never mind."

"Anyone else know about it?"

"Don't know. I only realized how big it is from in here. Outside it was just an interesting opening with some possibilities. But I was looking for it, I doubt anyone else will. So your answer is, no one is going to be looking for us where this hole comes out."

Finn brushed her elbow with his in an oddly endearing caress. "We're going to make it out of this clusterfuck in one piece. Trust me on this. We *will* get out, I promise. Through that hole, and out onto the cliffside. Keep climbing."

He followed suit, and Peri, who'd rested her hot cheek on the cool granite to look at him, felt a new burst of energy and reached up for the next hold.

"I have a comm device, doesn't work inside. But as soon as we're clear of all this rock, I'll try contacting McCoy, let him know where we're headed." Finn waited for her to get a good foothold. "Up there the Cutters and your brother and dozens of assorted, well-armed men, are dealing with Núñez's soldiers. They're coming now to pick us up."

"Psychic premonition or wishful thinking?"

"I hear a helicopter."

Hand. Foot. Hand. Foot.

The drop from *here* would most certainly kill them on impact. Which Finn already knew, so no point belaboring it.

Hand. Foot. Hand. Foot. "I don't hear anything other than my breathing."

"The good guys are getting closer." Finn glanced down over his shoulder. "And so are the fucking bad guys. Looks like Núñez's men didn't get the memo about leaving."

"So much for that plan." She held on with her left hand a little longer than she should because her arm shook. Finn waited until she started moving again.

"Nobody would believe that bullshit about sticking with him. He's seen how we can't keep our hands off each other. Even he's not *that* much of an idiot."

"I thought it would buy us a few minutes while he digested it." Her ruse hadn't worked worth a damn. Theo's men *had* clambered down to the water, but they were all still *there*. Waiting near the entrance. They were training the bright white spotlight on the two of them so they took center stage like bugs under a microscope.

Finn climbed beside her, the heat of his body warming the musk of his skin, the starch on his shirt and sea spray-scented soap. Her throat tightened with emotion. She wanted to be wrapped in his arms on cool sheets in a dim room. Not clinging like a frightened monkey to a rock-face.

"You didn't really think it would work, did you?" He adjusted the tablet between himself and the rock as he climbed. Every now and then Peri heard it *thunk* as marble bumped stone.

She didn't know how he was doing it. That tablet weighed at least twenty-five pounds. Dead weight. Unnecessary freaking dead weight. Every time he moved, Peri anticipated the heavy tablet pulling him backwards. She hefted herself up to the next toe and fingertip hold and looked up to gauge the distance. Only about twenty more feet. *You can do this*. One foot, one hand at a time.

"Had to give it a sho-" Now she heard the whop-whop-whop. It sounded as though the helicopter was right there in the cavern with them, and they were right inside its spinning blades

"Cavalry arrived," he shouted with satisfaction.

Lights from the hovering helicopter shone through the jagged hole directly onto them. The bright light blinded them as they continued to climb. Finn waved to acknowledge the rescue party as Peri glanced down to see if Theo was with the men who'd returned.

"McCoy, do you c--?" As he tried his comm, Finn's body suddenly jerked as though he'd gotten an electric shock. He said, "Ah, fuck."

Peri gave him a worried look. "What is it? Cramp?"

His pause was long enough to concern her. Then he said, "Checking to see if I have contact. I don't. Keep going."

Squinting, she looked up. Ten feet. They *were* going to make it. A wash of elation gave her a spurt of much-needed energy. Spurred on, keeping her eyes front and center so she wasn't blinded, she climbed for all she was worth. Until she realized Finn was no longer keeping pace.

"Finn?" She looked down at him from under her upraised arm. He wasn't moving, just clinging to the wall, forehead on the rock, immobilized. Her heart trip-hammered. "What's ha--"

She didn't hear the next shot over the deafening whop-whop-whop of the rotors, but suddenly a chunk of granite near Finn's left hand exploded. Scared the freaking crap out of her. With a jerk of surprise she almost lost her grip. They were damn-well shooting at them again from below. *Bastards.*

"Are you hurt?" Hell, she was already feeling downward with her foot, testing for a new foothold in the opposite direction.

"Don't come down for God's sake!" He sounded absolutely livid as she closed the distance between them. "Get up there. I'll be right behind you."

Peri found a solid hold, and gingerly lowered her body before swinging the other foot searching for purchase. "You're a damned liar, Phineas Gallagher."

Oh, God, he *still* wasn't climbing. Her entire body itched with prickly heat and her heart went manic at the ramifications. With bloody fingers latching onto a small outcrop, Peri tested her weight on it, then inched her way down to him.

"Jesus, woman, don't you *ever* fucking listen?"

"How badly are you hurt?"

Surrounded by noise and brilliant lights she got a good look at his face. Lips in a tight line, his forehead slick with sweat, Finn glared at her.

"Tell me," she demanded, tracking her gaze over him until she saw the sheen of wetness spreading over his right shoulder. Goddamnit, she wished that freaking helicopter would just *move away* and take the noise for a few minutes so she could *think*.

His breath *looked* ragged, she couldn't hear it over the din.

"Shot. Give me a minute. . ."

Shot. She anchored herself. Two feet. One hand. Cupped his cheek. His skin felt clammy and cold. He was in shock.

She gnawed her lower lip. Crap crap crap. Wouldn't leave him, couldn't carry him. Could the guys in the helicopter see them down here? "I see a tunnel off-shooting to the left about four feet, looks like it goes horizontal, not vertical. Big enough for us to fit in until they can come down and get us."

I hope. She dared not go to reconnoiter to make sure. She prayed it was at least big enough to allow Finn to rest on a flat surface until help arrived. "Drop the tablet, Finn. We'll retrieve it from the lake later."

"It'll break into a million pieces."

"And you call *me* stubborn? That damned tablet isn't the Holy Grail. We have *four* of them. That's good enough for me. Drop the damn thing and let's move before you lose your grip."

"How. Far?"

"Four feet." At least ten. "Left." Sixty feet down.

"Go."

Peri removed her hand from his cheek, to place it over his straining fingers. She gave a hard squeeze. "Hold on and shut up. Save your strength and move. Don't you realize that if anything happens to you it'll kill me? I love you. I have demands that need to be met. A life I want to share with you. If you fall, I'll never forgive you."

His lips twitched. "Are you proposing, Miss Case?"

"Ariel!" Theo's amplified voice boomed like the voice of God from above. "You're surrounded, and out of options. There's nowhere for you to run."

"Aw, shit. That's *Núñez* in the fucking chopper!" Finn's fingers beneath hers flexed. "That fucker is seriously pissing me off."

"Then let's go. See where that tunnel leads us because right now we're between Scylla and Charybdis. That's our only option. Ready?"

"Yeah."

Finn's loss of blood, and all the shouting they had to do to hear each other, worried her as she was acutely aware of his waning strength. Peri stayed by his side, so close she was touching him somewhere at all times as they inched their way sideways.

His foot slipped, and he looked at her with glassy eyes. "G—"

"One more hold and we're home free." She shot out her hand to hold his fingers in place as he lost hold. "I've got you, Finn. I'll climb in first and help you up." Clawing her way to the edge of the opening, Peri levered herself inside, then turned around to lean down. "Can you lift your body one more time?" Wrapping both hands around his wrist, she leaned back, pulling with all her strength.

With almost superhuman strength, Finn climbed inside beside her. It was a tight fit.

He lay on his side, his breathing shallow and too fast.

"I have to stop that bleeding before we do anything else." Peri pulled her arms out of the long sleeves of her T-shirt and undid the back clasp of her bra.

His eyes looked eerily silver and intense as they traced her naked breasts. "Beautiful. But. Don't-" His eyes drifted closed. "Have. . ."

"Let's get this off you, big boy. See what I have to deal with here."

"In. There." He didn't open his eyes.

He meant the bullet was still in his shoulder. Peri undid the buttons on his shirt with difficulty. Her fingers were raw, some bleeding, and fear and exhaustion had her fumbling for the small buttons. The buttonholes were pulled tightly because of the damned tablet strapped to his chest, making it harder to squeeze the buttons free.

Using both hands, she slipped her fingers between the fabric and his skin, gripped the edges of the placket, and tried to rip them free. The quality of the fabric wouldn't allow it. "Instead of bespoke shirts, shop at a regular store like everyone else," she told him, disproportionally furious at his damned recalcitrant buttons. "I wish we'd never found these freaking tablets."

"Mmm." His fingers curled around her wrist, his grip terrifyingly weak before his hand dropped to lie on the ground beside her hip.

He'd lost a lot of blood. There was a chilling, real possibility that he could die here.

She needed a plan. A strategy.

First things first. Stop the bleeding.

She'd figure out how to get him from here to there after that.

His lashes made black crescents on his cheeks. Finally, she got all the buttons undone. It was laborious and took up way too much time. Hurrryhurryhurry.

Quickly she spread open the unbuttoned shirt, then rested her fingers on the unsteady pulse at the base of his throat. Hurryhurryhurry. The tablet looked incongruous, warm shiny gold, against his tanned, cold skin. Peri hated the damn thing right then. She had to sit up on her knees to get a two-handed grip on it.

It winked gold as if laughing at all the trouble they were going through to save it. It weighed a ton as she lifted it free of his chest. It left a white, pressure indentation across his chest and belly. His chest, slabbed with hard muscle barely moved as he breathed.

This was bullshit. Finn was invincible. Powerful. Freaking bulletproof—

Not invincible. No longer bulletproof.

The knowledge that he could die terrified her. Her arms shook as she propped the tablet, none too gently against the wall beside her. Beyond their little refuge, bright lights shone. The sound of the blades was muted. Had they gone?

The world was still out there, waiting to bite them on the ass.

"I will be *so* pissed if you bleed to death right here under my house-Finn?" He was out cold.

She needed something to pad the wound so it would stop bleeding. His shirt? Damp with sweat and half covered with blood already. Her T-shirt would be perfect. Absorbent cotton. But she was loath to be bare-breasted in case Theo and his goons captured them, so she quickly put her shirt on again.

The t-shirt was long enough to cover her to mid-thigh. "As good as a mini skirt to cover the thong I put on a lifetime ago. This little piece of expensive lace was intended to give me confidence in anticipation of the confrontation I expected from you after the Cutter revelation. Instead, you walked out, I had very little confidence, and that wasn't even the freaking worst part of this hellishly long damned day."

She unzipped her jeans. "Given all that, one would think you'd at least be considerate enough not to die on my watch. I'd have to sell the house of course." She kept up the chatter as she wiggled the denim down her legs. Paused to remove her boat shoes, then pulled the jeans down her legs. "I could never live here with my dead lover's bones entombed in the cavern forever. Too creepy. On the plus side, you and our pal, Blackstar could keep each other company."

She folded the denim into a thick, flat pad, then climbed gingerly over his hip to get behind him. The back of his shirt blood-wet. She felt sick to her stomach as she eased his shirt off the arm he wasn't laying on.

He didn't utter a sound as she gently rested his bare arm on his side.

"This salvage will take us well into our old age." She wiped the blood off his skin as best she could with a section of her jeans. Blood welled from a hole high on his shoulder.

She tried to remember what arteries were in the shoulder. Her mind was blank. If she'd ever known she couldn't remember now. She blotted more blood. "Hell, by the looks of things, our grandchildren will still be pulling up artifacts right here off the coast of Patagonia. Besides, I love this house. The location is perfect, it's c-convenient, I don't want to move, Finn."

Her vision blurred, but she blinked it clear. *Buck up buttercup. You're the only game in town.*

Using her bra to secure the thick unwieldy pad in place, Peri applied pressure with her palms. How hard? Damn it, for how freaking long was she supposed to keep this up?

Finally, she sat back on her haunches to check her handiwork and whispered, "Now what?"

௵

For a moment Finn was disoriented and had to refamiliarize himself with where in the fuck he was. Hard cold floor. Stale, cool air on his hot skin. Yeah. Tunnel. He jerked into full consciousness, heart pounding as his eyes flew open.

No sound of chopper blades. Just his own uneven heartbeat pounding in his ears, throbbing with agonizing regularity and pain in his shoulder.

Oh, Jesus. Oh, shit. . ."Peri?"

When her fingers curled into his, Finn opened his eyes, blinking her into focus. He lay on his side, his head supported on her bare thigh. If he moved his mouth a few inches. . .

He looked up to see her face. Her hair fell in a wild fiery nimbus around her head and shoulders, and her freckles stood out in sharp relief against her paler than usual skin. "Are you okay?"

She nodded, exploring his face with cold, but gentle fingers. "Better now you're awake. You scared me there for a bit."

The tunnel they were in blocked most of the light coming from the cavern. But there was enough to illuminate her worried face, and the stark fear in her eyes. He tightened his fingers around hers, giving a reassuring squeeze.

He kissed her smooth thigh because it was the closest body part. "Darling? Are you aware you're not wearing any pants?"

She drew in a shaky breath. "Used them to pad your wound." Leaning down, she brushed a soft kiss on his mouth, her lips lingering for a few moments. "Think you can walk?"

Feeling annoyingly weak and lightheaded, he said, "Yeah." *Give me a minute.* Not gonna happen. The lack of sound from Núñez's chopper was a throbbing silence. Finn sat up. Fuck it hurt to move, his shoulder begged for mercy, and he almost blacked out. But he was upright.

"How long was I out?" he asked, buttoning his shirt.

"Seven-ish minutes."

"Shit. Where's the tablet?" He'd risked his ass bringing it with them. He hoped to hell he hadn't dropped it.

"I took it to the other end of the tunnel. Faster for me to move alone."

"Jesus, Peri, I'm sorry." Sorry for too many things to tick off right now. Bracing his hand on the wall, Finn staggered to his feet. His head swam. Enough of this shit. "I have a pretty good idea where the Cutters and your brother are. But I can't make communication in here. We need to move."

"You're sure they're coming?"

"Bank on it. But Núñez's men are trained professionals, and there are a crapton of them crawling all over your peninsula. The Cutters and your brother know what they're doing. I wouldn't be surprised if it's a fucking bloodbath out there, but we won't know until we're clear of this place. Did you notice they all have the same tattoo on the web of their thumbs? That indicates to me that they all follow Núñez, and they're not just hired guns."

"That tattoo's a *whirlpool.* It glows in the dark, which is creepy as hell. Theo's had it as long as I've known him."

"Which means those men are members of his Chosen sect," Finn said. "Marry religious zealots with heavy weapons, and you have what we're dealing with here. Trigger happy acolytes who will stop at nothing to give their Supreme Leader what he needs to fulfill his- and their- destiny. Núñez has obviously drummed into them who and what you are. That you're part of the prophecy. They won't stop until he has you and the tablets." Finn cupped her chin. "Not going to fucking happen in this lifetime or the next."

"Agreed. I explored this tunnel while you were out." She pulled his arm over her slender shoulders and took some of his weight. "It curves parallel to the main cavern, with a pretty steep downward slope in places, but I now know where it goes, and how to get us outside. The question is, will Theo and his goons be waiting for us?"

Even though her support was welcome, Finn removed his arm. He'd walk on his own. His warrior had enough to handle without dragging his sorry ass for miles. Although the thought was daunting, he put one foot in front of the other. "Let's find out."

It was a no-brainer that he was still losing blood. He'd said nothing, but the thick pad, she'd secured with her bra, and the bra itself, had fallen off, way back. He could feel the heated liquid bubbling sluggishly from the bullet hole in his shoulder, and felt the sticky warmth as it soaked the back of his shirt.

The ceiling of the tunnel was high enough for him to walk upright comfortably. Comfortable being a relative term. And wide enough for them to walk abreast, most of the time. In some places, the floor was even, with just a gradual slope. In others, a steep thirty-degree plus drop meant sitting and walking themselves down on their asses.

The farther in they went, the darker it became as they moved away from the main cavern and, he thought, deeper into the mountainside.

"Want to rest?" Peri touched his uninjured arm. His body reacted to the warm female musky scent of her skin, mingled with the evocative scent of lilies. Despite where they were, their physical condition, he wanted her as much as he ever had.

Finn shook his head, realized she couldn't see him, and said, "I'm good." He reached out to touch her shoulder. It didn't take much to draw her closer. Combing his fingers through her loose, silky hair, he shivered when the strands blanketed his hands and forearms as he cupped her cheeks. "Better than good."

Her lips opened under his. What he'd anticipated as a gentle kiss, became hungry and urgent as their lips, tongues and teeth clashed and for a few moments they melded together and forgot their dire situation.

Her fingers brushed over his damp mouth after they eventually broke apart. "To be continued. But for now, we're almost there."

When he realized he could see the heat in her eyes, Finn knew there was an ambient light source. "How close?" he asked as they turned in unison to continue walking. Here it was flatter, easier to pick up the speed.

"Round this corner. See? There's the tablet."

Propped up against the wall, the tablet seemed to glow with an inner radiance. Beyond it, the thin, lighted outline of a large flat square on the ground marked a dead end.

Peri pointed. "Freight elevator. It'll take us back down to sea level."

Finn raised a brow. "You have *two* elevators in your house?"

"You have four onboard *your* house." She placed her hand on his chest. "Stay put."

Not willing to let her do anything more without his help, he ignored the order and stepped onto the metal plate with her. It gave slightly with their combined weight. Now he saw the thick cables running up the vertical shaft over their heads.

"Trap door. You in?"

"Hell yeah," he smiled.

With a small grunt as she put her back into it, they pulled open a trap door. The interior was dimly lit with some sort of night light and showed mysterious shapes.

"Seriously, this time *stay put*. I want to rearrange a few things down there, and then I'll help you down." Sliding feet first, she disappeared into the opening. A second later the area where he stood lit up more brightly as she turned on an interior light.

Finn went back for the damned tablet. Might as well take it all the way home.

"Finn?"

He walked back, hefting its weight in both arms. "Here."

"Turn around and lie on your stomach. Drop your legs down, I've piled up some stuff for you to step on so you don't pull open that wound and make it bleed worse. Let me know when you're ready."

"Take the tablet first."

"Hang on a sec."

He heard the scrape of something heavy being dragged. "Okay, if you drop it straight down I have a soft landing for it." She sounded slightly out of breath.

Finn held the tablet over the lighted square, saw white cloth and Peri's bright hair, then let go.

She grunted. "Got it. Now you."

He was a little bit more difficult to maneuver, but he slid to the edge, dangled his legs, and dropped onto a blanket-topped crate. Even with the soft landing, and Peri's steadying hand, his body jarred painfully, and he had to grit his teeth.

"I made some stairs here. Come down."

She'd stair-stepped packing crates, and Finn walked down to stand beside her.

"Here are our choices." Gathering the wild mass of her hair with both hands, she twisted and tucked it into a messy bun at her nape. "Right now we're at ground level. If the doors open, we'd be in the garage with access to your helicopter."

The muffled sounds of gunshots and men shouting was an indication the shit was still hitting the fan in and around the house.

"They think the tablets are in the chopper, but they know it's rigged to blow. They'd presume I'd try to get back to the chopper. Ground level isn't an option since we don't know how many men might be waiting for us. But we'd have the chopper and the backup of at least my two men ...

"If we go down, we'll have my *Sea Witch* and the open sea. Either place could possibly be swarming with Theo's soldiers. Which odds should we go for?"

"Sea level. It's a clear way out, right? No idea if the chopper is still a viable option. It might be disabled."

"As might be the case for *Sea Witch*," she pointed out.

"I vote down to the open water."

"Me, too." She pressed the only button, and the elevator started to smoothly descend.

Finn glanced around. The freight elevator was packed, practically ceiling to floor and wall to wall with heavy crates. She'd managed to clear a space big enough for them to stand, near the door. "What *is* all this?" He had a damn good idea.

"Cutter artifacts." She squeezed behind him, took the small Glock from beneath his shirt. "Packed and ready to deliver to Cutter Cay at my earliest convenience."

He curled a strand of her hair around his finger, his knuckle brushing her smooth cheek. "Was it worth it?" he asked, taking the gun she handed him, even though he knew it held no bullets.

"Yes." Her eyes met his. "Unequivocally. It was fun at the time, and, if not for all this, I probably wouldn't have met you."

Finn shook his head as he leaned against a pile of heavy crates, pretending to himself that he wasn't lightheaded. He needed his wits about him, no time for wimping out. "If not here and now, we would've met somewhere else. Even Blackstar prophesied it."

"Funny." she shot him a sassy smile that sweetly pierced his heart like an arrow. "Theo had the same strong belief that *he* and I were soulmates."

"Núñez is a psychotic, fuckhead screwed up on numerous levels. If he so much as lays one more finger on you, I'll gut him like a fish." Bending to get the knife out of his boot almost had Finn puking. He straightened slowly, swallowing hard as black dots swirled in his vision.

Peri took his arm, eyes troubled. "Can you make it to *Sea Witch*? Never mind. That's rhetorical. Lean against the box behind you, I just remembered something."

Finn leaned back, letting the heavy crate at his back take most of his weight as Peri disappeared between the packing crates.

The sensation of floating didn't dissipate, but the pain at least kept him focused.

"Damn it," she murmured, hidden from view. Wood scraped against wood "Where the. . .*Yes*!"

She returned to his side brandishing a lethal looking dagger.

"Jesus-"

"Side-arm for a knight back in the day. This will go back to Zane." She did a few parries. "But in the meantime, we have use for this beautifully preserved fifteen-century Rondel dagger, and its tapered twelve-inch steel blade. Too bad the wooden hilt got eaten underwater over hundreds of years." She used it to slice a strip of cloth covering a nearby crate. "Woo hoo, and still wicked sharp." She wrapped the strip off the cloth around the bare steel of the hilt and secured it as she'd done with her hair. "I can do a lot of damage with this."

Unless someone took it from her- Fuck. "Make sure you have a sure grip on it," was all Finn offered. "Tell me where and what to expect when the door opens." He hoped to hell there weren't a dozen men waiting for them.

Peri readjusted her fingers on the fabric wrapped hilt. "Opens into a wide tunnel. Turn right. Walk twenty-five feet, first opening turn right again, enter cavern where *Sea Witch* is docked. Two ties. Then about a hundred feet straight out into open water."

"Weapons on board? Núñez was in the helicopter. There's every chance they'll spot us out on open water and he'll alert his people to give chase. "

"A Taurus 9 millimeter under the dash. A semi-automatic in the top left dresser drawer in the master cabin. Same in the guest cabin. All fully loaded. And of course, a galley full of sharps."

Finn smiled. "Better than I hoped." The elevator stopped with a small jolt. *Show time.* "Ready?"

TWENTY-FOUR

So tense her jaw ached, Peri doused the elevator lights seconds before the heavy door slid open. Cool, salt-scented air almost masked the metallic tang of blood. Finn's blood. She tightened her fingers around the hilt of the dagger as she wedged her way to stand beside him to peer into the near darkness. She cocked her head and after a few throbbing moments of silence, whispered, "I don't hear anything. There's no one here."

"That doesn't mean they aren't lying in wait for us," Finn's cautioned, voice low, breath warm against her cheek. "Move fast."

There was no way anyone could be waiting to jump out at them in the dark narrow tunnel, but she was braced for a Jack-in-the-box anyway. "Another fiftyish feet and we'll reach the dock," she said as softly as she could. The ceiling was low enough that Finn, while able to walk upright, had to bow his head.

There wasn't a soul around when they emerged from the tunnel into the cave. "Holy shit." Peri sucked in a breath, and then wished she hadn't. Evidence of a well attended, and bloody fight was everywhere. The stink of blood - and worse - choked off the fresh air. Bile rose in the back of her throat at the evidence of carnage that greeted them.

"No bodies?" she whispered, staring aghast at pools of dark blood, smears as though something - or someone- had been dragged across the rock floor. Some of her once neatly stacked supplies, under tarps along the wall, ready for loading, had been knocked over. Spewed dry goods like rice and beans crunched underfoot as they moved quickly to reach the dock.

"Looks as though the Good Guys came and went." Finn urged her to move more quickly with his hand on her back. "Or the Bad Guys came and went."

"God, there was plenty of bloodshed here, but where are the *bodies*?" Was Ry one of those bodies? God, she prayed not. She grabbed Finn's hand. "Let's get on board before the bad guys decide to come down here to look for us."

The wide opening in the cavern led out to the sea, and the vast expanse of moonless, star-studded black sky. Weird. It felt as though they'd been inside the caverns for months instead of hours. Shocking to discover it was still night time.

Peri breathed a big sigh of relief seeing *Sea Witch* right where she'd left her. Apparently undamaged.

"She's a beauty," Finn said, admiring her ship as she gently rose and fell on the incoming tide. "Same sleek lines as *Blackstar*, same black hull. They're a matched set."

The smell of fresh air and salt spray made Peri's shoulders un-hunch and allowed her to take a few cleansing breaths. "2010 Sunseeker Predator, sixty-four feet," she told him, proud and happy to show her off, even under these circumstances. "Twin inboard. Diesel. Cruising speed twenty-eight. Let's crank her open to her max speed of thirty-two and get the hell out of Dodge."

"Yeah, let's."

After quickly untying her, they climbed on board and Peri started the engine. "Want to pilot her out? I'm going below to put on some pants and get my first aid kit. I don't want you bleeding to death when we're so close to help."

Finn took the wheel, but snagged her arm as she walked past him. "I need a kiss to keep going."

She stood on tiptoe, kissing him hard and fast. "That's going to have to hold you for a bit."

Finn gave her the number for *Blackstar*. "Tell them we're coming in. I'll try McCoy on the comm to get an update."

Peri stayed where she was for a moment, to call the Captain of *Blackstar* to inform him of their location and eta, and that they were both alive, but Finn urgently needed treatment for his gunshot wound.

Finn settled into the comfortable Captain's chair, spoke briefly to McCoy via however he was communicating with the others.

"Everyone is okay. They have your tablet. Núñez left it with his men in the house. Your brother retrieved it. The bad guys have been rounded up, the authorities are on their way."

"What about Theo?"

"They have people watching for his chopper," his voice was grim, his jaw set. "They'll find him and bring him to justice." Finn headed out of the mouth of the cavern into open water. His smile was a little strained as he turned to find she hadn't moved. "You don't have to stay. I've done this before."

"Not with a bullet wound, you haven't. I'm going down to check my security cameras etcetera. Don't pass out before I get back." She reached over and kissed him again before going below. As she passed through the galley, the fragrance of her shampoo and soap lingered in the air. Odd. She hadn't been on board for days. Peri frowned as she walked through her midship salon toward the master stateroom, then stopped as the hair stood up on the back of her neck.

Someone was in her cabin. She heard them moving around. A soft footfall on the carpet, a drawer opened, then softly closed.

She darted into one of the guest cabins. It was empty of furniture other than the built-ins. Slowly, carefully, she slid open the top drawer of the dresser where she kept her log books and a sem-automatic pistol. The black polymer grip S&W compact rimfire fit her hand nicely. Her brother had trained her on one similar years ago, warning her of the dangers of sailing alone unarmed.

The magazine was already inserted. She was always prepared to fend off pirates and thieves, and she wasn't fooling around. If she picked up any of her guns, Peri was prepared to shoot.

There was nowhere to stick another magazine, and she hoped like hell she wouldn't need it as she eased open the cabin door. With a two-handed, grip she padded into the middle of the short corridor, the barrel pointed at the open bedroom door. "Come out with your hands up."

Theo stepped into the doorway, not looking in the least surprised to see her. Dressed in a pair of her sweatpants which were too short on his hairy legs, and an old sweatshirt of Ry's she liked to sleep in. He pointed the business end of a black gun at the middle of her chest as he casually rubbed his hair dry with one of her favorite purple towels. No wonder she'd smelled shampoo when she'd come downstairs.

"Did you just *shower* in my bathroom?" Thank God he was dressed, but still. "You're wearing my damn *clothes*?

"What is yours is mine." His eyes scanned from her face down her bare legs. His look felt like spiders crawling on her skin. His gaze lingered on her unfettered breasts, then tracked down her body. He frowned. "Why aren't you wearing any pants?"

"What are you doing here, Theo?"

"Where do you think you're going, Ariel?" The gun pointing at her didn't waver. "Gallagher's fancy ship was *destroyed* hours ago. Bombs. Such a big ship, it took several to do the job. And since my people were never able to break into his helicopter, because he made sure anyone touching it detonated explosives, all we have left of Blackstar's prophecy is *your* tablet. It's time to introduce you to my people, Ariel. We'll tell them what the tablet says, and start the New World Order. Put the gun down, *novio*.."

"Will you put yours down?" As exhausted as she was, her arms didn't waver either. Like Ry had taught her, she watched Theo's eyes for any telegraphing that he'd pull the trigger. "No? Neither will I." She was by no means a crack shot, but she couldn't miss at this range. But since his gun was bigger, his determination stronger, she figured she'd try talking first. If nothing else it would distract him until she shot him.

"I have serious issues with that ridiculous speech. Let me enlighten you, Theo." She stood her ground. Wondered why she'd never noticed how close-set, and reptilian his eyes were.

"They discovered the bombs on *Blackstar*. There *was* no explosion. The ship's perfectly intact."

"No." He shook his head. The towel in his hand dropped to the floor and he finger-combed his hair. "I saw the explosion with my own eyes from the helicopter earlier."

"I just talked to the captain. I'm pretty sure he'd have mentioned if Finn's billion- dollar ship had recently exploded." She let that sink in, while she tried not to hyperventilate. Did Theo have more men on board? Were they, as she and Theo spoke, with Finn? Or was he up there, slowly bleeding to death because she was down here, instead of with him administering first aid?

She was damn sick of having her heart knocking so hard she could hear it throughout her body. Sweat stung her eyes and she blinked them clear. The muzzle of her gun stayed pointed at his chest. "We have all the tablets. All *five* of them. Yes, Theo, *five*. Because when you and your band of dipshits were shooting at us in the cavern, we had to improvise. And guess what? We *found* your prophet. That's right. We found Blackstar. We almost fell over that poor little boy's ancient bones. He was clutching the fifth gold tablet. So you see, that cavern you were so intent on shooting up, *was* your Holy Lake, and *he* was on his High Altar."

Theo's eyes burned as if he had a fever. "I must go back."

"Sure. I have a dinghy I'll lend you. Oh, wait. You don't sail, do you? And the High Altar is sixty feet up. Ditto for your ability to climb since you don't like heights. Guess you're shit out of luck."

"You'll return with me. Retrieve Blackstar and all the tablets."

"Not to going anywhere with you. Now or ever. And you're delusional. Not only can Dr. Vadini corroborate what the tablets *really* say, dozens of people are witness to that *correct* interpretation. It's the Protector's that win for the correct reading of the prophet's words. Not the Chosen. Who, apparently were only chosen by *you*. Your version has been proven as bogus and filled with misinformation as you are. If necessary I'll put a full-page ad in the local paper to that effect and expose you for the fraud you are. Oh, and for the last damned time. My name is *not* Ariel, and I will never- I can't say this strongly enough- be your *anything*."

His gun wavered for a moment, then steadied as he brought it up. His eyes telegraphed his intention as he said, his voice silky, "If you have nothing to offer me, why shouldn't I k-"

His words were cut off by a muffled *pop*, and the sudden appearance of a small black hole in the middle his forehead, like a slightly off- center bindi. Peri let out a little shriek of surprise as Theo collapsed like a felled log at her feet.

"More often than not, certain negotiations go sideways, and we need to bring them to an expedient end." Finn said from behind her.

Body hot, then cold, then hot again, Peri turned. "Remind me never to negotiate with you!"

Finn gently removed the gun from her white-knuckled grip. "I have better ways to expedite a negotiation with you, darling. Want to go up and pilot your boat while I take care of the garbage?"

She liked the way he phrased that as a question. He was getting to know her. "Throw him in the dinghy, and light the damned thing. We'll give him a Viking's funeral. Not for the glory, but because I want to kill the son-of-a-bitch *twice*."

Dr. Gayle, a short, bald guy with skin the deep, golden brown of an acorn, and a strong Jamaican accent, called a couple of Finn's security people waiting outside to come in and haul an unconscious Finn onto his exam table. His arm hung limply off the edge, blood dripped sluggishly from his fingertips. He'd opened the wound again when he'd dealt with Theo's body on board *Sea Witch.*

God. How much blood did a person have in them? Peri was certain he'd lost at least half of it on the floor of the cave, more on her ship, more when they walked from the garage up to the infirmary.

Drip. Drip. Drip.

The doctor was wearing black, Hawaiian surf shorts with big pink flowers on them, and a black muscle shirt. He quickly and efficiently cut away Finn's shredded, bloody shirt, clearly unfazed by the man she'd watch nearly bleed out. After examining and cleaning his wound, he set up an IV for a blood transfusion and turned to her.

"Are you really a doctor?" Peri eyed his outfit.

"Sure. Certificate over there cost me a hundred bucks. Extra for the gold seal." He cocked his head, eyes sharp as he looked her over. "You look like crap. Let's take a look at you then," the less than charming doctor said. He examined her various scrapes and cuts and slapped four cartoon Band-Aids on her fingers then gently cleaned the raw, painful, red skin on her wrists where Theo's men had tied her. "Go take a shower. Get some rest. I'll send word when he's up and about. Want a tranquilizer? You've had enough trauma to warrant one. "

"Never again, thanks." She shuddered. "They shot me with a sheep tranquilizer. I hope I don't start baa-ing soon."

"That's why I did the blood draw," he said, not smiling, but his eyes twinkled. "I'll let you know if you need to worry. If you need something to help you sleep, let me know. Now scat."

Peri didn't appreciate being shooed out of the exam room while Finn lay pale and still, and she didn't appreciate the doctor's cavalier attitude. Lacing her bandaged fingers with Finn's, she lifted her chin, standing her ground. "Thanks for your medical opinion, but I'll stay until he wakes up."

"You won't be any damn good to him if you pass out, too."

"I won't pass out." Peri leaned her hip against the side rail of the hospital bed, tempted to hop up and stretch out beside Finn. A: she didn't have the energy, and B: she'd be asleep in about eight seconds. "I'm staying."

"The local police are waiting outside the door to talk to you. Go. Get that over with, I'm sure it'll take a while. Then rest." He opened the door to show her the two officers standing outside, gently pushed her out, then closed the door in her face.

She did need a shower, and crawling into bed, and closing her eyes, held a lot of appeal. But she had to thank the brothers, tell them what had happened inside the cavern. More importantly, she wanted to contact Ry to make sure he was okay. *Then* she'd go to Finn's cabin, shower, and wait for him in his bed.

But first, the police escorted her to an empty conference room one deck up. *Blackstar* Group's business offices apparently. Peri told, and retold her story to several officers, and finally was allowed to leave. Her brother was waiting outside in the reception area to go in next.

Peri gave him a tight hug the second she saw him. "Thank you for coming to find me." Stepping out of his arms, she assessed his drawn features and filthy clothes. "Please tell me you're undamaged, I've had about as much bloodshed as I can handle for the year."

"Other than being pissed at you, at those fucking Cutters, and at that boyfriend of yours, I'll live." His voice was harsh with worry, and she saw the concern in his eyes. He softened his tone and touched the small nick on her bruised cheek. "I had a brief chat with Dr. Gayle. He says you have no serious injuries and should be one-hundred-percent after you get at least twelve hours sleep. Come back to *Tesoro Mio* with us after I'm done making my report. You've had a hell of a day. You can sleep for twenty-four hours if you like."

"Thanks for the offer. But I'm staying right here."

The door opened and an officer waved Ry inside. Her brother turned to her with a scowl. "With Gallagher and the *Cutters*? You're shitting me, Magma. Have you forgotten who and what these people are? The clusterfuck they embroiled you in today? You could damn well have died! Think about that so you can explain it to me later." He closed the door behind him.

She wasn't particularly looking forward to that conversation, but right now she needed to find the biggest, blackest cup of coffee she could wrap her hands around, and then thank the Cutters. Which was going to taste a lot more bitter than the coffee, or anything Ry could dish out.

Then she was going back to the infirmary to see how Finn was doing. It had been thirty minutes or so, he should be awake by now.

Finn cracked open his eyes. He lay in one of four hospital beds in Blackstar's infirmary. A half-empty IV bag dripped blood into him. Other than a sharp pain in his shoulder when he moved, he felt pretty decent.

They'd left Núñez where he lay and hightailed it to *Blackstar*. Since his people had already contacted the authorities, who were on their way, Finn had accompanied Peri down to the infirmary so they could both be checked out. He'd passed out before he made the introductions.

"Where's Peri?" he demanded of the doctor, who sat on the bed across from him, feet swinging off the floor as he keyed something into his iPad.

Finn had hired Arley straight out of med school, where he'd ranked top in his class, almost a decade earlier, and they'd become good friends. In the space of two weeks, his ship's doctor had met, fallen head over heels, and married *Blackstar's* chief steward. Britt, a tall Norwegian blond, was a foot taller, and more than a decade older than her new husband. They were still blissfully in love.

Dr. Arley Gayle had the shittiest bedside manner Finn had ever encountered, and he didn't disappoint now. He glanced over at his patient, and said something - for sure something damned rude, in Patios, then translated in perfect English, "You fainted like a girl."

"I didn't faint. I passed out."

Arley hopped off the bed and placed his hand on Finn's chest to prevent him from rolling to his feet. "Same thing. I cleaned out the wound, dug out the bullet," he said unsympathetically as he efficiently removed the IV and slapped a band-aide with a Disney princess on it over the small puncture wound. They were the only bandages on board, and everyone got a damned princess. Wounds tended to heal fast on *Blackstar*.

"Took a bit of excavating. But I'm *that* good that I didn't do more harm than good. Saved the bullet. A giant-sized sucker. You could frame it and tell your children about your misadventures. Did I mention you fainted like a girl?" Arley's grin was wide, white and evil.

His features softened as he gave Finn a mildly sympathetic look, and squeezed his uninjured shoulder. "Lucky man you is. She's *anise*." His friend doctor dropped the accent. "A fiery beauty."

Anise. Jamaican slang, and high praise, for beautiful princess. "She is that." *And more*.

"I like her. Don't fuck that up. She was worried, and I had to threaten her with bodily harm to get her to leave you to my tender mercies."

The doctor checked his pulse, shone a light into his eyes. "I patched up her cuts and scratches while she held your hand, and watched every move I made with threat of dismemberment if I made a wrong one. Not that I would ever make a wrong move. Rumors of me killing my patients are grossly exaggerated. Which I told her. She was brave and stoic. I like that about the woman. No crying or winching as I stitched you up. Insisted I deal with you first since you were bleeding like a stuck pig. The worst damage was to her hands. Nothing that a half dozen princesses and a good manicurist can't fix. She needs to be taken to bed. And allowed to *sleep*."

"You're a prick, Arley. Help me up."

The doctor helped him sit up, holding on to Finn until his head stopped spinning. "You lost a bucket or two of blood. You'll feel weak for a while. No stitches. Leave it open to drain, let it dry out naturally. Less likely to become infected and kill you. It'll hurt like a fire-breathing dragon is kissing your shoulder for a while. But man up. You can take a little pain. Abstain for at least ninety days to be on the safe side. Doctor's orders."

Finn laughed. Wearing just the black slacks he'd worn before he left, he swung his bare feet to the floor. A fire-breathing dragon did indeed kiss his shoulder. *Hard.* The room bounced several times. "Where's Persephone?"

"Everyone's waiting anxiously in the salon, *mengkeh*. Lots of wringing of hands, and pacing. I ordered the lot of them to get blind drunk and sleep it off." His friend sighed. "Favor it if you plan on rolling around on a soft surface anytime soon. And don't get any long hair stuck to it. It'll be a bitch to get that out. Like spider webs, you know. Drink liquids, no alcohol. Sleep. Don't call me in the morning unless your arm falls off. I'm going back to a lonely bed since my wife is on duty for another hour. Off you go."

Finn padded down the corridor from the infirmary. He had no idea what the time was, Arley had probably stolen his watch as he frequently threatened to do when they played poker.

Dragging his bone-weary ass, he took the elevator, instead of walking up two decks. He needed to hold Peri in his arms. Had to see her beautiful face, and touch her hair. Then they'd go to his cabin and sleep, wrapped in each other's arms, for about a week.

Her steps faltered when she saw that the salon was crowded with people milling about. Everyone was there. The Cutters, Addison, Callie, and a bunch of black-clad men, all helping themselves to coffee and sandwiches. Finn's salon had apparently become a deli.

A strange, dark-haired woman stood beside Logan, a giant tabby cat apparently asleep in her arms. "This is my wife Dani."

"Hi." She looked like a pleasant woman, but hi was all Peri could muster.

Dani gave her a sympathetic smile. "We can meet again tomorrow after you've rested. It sounds as though you've had a hell of a day."

"Yes. . .that." Peri made her way across the room. It shocked her that the blackness of night still pressed against the windows. She felt as though days had passed since she'd set out to the mainland followed by everything that had happened. Instead, it was three am. She'd been awake for *years*.

"How is he?" Jonah sat on the arm of Callie's chair, and she had one arm draped over his knee.

"He lost a lot of blood, and he's getting a transfusion." She'd already pretty much experienced the apocalypse in the last six hours. She was braced for anything as she went to pour herself a mug of coffee, then went to sit beside Addy, who cradled a sleeping Adam.

"Have a sandwich." Callie frowned. "They have grilled cheese, your favorite."

"Thanks, but only if someone else chews and swallows for me. I'm so freaking tired all I want right now is this coffee."

When she sat down, Addison took her free hand and inspected the raw tips and assorted bandages, and the angry red marks on her wrists. Trust her sister-in-law to sit there looking serene while surrounded by Cutters. If Addy felt uncomfortable, she didn't look it. Wearing white shorts, and a sage-green t-shirt, with her strawberry blond hair up in a ponytail, face makeup-free, she still looked like a million bucks.

"Oh, honey, look at you. That *bastard*. I'd kill him myself if he wasn't dead already."

Peri drank half the hot coffee in one giant gulp, hoping for the instant jolt of caffeine. "Ow. Hot!" She fanned her mouth. "This is nothing. Finn was shot. It was sheer luck that the bullet didn't hit anything vital, but he lost freaking *gallons* of blood." She looked around the room. "Was anyone else hurt?"

"Not on our team," Zane said dryly. "Nunez's soldiers were either killed or rounded up. Your brother retrieved the tablet from your house, as you can see."

Addison gently squeezed her hand. "I heard about Finn. I'm sure he'll be just fine. They say the doctor on board is first class. But, how are you?"

"Yes, Persephone." Nick sent her a frowning glance from his position near the windows where he had an arm wrapped around Bria's shoulders. "How *are* you?"

Peri smiled. "I feel exactly like you guys *look*. Tired, filthy and ready to sleep for twenty-four hours."

"We're just hanging to see how Finn's doing, then we'll return to our ships. We can catch up tomorrow."

"First *signore* Gallagher must be informed of the message carved into the new tablet." Dr. Vadini didn't look up as he spoke. Crouched beside the marble-topped coffee table, in what looked likean uncomfortable position, he had all five tablets propped up on easels. With his hands encased in pristine, white cotton gloves, he was looking at the new one through a lighted jeweler's loupe.

"Perhaps it could wait until tomorrow, *signore*?" Bria suggested gently. "I don't think any of us can stand any more excitement or input into our weary brains for today."

"Amen." Nick kissed the crown of her head, tucked beneath his chin.

"No. It must be tonight," Dr. Vadini said, firmly, then seemed to forget they were there as he went back to writing notes with one hand and inspecting the tablet with the other.

"Have you been able to read the fifth tablet, doctor?" The glossy gold of the five tablets gleamed in the glow of the overhead lights. The one she and Finn had retrieved from Blackstar, was as shiny as the other four and needed no cleaning. Unlike the rough square shape of the others, this was oblong, eighteen inches wide, and five or six inches deep. There didn't appear to be any writing on it, but it was perforated by series of unevenly spaced holes.

"This is an extraordinary find, and the tablets, *together,* tell a riveting, and complete, story now that I have more words translated and interpreted." Dr. Vadini was almost quivering with excitement. "How long do you think it will be before signore Gallagher joins us?"

"I'm not sure." Peri covered a yawn. "He was having a blood transfusion when I left. It's possible he'll stay in the doctor's quarters until tom-"

"No no no." Vadini scowled. "He must be made aware of the situation *tonight.*"

"I'm sure he'll come and say goodnight if he's able," Peri said soothingly. Raising her eyebrows at the curator's vehemence, she met Nick's smiling gaze across the room.

With a small shrug, the middle Cutter indicated her bandaged fingers with a jerk of his chin. "I see Arley took good care of you."

"His bedside manner could use a little polishing, but as long as Dr. Gayle takes good care of *Finn,* I'm good." She drained the mug, then lowered it to her knee, cradling the warm ceramic between her hands. "I want to thank you guys for coming to the rescue." She looked from Nick, to Jonah, to Zane, to Logan. "I don't know what Finn could possibly have said to convince you to come out, guns blazing, but I'm really grateful that you did."

"Ready for a refill?"

Peri looked up to see a tall, gorgeous blond standing beside her holding a large black thermos of coffee. "God, yes." She held her mug aloft.

"I'm Britt Gayle." The woman had a stunning smile, wide and white. Even at three in the morning, she looked as fresh as a freaking daisy in her crisp black shorts and golf shirt, her pale blond hair swirled in a tidy coil on top of her head.

Peri wondered if Finn had slept with her. She scowled. "Wait. Did you say, *Gayle*? You're the *doctor's* wife?" This tall, beautiful *pleasant* woman was married to the cranky doctor?

Britt smiled even wider. "We get that shocked response every time. He sent you a message. Finn's doing well, and he'll come to you here in a little while." With a smile, she filled Peri's mug almost to the brim.

"Thank you."

Britt went around to refill mugs as another steward circulated offering sandwiches and freshly baked chocolate chip cookies.

What was a 'little while'? She should meet him halfway. Peri was about to get up and do just that when Logan spoke.

"Want to fill us in on what you and Finn were doing while we were doing what we were doing?" Logan asked, holding a sandwich to his mouth.

Peri sipped the hot coffee before responding. "Honestly? Not now." *I want to drink another gallon of coffee, struggle to keep my eyes open, and sit right here waiting for Finn.* The loveseat was soft and comfortable, and it would take just too much effort to speak, let alone go in search of him. "Maybe when Finn's with me, and we have energy to rehash the whole thing."

"Then we'll fill *you* in while we wait."

The men took turns recounting their individual stories, while Peri pretty much went into a semi-comaleaning her head back on the chair's soft pillow and watching everyone through gritty eyes.

"You really should go to bed, honey," Addy whispered as the others talked around them.

"In a bit." There was no way she'd sleep until she knew Finn was out of the woods, and lying beside her.

“Landed the chopper a couple of miles from the house,” Logan told Teal who'd just demanded 'Details!' “Walked in. Took out my fair share of the bad guys-“

“Logan!" Teal sat on the edge of her chair. "I don't want the Cliff's Notes version. Give us the specifics, please.”

"Sweetheart." Zane cupped the back of his head with both hands and gave his wife a tired smile. "Let the autopsy wait until tomorrow. We're all wiped out. We're going to split in a bit."

While the conversation swirled around him, Dr. Vadini continued his inspection of the new tablet. Every now and then excitedly writing something in his small, neat handwriting in his little red notebook. He appeared oblivious to everything around him.

"We have to stick around, might as well go over what we know and compare notes. Coffee? Cup five? Sure, why not? Thanks, Britt." Logan started from when the men, loaded up with weapons, departed their respective ships to go to her house. Apparently, the women, none-too-pleased to be left behind, had gathered on board Blackstar, awaiting word.

The Cutters and Ry had, shockingly, worked together. Using Finn's resources, including a very sophisticated satellite, they were able to pinpoint how many, and where each of Theo's men were located.

Peri frowned as Logan took a sip from his steaming mug. "I knew there were a bunch of them. Sounds like Theo had an army?"

"The army of the Chosen," Dr. Vadini said in his quiet, calm manner as he looked up. "The Chosen have been preparing for the war that would precede the end of the world for hundreds of years."

"A war against who?" Zane asked, making no comment on Dr. Vadini's unshaken assurance that there was going to *be* an imminent end to the world.

Vadini shrugged. "The Protectors. We too, have trained all our lives for the confrontation."

"You *have*?" Bria's eyes widened.

"Sí, Principessa. In secret, of course. And we do not have as many men as the Chosen. But our small army had access to Israeli weapons, and we have trained all our lives to protect Blackstar's legacy. To us, the Chosen was but a part of the myth of Blackstar. We didn't really believe we would ever have to fight to protect and preserve the truth from the Chosen."

Teal was the only person in the room who looked and sounded wide awake. "Just like you, Dr. Núñez believed his truth *was* the truth."

"The Chosen believed that they would rule eleven thousand true believers," Dr. Vadini said. "That this manifestation of the prophecy would secure their rule. The problem came when Dr. Núñez realized that what he had always believed, was in fact, *false*. Blackstar's prophecy was much different from what he'd been led to believe. And since his belief was unshaken, he couldn't allow what the tablets truly say, to become known to his followers."

"You think he was trying to steal them to *destroy* them? To destroy the truth?" Jonah asked.

"He was prepared either way. He set two bombs on board to destroy the tablets if Mr. Gallagher didn't bring them to him. Or he was willing to lie to his followers, cognizant of the fact that none of them would be capable of reading Abipón., He could've told them anything he needed to, to confirm the Chosen's beliefs. His people would've had no reason to doubt him."

"That's chilling," Bria said.

"Dr. Núñez was obsessed with the Chosen. It is my supposition that he'd been sending men away from Patagonia to be trained in various forms of combat for many years."

"They could've been trained in the Ukraine," Nick said, leading Bria to the sofa, her hand in his. "The last time I saw that many H&K G36 assault rifles was a skirmish in Cosio a few years back. That was a major clusterfuck."

"Stylistically their methods were very much Maza's M.O., so yeah. ANLF instructed," one of the T-FLAC men lining the wall, agreed. Most of the silent men standing against the back wall were unfamiliar to her. But she recognized several of Finn's security people, and one or two from Rydell's ship as well. Peri let the rumble of words wash over her, as the men's voices ebbed and flowed. Right now, she didn't care who'd done what- or how it had gone down, although the fact that the Cutters had jumped in to help astonished her.

Rydell strolled into the room, his gaze going directly to Addison.

"Ry!" Addison handed Peri the sleeping baby before jumping to her feet and racing across the room. Peri's hands automatically clasped the baby.

She, who'd never held a baby in her life, froze with the responsibility just foisted on her. Staring at Adam's sleeping face Peri hoped to God she wasn't holding him too tightly. Addison flung herself into her husband's arms. Ry wrapped his arms around her, resting his chin on the crown of her head as his eyes sought Peri.

Her brother, his arm around Addy's slender waist, scowled. "I thought you decided to go to *Tesoro Mio*, Magma."

"*You* decided. I'm incapable of moving."

Ry gave her a half smile and held out his hands. "Here, give him to me."

Peri couldn't move. "Take him. I don't want to drop him."

Her brother's large hands cradled his son as he lifted the child from her lap, then as he'd done on board his ship what felt like a lifetime ago, held him in one hand like a football. The baby slept blissfully on.

"Sit here." She rose from the loveseat. "I need to stretch my legs for a bit."

He gave his head a slight shake, his eyes hard. "We're going back to *Tesoro Mio*."

"Stay," Peri asked softly. "Please."

Addison and Ry took her seat and Peri went to pour herself another cup of coffee. Her exhaustion was now compounded by a case of the jitters and her nerves raw waiting to see with her own two bleary eyes that Finn was okay. Her hand shook as she returned the carafe to the table.

There was a sudden hush in the room. "My sister's alive, no thanks to you, Gallagher." Her brother's voice cracked with fury. "She saved your sorry ass." Ry glared at Finn who'd just walked in.

Finn put up a 'stop' hand. "True, but I'm not going to fight you." His eyes met Peri's across the room. Fumbling to set down her full mug without looking away, she walked toward him. They met in the middle of the room. He was favoring his shoulder, and his face was paler than usual, but he was the most awesome sight Peri had seen in days.

He was barefoot, but had on a clean black t-shirt. She wasn't too tired to notice, the fabric did nice things for his broad shoulders and tight abs.

"Thanks for sticking around," Finn addressed the others as he slung an arm around her shoulders and hugged her against his side.

Peri looked up at him. His color was better, but there was a tightness in the muscles along his jaw and down the column of his neck. He was tired and in pain.

Finn's fingers gently gripped her side ever so slightly more as he began to speak. "Now that you see I'm fine, and know this is over, would you all bugger off? I want to get Peri tucked into bed. She's exhausted."

Dr. Vadini staggered to his feet from his crouched position. Teal rushed to lend him a helping hand as he wobbled for a moment. "It is not over. You must let me read Blackstar's last message. For that, we must go outside."

"I'm not up for bedtime stories. Perhaps in the morning, Dr.—"

"No. No. It must be tonight! You must see it outside. *Tonight*!"

TWENTY-FIVE

Even though all the lights on board had been turned off, per the curator's urgent instructions, the bridge deck was awash with starlight. They headed for Finn's telescope near the empty helipad.

A shooting star arced across the blackness of the sky then disappeared. If Peri had the energy, or believed in such things, she would've made a wish. Instead, she observed the way the starlight played on Finn's features, painting them in stark relief. She worried about his shoulder.

Without revealing what was clearly a big deal, Dr. Vadini insisted the tablet be brought outside with them. Perspiration gleamed on his face, and his hands shook with excitement as he instructed the three men carrying the tablets how to position them on the table brought outside with them. "This one and this one at the top. *Sí*, just so. Now Blackstar's tablet in the middle, and the other two below it." He stood back, arms folded to ensure they'd been positioned as he wanted them.

Dr. Vadini adjusted them slightly, matching up the top and bottom edges.

"All right." Jonah stuffed his hands into his front pockets as he looked over the doctor's shoulder. "We're all out here. The tablets are all out here. Tell us what the fifth tablet says, Doctor."

"There's no text, right?" Peri asked around a yawn. In the center; a series of small randomly spaced holes looked as if a pencil-point had pierced the gold-covered marble. "Just holes?"

"There *is* a little text here." He brushed the faint, decorative border around the outer edges. "Instructions on the positioning of the perforations." Drawing in a deep breath, Dr. Vadini traced a white-gloved finger along the left-hand edge of the new tablet, and read, "*In the eleventh month when Mercury, Venus, Saturn, Mars, and Jupiter align-*"

"They align once *every* ten years, and have done so for hundreds of years." Finn adjusted the knobs on the massive telescope. "We'll be able to see them clearly, even with the naked eye and of course through this they'll look as though we can reach out and touch them. The timing is excellent. This configuration is best viewed just before sunrise, so we have a couple of hours to enjoy them."

"The five planets may very well align every ten years, signore, but five hundred years ago, Blackstar predicted this event," he said, pointing to the tablet, "would occur exactly as it has unfolded. Tomorrow night. It is not happenstance that the two of you found the seer when you did. Nor was it a coincidence *where* he was found."

Dr. Vadini's eyes gleamed in the semi-darkness. His hand rested on the new tablet as if it were a helium balloon about to drift into the sky if not anchored. "Blackstar prophesied this event. *This* night. *This* month. *This* year. Above all. *You, signore* Gallagher, and you *signora. Two stars converge, one red, one black*." He indicated where the words were on the tablet Finn had found. "The two of you - *You* are the red and black converging stars."

"If you say so." Despite all that had happened, Peri saw by Finn's small frown that he was still having a hard time believing everything wasn't coincidence. Or a well-hatched plot.

The air was dead still on the top deck, no sign of the high winds they'd experienced earlier. The black dome of the sky was studded with crisp, white stars. The air smelled fresh and salty, and of the strong black coffee Finn's staff had set up nearby. Everyone was mainlining the coffee now that the adrenaline rush had dissipated, and exhaustion was evident on the faces of all of them as they hung around to hear how Dr. Vadini was going to interpret the last tablet.

Peri inhaled deeply. On a night like this, anything was possible.

"The stars look like diamonds scattered on black velvet." Bria leaned both arms on the rail as she stood beside Nick looking out over the water.

The ocean, black, tipped with gleams of reflected silver from the stars, lapped the hull in a soothing lullaby that made Peri not *want* to talk. She wished she and Finn were alone. She'd give anything right now to spread a blanket out on the deck, and lie there in his arms, gazing up at the stars. Until her eyes slammed shut.

She wouldn't trade the view of the night sky for any amount of diamonds. Far from diminishing her, seeing this many stars made her feel as powerful as a pagan goddess. Lifting her arms to the heavens she swirled around until she felt dizzy. With a laugh, Finn captured her in his arms.

"*'Raise the compendium to divine the truth'*," Dr. Vadini quoted. "You need to look at the sky through the holes in the tablet, signore."

"What are we supposed to be seeing?" Rydell asked over the head of his sleeping baby. Addison was curled up on a lounge chair, fast asleep and missing all the fun.

"Spectacular shooting stars, for one thing," Finn told Peri's brother as he adjusted the complicated knobs on the telescope and looked through it. "Not only are we able to observe this rare juxtaposition of the planets, but the Graphton Meteor Shower peaks tomorrow. As you can see, we're observing a spectacular show of hundreds of meteors per hour as they vaporize on entering the Earth's atmosphere."

"I've never *seen* so many falling stars." Teal's head tipped back against Zane's shoulder as he leaned against the rail. "This is breathtaking. Is the meteor shower what *Blackstar* wanted us to see, signore Vadini? "

"No, it-"

"This shower is unique," Finn interrupted, his tone dry. "It has a cyclonic peak of about every thirty-three years. Unusual, but anticipated. I doubt Blackstar knew about a meteor shower five hundred years in the future."

"Why *are* there so many falling stars tonight?" Peri asked.

"We see meteor showers, shooting stars- every year at this time, but the Graphton comet makes its way around the sun every thirty-three years, leaving a trail of dust rubble in its wake. When the Earth's orbit crosses the trail of debris, pieces of the comet fall toward the Earth's surface. The Earth's atmosphere causes the comet's debris to ignite into burning balls of fire."

Peri loved watching Finn's expression as he talked about his passion. The stars.

"That sounds ominous." Bria frowned

"Is that what the tablets say, Doctor? That a meteorite is going to hit Earth?"

"No," Finn assured her, before Dr. Vadini could speak again. "Anything heading this way will burn up in the atmosphere. None will make landfall.," He tugged her closer by curling a strand of her hair around his fingers. "Hundreds of scientists, and many other assorted professionals, and God only knows how many amateur astronomers, watch the sky 24/7. We're safe from space debris."

"*Seek the High Altar to discover the answers written in the stars*," Dr. Vadini quoted, clearly undaunted. "This was of course done." He threw a pleased glance at Finn and Peri. "*In the eleventh month when Mercury, Venus, Saturn, Mars, and Jupiter align.* If you look here along the edge." He ran his gloved finger reverently across what looked like decorative border that matched that on the other four tablets.

"Blackstar gives us an exact measurement from the horizon. And here it says; *If not stopped, oceans will rise, mountains will topple, the mighty and innocent alike will perish. Raise the compendium to divine the truth.*"

"And you think Blackstar predicted a meteorite would strike the Earth?" Finn wrapped his arm around Peri's waist, tucking her against his side. "Sorry, not happening. Comet crumbs are usually the size of a pea. If a near earth object were to come our way, we'd know about it *years* in advance. Trust me, there's absolutely nothing threatening us. We have thousands of astronomers watching the skies, being ever vigilant, and we have so many failsafes, nothing can enter the Earth's atmosphere without being spotted *years* before it hits and becomes a danger."

"Please, signore. I entreat you. Pick up the tablet. Hold it up to the sky. *See* for yourself what Blackstar prophesied."

"Sure. But let's wrap this up. Everyone needs some shut-eye. It's been a hellishly long day." Finn reached over and plucked the long tablet from between the others.

When his injured arm dipped, Peri braced the bottom of the tablet with both hands. They shared a smile that sliced her heart.

Dr. Vadini's hands hovered under the tablet as Finn raised it to eye level. "No. The other way- Sì," he said as Finn rotated it. "Like so."

"What do you see?" Peri demanded, trying to see through the holes as he was doing.

"Intriguing," Finn murmured, shifting his left hand a few centimeters to slightly reposition the heavy tablet. "Mercury, Venus, Mars, Jupiter and Saturn line up perfectly. It's as if. . ."

"As if *what*?" Nick demanded.

Peri wished to hell she could read the word bubble she imagined she saw over Finn's head as he stared intently through the unevenly spaced holes in the gold tablet.

"As if someone spaced these holes purposefully, and with intention, in concert with the planets." He sucked in a breath, narrowed his eyes. "God damn- *Take* it," he instructed Jonah, standing closest to him. Jonah grabbed the heavy tablet with both hands before Finn turned to his telescope.

At the concern in his voice, Peri, like everyone else straightened, moving closer to him as he adjusted the telescope to peer intently through the viewfinder.

She tried to peer around his arm to see what he was seeing. Of course, she couldn't see a damn thing. "What is it?"

"*Asteroid,*" he told the assembled group as he made small adjustments to the telescope. "It should be hiding behind the moon, but it's visible tonight. There are ten to fifty thousand asteroids out there. This one shouldn't damn well *be* where it is, but God damn it, it's exactly where the *hole* indicates it would be. Heading straight for Earth."

"Holy shit," Peri said, reacting to his ominous tone. "It'll burn up in the Earth's atmosphere, right?"

Finn looked grim as he reached for his phone in his back pocket. "Not one of that size, no."

Finn held up a finger for everyone to hold their comments as he contacted his assistant on the phone. "Come up to the helicopter bridge right away," he instructed Walker after the phone rang once. "On your way, get California on the phone. We have a critical situation. Bring in all relevant leaders of our allies for a teleconference call in ten. Add the usual suspects as well." Every one of his competitors in this race to Mars. "We'll need every brain we have on this. Keep everyone on mute until I've talked to Halperin."

Yeah. This was serious enough that all world leaders had to be notified immediately. The world was in jeopardy – not just one country or another.

Finn never thought he'd be the one instigating the call. He rang off, but kept the phone in his hand. This hellishly long day and night wasn't over yet. The cool, salty air was dead still, and for several moments the near silence throbbed in his ears in time with his staccato heartbeat. The rapid pulse shot knives into the fucking hole in his shoulder, which had suddenly become the least of his problems.

The lights of the police boats, disappearing in the distance, as they returned to base with Núñez's body, winked against the darkness.

"You're scaring the living fucking crap out of everybody, buddy." Logan, jaw tight, suddenly looked alert. "Give us the shorthand facts, and tell us what we need to do to help."

"The facts are simple. Despite the complexity of the language that sets forth the facts," Vadini responded to Logan, but had eyes only for Finn. "Blackstar foretold that *signore* Gallagher will prevent the annihilation of our planet."

Simple his ass. While Finn appreciated the man's unwavering faith in him, Vadini didn't understand the astrophysics of what needed to be done – if it could be done.

"You can do this, *sì*?" Vadini asked when Finn didn't say anything.

Finn slid his arm around Peri's shoulders, tugging her against his side. The faint scent of lilies calmed his racing heart. His chest ached with intense emotion, as she rested one hand over his heart.

"Did it suddenly appear out of…thin air? Where did it come from?" Peri's eyes said she was counting on him to have all the answers.

"As we do for all NEOs- near-Earth objects, they'd been keeping a close eye on this asteroid for years before it hid behind the moon. We couldn't see it, but we knew its path. This isn't that fucking path. Something knocked it out of its regular orbit, and it's visible now, and traveling at approximately forty-three thousand miles an hour, give or take." Unprecedented and alarming.

Walker arrived on the helicopter deck and strode to the large gathering near the telescope. He held out a phone for Finn. "Dr. Halperin."

"Brock," Finn said by way of greeting. "DW17C is visible and off course." After the lead scientist at the launch facility in the Mojave Desert sucked in a shocked breath, Finn shot off the coordinates like bullets. "Yeah, impossible as it may seem, you can *see* how it dramatically veered off course. *Not* fucking impossible. How long until impact? I need solid numbers and our team's best/worst case scenarios. Is the possibility of deflection or obliteration even on the table at this time? Good man. I'll observe in real time." He handed Walker back his phone. "Set up the conf-"

"Done."

"Anyone who wants to come downstairs and observe, follow me."

"Hell yes," Zane said. "If this is doomsday I want to be at ground zero facing the fucker head-on."

"Not fucking funny, bro." Jonah, standing behind his new wife, circled Callie's shoulders with both arms as if protecting her from whatever the fuck was going to rain Armageddon on their heads. "What's actually happening here?"

"A thirteen-mile wide asteroid has been knocked out of its orbit and appears to be heading for the Earth." Finn figured they could all take the unvarnished truth.

Peri's arm tightened around his waist. "Okay, that is really, *really* freaking terrifying."

"What are you thinking?" Rydell asked, looking up at the starry sky. He'd woken a sleeping Addison and was helping her to her feet. "Clearly something catastrophic since you put in a call to World leaders."

"This is a situation that warrants immediate attention from decision makers. If none of them have contacted me, as yet, then they aren't aware of the situation. And that's extremely troubling. We aren't the only ones with telescopes and knowledgeable people. Someone else should've seen this *before* now."

"Would it make any difference?" Logan asked. "Is anyone ready for something like this? Think tanks speculating opinions, but anyone have what's necessary to destroy or deflect this fucker?"

Finn dragged clean sea air into his starving lungs. "We're going to find out."

"Just how bad are we talking, here?" Nick asked.

"It's big enough to take out half of South America on impact, cause global earthquakes, tsunamis several hundred feet high, and set off major volcanic activity. The dust cover would do the rest. Think the last of the dinosaurs, then *double* the destruction."

"Jesus," Jonah said harshly. "Don't sugar coat it."

Finn didn't bother trying to rationalize. Bizarrely, the coincidences kept piling up. Yet a child had seen these events unfolding more than five centuries years ago. It was now hard to find fault with the message of the tablets. He indicated they take the outside stairs to the third deck where the Blackstar Group's business offices were located. The same deck the authorities had used just an hour earlier to interview the principal players in what had gone down at Peri's home.

Was he reading too much into the shift of the asteroid? Perhaps his calibrations on the telescope were off. . . No. No, they weren't. Halperin's equipment in California made this telescope look like a Tinker Toy. He'd confirmed the unexpected shift. Not wrong. Terrifyingly right. Yet *his* people hadn't noted DW17C shift either. Was it possible that he'd observed the shift of trajectory at the exact moment of change? What were the astronomical odds of that?

"If it's near enough to see with the naked eye," he told them as they walked across the deck to get to the next set of stairs, "it'll be too late to do anything about it."

Peri, almost glued to his side, frowned. "*You* just saw it through the holes in the tablet. That was with your naked eyes, right?"

"No, I didn't see it through the holes. But when there were two holes through which I saw *nothing,* I looked through the telescope, positioned it to see the section of sky indicated through the top hole. That exact coordination was the last known location of DW17C, an enormous asteroid, a million miles from Earth. It wasn't there. But when I adjusted the telescope to look where the second hole in the tablet indicated- There it was. Knocked off its orbit. I believe that it was hit by another asteroid hundreds of years ago, and can only be seen now."

"Jesus. Thirteen miles wide?" Jonah asked. "How soon?"

"To give you perspective, the asteroid that wiped out the dinosaurs was about six to eight miles across. That event wiped clean thousands of square miles from the impact site. This will be worse, much worse."

He paused to look at each of the people gathered around him. His friends. The people he cared about. The woman he loved. Each looking at him like he had the fucking solution to save mankind. Fucking hell. The weight of his friends, his love, the whole damn world sat on his aching chest.

Finn sucked in a fortifying breath. "If the asteroid hits earth," he continued, "all life will be obliterated. Our entire solar system will be changed forever." The doors to his on-board control room stood open, the white light of the wall-sized monitors flickered, bathing the room in a surreal day-light glow.

"How long?" Nick asked as they entered the room. Finn didn't answer right away. He had to gather more information to answer that ominous question accurately. This was the place to do it. From this room, he had made video conference calls, observed all aspects of the Blackstar Group across the globe, and watched his divers when they were salvaging. Now, from here, he had to figure out when mankind would be obliterated.

Crystal clear, giant, rear-projection wall screens took up most of the four walls, now showing the interior of his Mission Control in the Mojave Desert as if they were inside the room. It was one in the afternoon in California. All the monitors there showed various locations for the Mars launch schedule five months from now. All activity brought to a screeching halt as everyone scrambled to change course.

"My people will give us their educated predictions, Nick." Letting everyone else find a seat, Finn reluctantly released Peri and pulled out a chair. "Sit here, darling." He thought better on his feet. He'd stand.

The image of the President of the United States flashed onto a side screen. The image split to show several Presidents and two Prime Ministers, the rest he knew, would follow. Walker would already have informed them of the dire situation and brought them up to speed before connecting them.

"Right now, you know what I know. Asteroid DW17C has changed course over the last few minutes, with a new trajectory toward Earth. If you would hold your thoughts until I've spoken to Dr. Halperin, I'd appreciate it."

"What can you tell me?" he asked, as Brock Halperin walked into view on the center screen. In his sixties, Halperin had the deep chest of a Brahman bull and the tenacity of a honey badger. The man rarely left his precious lab, hence his pasty white skin. The dandelion-fluff of his white-blond hair surrounded his head like a halo. Finn had hired him, one of NASA's top scientists, to run his space lab six years ago. Halperin was brilliant, tireless, and fearless.

"The point of impact is a direct hit to South America." Halperin gave Finn a pointed look, as he signed, without looking at it, something someone stuck under his nose and nodded at someone else off camera. He was like a conductor, not in the least distracted by handling questions, and requests from his staff on site as he talked to Finn. And aware that half a dozen Heads of State were in on the video conference.

"In fact, twenty nautical miles from *your* location." Cocking his head, Halperin narrowed his eyes. "That doesn't seem to surprise you."

"It doesn't, and one day, when I tell you why, your brilliant scientific brain will explode."

"I look forward to that 'one day'," Halperin said dryly. "Do we knock this thing out with a nuclear explosive? At NASA we did blast deflection studies for nuclear explosives, as you know. Might be the only strategy to effectively deflect something of this magnitude into a different trajectory and steer it away from Earth's orbital path. I think everyone would agree that this is an appropriate time to ignore the ban on using nuclear explosives in outer space." Halperin held up his hand, talked quietly to one of his techs, then returned his attention to his monitor to look at Finn

"Nobody will give a flying fuck about the illegality of it." Finn stroked his hand absently along the length of Peri's hair down her back. "My concern is, if the result of sending up a nuke *fractures the asteroid* instead of *deflecting it.*"

"Quite," Elon Musk, up on screen, said briskly. "The smaller pieces would still negatively impact the earth. Not a good idea."

Branson's light flashed. "Sending up nukes would be like sending a flamethrower to get rid of a moth instead of a flyswatter. Both would do the job, but the flyswatter and the person holding it can be more precise because we could control exactly where to hit the asteroid. Head it in the right direction."

"I agree," Finn said. "No nukes."

"Agreed," The President of the United States interjected. "We've anticipated this possibility for decades, and are still studying methods we would use in the unhappy eventuality that we are attacked from deep space. But it's as expensive as hell, which is why we've privatized most of our space programs.

In other words, 'I'm scared as shit, it's all yours Finn.'

Finn met the eyes of Branson, Bezos, and Musk. "I understand, Mr. President."

The President of France lit his screen to indicate he wanted to speak. "I concur, *monsieur* Gallagher," he said, his features conveying the seriousness of the situation. "We have neither the expertise nor finances to get the job done within the time constraints."

"I agree," the Prime Minister of England added. "You gentlemen are years ahead of any government program. Clearly, we do not *have* years. I hope to God you have a solution to this dire situation. I'm going to go and kiss my grandchildren now. Keep me apprised of progress." Her portion of the screen went dark.

"Who else has a spaceship ready to launch *today*?" Finn addressed the other three men in the competitive manned space flight race with him. He enjoyed the neck and neck competition. They challenged each other to be first to take passengers to the moon. Of course, he enjoyed it more because so far he was miles ahead of his competition. Still, they kept him on his toes.

"We're a year out," Musk said.

Branson, never one to show his hand, merely said, "At *least* that."

Bezos shook his head. "Not even close. Are you saying *you're* capable of sending up a ship right now? *Today*, Gallagher?"

Finn nodded. "We are." He'd kept that information top secret, they'd had no idea how close he was.

There was a trio of *Fuck!*

"How soon can we launch?" Finn asked Halperin.

"We have her on the launch pad now, prepping for next week's Mars test. At your word, we'll have her in the air in three hours."

"Word."

Halperin nodded to someone out of camera view. Above each screen in the room where Finn stood, a large digital clock started counting down the hours, minutes and seconds to launch. "We're calculating the coordinates necessary to make impact to knock DW17C off course. We're removing all safety checks. Have that info to you within the hour."

Using the latest iteration of a rocket that had taken almost a decade to build and test, and cost multi-billions, as a kinetic impactor, suddenly seemed like a good fucking investment.

"Gentlemen, if I may, I'd like to confer with the experts privately. We'll keep you apprised of our progress every step of the way."

The President of France rubbed his jaw nervously. "When should we alert the public? Too soon and we instill panic and pandemonium."

"Hold off on that. The fewer people who know about this-" He didn't need to finish. In this case, ignorance was bliss if this thing went sideways. "I'll let you know if it becomes necessary." Finn sounded a whole lot more confident than he felt. There were so many fucking ways this was FUBAR.

The group of World leaders reluctantly signed off.

There would be no need to alert the public if things didn't go as planned. They'd know when a fucking thirteen mile wide, flaming rock landed on their house and shoved it miles deep into the Earth's crust.

"Gentlemen, I'm sure you all have thoughts and theories as where best to target the asteroid," he addressed his competitors, now we're all in this together. "We *have* a rocket. Now we must know *precisely* where to hit DW17C to have the most impact. Literally. Let's reconvene in one hour with a consensus."

The wall monitor went dark as the men went to consult with their own teams.

"How long until the rocket achieves impact?" Finn asked Halperin, knowing he, and his fellow scientists, were already calculating, velocity and area of impact. In the background, he could see various computer monitors spitting out information. That same information was being relayed to Finn's computers on board *Blackstar* and showing on a side screen.

"Fourteen hours, plus the three readying the launch."

Finn scrubbed his rough jaw. "Keep me apprised every step," Finn paused, "Brock. I'm *damn* glad to have you at *Blackstar*."

"Big bucks and this kind of excitement? Hell, happy to be here." Brock Halperin disappeared from view. The cameras panned out to encompass the entire Mojave control room, which was now a hive of activity as his staff readied themselves for an early launch.

"Jesus," Rydell Case said. "This is surreal. The time frame is- Terrifying."

"Seventeen hours and this should be over." *Should.* There was no need to tell them that the kinetic impactor may very well *not* be effective in changing the orbit of such a large asteroid.

Peri looked up at him, eyes large in her pale face, freckles standing out as if they were floating above her skin. Dark circles made her eyes look more blue than jade, her hair was a wild, flaming tangle down her back. All she needed was a flaming sword in her hand, and she'd be the warrior woman foretold by Blackstar.

"Now what?"

"Now, my love, on the off chance the world really is going to end, we're getting married."

Halfway out of her chair, the blood drained from Peri's head. "Marr—What's this? An *Armageddon* proposal?"

Cupping her jaw, Finn smiled. "If there's a scintilla of a chance that happens, I want to make sure we're bound together for the time we have left."

Her brother strolled over to narrow his eyes at them.

"Whatever you have to say, Rydell," Peri told him, keeping her attention on Finn. "Hurry up and say it. We might not have tomorrow. I refuse to die fighting with you. And would you please hurry up about it? I'm being proposed to right now."

"I just want you happy, Magma. I love you. Always have. That's all that matters. If the world's ending, I'm not wasting time being mad. I have no beef with Gallagher, if you love him, he's family. But just because you seem to have embraced the damned Cutters, doesn't mean *I* have to. But my love for you will never change."

Peri turned to face Ry. Linking her fingers with Finn's, drawing strength from him. A united front. She held her brother's gaze. "It might when I tell you a secret I've never told a soul."

"Never happen."

"Before you tell anyone else anything," Finn said, putting a finger under her chin, turning her face to him, "answer *my* question." His face was serious, his eyes intent.

Peri turned to wrap her arms around his neck and peppered his face with kisses, each one punctuated with, "Yes. Yes. Yes." Marriage had never crossed her mind. She'd never wanted it, or *not* wanted it, it had just never been a *thing* for her. Now she wanted to marry Finn with every fiber of her being.

"Okay, everyone let's get ready for another wedding," Callie said cheerfully clapping her hands. "The priest I brought with me is still on board, I think."

"No, he left with the police," Bria told her, sending a worried glance Peri's way. "But I'm sure Finn's captain can marry them."

"*What* secret, Magma? What could you possibly have kept hush-hush from me that would matter now?

The women were trying to defuse a tense situation, but their cheer actually made Peri feel bad. Mouth dry, she pushed out the words she'd sworn to herself she would never utter out loud. To anyone. Of course at the time she hadn't known the world was about to end.

Maybe she should just shut up and take the secret to her grave. And maybe not. Locking eyes with her brother, tightening her fingers between Finn's, Peri said, "Mom had an affair with Daniel Cutter."

TWENTY-SIX

Ry frowned, attempting to interpret the words as if she'd just spoken in the Abipón.

A sense of dread filled her, pressing down on her chest, making her eyes sting. She hated reflecting on her childhood, and she'd never, ever thought she'd mention this to another living soul.

"Say what?!" Logan's voice was dangerously low as he came closer.

"You heard her." Nick gripped his older brother's shoulder, holding him back.

"Are you saying … yeah, you are, aren't you?" Zane took an aggressive step forward, but Teal grabbed his arm and halted him in his tracks. "You think our father was *your* father?"

"I *know* he was. My *mother* told me so."

"Magma, that's just not true. There was trouble in their marriage. Yeah, they fought all the time, but they loved each other. Loved us.."

Her throat tightened, and her eyes burned with unshed tears. Vulnerable emotions she'd kept at bay for years, were exposed, leaving her nerve endings and emotions stripped of their protective coverings. She hated feeling this exposed.

"They loved *you*, Ry. Between one day and the next Dad refused to look at me. The next day he left. He'd found out that mom had lied to him from the moment I was conceived. Five years of lies. I knew *you* were aware of how she felt about me because you always tried to compensate for her coldness. I loved you for that and so much more."

Finn's hand tightened on hers. A small show of support, but huge for Peri. "After she died, I found the letters she'd written, and never mailed, to Daniel Cutter. They confirmed what she'd told me. She wrote that she loved him, sacrificed her marriage, was saddled with a kid she didn't want, based on his promises to return for her. Each letter got progressively angrier, more desperate. In the end, she told him he'd ruined her life, and she was left with *nothing*. She hated him. She hated m-*me*."

"Ah, Jesus, Magna. That's not true."

"She told me she did. I was twelve." Peri gave him a steady look, seeing the pain of belief in his eyes. The dawning realization of why their mother had treated them so differently. "*I* was the nothing she was left with."

Rydell winced. "She had emotional problems, love. I should never have left you with her."

"Of course you couldn't have taken a little girl with you for months on end. I wouldn't've left Adam with her anyway. Half the time she forgot his damned doctor appointments. I forgave her a long time ago. But I can't let this secret follow me to my grave."

"Why didn't you tell me this years ago?"

"Because I didn't want to see you looking at me as you're looking at me now. I didn't want you to hurt because you thought I was hurt. I never planned to tell any of you. But just in case-"

Finn squeezed her hand. "No one's dying today."

"I know," Peri said with confidence before turning back to the others. "Despite my preconceived ideas, I was shocked myself when I discovered how much I *like* you, guys. You deserve the truth." God, it felt good to be free of the burden of holding the secret inside for so long. Peri felt a little like a helium balloon as her guilt lifted, giving her an unfamiliar feeling of lightness and buoyancy that was intoxicating.

Releasing Finn's hand, she went to hug her brother tightly, whispering in his ear, "You'll always be my hero, and obviously, my favorite brother. Please tell me this doesn't change how you feel about me, now."

Ry took her face in his big hands. "I've loved you since the day you were born, Persephone. Nothing, and no one, can change the bond we've always had. Love isn't finite, it expands to encompass as many people as you want. Your happiness makes everything else noise. Now go. Everyone is waiting to participate in the love-fest."

"I love you."

Her brother ran his finger down the slope of her nose. "Ditto." As soon as Peri turned around, Bria came over to give her a tight hug. "Welcome to the family, Peri. We can never have too many sisters."

Callie came in next. "Thank God," she said against Peri's hair. "I hated that my love for Jonah kept us apart. You're the sister of my heart, and I love you so damned much, and my loyalties being torn, was breaking my heart."

Peri's eyes blurred. "I'm sorry."

"My turn," Teal said, coming forward. "I'm not a hugger, but with this family, I'm learning." She gave Peri a quick catch and release. "Welcome to the family." She stepped out of the way for Nick.

Nick lifted her chin so Peri looked directly into his startling blue eyes. "You spent all those years baiting us to see if we would come over to *Sea Witch* and demand to know who you were and why you were stealing from us, didn't you? You *wanted* us to come to you. I wondered if you'd ever tell us."

"Wait. You *wondered*?" Zane demanded, grabbing his upper arm. "*You* knew about this? How and why the fuck didn't you tell us?"

Nick lifted a brow, his lips twitching. "You forget that I do work for a counterterrorist organization, brother. I knew within days of her pirating you. Seven years ago."

"And it didn't occur to you to *mention* it to the rest of us?" Jonah said mildly. "Especially considering how *I* came to be in the family."

"It wasn't my secret to tell. Just as your secret wasn't mine to tell," Nick told Jonah. "Come and hug your sister so she can get ready for a hasty wedding. We have more pressing issues right now."

"If she's getting married, they should do the deed at Cutter Cay, it's only fitting," Zane announced.

Nick smiled. "That's something we will definitely plan for- later."

For the next few minutes Peri was swept into the arms of her half-brothers and passed along like a birthday package.

Jonah wrapped his arms around her and kissed her temple. "One of these days, I'll tell you how I introduced myself to our brothers. Half brothers. Daniel was my father, too. You aren't the only one in the family with acting chops." His smile reached all the way to his devilish, Cutter-blue eyes as he released her. "Welcome to the family, *Sea Witch,* glad to have you."

When Jonah let her go, Peri's gaze went to her brother, who stood apart from the activity, to gauge his reaction to all this. It would break her heart if Ry felt as though, now that she had this big happy family, he was excluded. She sent him a look filled with questions which, knowing her as well as he did, he easily read.

He smiled and gave her a thumbs up.

She cocked her head, trying to read any nuances in his expression. *Really*?

Ry mouthed, "All good. Swear to God." And twirled a finger to continue.

"My turn." Logan took his place, hugging her with a genuine warmth. All this emotion made her chest hurt. It was almost too much, too soon. She lived on her own, sailed on her own, went weeks without speaking to a single soul, and now she had an entire army of family and a man who loved her.

She emerged from the tight hug with Logan. "Now you have *five* brothers to watch your back. Good thing we already like Finn. We'll need some time to work with Rydell, but we're Cutter's we can do this."

Laughing, Peri pushed her hair over her shoulders and returned to Finn's side. "God help me. I'll never get away with anything."

"When were you born?" Zane asked. "Checking birth order here." When Peri told him, he shot her a smile. "Excellent. Now, *you're* the baby of the family."

She smiled back. "Weird, but surprisingly wonderful."

Her smile faded when she noticed Finn was on the phone. When it looked as though he was finished, she gave him a worried glance. "Is something wrong?" She rolled her eyes. "Is something *more* wrong?"

"The captain will marry us on the bridge in thirty minutes. It's going to have to be quicker than Elvis marrying us in the Chapel of Whatever in Vegas. I want to be there for the launch."

Shoulders hunched, Ry said thickly, "Jesus, this is all happening so fast. This isn't what I wanted for you, Magma. I've only ever wanted you happy, and knowing that you've kept this secret for most of your life - that you were *un*happy, kills me.

"I want you to be happy now. God only knows you deserve every scrap of happiness thrown your way, not rushed into a decision you don't have time to consider because we're about to be obliterated." His voice was choked with emotion as he ran his finger down the slope of her nose. A uniquely Ry display of affection. "At any other time, I'd want you to have the wedding of your dreams."

"Any wedding where I'm marrying Finn is the wedding of my dreams. I don't need time to consider. I knew the second I set eyes on him that he was the one." It was wise not to tell her brother that she'd fallen hard when Finn had awakened, for the first time in her life, the feeling that she *was* loveable.

No, she thought, as she studied her brother, who carried a world's weight of worry as his eyes bounced from Finn to her. And back again. Best not to tell Ry what Finn had done for her when Ry had tried all his life to give her all the love no one else ever had.

She cleared the gruffness out of her throat. "I don't need fancy. I just need Finn. I'm making the right decision, Ry. But it would be even sweeter if I had your support."

"We'll make *sure* Peri has the wedding of the century," Callie assured Ry. "At *Cutter Cay* after Finn saves the world, and we catch our breath. Right?"

Wrapping an arm around her shoulders, Finn drew her away from the others. His face was serious as he said, "There's a 50/50 chance this'll work. You don't have to m-"

Standing on her toes, Peri drew his head down and kissed him. Not a peck, not a gentle kiss. A full out, erotic, tongue and teeth kiss that took up at *least* half her allotted time. They were both a little breathless when their lips parted.

"Shut up, Finn Gallagher. If you don't marry me in the next half hour, I'll sue you for breach of promise. I also have five brothers who'll march you down the aisle at shotgun point should you change your mind." Just *saying* five brothers boggled the mind.

Finn brushed long, untidy strands of her hair behind her shoulder, then slid his hand around the back of her neck. His thumb did a lazy sweep up her nape that made her heart flutter. For a moment he said nothing as his eyes caressed her features.

"I love you Persephone Case. I have pretty much since I saw you in the museum. Even the end of the world won't change my mind." He brushed her lips with an achingly gentle kiss. "See you on the bridge in nineteen minutes, my love."

She was two minutes late, and when she arrived she took Finn's breath away.

Barefoot, Peri ran through the open door into the solarium, which was still decorated for the previous wedding. Seeing everyone gathered there, she hesitated. "Had to shower, find something to wear. . .Thanks, Callie. . .God, I'm nervous."

Heart beating, slow and steady, Finn wordlessly held out his hand as he walked to meet her halfway. She crossed the long room with confident steps, her eyes locked on his. No matter what she wore, or didn't wear, she was, without a doubt, the most beautiful woman he'd ever seen, despite the nick on her cheek, and raw wrists, which spiked his blood for a different reason. Her damp hair hung down her back, a dark copper skein that would dry to the wild, flame-colored mass he loved.

Finn took her cold hand, opened her fingers, then pressed his lips to her palm. "I'm not nervous at all, this is the easiest decision I've ever made in my life. Let's get married, then go save the world. Captain?"

Rather than experiencing the Mojave Desert launch on site, firsthand, Finn watched the prep work for the blastoff of his multi-stage rocket on a flat screen thousands of miles away. With his *wife.* Marriage didn't feel odd, but being here, on the other side of the world, when this momentous event had consumed him night and day for years, did.

Everyone was gathered in the conference room to watch *Red Star* on the giant monitors. They all stood, too wound up to sit. Tension filled the air, vibrating as if it was alive and had infected the entire group. Calculating had been done, by dozens of people across the world, yet minute adjustments would be made on *Red Star's* path to the comet. There could be zero room for a miscalculation.

The weather in California was ideal; seventy degrees, winds twenty-nine knots, wind direction eighty degrees.

With Peri tucked against his side, Finn checked the numbers and stats scrolling to the left of the main screen. *Red Star* stood on the launch pedestal, a pad that was roughly a mile and a half round. Huge propellent tanks, and a water tower to deluge the pad to suppress sound prior to liftoff, were housed inside the circle. Hold down arms, to cradle the rocket prior to launch, dropped away, umbilical connectors were released to snake to the ground.

"Launch commit criteria met. All systems go," Halperin said, off camera, his usually calm voice holding a thread of excitement.

Less than a month ago, Finn would've stated emphatically, and unequivocally, that nothing, and certainly no *one*, could derail his mission to be the first to colonize Mars.

He hadn't counted on a beautiful redhead, an ancient seer, or a five-hundred-year-old prophecy.

Peri twisted her head to look up at him, and mouthed "Okay?"

He realized he'd been holding his breath and released it. "Everything I could possibly want or need is right here in my arms." *Truth.*

Her arm tightened around his waist. "I'm sorry you couldn't be there in person. This has got to be really hard for you."

He squeezed her shoulder. She got him.

"Five. Four. Three. Two. One." An automated voice from the launch site counted off the seconds. "We have lift off."

There was a spontaneous round of applause as seven million pounds of thrust erupted from the launch pad in a fiery display. Flames shot out of the bottom of the shuttle, scorching a line through the clear blue sky as a thick trail of orange smoke billowed behind them.

Even Finn's state-of-the-art audio equipment couldn't recreate the *feel* of the shock waves blasting through the air by all that energy. The familiar, Earth-shattering rumble, a wall of sound, was a prelude to the reverberation building to a crescendo of popping. That was followed by a loud, relentless, crackling roar, as if someone was shaking a metal sheet.

"Holy shit." Rydell's quiet voice was filled with awe. "Sounds like the sound waves are literally ripping through the air."

"If we're still around for your next launch, can I be there, boots on the ground up close and personal?" Teal's eyes were fixed on the brightness of the flames from the solid rocket boosters as it shot vertically into the air. "What's the method of spacecraft propulsion?"

Finn smiled at her enthusiasm. "I'll let you handle every one of the over three million bits that make up the rocket." *If* they were around for another launch. He explained the propulsion and various specs to Teal and the others, but his entire focus was on his hopes and dreams, and the billions of dollars, going in the opposite direction of what had been so painstakingly planned.

"Thousand says your rocket makes contact exactly on time," Zane bet.

No one was going to say otherwise.

"Four minutes *under*," Jonah offered, expression intent as he watched the screen. Callie winced slightly, and he eased his grip on her shoulder, then pulled her in to kiss her temple.

Logan wrapped an arm around Dani's shoulders, cocked his head, and watched the scrolling numbers. "Eight seconds over."

"I'm out. This is a no-brainer." Nick rested his chin on top of Bria's head as he held her flush against his chest, both facing the screens. "I trust Rocketman. Not to mention, Blackstar predicted the outcome."

Finn trusted his people. Trusted his own estimation of the success of this launch. He watched his pet project arc across the sky as the rocket boosters successfully separated and the rapidly decreasing point of orange hurtled faster and faster toward space.

He felt a sharp pang of loss for what *could* have been. He'd planned, *anticipated*, this Mars launch for years. Now, most of the safety controls had been abandoned, the payload lightened as much as made sense, and the direction markedly altered. This precipitous launch would effectively set them back at least five years if not longer. But then, considering what would've happened if he *hadn't* had a rocket sitting ready on a launch pad, was unthinkable.

A passenger trip to Mars wasn't that important in the grand scheme of things.

"How long until it hits?" Jonah asked as the onboard cameras showed the decreasing size of the Earth in the rearview mirror.

"Twelve hours eighteen minutes and eleven seconds," Finn told him, seconds before the new countdown clock appeared on the screen. "We won't know the result until tonight. I suggested everyone use the time to get some sleep. We'll reconvene here this evening."

There was nothing more they could do but wait it out and see if the calculations had been correct. See if they could nudge the giant rock sufficiently to change its trajectory.

"I'm too wired to sleep," Peri told him as they made their way up to his cabin, letting the others leave, or not leave as they chose. "If it works, which it *will*, we can sleep tomorrow. If it doesn't, then I don't want to waste a second I can spend with you."

Flooded with pearly early morning light, Finn's cabin looked jarringly normal after all they'd been through in the last twenty-four hours. Yesterday, she'd thought she'd never see it again. Never see *Finn* again. A lump formed in Peri's throat.

"We'll lie down and close our eyes," Finn told her. "If we sleep that'll be good."

"Trust me," she told him, padding barefoot into the bedroom ahead of him. "I *won't* sleep. We should just go back and watch your rocket while we're waiting."

Stripping his black t-shirt over his head as he walked, he tossed it onto a nearby chair. "Not much to see for the next twelve hours."

His hair was mussed and he desperately needed a shave. Peri's heart filled to overflowing. Love, lust, need, tangled together inside her in a warm glow. "I don't know about that, I'm enjoying what I'm seeing right now." His tanned skin looked like bronze satin, his broad chest roughened with dark hair which arrowed between his cut abs. She touched the bandage high on his shoulder. "Except this. I'm not enjoying that you have a bullet hole in you."

"I forgot I even had it."

Sitting on the edge of the bed, he slung one arm around her hips and activated the remote to shut the drapes. The thick white sheers glided with a faint susurrus across the ceiling to floor window, wrapping them in a hazy white glow.

"Liar." Peri stood between his spread knees, then combed his hair back off his face. His hair felt thick and silky between her fingers.

Gently, he reached up to touch under the cut on her cheek. His touch was achingly tender, but his expression was murderous. "I will never, as long as I live forget *this*. Nor will I forget every fucking second you were in danger." He brushed a kiss to the rope burns on her wrists, and one to each raw fingertip. "I want hours, days, months, *years*, to make love to you."

"First you have to save the world." Peri took his hand and linked their fingers. "You have to forget what happened today. It's over. *He's* over. Thinking about it won't change history. We just go forward, and live each moment we have a hundred and ten percent."

"You're very wise."

She smiled. "I'm very *lucky*."

He winced as he moved, and her smile turned into a concerned frown. "How badly does it hurt? Don't go all macho. Tell me, seriously."

He smiled as he placed his hands on her hips. "Every ounce of feeling in my body has traveled somewhere a lot more interesting. And there's no pain involved."

"So, lust works like a pain killer?" She let the strands of his hair drop, then combed through them again as if she were petting a cat. A large, panther with an erection tenting his pants. "Good to know."

He urged her closer into the V of his body. His fingers hot through the thin fabric of her dress as he anchored her against him. "We've been up for eons," he reminded her, running his palms from her hips down the outside of her thighs and back again. "And *exciting* eons at that," he said, voice husky as he stroked his hands higher. "The adrenaline surging through us has dissipated. We'll feel like leaked balloons soon enough." He slid the fabric up her bare legs, then sucked in a breath when he saw she was naked from the waist down.

"I love that you didn't bother with underwear."

Peri's nails dug into his shoulders as her nipples puckered. Anticipation. "*You* have on too many clothes." Her voice sounded thready as the blood pounded through her veins. "I don't have any clothes on board, remember? I had to borrow this dress from Callie. I wasn't about to borrow her underw- Oh God." All the breath left her lungs as he dipped his head to brush his lips across her stomach, his breath hot and moist against her sensitized skin, his rough jaw in counterpoint to the smooth glide of his tongue.

"Sexual satisfaction cures almost all ills I've found."

"I know." She braced her hands on his shoulders. "You've kept me in a constant state of arousal from the moment we met. Do you believe Blackstar predicted- *us*- five hundred years ago?"

"I *won't* say I *don't* believe."

Her eyes widened as his tongue explored her navel, sending shivers over her skin. "Really? Scientific, skeptical you?"

He shrugged. Lifting his head to speak left a cool damp place on her stomach. "Everything else he predicted seems to have come to pass. Why not us?"

"This *has* been incredibly fast."

He looked at her. "Preordained?"

She cocked her head.

"I won't say *I* don't believe. It doesn't matter if it is or isn't. We're joined together now, no matter how it came about. Are you happy, Persephone?"

"Overwhelmingly so. Are you?"

"More than I ever thought myself capable of being."

"So you're happy being stuck with me until the end of time?" Of course, the end of time might come in twelve hours.

"And beyond," he said, as if reading her mind. He scanned her features with humor-lit eyes. "I'm into this for the long-haul. My rockets always go where I send them."

She gave him a sassy smile as she pushed his shoulder to topple him onto his back. "That sounds very sexy," she said, resting her knees on the bed on either side of his hips. "Let's see what you've got, Rocketman."

"I have everything you need, darling." He drew her down on top of his hard body, then rolled so that they were side by side on his lovely wide bed.

They finished stripping each other, slowly, kissing , as if they had all the time in the world to explore each other's body. His movements felt languid, but his silvery eyes were all hot, black pupil. Warm honey flowed through her veins and her heartbeat did flips. They made love dreamily, the heat banked. Then climaxed together. Even when Finn disengaged, they stayed facing each other, pressed together from chest to ankles.

The room was getting lighter as the sun crested the horizon. Peri felt absolutely content. "Should we go downstairs to check the monitors?" she murmured, tracing a zig-zag path across the dark stubble on his jaw from his ear to his mouth with a finger tip.

"Halperin will contact me if something goes awry." Finn was draping her hair over his chest, and didn't look up. "We're here to *rest.* You don't have to sleep, but close your eyes."

"Are you saying *you're* going to try to take a nap right now?"

His leg slid between hers. "Why not?"

"I don't want to miss anything." Her eyes felt gritty, her body lax and replete. His erection pressed against her mound. "If you want to make love again, you're going to have to do all the work," her words slurred. "The spirit is willing, but my body is just going to lie right here. . . She closed her eyes with a small sigh as he stroked his hand up her back under her hair in a slow sweep. "Love y-"

She slept for ten hours and came up on the helicopter deck yawning, blinking the sleep from her eyes. She wore white shorts and a black tank top that Addison had sent over. Her hair, flowed wild and loose down her back, just as he liked it. She glanced around. "Holy crap. It's night again! Why didn't you wake me?"

Finn met her halfwayand wrapped his arm around her waist. "No need. Anything that's going to happen is going to happen within the next hour. The others will be rendezvousing here in the next twenty or so minutes. Your timing is perfect. *You're* perfect." She was warm and soft and smelled of the lily shampoo she'd left in his bathroom what felt like a lifetime ago. "Hello, wife.

"Hello, husband." Reaching up, she brushed a toothpaste-scented kiss to his jaw. "It feels perfect being in your arms." Worried eyes searched his face. "And?"

"And *Red Star* is on time and on target."

"Yes, but will it make it before we go the way of the dinosaurs?" Peri wiped the words away with a sweep of her hand. "Sorry. Of *course* it'll do exactly what you want it to do. You're Finn Gallagher." She glanced around the empty deck. "Where's everyone?"

He loved her faith in him, and even though he and his team had crunched numbers, and made minor adjustments, all day, there was still a chance that things might not work.

"Showering, napping, grabbing a bite to eat," he answered. "The women went back to their respective ships. They'll all be here soon." He pulled her in front of him, circling her waist with his arms, and nestling her sweet butt against a hopeful erection.

"Your brother is an amazing man," he said nuzzling her cheek. "We had a long talk while you were sleeping. He grilled me like a cheese sandwich, but the bottom line was; do I love you more than humanly possible?"

She turned her face to look up at him. "Do you?"

"Hell yes. He believed me. We talked salvage, business, and rockets. Every thread of the conversation was in a veiled and not so veiled, reference to you and your well being."

"Then the Cutters joined us, and he told them, without frills, his side of the story and they did the same. Cleared the air. They all came to realize most of the animosity stemmed from their fathers' bitter feud."

"I know your brother's reaction and feelings concerning your relationship with the Cutters worries you. He knows it too, and assured me, he's okay with it. His feelings for you haven't changed, you must know that."

"I'm glad they talked and cleared the air. That's been a long time coming. How *do* the Cutters *really* feel?"

"They're tickled to have a little sister," he told her.

She smiled. "Really?"

"Yeah, really. They feel as though they have years to make up for."

"They don't. I should make it up to them for hating them because of something they had no control over. I wanted to hurt them because I was hurting. It was stupid and childish, and I feel like a complete moron for not just boarding one of their ships and *telling* them flat out years ago. My anger and pain was mixed up with my love for Rydell. He adored our Dad- *his* dad. I didn't want to tarnish that."

Finn tenderly stroked his palm up and down her bare arm. "You'd been fending for yourself for so long you thought you didn't need anyone, *macushla*. But you went to extraordinary lengths to make a connection."

"Pretty damn stupid. My rational brain told me time and time again they weren't responsible for their father's actions. But he was dead. They were the only connection I had to take out my-"

"Pain."

"*Frustration*. Pain. Yes, I suppose so."

You want to be *loved*, to be acknowledged. To know you had worth. I think you stole from the brothers hoping for acknowledgment. It was as though you were daring them to come to you, to demand to know who you were and why you were doing what you were doing. You wanted them to *see* you."

"All little girls need to feel safe and wanted." Finn turned her in his arms. "The props were knocked out from under you at a young age. When you grow up without something, the lack is always with you. I know better than most. Even when you finally have it. I understand that it's hard for you to trust. Give me another chance to prove to you that I'll always be your rock, and I'll stand by your side no matter what."

Peri wrapped her arms around his neck, a wicked gleam in her eyes. "Even if I fib?"

Love swelled his heart. He was in for a lifetime of fabrications, and whimsy. "How about this? If I ask, 'honestly?' you'll tell the truth."

"Okay."

"Honestly?

She laughed.

Shaking his head, amused, happy, and crazy in love, Finn kissed her soft mouth.

"Hey, you two," Ry said as he and Addison came over to the rail where they stood. "You have an audience."

"You shouldn't be supervising my honeymoon, big brother." Peri, arms loosely looped around Finn's neck, stayed in his arms as she turned to smile at the couple.

"We want Adam to witness the non-apocalypse," Ry said dryly. Cradled in his arms, the baby wore a swimsuit covered diaper, and a minuscule blue t-shirt that read, 'Dive Baby'. He waved his little arms and legs and gave a gummy smile.

"How long?" Ry asked Finn.

"Twenty minutes and a handful of seconds, give or take." Walker set up a couple of monitors over there. We can watch from the onboard cameras."

About to leave, Case hesitated at a nudge from his wife. "I've been reaching across the aisle, Magma. We have a long way to go to trust each other, it'll take time. But the Cutters and I have two people we love in common. That makes a strong, unbreakable tie, binding us together. Either I embrace them as family, or I lose both my sisters. And that's unthinkable."

Peri's eyes filled as she said simply, but with great depth of feeling, "Thank you."

"I want a couple of those," Finn said softly as Ry took Addison and the baby and went to where three giant monitors were set up. Lounge chairs were arranged so his guests could see the monitors, or lie back and watch the sky.

Either they'd get a show. Or it would be a giant curtain call.

"You do?" Peri kissed his chin.

She sounded as surprised as he was. But the desire to have kids with Peri was as strong as he'd felt about any of his passions.

"Hmm. You realize that we haven't used a condom for the last nine hundred and ninety- eight times we've made love, right?" Peri murmured, tracing a zig-zag path from his ear to his mouth with a finger tip through the dark stubble on his jaw.

"Do you think we made a baby?"

Her hand stilled. "You don't sound worried about it."

"I'd love a daughter with your red hair and pioneering spirit, and a son with your jade eyes who'll colonize Mars. Or the other way around. I want to watch our children grow, and thrive. I want to teach them, and make sure that they know from the moment of conception that they're wanted and loved."

"We'll have to keep trying." Her jade eyes sparkled.

In the background, he heard the footsteps and low murmurs of the others coming out on deck for the final showdown.

Family. *His* now, too. An unexpected bonus.

In Finn's ear, Mission Control started the countdown, "Impact minus five minutes."

"It's time." Gently, he led Peri to stand near the others. "Kill the lights," he instructed the captain via his headset.

The ship instantly went dark. It was an eerie sight. In the distance, the other ship's lights were pinpricks of gold dust, but the surrounding water was sprinkled with diamonds of starlight in the black dome of the sky.

Lining the port-side decks below, the entire *Blackstar* crew, and all his office staff, looked out over the dark water. Tension pulsed in the near silence. No one spoke, people barely breathed.

"Point to exactly where we should be looking." Jonah's voice was hushed with anticipation. Finn indicated the location. "What do you expect to see?"

If they saw nothing it meant his rocket had missed its target. Hundreds of powerful telescopes around the world were focused on the same point. "A brief ball of fire as the rocket hits the asteroid, followed by a streak of fire as it harmlessly bounces on the atmosphere and hurtles into space."

Logan drew in a breath, tightening his hand in that of his wife's, who stood by his side. "From your brilliant mind to God's ear."

"Amen," Dani whispered.

"Holy shit, Rocketman, this is goddamned nerve-wracking!" Nick said quietly, arms wrapped tightly around Bria as they stood beside Finn and Peri at the rail.

"It is *exactly* as Blackstar prophesied," Vadini said reverently, his gaze intent on the sky. He dropped to his knees, clutching one of the tablets tightly to his chest, his lips moving in prayer.

"He predicted that Finn would save the day, right?" Rydell, standing on the other side of Peri, had his arms around Addy and Adam as they too looked over the vastness of the dark ocean.

"I have every faith in you, Finn," Teal said. Zane stood beside her, their arms around each other's waists. "This is *epic*, and I'm proud to be standing here at this very moment in history. Watching you *make* history."

"Two minutes to impact," Finn repeated Halperin's words, then held his breath, tightening his arm around Peri's shoulders.

"I take the pot," Jonah said with satisfaction.

Logan gripped the rail. "Hasn't hit yet."

"It will."

"Don't spend your ill-gotten gains yet," Zane told him. "It might be over."

All eyes went to the monitors. Real-time images from the onboard cameras in the nose of Red Star showed every detail of the comet in living color as it closed the distance to the giant rock hurtling toward them.

Everyone tilted their heads to the sky. More reassuring, Finn thought, than seeing what was about to happen in real time on a giant screen. Millions of miles away, seen with the naked eye, was less threatening.

"Watch the sky. Fifty-six seconds."

"Come on come on come on," Peri whispered, fingers bunching his shirt, as she pressed tightly against his side. Fin tightened his arm around her shoulders.

Finn continued the countdown, his own calm voice settling the threat of jitters in his gut.

A flair of red sparked in the blackness, minutes earlier than predicted. Jonah was right. He'd won the bet. Finn's breath left his lungs in a rush, as he continued to repeat what Halperin was saying in his ear. "We made contact!"

A bright orange ball of fire flashed, as Finn's multi-million dollar rocket struck the asteroid.

Zane whispered, "Did it -?"

"It hit!" Laughing, Finn swung Peri in a circle.

"*Damn*, that was close." Rydell slapped Finn on the back. "Congratulations to the man who saved the planet. Literally."

Everyone cheered as a tail of fire streaked across the blackness of the sky indicating the asteroid was bouncing on the atmosphere, as it harmlessly hurtled into space.

"Shit, that was almost the end," one of the Cutters said, voice hoarse.

Gathering Peri into his arms, Finn whispered, "No. It's only the beginning."

EPILOGUE

Cutter Cay
One Year Later

Finn had flown everyone, including Addy and Rydell, to the island on his fabulous jet, for their First Annual Cutter Cay Family Vacation. The word *family* had been stressed. Peri smiled. *Repeatedly.*

It was late afternoon on the fourth day and they were all on the beach. Her skin felt pleasantly tight from an afternoon in the sea and the sun. She and Finn sprawled on a blanket in the deep shade of the fern-like leaves and brilliant clusters of red/orange flowers of an enormous Flame tree on the edge of the sand.

Three-month-old Samantha, Zane and Teal's daughter lay on the blanket next to them, cooing and waving her arms and legs as if trying to catch the shifting light and shadows from the overhanging branches.

Finn leaned against the wide trunk, Peri between his upraised knees, using his bare chest as a backrest. Relishing the smell of the ocean and evocative smell of recently lit charcoal, Peri lowered her sunglasses so she could see the true colors spread before her. The brilliant white sand, translucent, aquamarine water and a cloudless bowl of robin's egg blue overhead, were picture postcard perfect.

Hiking her sundress a little farther up her thighs to catch the breeze, she inhaled, her mouth watering at the smoky, savory smell of grilling meat. Then smiled at the shouts and laughter from Zane and Teal, Jonah and Callie, as they ran back and forth, whacking a volleyball across the net. There was, of course, a bet riding on the winners, and a lot of trash talking accompanied by laughter.

Peri breathed deeply in wonder at the carefree, happy sounds of her family. Takig a moment to absorb the sheer happiness of it all as she rested her head against Finn's chest and sighed with contentment. The babies rested on her bladder, and she really needed to pee. But she was too content, too lazy to move.

One of the babies in her womb did a backflip. Her throat caught with emotion, and she moved Finn's hand, guiding it low on her belly so he could share the baby moving. "Woke up from your nap, did you, sweet pea? Oh. You're brother's coming to play, too."

"How do you know which is which?" Finn rubbed his hand gently over her belly as one baby kicked, and the other rolled.

"Your son's the soccer player. You're daughter's the gymnast."

She felt Finn's smile as he rested his cheek on her crown. "Last week it was the other way round."

"They'll keep us guessing 'till we meet them." Her stomach joined in the activity by rumbling. She seemed always to be starving. "Maybe they're responding to the smell of food. Hey, Dani?" Peri raised her voice to be heard. "Is my root beer in the cooler?" A disgustingly sweet soda that Peri had always despised, and now craved like an addict.

"Yes, right next to the milk," Dani yelled back. "Want a drink now?"

Her mouth watered. "I'll send Finn in a bit, thanks." Her bladder wasn't ready for her milk and root beer concoction right now.

Logan and Nick flipped burgers, as Dani and Bria set up the rest of the food on a long trestle table in the shade of a nearby tree. Logan's dog, Buoy, barked as he darted between the table and the tempting smells from the grill.

Lazily scooping sand into her palm she sifted the powder-soft grains between her fingers as she leaned against the solid bulk of Finn's chest. "Who, in a million years, could've imagined the two of *us* on vacation, let alone a *family* vacation?"

He kissed her on the top of her head. "I'm not complaining. It's ironic, isn't it?" Finn rested his hand on her belly as they stared out at the placid Caribbean water lapping the sand. "We both ended up with the one thing we never dared dream of- *family*."

"I never knew how lonely I was until I -*wasn't*. Talk about my cup overflowing."

"You'll never have to be lonely again," Finn murmured against her temple. "Good thing this lot respects boundaries."

Farther down the beach, Rydell and Addison splashed in the shallows swinging a giggling Adam between them. Her brother carried Antonio, Nick and Bria's five-month- old, in one arm. Peri's eyes rested on her brother as he flung his head back and laughed at something his wife said. "I don't want him to feel left out. . ."

"Look at him, love. He, Addison and Adam have been assimilated seamlessly into the Cutter clan. We've *all* been integrated as if it were meant to be."

Turning her head, she smiled at him, loving the way his silvery eyes softened when he looked at her. Even after a year, their physical response to each other was off the charts. He was always touching her, as if she were his lodestone. She reached up to stroke the stubble on his jaw because she couldn't keep her hands off him either. "I've never seen you this relaxed." He'd even left his phone at Logan's house where they were staying, which was unprecedented.

"I'm pretty damned relaxed after we make love."

"Then you must be the most freaking relaxed man on the planet," Peri teased as she returned her attention to the strenuous volleyball game down the beach. The two couples had way too much freaking energy for a hot afternoon as they raced back and forth like crazy people, trying to spike the ball.

"Sam's having. . .issues," he told her as the baby gave a mewling little whimper, that threatened to get louder.

"Hand her over. It isn't rocket science. She's either hungry, needs a diaper change or wants a cuddle."

Finn settled the baby in her arms. He shifted her so she could hold the baby more easily. "I'll be ready when ours arrive. I promise."

Peri checked the baby's diaper, and since it was dry, and Sam still fussed, reached for her bottle. "Sure. I can imagine *that* being part of your daily calendar." The baby latched onto the bottle's nipple as if she hadn't eaten all day. Peri knew the feeling.

Finn pulled the diaper bag over for her to brace her elbow on as she fed Sam. "I'm already reallocating the time," he told her. "We can negotiate when the time comes, but for now I've estimated eight diaper changes per day for me. Four per baby. Ten minutes apiece."

Peri suppressed a smile. "I don't think you can schedule a diaper change."

"They said I'd never make it to Mars."

"Hmm. I don't even want to know how you propose making them poop on schedule. But even if you could- and you'd make an untold million sharing the secret with other busy parents- a diaper change won't take ten minutes."

"Figured there'll be cuddling time at each one."

The baby spat out the nipple. Peri lifted her to her shoulder, waited for the bubbly burp, then handed her over to Finn. "Practice."

Finn, used to holding an infant, held Sam upright, gently rubbing her tiny back. Peri's heart melted.

Dani and Logan were still trying to get pregnant, and as promised, Callie and Jonah were the doting uncle and aunt, already spoiling eighteen-month-old toddler Adam, and taking diaper, and babysitting duties when called on, for Sam and Antonio. And in about three months, if she didn't get so big she floated away like the Goodyear blimp, she and Finn would add their two babies to the pack.

There'd be a *lot* of diapers involved. But they were all in it together, all of them used to the erratic, crazy wonder of it all. After some instruction from Rydell on the care and feeding of a baby, Finn had taken to handling all aspects of babyhood like a duck to water.

"Hello, Samantha," he said, holding the baby so she could see his face, "You're getting stronger every day, aren't you?" His tone wasn't baby talk, but as if he were speaking to an intelligent adult. The baby stared into his eyes, her little hands waving. "Yes, pretty girl, I saw you lifting your head just now. Any minute now you'll be running around with your cousin, Adam, won't you? And when you're ready for school, I'll help you with science and math. "

"She understands you," Peri said, amused as the baby cooed and gave Finn a gummy grin.

"Of course she does. And if I speak to her like an adult, then when she starts speaking, she'll speak more like one, too."

"Really? And where did that fascinating parenting tip come from?"

"I've been doing research."

"Of course you have." Peri laughed softly. "You don't do anything halfway." It didn't matter if Finn was in a boardroom, directing a missile to intersect with an asteroid, or holding a baby, Peri had never seen him out of his element.

"You're a very pretty girl, Samantha Cutter," he told the baby. "And I can see you're going to be as smart as your Mom and Dad. Being so pretty won't hurt. You're going to be a heartbreaker, yes you are."

Peri laughed. "You're going to be a terrific father." He was so good with all the babies. Peri could barely wait for their own to be born. She was six months pregnant with twins and felt as big as a whale. She never considered how much of a challenge it would be to walk around when her center of gravity was shifted.

"We could stay here—"

She shook her head. "Not for three freaking *months* we can't. As idyllic as the island is, we'd both go nuts if we had to stay here for any longer than this couple of weeks. This is the first vacation you've taken in your life, you have to *ease* into it." The man barely slept and had the energy of a hummingbird on speed. That was going to come in handy with two babies. "I want them born on *Blackstar* where they were conceived. Arely will make a fine midwife."

"I defer to your decision. *Blackstar* it will be." He stroked her tummy. "This is pretty damn perfect. *Your* pretty damn perfect, Mrs. Gallagher." Finn shifted her so he could rub the exact spot on her back that ached. Peri hummed her pleasure.

"Want to walk to the Counting House after we eat?"

"If I can move, sure."

Standing at the top of a long jetty, on the west end of the island, the two-story wood structure of the Counting House looked as though the next tropical hurricane would blow it away. But like Zane's *Decrepit*, its rickety looks were deceiving.

Logan and Nick had taken them on a tour of the island and building the day they'd arrived. The Counting House was used to compare notes at the end of a salvage operation, drink beer, tell tall tales and process the artifacts before they were sold worldwide. The fifty permanent island residents, their homes scattered on the slopes, gathered there for birthday parties, hurricanes, and funerals. The sturdy building had been constructed by Daniel Cutter to store his priceless treasure.

It housed some fascinating artifacts that she'd like another look at.

The more Peri learned about Daniel Cutter the less she liked him. The brother's had no illusions about his drinking or womanizing. Only Zane had a slightly romanticized memory of his father. He had a right to hold onto his good memories. Peri was glad she'd never met him.

Beyond the dock was a small marina with a few fishing boats of the locals. The Patagonia salvage continued unabated in their absence. Their ships were all still anchored over the wrecks three thousand miles away. The value of the artifacts salvaged so far was unprecedented. They'd be anchored there for years, if not *decades*. The Cutters and Rydell had all bought property along the coast of Patagonia to give them a home base nearby. Unlike Finn, they didn't relish living year round on their ships.

Of course, Finn had considered the inherent dangers of having toddlers/small children onboard. All the guys had pitched in too, to retrofit *their* ships with Finn's clever solution. Secure safety lines running along the outside walls on every deck, so that a child could be harnessed, with free range, and not get anywhere near the rails. It was genius, and eased Peri's mind considerably.

Instead of shipping the artifacts being held at her house on the bluff, back to them on Cutter Cay, the brothers had voted that the artifacts be displayed permanently at Bria's museum on Merrezo along with the five gold tablets. A win-win for all of them.

Dr. Vadini, his daughter and grandson, the *future* Protectors, were industriously further studying the tablets and developing a dictionary of sorts for the Abipón language. Theo's house in the hills of Patagonia had given them a treasure trove of invaluable books and manuscripts to aid their studies.

Zane gave a triumphant yell as he volleyed the ball over the net in a blizzard of white sand and a flash of tanned skin. "Score!" He punched the air. "Match, set and game. Hand over the dough, bro!"

"I love you when you're all sweaty." Teal laughed, cheeks flushed from the energetic game. Her shaggy hair clung to her cheeks and neck as she flung her arms around her husband's neck. "I love when *we* win." They grinned at each other, as they returned hand in hand to their shady spot beside Finn and Peri.

Nick and Bria went down to the water's edge to retrieve their son and stayed to have an animated conversation with Ry and Addy, which made Peri's heart swell with love and gratitude.

"Don't tell Jonah." Zane flopped down on his back, one elbow covering his eyes. "He almost killed me out there."

Teal shoved her hair out of her eyes, then took Sam, named after her paternal grandfather, from Finn. "I'm buying that universal diagnostic tool with my winnings." Sitting next to Zane, Teal punctuated each word with noisy kisses to her laughing baby's belly.

Zane leaned in for a couple of kisses, too, then pulled both his wife and child against his side. "Isn't half the win *mine*?"

"What's yours *is* mine, Ace."

"Well in that case," he laughed, cupping the baby's downy head. "You only won a hundred bucks. I'll buy the expensive tools for your birthday, how's that?"

"Deal."

Zane looked over Teal's head at Peri and Finn. "Did you two decide where you want to build?"

Peri had been stunned when the brother's had gifted her several acres of land on Cutter Cay. They'd told her Finn's ship was a great home, as was her house on the cliff of Patagonia, but she was a Cutter, too, and part of the island belongs to her. A perfect place to build a vacation home, or a permanent, land-based home, if they ever wanted to retire and laze on the beach all day. Peri could never imagine that day ever coming for either herself or Finn, but it was incredibly generous and sweet of them, and she and Finn had accepted their offer.

More astonishing, they'd gifted Ry and Addy with land as well, and after some convincing, Ry had accepted their offer when they assured him it was the least Daniel Cutter owed him.

"We like that spot on the windward side near the hill that looks like a camel." They'd hire an architect when they got back home, and on their Second Annual Cutter Cay Family Vacation, they could sleep in their own bed, in their own house. Peri's heart filled with happiness.

"Good spot," Zane said, lazily stroking his wife's back, eyes closed.

Jonah and Callie returned from a quick dip, and Jonah grabbed up a couple of nearby folded towels to dry off. Callie blotted the water from her face. "We need a rematch," she told Teal, eyes glinting with challenge. "Best out of three?"

"You're on. Tomorrow. Same place, same time. *Five* bucks."

Shaking his head, Zane laughed. "We've created monsters!"

Peri and Finn shared a smile. "Since we have no horse in the race, let's go for a walk." Finn gave her shoulder a nudge.

"A waddle you mean." She let him pull her to her feet, which she hadn't seen in months.

"Head to the right," Teal told them. "There's a great tide pool about quarter of a mile down the beach."

"Don't go far, you two," Nick yelled after them. "We're eating in half an hour."

Finn did a back- handed wave to acknowledge him. Hand in hand they strolled down to the water's edge, then walked on the wet, packed sand, leaving their footprints in their wake. Beyond the edge of the beach and the tree line, lush, jungle-like vegetation and tall trees obscured Logan and Nick's houses from view. On the other side of a three-hundred-foot-high, extinct volcano in the center of the island, Zane and Jonah had built their houses with more, spectacular, views.

Sun hot on her head and shoulders, the warm water foaming around her ankles, Peri paused to turn into Finn's arms. "Do you think all of us staying on the island at the same time will make us homicidal?"

With a smile, Finn smoothed her hair over her shoulders, his hands lingering on her sun-warmed skin. "Already ready to kill someone?"

"No. Not at all. Actually, this is. . .I don't know. *Nice* is too tame a word. Magical. This past year has been an eye-opener. We genuinely like each other. Even Ry is looking more relaxed and less stressed these days."

"We don't live in each other's pockets onboard," he pointed out. "Over the past year, we've all gotten into a rhythm, and not encroached on anyone's privacy. We respect each other's space. Boundaries. This looks as though it'll be a once a year thing for just a couple of weeks at a time. Different playing field, different environment. We don't always have to come with the entire family if it's too much."

"Are you kidding? I *love* the whole family. I love *you*. I'm in love with—" her voice broke. Oh, crap, pregnancy wreaked havoc with her hormones. "Our twins. It's as though I've found a magical answer for things I didn't know I'd been searching for my entire life."

"I feel exactly the same way. I love you." Finn's smile was tender as he brushed a damp spot on her cheek. "Now." He kissed her forehead. "Forever." He kissed the tip of her nose. "Always. You are, and will always be my soul mate, my *anamchara,* Persephone Case-Cutter-Gallagher." His eyes gleamed silver as he cupped her cheek.

"You are my love." The Irish in his voice was always more pronounced when he felt strong emotion. "There can be no doubt about any of this magic. It, *we*, were written in the stars."

The End

About Cherry Adair

Always an adventurer in life as well as writing, New York Times best-selling author Cherry Adair moved halfway across the globe from Cape Town, South Africa to the United States in her early years to become an interior designer. She started what eventually became a thriving interior design business. "I loved being a designer because it was varied and creative, and I enjoyed working with the public." A voracious reader when she was able to carve out the time, Cherry found her brain crowded with characters and stories of her own.

"Eventually," she says, "the stories demanded to be told." Now a resident of the Pacific Northwest she shares the award- winning adventures of her fictional T-FLAC counter terrorism operatives with her readers.When asked why she chooses to write romantic action adventure, she says, "Who says you can't have adventure and a great love life? Of course, if you're talking about an adventurous love life, that's another thing altogether. I write romantic suspense coupled with heart-pounding adventure because I like to entertain, and nothing keeps readers happier than a rollercoaster read, followed by a happy ending."

Popular on the workshop circuit, Cherry gives lively classes on writing and the writing life. Pulling no punches when asked how to become a published writer, Cherry insists, "Sit your butt in the chair and write. There's no magic to it. Writing is hard work. It isn't for sissies or whiners."

Cherry loves to spend time at home. A corner desk keeps her focused on writing, but the windows behind her, with a panoramic view of the front gardens, are always calling her to come outside and play. Her office has nine-foot ceilings, a fireplace, a television and built-in bookcases houses approximately 3,500 books.

"What can I say? My keeper shelf has been breeding in the middle of the night, rather like drycleaner's wire clothes hangers."

Where can we find out more about you Cherry Adair?

On my website: www.cherryadair.com,

Twitter and my beloved Facebook. I love hearing from readers – wherever you may find me.

Paranormal

Dark Prism

Writer's Tool

Cherry Adairs' Writers' Bible

Connect with Cherry on CherryAdair.com for info on new releases, access to exclusive offers, and much more!